THE VISION OF A VISCOUNT

LINDA RAE SANDE

Twisted Teacup
PUBLISHING

The Vision of a Viscountess

https://www.lindaraesande.com

To the cover models who bring my characters to life

ALSO BY LINDA RAE SANDE

The Daughters of the Aristocracy

The Kiss of a Viscount

The Grace of a Duke

The Seduction of an Earl

The Sons of the Aristocracy

Tuesday Nights

The Widowed Countess

My Fair Groom

The Sisters of the Aristocracy

The Story of a Baron

The Passion of a Marquess

The Desire of a Lady

The Brothers of the Aristocracy

The Love of a Rake

The Caress of a Commander

The Epiphany of an Explorer

The Widows of the Aristocracy

The Gossip of an Earl

The Enigma of a Widow

The Secrets of a Viscount

The Widowers of the Aristocracy

The Dream of a Duchess

The Vision of a Viscountess

PROLOGUE

*S*pring 1796, Rome
       A young man watched from the stairs below as tears streamed down Chiara Ferraro's face and sobs racked her body. She didn't seem to care that her tears were staining her gold silk gown, or that an escort or lady's maid was nowhere near, or that a *piastra* had fallen from one of her gloved hands and was clattering on its way down the stairs.

This is why I'm here, Antony remembered. A visiting British archaeologist had begged Antony to be at the steps of the Forum no later than four o'clock that afternoon.

I will see to it you shall have your opportunity to make your affections known to the young lady. Her father will give you his permission to marry her if you wish to do so.

Or, at least that's what he thought the foreigner had said. His Italian was abysmal, and Antony's command of English wasn't much better.

More than a little curious and ever so anxious to learn if the Brit's words were true, Antony had made his way down the partially colonnaded *Via Sacra* to the Forum and surveyed the scene of *turistas* and young lovers enjoying a fine afternoon in one of Rome's most historic sites. A quick glance at his pocket watch had him frowning when the hour was nearly four o'clock, and there was no sign of the young lady.

And then she was suddenly there, the sounds of her sobs alerting him to her presence.

He hurried up the steps, retrieved the *piastra*, and bowed before her, helping himself to the gloved hand that wasn't wiping tears from her cheeks. "*Non piangere, signorina,*" he pleaded. *Do not cry.*

Chiara blinked and stared down at the young man who knelt before her. She recognized him, of course. He had been a guest in her father's villa on many occasions, his wealth providing patronage for archaeological expeditions and money for ancient artifacts in need of a safe place to be housed.

"Signore Romano?" she whispered, blinking again before she sniffled.

A fine lawn handkerchief was pressed into her hand along with the wayward *piastra* before he straightened from his bow. Despite standing on the step below the one on which she stood, he was still taller than her. Taller and more handsome than she remembered, with his jet-black hair and brown eyes, a square jaw that might have been clean-shaven this morning, but was now displaying dark stubble. He had a mouth that smiled easily because, well, the dental gods had blessed him with straight, white teeth and lips that she just then noticed seemed perfect for kissing.

"*Sì,*" he replied as he angled his head. "*Cosa ti ha turbato?*" he asked. *What has upset you?* He still wasn't sure from where she had come. He had half-expected to find the Brit escorting her, so discovering she was by herself was a surprise.

He had seen the two in each other's company at her father's home, although it was possible she was merely playing hostess on her father's behalf. If the two had engaged in any kind of *affaire*, they had certainly hidden it well, for there was no scandal surrounding the young woman. Besides, when would they have had any time? The archaeologist was off surveying digs all around Rome and had been for months.

Using the corner of the handkerchief to dab at her eyes, Chiara regarded Antony with a watery smile. "*Niente,*" she said with a shake of her head. "*Anche se ho bisogno di una scorta a casa,*" she added, glancing about as if she just then realized where she was. *Nothing. Although I am in need of a ride home.*

Ah, Antony realized. This was the Brit's plan all along. A way to arrange for Samuele Ferraro's daughter to require an escort to see her home. A way to give him time to spend with the beautiful young lady with the dark brunette hair, golden eyes, and lips he wanted to kiss every morning and every night.

But would she want to kiss him?

"*Sarò onorato di prenderti,*" he replied as he held his arm for her. *I shall be honored to take you.*

Placing a gloved hand on his arm, Chiara joined him on the same step and dared a glance up at him before turning her attention to the sleeve on which her hand rested. The quality of the superfine of his topcoat was a testament to his means. His embroidered waistcoat was just as expensive, although not a bit ostentatious. His leather boots were shined to a gloss that might have blinded her should the sun's rays reflect from them.

But most important of all was how he looked at her. As if he loved her.

Perhaps he does, she considered, before she sniffled one last time.

If she couldn't have the man to whom her heart had pledged itself, then she could have a man her head deemed a good match. Sometimes the second-best was really the right choice, after all.

So when she raised her gaze back up to meet his, she allowed a brilliant smile. "*Grazie, mio eroe,*" she said with a sigh. *My hero.*

Antony Romano never thought to hear such an endearment from Chiara Ferraro. His heart soaring as he led her to his carriage, Antony planned how he would ask her father's permission and propose later that night.

*F*rom where he stood hiding behind the base of a statue, Lord Darius blinked back tears. He could barely breathe as he watched the wealthy Italian escort the love of his life to a waiting town coach, the expression on her face and the way she was gazing up at Antony Romano suggesting she had already forgotten about him.

Perhaps it is best this way, he thought. It's not as if he could offer for her hand, after all. And although he had offered *carte blanche,* part of him hoping she would join him in England, he was relieved she hadn't accepted. She deserved better than him. Better than a life as a mistress.

Chapter 1

A CHANCE SIGHTING AT A BALL

L *ord Attenborough's annual ball, 1816*
      Despite the French doors having been opened
to the gardens behind Lord Attenborough's
mansion in Park Lane, Jasper Henley still found the crush of
the ball nearly unbearable. The cloying scents of perfumes
and colognes had the champagne tasting rather odd. His
heart was racing far faster than it should considering there
wasn't a single woman within his line of sight who could
elicit such a response. And it was growing progressively more
difficult to breathe.

The orchestra, seven musicians seated on a raised dais at
one end of the ballroom, was in the middle of the third
dance set of Lord Attenborough's annual ball when the
viscount realized he needed air. Fresh air. His fear of crowded
spaces was about to send him into a state of panic.

Winding his way through the members of the crowd not
dancing the cotillion, he managed nods of acknowledgement
to those who waved or called out to him. At the site of Alistair Comber, he paused and angled his head. "Comber?" he
questioned just as he came to a halt.

"Henley! So good to see you," Alistair replied, clapping a

large hand against Jasper's upper arm. "I thought you were in Italy."

Jasper gave a start. He had been in Italy. Some three years ago. "I was. Finished the dig and returned with some magnificent pieces for the collection," he said, referring to the Roman artifacts he brought back on behalf of the British Museum.

"But you're going back, aren't you?" Alistair countered.

Jasper blinked. "I am. I leave for Sicily next week," he acknowledged. "Lord Darius—Dr. Jones—has sent word of a find near Girgenti. Said there is a potential for finding hundreds of mosaics in an ancient Greco-Roman site." He suddenly frowned. "I thought you were on the Continent."

Alistair nodded, realizing it had been a long time since they had seen one another. "I was. Just got back in February." The second son of an earl, Alistair Comber had been an officer in His Majesty's army. His last assignment had been in Belgium for some of the final battles against Napoleon's forces. "After Father disinherited me for selling my commission..."

"He didn't," Jasper replied in shock.

"I took a position as a groom for Lord Mayfield, married his daughter, and now I'm in charge of his stables."

"Your mother wouldn't have allowed Aimsley to disinherit you," he argued, remembering how Patience, Countess of Aimsely, doted on her sons. Besides, it was well known the woman had her husband wrapped around her pinky.

Alistair grinned. "I'm back in my father's good graces, it's true," he admitted. He sobered when he noticed the fabric band wrapped around Jasper's upper arm. The black arm band that signified mourning was barely visible given the formal topcoat Jasper wore was black. "Oh, I apologize. Who... who died?"

Jasper's eyes widened a bit at hearing the young man's query before his brows furrowed. He wondered how Alistair knew he was supposed to be in mourning. Then he remembered the arm band. "My wife. Sophie. The damned influenza got her last fall," he murmured.

Although most men would have removed any evidence of their mourning after only a few months, Jasper found he couldn't. Not just yet. As for why he would attend a ball, especially a crowded one, he hadn't planned to do so. Their host, Lord Attenborough, insisted that he at least take a look at the current crop of *demoiselles*. "You need to consider your duty, Henley. Time to find another wife and get a child on her," the older earl urged. "Start your nursery."

Not that Jasper was interested in the current crop of young ladies. They always seemed so *young*. At one-and-thirty, he figured he would be happy finding a widow, or a young woman who had maybe been missed by others intent on marrying for beauty or blunt. Someone who was over three-and-twenty. Someone who wasn't made too independent by having come into their majority and therefore taken possession of their dowry and a companion.

And a place at the gaming tables.

"How awful," Alistair remarked. "I cannot imagine losing my Julia," he murmured with a shake of his head. "I do hope you're here for a bit of respite," he added, his gaze attempting to take in the entire ballroom. "Although, in this crush, I'm not sure how that might be possible."

Jasper could think of a couple of places where he might find respite this very moment. The library, if it wasn't occupied by an amorous couple intent on a coupling. Or the gardens, where at least he could get some fresh air. Maybe commiserate with Cupid, who stood poised to shoot an arrow from the top of the garden fountain. That cur had been responsible for his marriage to Sophie, for Jasper had been kissing his late wife next to the fountain when they were caught in the act.

He had already planned to ask for her hand, of course.

But being forced to do so because of an innocent kiss took away any romance from the subsequent proposal. At least Sophie didn't seem to mind too much. She was an agreeable wife. A happy wife. At least, Jasper hoped she had been.

"Congratulations on your marriage. I'm off to the gardens. I need some air," Jasper announced before he gave a nod, made his way around Alistair, and headed toward the French doors.

Just as he was about to step outside, a most odd sensation —a sort of niggling at the nape of his neck—had Jasper pausing. He turned around to find he was being watched by a young woman sitting beneath a potted palm not ten feet away. Dressed in a white gown, she could have been any one of the dozen or so *demoiselles* in attendance, except she seemed a bit older. Her honey blonde hair framed an oval face that would have been nondescript except for her eyes. Their bright blue was arresting, and yet he was quite sure they were also unseeing.

How was it then that she seemed to be staring at him, a rather besotted look on her face? Perhaps she could see and was merely lost in a pleasant thought.

His phobia forgotten, Jasper weaved his way through the crowd to where the young lady sat, glancing about in search of a companion or chaperone who might introduce them.

"Hello," she said, coming to her feet in a graceful move that segued into a deep curtsy. Her gown, a column of white silk de Naples embroidered with white silk threads, had obviously been made by one of the best modistes in London. The fact that it was white suggested she was unmarried.

"Hullo," Jasper managed as he gave a bow. He dared a glance to his left and then to his right. "Pardon me, but I... it looks as if your companion, or chaperone—"

"Aunt," she interrupted with a sly grin.

"Has gone missing," he continued, worry evident in his voice. How could such a delectable creature be left alone among the palm trees at the back of Lord Attenborough's ballroom?

"She's dancing with Lord Devonville."

One of Jasper's eyebrows cocked up. "Ah. Poor thing," he murmured, not intending for her to actually hear the comment. Her brilliant smile had him a bit mortified when he realized she *had* heard. Besides the dimple that appeared in her left cheek, her porcelain skin bloomed with a pretty shade of pink while her bright blue eyes focused on him to the point he realized she could see, although perhaps not well. "Oh, pardon me. I didn't mean it like that," he said with a shake of his head.

"Oh, I won't tell him. I promise," she countered, her face still displaying an expression of delight.

Jasper blinked. "You know him well enough to tell him should you wish to?" he wondered aloud, daring a glance at the dancers who were still performing the cotillion. They would continue to do so for at least another fifteen minutes.

The young lady nodded. "Devonville is my uncle."

Blinking again, Jasper had to resist the urge to say, "Poor thing," again when he realized two things at once. The woman who stood before him had to be Lord Donald Slater's daughter. The woman who was dancing with Lord Devonville was either his marchioness, Cherice, or else his sister, Adele, Countess of Torrington.

No wonder this young woman's gown appeared so expensive! Donald Slater was a distiller of some of the finest scotch in all of the kingdom. His home and the base of his operation was somewhere barely over the border of Cumberland. Prinny had once suggested the border be moved so that Slater's scotch could be considered a product of England. "It's very good to meet you, Miss Slater," he murmured as he lifted her gloved hand to his lips. "Jasper Henley, at your service."

Her suddenly widened eyes gave away her momentary

surprise at Jasper's ability to sort her name. That she didn't immediately excuse herself and return to her chair had Jasper feeling a bit of satisfaction.

"Then perhaps you could escort me on a walk through the gardens?" she replied. "It's rather warm in here, and I could use some air."

Rather surprised at the request—when had a young woman ever asked him if they might take a turn in the gardens—Jasper dared another glance at those who were dancing, wondering if he could catch Lord Devonville's attention and attempt to let him know he would be removing the young lady from the ballroom. When he couldn't find the marquess among the dancers, however, he had a thought the man and his new wife might be in the library.

Probably enjoying a tumble this very moment.

"Would you like me to fetch your shawl? It's a bit chilly out there," he warned, half-turning as he continued his attempt at locating the Devonvilles.

The woman shook her head. "You're most kind to offer, Lord Henley, but truly, I will be fine. It is *Lord* Henley, is it not?"

A bit hesitant, Jasper finally turned around and offered his arm. "If you insist," he finally replied "And, yes, I am a viscount."

*M*iss Marianne Slater placed a white kid-gloved hand onto Lord Henley's arm and allowed the viscount to lead the way to the French doors. Why she had decided to fix her gaze onto the man who now escorted her to the back of the Attenborough's ballroom, she wasn't quite sure. When he had walked past her, he hadn't been close enough for her to see him with any kind of detail—he appeared as blurry as any other attendee at that night's ball—

but the faint scent of lime briefly freshened the air around her. There was also his determined gait as he hurried to reach the exit, a rhythm to his walk that was unlike any of the aristocrats who were in attendance.

Whatever could have captured a man's attention so thoroughly as to have him rushing to leave a glittering ball such as this?

A liaison in the gardens? Illness? Extreme boredom? Heat?

Well, Marianne could certainly understand if heat was the cause. Although she dearly loved the gown her aunt had arranged for her—Madame Suzanne assured her it was beyond *au courant*—the long sleeves and silk fabric were rather warm. She couldn't imagine dancing in this crush. She would probably faint.

So, out of curiosity, she had allowed her gaze to follow his retreating figure. When he suddenly turned around and made his way back to stand before her, she thought perhaps he recognized her. That perhaps she had been introduced to him at some point in her past and simply couldn't see him well enough to discern his identity.

But how was that possible? She had just come from Canobie in southwest Scotland for only her second time in London since her birth, the first one having been the occasion of her birth at Devonville House.

No one from Canobie would have received an invitation to Lord Attenborough's ball. Well, perhaps her father would, but only if it was known he intended to be in London this week. And he hadn't paid a visit to the capital since his oldest nephew, William, joined His Majesty's Navy, and that had been six years ago.

But Marianne was sure she didn't recognize the lime-citrus scent of this man's cologne, nor his light brown hair. When he spoke, she was very sure she hadn't heard his voice before.

Her body seemed to think otherwise, however, for she was acutely aware of the precise fit of her gown, of how her gloves hugged her arms, of how a few of the pins in her coiffure dug into her scalp, of how her breasts seemed to swell beneath the corset her aunt had insisted she wear.

Aware, and rather uncomfortable in a manner she had never before experienced.

It's entirely too hot in here, she thought at the very moment he was close enough that she could make out his features quite clearly. Aristocratic, but not proud. Green eyes, straight nose, high cheekbones, and a complexion that suggested he spent a good deal of time out-of-doors. *Riding horses, perhaps*, she thought, which would explain the snug fit of his formal attire. His expression suggested a practiced friendliness to which she was immediately attracted.

So what else could she do but say, "Hello," and dip a curtsy?

Then Marianne remembered she had no business introducing herself to a strange man.

Where are you, Aunt Cherice? Aunt Adele? Uncle William?

*T*he cool air had Jasper inhaling a deep breath even before his feet hit the flagstones leading to the gardens. Unlike Lord Weatherstone's gardens, the Attenborough gardens featured row upon row of Japanese lanterns. The ethereal glow from the paper globes lit most of the area behind the house, including the fountain. A statue of Cupid —the very same Cupid who had paid witness to Jasper's first elicit kiss with Sophie Knox—hovered over the double-decker dishes that made up the base of the fountain. Despite the blindfold wrapped around his head, he seemed poised to shoot an arrow into the heart of whomever dared pay him a visit.

"Are you sure you're not too cold?" Jasper wondered as

they made their way to a parterre garden featuring tulips and bluebells. Due to the cooler spring weather, few of the flowers were actually in bloom.

"I'm quite comfortable," Marianne replied, a sigh escaping as she took a deep breath and reveled in the scents of spring flowers and fresh greenery. "Although I appreciate Madame Suzanne's creation..." She indicated the gown she wore. "I fear it's more appropriate for a winter ball."

Jasper paused a moment, his gaze traveling over her gown. Try as he might to seem unaffected by the gown—or her in it—he found he couldn't help but admire her. "Given how chilly it is tonight, you may find Madame Suzanne's beautiful creation a blessing before the night has ended," he countered with a grin.

Marianne angled her head and regarded him for a moment. "Thank you, my lord," she managed. "Truth be told, I had no idea if it would suit, since I haven't attended a *ton* ball before."

Jasper considered her claim. "But you've been to balls in... where do you live exactly?"

"Canobie," she replied. "Every district ball, and all of my father's soirées, of course. He likes to host one every time a batch of scotch is ready for shipment."

Wondering if the attendees at those particular soirées were gifted with any of the casks of scotch, Jasper was about to ask when Marianne suddenly stopped and inhaled. "Roses?" she whispered, her gaze darting about as if she were trying to determine from where the scent of roses had come.

Jasper did a quick survey of the immediate area and finally found a single bush displaying just two peach roses. Far too early and too cool for the flowers, he wondered how these two had managed to bloom. "Over here," he said as he led them to the rosebush. He watched as Marianne sought the roses with her free hand, her fingers seeming to first caress the leaves surrounding the meager blooms before they touched the petals. She lowered her face until her nose grazed a peach velvet petal.

A frisson shot through Jasper as his body imagined how it would feel to have those two fingers caress his body as she was caressing the rose petal. Even gloved, they promised a sensation he hadn't realized he missed.

Sophie rarely touched him so. She had never been comfortable seeing him shirtless. Never been comfortable in the marriage bed, although she was willing on the nights he asked if he might join her. He was determined to get a child on her if for no other reason than he believed she needed someone to love.

Long after what had happened in these very gardens, he discovered she didn't marry him because she felt affection for him, or because she aspired to marry a lowly viscount, or because he wanted to marry her, but because she had been forced to do so.

Her father had caught them kissing next to the fountain of Cupid.

It wasn't until after Jasper buried her in the family plot in Kent that he discovered she had felt affection for another. A young man who had departed for the Continent as part of Wellington's army and died near Ligny.

Jasper never learned the identity of the other man. Sophie had accepted her fate with such grace, he had no idea she loved another. Even so, he did everything in his power to see to it she didn't regret their forced match.

He certainly didn't.

Marianne raised her face to his, a brilliant smile appearing. "They're beautiful," she breathed.

Jasper nodded, although he couldn't take his eyes off of her to even look at the roses. By the dim light of the Japanese lantern nearest them, he still found her eyes arresting. He knew from how she gazed at him that she could see him clearly, so he smiled in return. "There should be some tulips around here," he murmured as he led her along the crushed granite path to another flower bed. "Do you have a favorite color?" The small parterre garden was edged in tiny clusters of white flowers, but behind those, a row of red tulips were open.

"I've only ever seen red ones," she replied, bending over to study a tulip, her hand nearly clutching his arm as if she needed it for support. From how close her face was to the tulip, Jasper wondered if she was studying the stamen inside the bloom.

"There are yellow ones in the next section," he commented, his gaze taking in as much of the garden as he could make out in the candlelight from the lanterns. He listened for the strains of music that would indicate it was time for the next dance—and the cue that he needed to return the young lady to the ballroom. At some point, her aunt would discover she was missing.

From the sound of her gasp and the smile she displayed, Jasper realized her delight, and he led her to the next section of the parterre.

Once again, she bent down and studied the flower, her gloved hand barely touching the bloom. "They must be bright yellow by the light of day," she commented as she stood up.

"They are, indeed," Jasper agreed, as much amused by her enthusiasm as touched by it. He returned her to the path. Directly ahead, Cupid loomed, his bow drawn back as if he were taking dead aim in their direction. "Ah, we're in the middle of the gardens," he said with a sigh.

Blinking when he realized they had come to the scene of the crime, so to speak—the fountain next to which he had been caught kissing Sophie just before he was about to propose marriage—Jasper stared up at the statue of the diminutive Greek god and wondered what to say. Marianne saved him from having to make a comment, though, when she asked, "Is he aiming his bow in our direction? I apologize, but I cannot make out the details from this distance."

Jasper allowed a chuckle. "He is," he admitted. "But whatever do you mean you cannot make out his details?" he asked. Did she refer to Cupid's rather small genitalia? *He is just a boy*, he thought.

Or was she referring to his arrow?

"I am possessed of very poor eyesight, my lord," she answered as she turned her attention to him. "I only know it is a statue of Cupid because my aunt warned me I might be kissed in his presence."

Jasper furrowed a brow, a bit bothered by both of her comments. "What do you see of him, then?" he asked as he turned his attention back to the marble god, ignoring the comment about the warning she had been given.

"A blurry white... thing," she managed to get out. "I can see this bowl in which the water collects," she added as her gloved hand brushed over the lip of the fountain's lower bowl. "But he is entirely out of focus."

Watching as her gloved hand grazed over the marble's edge, Jasper once again felt the need to tamp down his sudden arousal. Goodness, but if her fingers touched one more thing besides him, he would be quite jealous!

What had she just said?

Something about focus.

Something he needed to do, it seemed.

Remembering how she was able to see him clearly up close, he realized she was near-sighted. He moved a bit closer. "Have you been to see the Townley Collection at the British Museum?" he asked in a hoarse whisper, attempting to keep his contempt for the collection's namesake from coloring his question. The man's money had been responsible for the plunder of statues from several countries—mostly Italy—and resulted in a plethora of poor copies and stolen relics throughout England and Northern Europe.

Marianne turned to him as her face brightened in delight. "Why, just yesterday, in fact. My aunt, Lady Torrington, took me to the museum. The manner in which the exhibits were displayed allowed me to see everything in great detail!" she enthused.

Jasper blinked, well aware he no longer had any control over what was happening behind the placket of his breeches. "So, you found you... enjoyed your visit?" he asked with a arched brow.

"Oh, *enjoy* is not the word I would use, my lord—"

"Jasper," he interrupted. "Call me Jasper."

Marianne blinked. "Jasper," she repeated in a whisper, her expression suggesting she was testing the name in her mind. Her eyes brightened again. "*Thrilled* would be a more appropriate term. "Why, I was allowed to stand so close to each and every statue, I could actually see them clearly," she claimed happily.

The viscount regarded her for a moment, stunned that a lady would find statues in the British Museum *thrilling*. God, but she was beautiful when she made such a claim. Happy, too, which was so infectious, Jasper found he could do nothing but smile. And then, when she angled her head and regarded him with an expression suggesting she could see him quite well, his lips were suddenly on hers.

Despite knowing exactly what could happen if he was caught kissing a young lady in front of the statue of Cupid in the gardens behind Lord Attenborough's mansion in Park Lane, Jasper Henley could not help himself. Miss Marianne Slater was a jewel. Even if she wasn't a diamond of the first water, she was of the second, and he wanted to taste her delight. Partake of her joy. Revel in her discovery of the statues in the British Museum.

Even if they were those from the Townley Collection.

She seemed just as willing to learn his secrets, for she returned the kiss within moments of their lips touching, and she did so in equal measure. She tasted of champagne and strawberries, and smelled like jasmine in the summer. When one of his arms moved to pull her closer, she didn't resist but instead moved even closer until the front of her body was pressed against his.

From somewhere in the back of his brain, Jasper remembered the chill in the night air. He absently undid the button of his topcoat so that he could slip first one arm and then the other out of it even as he continued the kiss. He wrapped the garment around her shoulders, which had her breaking off the kiss to murmur a whispered, "Thank you," before her lips were once again pressed against his.

Jasper would have continued the kiss—Jesus, but she was the perfect panacea on this night—but he was suddenly aware that they were no longer alone in their worship of Cupid.

Not only had the twit shot one of his deadly arrows, but he had done so with witnesses present.

Again.

Jasper finally ended the kiss, his forehead pressed against Marianne's as his eyes squeezed shut.

Here I go again.

Chapter 2

BLINDED BY A KISS

a moment later
        Jasper didn't want to straighten and look over at whomever stood watching them. He wanted to renew the kiss. Wanted to pull Marianne Slater even closer to his body. Close enough so she wouldn't feel the least bit of chill. Close enough that they would appear as one body to whomever stood staring at them.

But propriety had him realizing it was too late for either of them.

They had been caught.

Shot by Cupid and caught by...

Jasper lifted a hand to the back of Marianne's neck and pulled her head against his shoulder, his lips briefly pressed to her forehead. "Courage, my sweet," he whispered, girding his loins for what was to come. He finally looked to his left to find not one, not two, but three people regarding him with various expressions of shock.

The former Cherice DuBois, currently the Marchioness of Devonville, displayed an expression of awe, as if she had just seen her favorite fairy tale come to life. Jasper was quite sure he heard her whisper, "How romantic," before she allowed an audible sigh.

Adele Slater Worthington Grandby, the new Countess of Torrington, blinked and thankfully appeared impressed, as if she might have doubted his kissing abilities.

William Slater, Marquess of Devonville, displayed an expression that might have been a cross between murderous resolve and disbelief. Or perhaps he was merely experiencing a moment of indigestion.

"Hullo," Jasper managed, not about to let go his hold on Miss Slater. Knowing she wouldn't be able to make out the identities of their interlopers—at least, not until one of them said something—he didn't want her falling into the freezing water of the fountain, or rushing off into a hedgerow, or trampling the few flowers that had managed to bloom despite the chill.

"Lord Henley?" Adele, Countess of Torrington, was the first to break the silence, a lorgnette held to her face.

Jasper managed a bow despite his continued hold on Marianne. "Good evening, my ladies, my lord," he replied.

"What do you think you're doing?" Devonville asked, his brows furrowed in a familiar frown.

"He's kissing your niece, of course," Cherice replied on Jasper's behalf, her comment loud enough to be heard by all five of them. "Cupid shot him," she gushed. "So romantic."

Devonville gave his wife a quelling glance. "So ruinous, you mean," he countered.

Jasper felt Marianne stiffen in his hold, but he didn't dare let go of her. "Miss Slater is completely innocent," he argued with a shake of his head. "This is entirely my fault. She claimed to find the statues in the British Museum thrilling, and I was overcome by her infectious enthusiasm." He moved an arm up to Marianne's shoulder, still covered with his topcoat, as if he expected she might try to escape his hold.

He felt a good deal of satisfaction when she made no move to do so.

She obviously didn't want to end up in a hedgerow.

Or in the fountain.

Devonville blinked. Jasper was fairly sure all three of them blinked, in fact, which could only mean they had absolutely no appreciation for the relics in the museum.

"You *do* know what this means, Henley?" Devonville asked, one hand raised to point a finger at him.

Jasper sighed, well aware of what it meant. "I do. I believe I have found a soulmate in your niece, Lord Devonville. Which begs the question. To whom do I ask permission to marry Miss Slater?"

Cherice's eyes widened as her clasped hands were suddenly beneath her chin. "Oh!" she managed, looking as if she might swoon at any moment. "It's only her first ball in London!"

Adele was far more practical, one finger raised to point at her brother.

Devonville lifted his chin—both of them, actually—before he furrowed his brows. "That's a good question," he acknowledged. "Normally I would say her father, but Donald isn't due here from Canobie for a week. It would take days for a missive to reach him, and by then, he'll already be on his way—"

"William!" Adele said in a hoarse whisper. "You outrank your brother. Give the poor man your permission," she insisted.

"Oh, yes, do!" Cherice enthused, her gloved hands clapping together as if she had just paid witness to the opening night of a play at the theatre.

At the moment, Jasper felt as if he was the star of the play and poor Marianne was the tragic chit about to be tossed into a volcano—or to the Kraken—to appease the gods. Since he was standing to her side, he had no idea what she thought of the proceedings. If she even agreed with what was about to happen.

"Very well, Henley. I give you permission to marry my niece," the marquess stated as he straightened in an attempt to match the viscount's stature. He frowned. "If I remember correctly, you're about to depart on one of your archaeological expeditions, are you not?"

Jasper nodded. "I am." He allowed a wan smile to form, rather relieved he had plans for the near future. Plans for an expedition to the island of Sicily. "Indeed. I have already booked passage to someplace warmer than here," he replied.

"Good. Then if we arrange a quick wedding, you can take my niece along. Make it your wedding trip," Devonville stated, his words more of a warning than a suggestion.

Jasper felt a good deal of satisfaction when his reply of, "The Kingdom of the Two Sicilies it is, then," resulted in a collective gasp, including one from the woman he still held in his arms. He could feel her gaze on him, feel how stunned she felt at hearing his words. "That is, if my future viscountess is in agreement?" he asked as he turned his attention back to Marianne.

Poor girl. Did she have any idea of what had just happened?

At least she seemed to see him clearly as she stared at him in disbelief before a brilliant smile appeared. "I am," she breathed, her words almost a question.

"Very good. Then, I do believe I have the honor of the next dance, my lady," Jasper said as he heard the unmistakeable tempo of a waltz. He gave a deep bow to their interlopers, offered Marianne his arm, and felt a good deal of relief when she dipped a curtsy and hurried alongside him back to ballroom.

He couldn't help but notice how she occasionally glanced in his direction as they made their way, as if she expected him to claim it was all a huge mistake at any moment. "I shall pay a call at the archdeacon's office on the morrow," Jasper said just before he opened the French doors leading back into the ballroom.

"Whatever for?" Marianne asked, stepping over the threshold and turning to regard him as she did so. She remembered she wore his topcoat and slipped it off her shoulders.

"For a marriage license, of course." At her blank stare and slight shake of her head, Jasper wondered if she just couldn't see him or if she was simply unfamiliar with marriage licenses. "It will also allow us to wed in five days, if we wish —without requiring the banns to be read."

Marianne could tell he was pulling on his topcoat— although her eyesight was poor, she was close enough to make him out with some clarity. "You truly intend to wed me?" she asked as he once again offered his arm. She wondered what he meant when he referred to the reading of the banns. In Scotland, there was no need for banns to be read.

Jasper blinked. "Of course." He captured one of her hands in his and brought it up to his sleeve, intending to lead her to where a circle of couples was already formed and performing the waltz. He stopped, though, and furrowed a brow. "Do you know how to waltz?"

Marianne shook her head. "I cannot even claim to have seen it performed, my lord," she replied sadly, still rather stunned she would be married soon. And all because of a kiss in the gardens.

Disappointment had Jasper leading her back to where he had found her, intending to simply stand with her during the dance. "I'll teach you," he said when they were at the potted palm where he had first found her. He wasn't about to give up on the idea of dancing with her.

"Here?"

"Indeed." He gently turned her to face him, placed a

hand at her waist, which had her giving a start, and then took one of her hands in his. "Put your other hand on my shoulder," he instructed as he straightened his body.

Marianne did as she was told, but from her expression, Jasper knew she wasn't comfortable. "Can you... see me?" he asked, one of his brows arching up.

She nodded. "Well enough," she replied, a bit hesitant. Although she couldn't make out his facial features with any kind of detail, she knew it was him from his height and breadth, the color of his hair, and the scent of lime that surrounded him.

"Perfect. You needn't see anything else but me." *For the rest of our lives*, he almost added. "Now, when I push your hand, you step back whilst I step forward..." He demonstrated the step, relieved when she managed to step back on the correct foot. "Step together," he said as he guided her somewhat to the side. "And you step forward as I step back."

Although she faltered a bit, he kept a tight hold on her and allowed a grin when they were back to where they had started. "That's it. We just do it over and over..." He continued the steps, rather pleased at how she followed his lead so well. But given her near blindness, he supposed she had no choice.

A nearby wallflower and her chaperone retreated farther down the wall when they perceived they were about to be trampled. "People are staring," Marianne whispered hoarsely.

"How can they not? You're the most beautiful woman in the entire room," he countered, silently counting the steps as they moved to the music. He wondered if perhaps her sight was better than he first thought. Otherwise, how was it she knew people were staring?

Marianne blinked, her face blooming with color as she dared a glance to her left and then to her right. Although she couldn't see anyone clearly, she was sure she and Henley were the center of attention. "You're a bounder, Lord Henley," she claimed.

"Jasper," he whispered. "Now I'm going to move us over to where everyone else is dancing," he added, his hand against her waist pushing her sideways a bit.

"What if someone...?" she started to ask just as Jasper avoided a collision by pulling her closer to him.

"I shall protect you, my lady," he assured her.

From the way he seemed to survey the space around them, Marianne realized he would protect her. Now that she had the steps down—the entire dance was rather simple— she found she could enjoy it as Jasper seemed intent on showing her off. Not that she could really see well enough to know for certain, but at no point did anyone step on her, nor did her shoulders bump anyone. Soon, she was displaying a hesitant grin.

A moment later, and they had merged into the circle of dancers making their way around in a huge arc. "I take it you don't have a subscription to Almack's for the Season," Jasper said.

Remembering the name from something her aunt had said when she first arrived in London only a few days ago, Marianne shook her head. "Aunt Cherice claimed we would be attending on Wednesday nights," she replied. "She wanted me to obtain some sort of... voucher?"

Jasper grinned. "A voucher to dance the waltz. Which you're doing rather well without," he said, the idea of wedding the young woman becoming more real. Not so daunting as it had been out in the garden, when he had simply put on a brave face and behaved as if it was his plan all along.

When they had made their way out to the gardens, he had no intention of being caught kissing Miss Slater. Certainly no intention of having to marry her. And now, not even an hour later, he was once again betrothed to be married because he had kissed a woman next to the fountain featuring Cupid.

The cur.

The chubby-cheeked troublemaker.

The doubly chubby-cheeked, multi-dimpled...

Jasper blinked as he realized Marianne was regarding him with the most brilliant smile. Christ, but she was beautiful, her bright blue eyes as stunning as her smile.

"What is it?" he asked as they whirled about in the wide circle of dancers.

"I do so love this dance," she replied happily.

"Then we shall do it at every ball to which we're invited," he replied. From the corner of his eye, he could see they were being watched, and not by someone who admired their moves. Given how the music seemed to be ending, Jasper slowed their movement and finally pulled them to a stop when the music ceased. He dared a glance to the man who watched them from the perimeter of onlookers.

William Slater, Marquess of Devonville, was regarding him with an expression that suggested he had better return Marianne to her aunt and see what his future... *uncle?* Faith! —His future uncle was a marquess!—wanted of him.

Chapter 3

THE SITUATION BECOMES
CRYSTAL CLEAR

*T*wo *moments later*
Jasper bowed to Marianne's deep curtsy and offered his arm. "I believe I must return you to your aunt now," he said as he leaned in her direction. "Devonville wants a moment of my time."

Marianne dared a glance in the direction he indicated, although she couldn't see anyone well enough to discern their identity. "Thank you for teaching me the waltz," she managed before she realized she was standing next to her aunt, Cherice.

Jasper had already lifted her gloved hand and was brushing his lips over the back of it before saying, "I shall call on you tomorrow afternoon. Perhaps we can ride in the park for the fashionable hour?" he suggested.

Giving her head a quick shake, Marianne's eyes seemed to widen with fright before she said, "I do not ride."

A twinge of disappointment had Jasper rethinking his plans. "Then I shall come for you with a carriage," he countered with a shrug, relieved when her grin returned, as did Lady Devonville's, he couldn't help but notice. As for a carriage, it might have to be his phaeton—he didn't own a barouche or a curricle.

He took the marchioness' gloved hand and quickly brushed his lips over the back, deciding it might be too soon to refer to her as 'aunt'. "Good night, my lady," he said with a bow. He gave his intended another nod before turning his attention to Lord Devonville. "You wanted a word?" he asked.

Devonville regarded the viscount a moment. "Indeed. Let's see if we might find a bit of privacy in the library."

Jasper nearly blinked at the suggested meeting place. Didn't the marquess know the room would be occupied by a couple in need of a tumble? Why, the marquess had probably been doing that very activity with his marchioness when Jasper took his niece into the garden! "The study might be less crowded," he suggested when they took their leave of the ballroom. As they moved farther from the crush and down the carpeted hall toward the study, the noise of the ballroom lessened.

"Pray tell, how long have you known Marianne?" Devonville wondered as they stepped into the study. Although no lamps were lit in the room, a fire provided enough light to see by.

Jasper was about to reply with, "Who?" when he realized the marquess referred to his niece. The woman to whom he would find himself married within the week.

Marianne.

He tried the name in his head and decided it suited his betrothed perfectly. "About an hour and... perhaps ten minutes. I just met her this evening, it's true," he admitted. "Where have you been hiding her?"

Devonville gave him a quelling glance. "She only just arrived in London three days ago," he replied, helping himself to a cheroot from the box atop the room's enormous desk. "This was the first entertainment to which we could escort her."

"For the purpose of finding a husband," Jasper stated, not making it a question.

Rolling his eyes, the marquess gave his head a shake as he regarded the cheroot. He set it aside, apparently deciding to forgo a smoke just then. "I'm sure that was my marchioness' intent when she invited the girl to spend the Season with us," Devonville replied with an arched brow. "Marianne has only been to the capital once before, and that was back when she was born."

"So you *have* been hiding her," Jasper accused lightly.

The marquess repeated the quelling glance. "My brother hasn't been in London for nearly six years, although he's due to arrive next week."

"So *he's* been hiding her."

Devonville finally shrugged. "Not intentionally, of course. But what's a widower to do when he lives near such a small village? Marianne is nearly three-and-twenty, but despite her beauty, she has no prospects in Canobie."

This bit of information explained much, although Jasper was surprised to learn she lived in the borderlands. Her speech held no suggestion of a Lowlander's lilt. "Is every man a monk up there?" Jasper asked, trying to lighten a mood that seemed to grow darker as the marquess continued to regard him.

"She's blind, Henley. Surely you noticed."

Jasper gave a start, despite his intention to appear nonplussed by the marquess' manner. "She is not blind," he countered with a shake of his head. "Near-sighted, surely, but not blind."

Devonville gave a shake of his own head. "She may as well be blind. She can only see things when they are close up—"

"A pair of spectacles will solve that problem," Jasper said

with a shrug. When the marquess' face appeared more pinched than normal, he sighed. "What is it?"

Allowing a sigh of his own, Devonville said, "Apparently, she has a pair. She was wearing them when she arrived in London, but ever since Cherice welcomed her into our home, she hasn't worn them. In his last letter, my brother mentioned she went about wearing them everywhere she went in Canobie. Wore them quite regularly. But since she's been here, she's quite stubborn about refusing to wear them."

Jasper frowned. Had Cherice spoken with her? Explained that eyeglasses were not regarded kindly by the Beau Monde? Which had him wondering why lorgnettes and quizzing glasses were acceptable eyewear for members of the *ton*, but spectacles were not.

Half the members of the Royal Society wore eyeglasses, and yet their use was expected if for no other reason than they added an aura of wisdom to men who were already seen as experts in their fields. "How bad can they be?" Jasper countered.

The marquess rolled his eyes. "Have you ever seen a pair of Martin's Margins?" he asked rhetorically. "With clear glass lenses?"

The viscount's eyes darted to one side, as if he thought he might find the offending eyewear standing next to him. "I may have," Jasper hedged, realizing he had never paid much attention to eyewear. A few of his colleagues wore spectacles. His uncle used a pair of bifocals when he was doing his books and for reading. They made him appear wiser. Older, too, but then the man was well into his fifties.

"They're hideous," Devonville stated, his thumbs and forefingers forming 'O's that he then raised to frame his eyes. "Ugly black circles with even uglier..." he motioned with his fingers to indicate the hinged sides that had to wrap around the head.

Jasper grimaced. "Surely an oculist can see to a pair that

wouldn't appear so... hideous," he countered. Most of the eyewear he had seen had lenses held in gold wire or silver or iron frames. The marquess no doubt referred to eyeglass frames made with tortoiseshell or horn, which would explain their dark color and thick circles.

Devonville gave a start, as if he hadn't considered that option. "Oculist?" he repeated.

"Of course. I'm a member of the Royal Academy. We have a couple of oculists in our midst. Waller is getting on in years, but he still has his practice. He's the oculist to the king," Jasper explained, referring to Jonathan Wathen-Waller, an eye surgeon of some renown. "Unfortunately, James Ware died last year," he added with a bit of sadness.

In the prior century, Ware had been a partner of Wathen-Waller's, and when Ware left to open his own shop, Wathen-Waller's step grandson, Jonathan Phipps, became his apprentice. The young man was proving as adept as his grandfather at treating eye diseases, performing surgeries, and fitting patients with corrective lenses—for those willing to wear spectacles.

These days, those who were willing were also on the older side. Less likely to be bothered by the dictates of fashion that eschewed eyewear of any kind—other than a lorgnette or a quizzing glass.

Why eyeglasses were considered a mark of wisdom in Italy, where they had made their debut over five-hundred years ago, but were considered unfashionable in England, was beyond Jasper's ken just then.

On his last expedition to Italy, Jasper had paid witness to a stage actress wearing a pair of what he just then realized had to be Martin's Margins. They featured green colored lenses as a means to protect the eyes from the bright sun. He had watched as she proudly made her way across a piazza to an outdoor cafe, the noon-day light rather harsh. During her luncheon with a friend, a half-dozen people approached her table and commented on how stylish her 'sunglasses' appeared.

Apparently a person blessed with some fame would have to be seen in public—in London—in order for public perception of spectacles to change in England, he realized.

Jasper didn't think it would happen in his lifetime, though.

"Perhaps you'll have better luck getting her to wear them then," Devonville replied with a shrug. He sighed. "Pray tell... when you escorted her to the gardens, you must have had an inkling something like this might happen," he half-asked.

"I did," Jasper admitted with a nod. "I found her company especially pleasant. She took such joy in the gardens. In the flowers. The entire time, I knew it was just a matter of time before you or Lady Devonville would make an appearance—"

"Then why didn't you return her to the ballroom?" Devonville countered, obviously miffed at the viscount.

Jasper gave a one-shouldered shrug. "I was enjoying her company." *Enjoying her kisses*, but the marquess didn't need to know that.

"Had it just been me, I would have given you an out," Devonville claimed, appearing rather apologetic just then.

Jasper frowned. "Why? I knew what I was doing was... unacceptable," he countered. "But, by then, I had already decided I found your niece quite agreeable."

Devonville rolled his eyes. "Let us hope you still feel that way after you've had to spend more than a day in her company," he said as he arched a brow.

Rather alarmed at the comment, Jasper angled his head. "Is she... a hoyden?" He had been about to say, "Fast," thinking perhaps this wasn't the first time she'd been caught with a man in the gardens, but he thought better of it.

"Oh, no, no, nothing like that," Devonville replied with

a shake of his head. "But she can be a bit... independent. Head-strong, even," he said in a hoarse whisper. "But I swear, should I learn you've raised a hand to do violence upon her—"

"I will do no such thing," Jasper interrupted, rather offended by Devonville's implication. "I'll have you know I never once touched my Sophie with anything other than a gentle hand."

How could he when she shied away from his hold?

The marquess furrowed his brows and finally nodded. "It's not that Marianne is spoiled, exactly, but she spends a good deal of time reading, and I fear she's become a bit of a bluestocking," he explained, obviously scandalized by the thought that his niece might be an intellectual. "I cannot believe my brother would allow it, but then he hasn't exactly had the benefit of a wife to help with raising her."

As a member of the Royal Society, Jasper found he preferred the company of those who were well-read. Those who were educated. Although Sophie had been taught a bit of arithmetic and how to read and write, she hadn't known enough of the world to be much of a conversationalist, and although she feigned interest in his archaeological expeditions and the two books he had written on Roman artifacts, he knew she hadn't read either one.

"Miss Slater sounds perfect," Jasper replied with a shrug. "I cannot abide the thought of having a stupid wife. Being headstrong is not necessarily a bad trait if she is merely standing up for her principles," he added, his chin lifted in defiance.

Devonville sighed, deciding he wasn't going to talk the viscount out of the marriage. Not that he wanted to—having Marianne betrothed only a few days into her first Season in London was a coup as far as he was concerned. Cherice would be thrilled, he was sure, which meant she would be especially attentive later that evening.

And probably for the next few days.

"When do you plan to marry her?" Devonville queried. "I'll be sure you receive a suitable settlement, of course. I'm quite sure my brother has a decent dowry set aside for her. Probably growing larger by the day," he added, *sotto voce*.

"If I can obtain a marriage license on the morrow, then we shall be married in six days" Jasper stated, ignoring the man's remark about the dowry.

Faith! Had Lord Donald given up all hope of marrying off his daughter? Jasper wondered. *How bad can she be?* Marianne seemed ever so pleasant. Ever so happy whilst they toured the gardens. Ever so willing as they kissed in full view of Cupid.

"Cherice will be at once happy and then all atwitter when she learns of your plans," Devonville replied. "I pity whatever modiste she calls on tomorrow. There are bride clothes to be made, you see, and clothes for the wedding trip." He sighed. "Are you quite sure you can't wait a few more days?"

Jasper blinked. *"The Fairweather* sails for Italy in just a week, so I can wait until then, I suppose," the viscount finally agreed. "As long as Miss Slater is in agreement."

Devonville frowned. "I will make her be in agreement," he stated. And with that, he gave a curt nod and took his leave of the study.

Taking a deep breath, Jasper watched the retreating back of the marquess before letting it out at the same time the door closed.

What am I getting myself into? he wondered. He had a thought to find Miss Slater to let her know of the plans. He didn't think it fair she would learn of them from her uncle.

Well, he would be taking her for a drive in the park tomorrow afternoon. The time on the phaeton would give him an opportunity to converse with the young lady. An opportunity to learn about her likes and dislikes, her faults and her foibles.

She'll learn about mine as well, he thought, wondering what she thought of him given they had only spent an hour and ten minutes in each other's company. Some couples he knew hadn't even had that much time together before they said their vows—their marriages had been arranged since they were barely able to walk.

If Marianne Slater decided he was lacking, or that she didn't like him, or that she had changed her mind about marriage, she would have to be the one to call it off.

Jasper had every intention of honoring his promise to marry her.

Chapter 4

FORESIGHT PROVES
FORTUITOUS

*M*eanwhile, in Sicily

"This came for you, Aunt," Angela Romano said as she handed a frequently franked missive to Chiara Romano. Although the words were said in English, they were stilted and careful in their pronunciation.

"*Grazie*," Chiara replied, turning her attention from her sewing to the note. She blinked as she turned it over, its red wax seal apparently still intact despite the number of hands through which it had passed on its way from England. She broke the seal and unfolded the parchment, furrowing her brows as she read the even script. Written in English, the note was embossed at the bottom and included a signature in a flourish of swirls that she supposed were meant to convey importance.

Dear Mrs. Romano,

I am writing at the request of my client, Viscount Henley, in regards to securing a villa for this lordship's use whilst he is engaged in an archeological expedition near Girgenti. Lord Henley, renown in his field of Roman ruins (specifically mosaics), was informed you have such a property and might agree to let it to him for the two months he plans to be in Girgenti beginning in early May. He has secured passage on The Fairweather, and expects to dock in Marina di Girgenti around the fifth of May.

My client's needs are minimal. A housemaid, a cook and a laundress, and the occasional services of a valet should be enough to see to his needs. His lordship will of course pay a deposit in local currency upon arrival and the balance before he departs. Please find enclosed a character as well as a cheque that can be converted to piastras in Girgenti. This is meant to convey the importance of my client's intent.

May I inform his lordship you are in agreement with his plan? A return note detailing your acceptance and your charges for his lordship's stay will be appreciated. My address is below.

Sincerely yours,
Andrew S. Barton, Esq.

Chiara re-read the missive three times to be sure she understood every word. It had been a long time since she had read anything written in English, and although she could speak the language and understood it well enough to interact with those who dared to visit Sicily since the wars, she struggled with the written language.

"What does it say?" Angela asked. She had been standing next to where Chiara sat for nearly ten minutes, her brows furrowed as she attempted to make out the strange words.

"It seems we're to have an Englishman stay at our guest villa," Chiara finally replied. "Lord Henley," she added, an elegant eyebrow arching as she said the name. She opened the character, once again frowning as she struggled to interpret the list of accomplishments—two books and several expeditions—and the associations to which her future guest belonged. An initial thought that the viscount was probably in his sixties was proved wrong when she noted his age listed in the midst of his details.

Thirty-one. Older than her son, but not nearly as old as she would expect from his credentials. Then she studied the bank draft, and her eyes widened.

"An aristocrat?" Angela asked.

"*Sì,*" Chiara replied absently, shaking her head at the amount written on the cheque. Then she grimaced when she re-read *why* Lord Henley was coming.

An archaeological expedition.

Chiara wondered what the man hoped to cart away when he returned to England. If he only studied the Roman mosaics, perhaps he would leave them—if he found any. Most of the excavations that had taken place in the Valley of the Templi had unearthed Greek artifacts, the work overseen by an Italian duke the decade before. The area had been home to some Romans back in the day, though, and there were the ruins of a Greco-Roman quarter mostly buried closer to Girgenti.

When her aunt didn't provide any more details, Angela asked, "May I work for him?"

Chiara regarded her niece a moment, rather surprised the girl seemed so anxious to work for a pompous English lord. But then, Angela had never been introduced to one. They hadn't had any visitors from England since the French invaders had been vanquished. "He'll require a laundress, a cook, and a maid," she replied as if in warning.

At fourteen years of age, Angela was too young to be the cook, but she could handle the other duties. Chiara had been seeing to her education in all matters of an Italian household since taking on the care of Angela when Chiara's brother died during the last battle against France. Thank the gods Ferdinand had been successful in driving out the latest invaders of Sicily. Now part of the Two Kingdoms of the Sicilies, the island fell under Spain's protection.

"I can do the laundry," Angela said with nod. "Aurora can see to the cooking, and Tamara can be the maid."

Grinning at her niece's words, Chiara realized the girl had made the work assignments much as she might. The girl's other two nieces, older and both seeing to a widow's household in Girgenti, might welcome the opportunity to earn some money. Neither had landed husbands, although it was just a matter of time before Aurora made a match. Her cooking skills had attracted the attentions of several young men in the city, a surprise since her mother had died giving birth to Angela.

"Then I shall write back to this..." She re-read the name of the solicitor who had sent the letter. "Signore Barton, and inform him we will have a villa for his lordship."

Angela beamed with delight. "Should I begin cleaning the guest villa?" she asked, nearly bouncing on the balls of her feet.

Chiara allowed a grin. "*Sì.*"

She could only hope Angela's enthusiasm wouldn't be crushed upon meeting their guest.

Chapter 5

ENVISIONING A PERFECT UNION

*L**ater that night***

Despite the glass of brandy he had downed after returning from the ball and the rather boring book he had been attempting to finish on the excavations taking place near Athens—it seemed as if everything ancient Greek was in the process of being dug up or crated for transport to England—Jasper found he couldn't get to sleep.

For the second time in his life, he was due to marry a young lady because he had been caught kissing her in Lord Attenborough's garden. Caught by Cupid as well as the man responsible for the young lady.

Although he had wanted to marry Sophie Knox—he had even planned to propose with a betrothal ring he had already purchased in Ludgate Hill—he hadn't wanted them to *have* to get married. He didn't want their union tainted by the events of that night.

As for Miss Marianne Slater, he had to admit he was experiencing a bit of a quandary. From the moment he thought she was watching him in the ballroom, he had been intrigued. Intrigued enough to stop his exit from the crush of the ball so that he might make his way back to the young lady with the arresting blue eyes.

Love at first sight? he wondered. He knew it was possible. Why, his fellow viscount, George Bennett-Jones, Viscount Bostwick, claimed he had fallen in love with his viscountess the very first time he spotted her at a ball. The man later admitted he had been predisposed to the idea of loving Elizabeth Carlington, though, when he learned her charity had helped his best friend. But Jasper knew nothing of Marianne Slater prior to this evening. He barely knew the Marquess of Devonville had a niece.

So when had he decided a kiss was warranted? Nay, necessary?

He remembered the way she had touched the roses, and a frisson passed through his entire body.

That was it then.

He had fallen in love with her fingers.

Jasper rolled his eyes. Her fingers had been encased in silk gloves at the time. But there was the way she had sniffed the rose and then lifted her face to smile up at him.

Oh, Christ. That had to be it.

How she smiled at him.

But there had also been the promise of a pleasing figure beneath her gown. A sense she was a bit older than the dozen or so young ladies in attendance at the ball. The unexplainable attraction he was sure they shared.

Now, every time he thought of Marianne Slater, a part of him reacted in a manner rather unexpected. A manner apparently of lust. A manner that had his bed linens tenting halfway down his body.

Jasper allowed a sigh of frustration, wondering if he should have made a trip to a brothel before returning to his townhouse in South Audley Street.

He hadn't bedded a woman since Sophie. And she had been the only woman he had bedded during their marriage, despite his married friends' insistence that he didn't have to remain monogamous. To have spent time in the beds of others whilst attempting to get a child on Sophie didn't seem right, though.

Before Sophie, there had been other women.

Back when his funds were more flush—before he had sunk half his viscountcy's fortunes into archaeological expeditions—he had at one time enjoyed the weekly company of a mistress at *The Elegant Courtesan*, a high-end brothel in Westminster. Flame-haired and green-eyed, with rather large breasts that bounced in rhythm to his thrusts, Miss Ann welcomed him with such enthusiasm, Jasper thought she found his lovemaking skills more than adequate.

Nothing could be further from the truth.

She admitted after a year of his regular visits that she appreciated his simple tastes. Appreciated that he didn't expect her to perform "unsavory acts," she later explained.

Which had him wondering what her other clients expected of her.

Miss Ann had started to list some of the positions in which she had to perform sexual intercourse, but then stopped and shook her head, claiming she didn't want to be giving him any "unsavory ideas."

He knew some members of his sex claimed to have insatiable appetites when it came to sexual congress. They spoke of their exploits at his men's club when they played cards. Described nights filled with too much drink and debauchery. Bemoaned the following days spent with headaches and hangovers.

Jasper rather preferred a clear head and the ability to remember what he had done the night before. Especially what he had been doing with Ann, even if it was "simple."

At least he didn't suffer aches and strains the way Lord Boomerant did after a night spent with Miss Boo. She was blessed with exotic eyes and upturned breasts, but challenged her clients with positions straight out of the Kama Sutra.

Jasper never had to worry about a snake bite, as did those who attempted to share Miss Debra's bed. The blonde with the dark almond eyes apparently spent her days and nights wrapped in a snake. Lord Everly never found the snake a challenge, but then he was a naturalist and probably had plenty of experience with the reptiles in the wild.

No, Miss Ann had suited Jasper just fine.

But will Marianne? he wondered.

Was she still a virgin?

Or had her headstrong manner or bluestocking reputation led to poor choices in men?

As a widower, Jasper found he didn't much care if she was a virgin as long as she didn't cuckold him. He couldn't abide the thought of sharing his wife with another man.

Wondering if he could bring up the topic during their ride in the park, Jasper rolled his eyes.

Why was he even concerned?

The poor girl would probably break off their engagement even before she stepped into whatever conveyance he might manage to borrow for the trip to the park.

He had a phaeton, but would Lord Devonville allow him to take Marianne on it? He would have to send a footman with a note in the morning and hope the marquess could respond before four o'clock in the afternoon.

About to drift off to sleep, Jasper suddenly blinked.

Oh, faith! I haven't even proposed to Miss Slater! he thought.

Jasper dared a glance at his Breguet and frowned. He was about to bolt out of bed when he realized he had the chronometer upside down. He flipped it around and stared at the jeweled face.

Three o'clock in the morning.

Miss Slater was probably sound asleep by now. To pay a

call on Devonville House and request a moment of her time in the mansion's parlor was probably out of the question at this hour.

Well, perhaps he could pay a call in the late morning. Or early afternoon.

What time did young ladies wake up these days?

If I don't go to sleep, I won't be waking up until it's time to leave for the park, Jasper thought in dismay.

Moving his thoughts to the boring book he had read before making his way to his bedchamber, he finally nodded off about the time the tented bed linens flattened out over his body.

*M*arianne regarded the leather binding on the book her aunt had just pulled down from the highest bookshelf in the library at Devonville House. "What is this?" she asked as she moved to open the front cover.

Obviously something important.

Aunt Cherice had seen to taking her to the library even before she had a chance to go up to her bedchamber to shed her ballgown in favor of a nightrail. The fact that the book was leather-bound made it even more important since not all books on the shelves had benefited from the expensive binding procedure.

"An attempt to quell your fears about the marriage bed," the former Viscountess Winslow replied with an arched brow. Her current title of Marchioness of Devonville seemed to suit her much better. "Seeing as how you don't have a mother to explain it." She furrowed a brow. "Come to think of it, my mum didn't explain it to me." Rolling her eyes, she finally directed them on her niece and gave a shake of her head. "I had to learn it all from Winslow," she said as her entire body seemed to quake with disgust.

Marianne was about to put voice to a protest at the same

time she was struggling to keep an impassive expression on her face. She hadn't said a word about the marriage bed whilst they rode home from the ball in the Devonville town coach.

She, in fact, hadn't had a chance.

Cherice had spent the entire time in conversation with Lord Devonville about the impending nuptials, although "conversation" probably wasn't the right word. The marquess was barely able to get a word in as Cherice espoused a series of "to-do's" she claimed were necessary to prepare for a *ton* wedding.

Her uncle had managed to remind his wife that Lord Henley wouldn't be *in* London much longer. "My love, do not fash yourself. There won't be time for a large wedding breakfast. Henley and Marianne will be departing for Italy in a week," he said as he patted Cherice's knee.

His marchioness blinked, as if she had to rethink every plan she had formulated. "But there will still be a wedding," she countered, her comment almost a question.

The way her uncle sighed had Marianne wondering if he thought Lord Henley would be sending his regrets. He couldn't though. If he broke off the engagement, she would be ruined! *I could break it off,* she thought. *Without so much as a logical reason.*

"I spoke with Henley—just to determine his willingness, of course—and he assures me he has every intention of marrying our niece. As for Marianne, I think we should ask *her* if she's truly willing to marry a man she hardly knows." He said the words as if his niece wasn't sitting just two feet in front of him in the coach.

"Of course, I am willing," Marianne piped up as she leaned forward a bit, her face illuminated by the carriage's interior lantern. Hearing that Lord Henley truly intended to marry her was a bit of pleasant news. She knew the two men had taken their leave of the ballroom, presumedly to discuss the terms of the marriage. "I feared he thought me... too old," she hedged.

Too blind would have been her first choice of reasons, but Lord Henley didn't seem bothered by her lack of eyesight. Had it been any other man, she thought he might find her near-sightedness a liability. That he might change his mind about wanting to marry given she was essentially blind. Hearing Lord Henley still intended to marry her even when given the opportunity to opt out had her assessment of the viscount changing.

He's honorable and *handsome*, she thought.

Relieved there would be a wedding—and within a week —Marianne settled back into the squabs and wondered at how her body had reacted to the viscount's kiss. She remembered how pleasant the kiss had been. Pleasant and exciting. Then she wondered if their marriage bed might be the same.

Pleasant and exciting.

Staring at the color plate that was on display in the book she was holding over one arm—she had allowed it to open of its own accord to the middle of a series of color images— Marianne suddenly wondered if the marriage bed might be a bit *too* exciting.

Embarrassing, actually.

Cherice must have noticed her look of shock, for she quickly said, "Oh, don't be alarmed. Some of those color plates are rather... well, the whole book is *French*, so there's bound to be some... *positions* you may find distasteful. But you'll want to give most of them a try as you'll find it necessary to keep your husband entertained in your bed. You don't want him to have an excuse to employ a mistress."

The spine still resting on a forearm and the book wide open to a rather salacious image, Marianne listened to her aunt's comments and found she couldn't *not* be alarmed.

Faith!

Were those two people?

And just what were they *doing?*

They looked as if... Marianne gasped despite Cherice's warning and shut the book. She blinked. "Necessary?" she nearly cried out, briefly trying to imagine the viscount to whom she found herself betrothed doing what the man in the painting was doing with some poor young woman.

Or perhaps she should be pitying the poor man.

"*Necessary*, or else someone *else* will be entertaining him in *their* bed," Cherice replied with an arched brow. She "tsk'd" and took the book from Marianne. Cherice flipped through several printed pages until the series of color plates flashed by. She stopped at one and angled the book so it faced her niece. "Now, this position is easy, and men love it because... well, let us just say I think Viscount Henley will appreciate it because you're rather well-endowed..."

"I am?" Marianne countered, one arm going up in an attempt to hide her bosom. The man in the painting had his face planted between the woman's breasts as she sat facing him, her bottom on his lap and her legs wrapped about his torso and the back of the chair in which he sat. "Oh, no," she whispered as she dropped her gaze down the front of her rather chaste gown. *Is that why Lord Henley saw fit to speak with me?* she wondered then. *Because he thought me well-endowed?*

"Oh, darling," Cherice sighed. "Most men love a pair of plump breasts. A pair of peaches they can't quite completely cover with their mouths but can hold in their hands," Cherice explained as one of her hands went to her own bosom. The tops of her rising moons were mostly on display in the bright pink silk deNaples gown she had worn to the ball that evening.

Had Marianne not become so flustered at hearing her aunt's outrageous claim, she might have countered it with her late mother's comment that men didn't appreciate women who were too fleshy.

Am I too fleshy? she wondered.

"They also love it if you leave your hair down at night. No mob caps. Ever. And don't braid it, either, for they'll just undo the ribbon, and then it will be lost in the bedding." She paused a moment before her face crinkled into a mischievous grin. "But if you do find it, you can always tie it around his..." She stopped when she realized her niece looked as if she was thoroughly scandalized.

Or about to faint.

"Well, never mind about the ribbon."

Marianne blinked, not about to ask how a ribbon might become lost. Or tied around... well, whatever her aunt was about to suggest it could be tied around. She could imagine what that might be, especially after seeing some of the images in the book she still held.

She rather doubted any of her hair ribbons would be long enough, though.

Marianne turned the page and blushed red at seeing a painting of a woman bent over a huge bed, her bare bottom pressed against the front of a man's nether region. "Surely he won't expect me to do *this?*" she half-asked. The woman in the painting obviously wore cosmetics and was probably a mistress or a courtesan engaged in a rather scandalous dalliance with a man wearing a periwig and nothing else.

Cherice sighed. "My mother always said it's why she gave birth to five boys and just one daughter," she claimed with an arched brow.

Her aunt's implication quite clear, Marianne tried to hide her look of shock as she once again shut the book. She ignored the puff of dust that blew into the air, her attention on the fact that she would be expected to bear an heir. And preferably a spare, as well, before giving birth to daughters.

Wouldn't she?

Cherice angled her head. "I remember my first wedding night, although I don't know how. I must have drunk an entire bottle of champagne. Thank the gods, or I think I would have fainted over what Winslow did to me," she claimed, referring to her late husband. She didn't go into detail, which suited Marianne just fine. "I know you'll be quite scandalized at some of the paintings in the book, but do read the narrative," Cherice encouraged. Then she paused a moment and lowered her voice. "After the first time, and if Henley is only a half-skilled lover, you'll find yourself enjoying the marriage bed."

Sure her cheeks were bright red, Marianne nodded. "I'll read some of it tonight," she promised, wondering why her aunt found it so important she know about such things when Marianne was still trying to decide if she should break off the engagement with Lord Henley.

For she just realized something rather important.

What engagement?

The man hadn't even proposed!

He had simply acquiesced to her uncle's implication that he was expected to marry her given they had been caught kissing.

I can call it off, she reminded herself. Women were allowed to break off betrothals without so much as a hint of scandal.

She dared a glance at the mantle clock, wondering if it was too late to ask for a carriage to take her to Lord Henley's residence—wherever that was—and admit it was all just a mistake. Apologize profusely for ever joining him in Lord Attenborough's gardens.

She blinked when she realized it was three o'clock in the morning.

Well, she could just have the coach take her to the nearest posting inn, board a stage coach, and make her way back to Canobie. Leave a note claiming she and Lord Henley wouldn't suit, although...

Who was she kidding?

If all she and Lord Henley ever did was kiss one another, they would have a happy union.

A frisson shot through her entire body, and she nearly put voice to a curse. The thought of Lord Henley doing to her what the periwigged man in that one painting was doing to the rather fleshy courtesan had her stays suddenly feeling entirely too tight.

She dared a glance down, wondering what was happening to her fleshy breasts before she returned her thoughts to the situation at hand.

Who even knew they were to marry?

There were just the three witnesses to her indiscretion. Aunt Cherice, Uncle William, and Aunt Adele. Surely Aunt Adele wouldn't say anything to the visitors she would be hosting for tea in the afternoon.

Marianne rolled her eyes. Of course Aunt Adele would mention it. Why, she probably intended to announce the impending nuptials to all her morning callers. And then, when she went to call on Lady Norwick in the afternoon, she would tell all the afternoon callers in the parlor at Norwick House. The next issue of *The Tattler* would feature an entire paragraph—maybe two—about them, if the last issue was any indication.

Sighing, Marianne bade her aunt a good night and made her way to her bedchamber, the book held under one arm. Despite not wearing her eyeglasses, she found her bedchamber and spent the rest of her waking hours reading and then studying the rather graphic paintings.

And feeling ever so scandalized.

Chapter 6

SEEING TO A PROPER
PROPOSAL

The following afternoon
Jasper regarded the missive a footman had just delivered to his study. The Devonville crest was emblazoned in the dark red wax that sealed the four corners in the middle. Popping the wax, he unfolded the parchment to reveal the marquess' reply to his earlier query.

> *Dear Henley,*
>
> *In response to your query as to the suitability of taking Miss Slater to the park on a phaeton ~ I give you my permission. Seeing as how you're betrothed, you have my permission to do whatever you see fit to do with her. She is yours now.*
>
> *Devonville*

Blinking at the short, rather curt reply, Jasper felt a combination of relief and dread. Of course Lord Devonville would think a phaeton a suitable form of conveyance. He had no doubt courted his second wife on his sporty red phaeton. Jasper's black model was as staid as they came. He chose it over yellow only because he thought the yellow would display the dust and dirt of Rotten Row to poor advantage.

Since Devonville's missive didn't mention anything about Miss Slater having changed her mind—or perhaps arranged to flee London on a stagecoach bound for Scotland in the middle of the night—Jasper had to assume she still wanted to ride with him in the park.

At half-past three o'clock in the afternoon, he took the reins from the stableboy in the mews behind his townhouse and tossed the urchin a coin.

"Much obliged," the boy called out as Jasper led his single horse into traffic on South Audley. He was leaving a bit early, to be sure, since Devonville's residence was just a mile away at the north end of Park Lane, but he didn't want to arrive too late. He figured Lady Devonville was probably a stickler when it came to appointments, and he didn't want her to develop a poor opinion of him. Even though Cherice DuBois Winslow Slater wasn't Marianne's true aunt, she was seeing to the young lady's come-out in London. Better he stay on her good side until he could wed Marianne Slater.

As to if he could manage the same *after* the wedding, Jasper felt a profound sense of relief when he remembered he wouldn't have to. He and Marianne would be on a ship bound for Italy, his archaeological expedition keeping him in Sicily at least six months. Possibly longer.

When he halted his horse in front of the white Palladian mansion bearing a brass lion's head knocker on a door flanked by spiral topiary trees, Jasper took a deep breath. He would be forced to wait for fifteen minutes or more in the vestibule of Devonville House, he was sure, but better he sit there than to wait out in Park Lane for anyone to see. He hobbled his horse and made his way to the front door, not the least bit surprised when Hatfield, the butler, answered his knock.

"Lord Henley for Miss Marianne," he said as he presented his calling card.

The butler gave a nod. "I'll see if the young lady is in residence, milord," Hatfield said as he took the card. At least the butler allowed him to enter the vestibule. Jasper didn't want to be seen loitering outside the marquess' mansion.

The fifteen-minute wait turned out to be only a few minutes when he realized the young lady was descending the stairs.

He gave a bow even before she had come to a complete stop in front of him. "My lady," he said as he reached for her gloved hand.

"You came," Marianne said as she dipped a curtsy and watched with fascination as he brushed his lips over her knuckles.

Jasper blinked. "Of course I came." He frowned. "Did... did you think I would not?" he wondered, rather dismayed by the thought that she didn't consider him honorable enough to keep their engagement.

Marianne gave a one-shouldered shrug. "I wanted to believe it, truly I did. But I fear I have become somewhat jaded since my arrival in London."

"Jaded?" he repeated, his brows furrowing.

The young woman colored up. "My aunt warned me that young bucks might find my lack of... clear vision... a detriment."

His frown still firmly in place, Jasper asked, "Do you lack vision?" he wondered. "Or merely the ability to see clearly?"

Marianne blinked, her gaze rising to meet his. "They are not the same?" she countered in a hoarse whisper.

Jasper allowed a slight grin. "They are not. If my lady will allow me, I shall explain their differences as we make our way to Hyde Park." He glanced around, rather surprised a lady's maid hadn't yet joined her.

"I will allow it, of course," Marianne replied, her manner most sincere. "I look forward to it, in fact."

"Very well. Will your lady's maid be joining us? Or... or a footman, perhaps?" He thought it rather unlikely he would be allowed to escort the young woman into the park for the fashionable hour without the benefit of a chaperone.

And then he remembered Devonville's earlier missive.

Seeing as how you're betrothed, you have my permission to do whatever you see fit to do. She is yours now.

"No," Marianne replied with a shake of her head. "Uncle William said the *ton* will simply know we are betrothed if I am seen without a chaperone."

Jasper blinked, rather surprised at this bit of news. If anyone from the Royal Society saw him with a woman at his side, they would probably pass out from shock. He had already been admonished for how long he had stayed in mourning, evident from the black arm band he always wore in public. Given the nature of his ride today, and the fact that he was due to remarry—and rather soon—Jasper had tucked away the arm band in the back of a dresser drawer.

He hoped that he might never have to wear it again.

With the assurance they didn't require a chaperone came Jasper's relief there wouldn't be one. He didn't know where he might have space for one on his phaeton. "Shall we?" he asked as he offered his arm.

"Yes," Marianne replied with a nod, placing a gloved hand on his proffered arm. "I would be remiss if I didn't admit I have been looking forward to this all day," Marianne stated as they made their way down the front walk to where his phaeton was parked. "I have spent at least three hours in parlors drinking tea and listening to old matrons repeat their impressions of last night's ball," she complained.

Jasper wondered how he was going to get Marianne up and onto the phaeton's high bench. He would have simply lifted her up there, but he wasn't sure she would welcome his hold on her waist. The safer alternative was to lace his fingers together and provide a step much like he would do for a lady mounting a horse.

In the end, he didn't have to do either, as Marianne simply raised her skirts and took the step up of her own accord, although she did place a gloved hand on his shoulder for support. "Were their impressions... agreeable?" he asked, having a hard time keeping his voice even.

The flash of a stockinged ankle had him taking in a breath rather slowly. *Steady*, he warned himself, even though he thrilled at the brief glimpse of the well-turned ankle above her slipper.

"For the most part," she replied. "Although there were complaints about the heat and the fact that the Prince Regent didn't make an appearance."

Was he supposed to? Jasper nearly asked. It was rare when Prince Charles attended a *ton* ball, and he usually only did if it was hosted by a duke. "It was rather warm in Attenborough's ballroom given how chilly it was last night," Jasper commented as he moved to the other side of the phaeton and climbed onto the bench. A jolt of something pleasant shot through him when he realized Marianne's thigh was pressed against his. She didn't even attempt to move away from him, although if she did, she would no longer be completely seated on the phaeton's small bench. She might actually topple off!

"Are you comfortable?" Jasper wondered before he took up the reins.

"I am," Marianne replied, daring a glance in his direction. "I must admit, I have never ridden in such a conveyance. It's rather... exhilarating," she claimed as the phaeton merged into the late afternoon traffic.

Exhilarating and frightening.

She wasn't wearing her spectacles, so she couldn't see anything clearly more than three feet in front of her face.

Beyond that, the other equipage and horses, buildings and streets, and costermongers and street urchins were just a blur of color and motion.

"Do you daydream?" he asked, remembering his promise to explain the difference in vision and seeing clearly. "Imagine things in your mind that you wish could be true?"

Marianne regarded him a moment, rather surprised he would ask such a personal question. "Sometimes," she hedged.

"So you see... visions. Like in your dreams."

"I do," she agreed.

"Do you see them clearly, or are all the edges blurry?"

Blinking at his query, Marianne gave it a great deal of thought. "I see them clearly," she admitted in awe, as if she had never given it thought before. She had spent hours daydreaming. Without siblings to play with, and living in a home on the outskirts of a border town, she had to use her imagination or suffer from extreme boredom.

"Then, just because you cannot see clearly does not mean you lack vision," he said quietly.

"Still, I rather wish I could see clearly," Marianne countered. "Although, given what I think is about to happen to that cart up ahead, perhaps it's better I do not."

Jasper allowed a quiet curse as he pulled back on the reins in an attempt to slow their progress, the move necessary to prevent a collision with said cart. Given Marianne could at least tell it was a cart up ahead suggested she could see better than he originally thought. "You can see that cart?" he half-asked.

Marianne dipped her head. "I can see a... a rectangular blob with round things beneath," she said. "Things come into focus as they get closer, which is why I was sure it was about to hit us."

Grinning, Jasper dared a glance in her direction. "I don't yet own a town coach," he commented. "But if I order one from Tilbury's this week, there's a chance it will be ready when we return from our wedding trip."

Marianne inhaled sharply. *He really does intend to marry me!* "I have been wondering something, and thought to ask if you object to my age."

Jasper blinked. "Why would I object to your age? What are you? Two-... three-and-twenty, perhaps?" he pretended to guess, remembering what Devonville had said in the study the night before.

Marianne gasped. "Now you're being a bounder," she accused, her chin lifted in the universal manner women used to display their displeasure.

Jasper blinked again. "Other than last night, I have never been accused of being a bounder," he claimed, not sure if he should be offended or amused. He dared a glance in her direction, rather surprised to find she looked as if she were about to cry. "Truth be told, your uncle said you were three-and-twenty. I had no reason to doubt his words," he said quietly.

"You should have," she replied with a sigh.

Frowning, Jasper wondered what she meant. "From your manner last night, I would have assumed you were a bit older—"

"Older?" she interrupted, her bright blue eyes wide.

"Accomplished," Jasper stated, about to curse when a nearby rider on horseback seemed intent on colliding with the phaeton. "Which has me hoping you're closer to five-and-twenty," he stated, deciding he couldn't offend her too terribly much. "But then," he hedged, rather hoping she would just come out and admit her true age. "I remember you have grown up without the benefit of a mother and may have gained your confident manner from necessity." He pulled back on the reins as a barouche cut in front of them when he negotiated the last turn before the park's entrance. "I will admit that since I am older—and a widower—I would prefer a wife closer in age to me." He knew Marianne had turned to regard him, her stunned expression finally forcing him to glance in her direction. "But if you are only three-and-twenty, I will not mind that either."

Allowing a sigh that had her shoulders slumping a bit, Marianne seemed to swallow a sob. "I am six-and-twenty."

Jasper had to suppress the urge to laugh, more relieved than amused by her manner. "You needn't make it sound as if you're *elderly*," he teased.

"Are you?" she countered. "Elderly, I mean."

About to curse at the driver of a landau who was about to sideswipe the barouche in front of them, Jasper frowned his offense. "Of course not!" he replied with a quick shake of his head. "At least, I've never thought of one-and-thirty as being *old*."

Marianne seemed visibly relieved by his assurance. "It's not. I just... seeing as how I cannot see well, I wasn't completely sure," she stammered. "Forgive me," she added as she turned her attention back to the road ahead, or rather the landau that now seemed determined to merge into the barouche so they appeared as one rather wide carriage in her limited vision.

Had she not been wearing a bonnet that covered the side of her head facing him, Jasper would have kissed her hair. He combined the reins into one fist and covered one of her gloved hands with the other, giving it a quick shake of assurance. "There's nothing to forgive. Besides, I am rather glad you are as old as you are."

"Truly?"

Nodding, Jasper managed to steer the horse away from the equipage intent on doing damage up ahead. "Older means you probably know more. You've had a chance to read more books..." He paused when he noticed her sudden look of surprise, as if he had caught her reading one that very instant. Probably an inappropriate book. Like the one she had read until five o'clock that morning. "You do read?" he half-asked.

"I do," she replied, rather hesitant with her response.

"I don't mind an educated woman. You know what you like, and what you don't like. You're less likely to do something foolish. You've already reached your majority and decided what to do with your inheritance. You may have already spent it on something grand or gambled it away." He paused again. "Do stop me if I've assumed wrongly," he encouraged, his manner once again teasing.

Marianne angled her head, rather amused by his list of possibilities. "It's true about the books. About the foolish behavior. As to what I like and don't like, I suppose it depends, for I have been known to change my mind."

Recognizing the opening for what it was, Jasper asked, "Will you be changing your mind about marrying me?" He had to turn his attention back to the landau that now seemed about to run over his horse. Glancing behind him, he had the gelding taking a right turn in an attempt to get as far from the suicidal landau as possible. "It's your right, of course, but... I hope you will not," he added in a soft voice.

Marianne considered his words, rather touched at how he said them. "As for my inheritance, I haven't yet collected it. I think my father was holding out hope I would be wed. So that means I haven't gambled it away," she explained before adding, "I know how to play some card games. I've even won a few pounds from my father, but that was a long time ago, and truth be told, I think he let me win."

Jasper chuckled, his gaze darting between her and the traffic ahead. "You needn't worry about my gambling. As a man of science, I know the odds are not in my favor, even in a game like faro, and so I do not participate."

The mention of him being a man of science had her furrowing her brows. "Are you truly planning a trip to Italy?"

she asked as they made their way beneath the gate that marked the entrance into Hyde Park.

"I am," he replied with a nod. "A colleague in my field of study is already there. Claims there are Roman mosaics buried in an ancient city. I have prints of old paintings and copies of drawings from the area. There is a well preserved Greek temple and some Roman ruins, but I am most interested in the mosaics," he explained. "I do hope you'll join me, seeing as how I've been able to obtain an extra ticket for your passage to Sicily," he added, daring another glance in her direction. "On *The Fairweather*. With me. I was able to secure a larger cabin for us."

Jasper had asked the ticket agent to hold his original cabin for his colleague, James Singleton. He had sent the man to Cambridge to retrieve a trunk containing another archaeologist's research materials. Dr. Darius Jones, who could usually be found excavating the remains of Roman forts along Hadrian's Wall, had already been on Sicily for a month. He had sent word to bring the trunk along, claiming he had already made discoveries in an old Roman city near Girgenti but wanted to compare his findings with those of an earlier archaeologist.

Singleton, Jasper's friend and fellow archaeologist for more than a decade, had never been a formal student of archaeology, but he had proven his worth on digs in the past. Jasper could only hope he could make it back to London in time for *The Fairweather's* departure.

As for the sleeping arrangements on board, Jasper now wondered if he should have secured yet another cabin for Marianne.

Will she be amenable to sharing one with me?

*M*arianne wondered at her future husband's words. The way he said he hoped she would join him.

Was he giving her the option to stay behind?

Did she want to remain in London? Doing so meant staying with her aunt and uncle, which, when she thought about it, wouldn't be such an inconvenience for her but certainly would be for a couple who were still enjoying their first few months of marriage. She already felt as if she was preventing them from displaying their obvious affection for one another. "I've never been to the Continent," Marianne finally replied. "Have you been before?"

The viscount nodded, well aware she hadn't responded to his query about joining him. "Twice. Both times for research. I'm an archaeologist, you see, so I travel a great deal."

"*Arky ologist,*" she replied, sounding out the word. Her brows furrowed. "Does that mean you study... ancient relics?" she guessed.

"Indeed," he replied happily, wondering who had seen to her education. She had obviously learned some Greek. If she knew any Latin, he would be in heaven. "I specialize in Roman artifacts. Their soldiers left behind a good deal of treasure here in England before they took their leave, but I prefer to study the artifacts in their homeland. In Rome and the surrounding lands," he explained.

"Where exactly will you go this time?"

"Girgenti. I plan to do some work I wanted to start the last time I was in Italy, but my finds north of Rome kept me there too long. This time, I hope to unearth the mosaic tile floors in what was once either a temple or the palatial home of a very wealthy citizen. It's possible there are many, so I hope to uncover what I can."

Marianne dared a glance in his direction. Despite her inability to see clearly, she was aware of a conveyance up ahead that seemed determined to collide with their horse. "If you haven't been, then how do you know it's there?"

Allowing a grin, Jasper sighed. "One of my colleagues informed me of the likelihood. He was in Sicily many years ago and has recently returned to continue his work. He'll be joining me on the dig, although he specializes in a different aspect of Roman culture."

Marianne gave his answer some thought before asking, "How long will you be gone?"

Jasper furrowed a brow. "*We* will be gone at least until winter makes it too uncomfortable to work out-of-doors," he replied, his emphasis on the 'we' unmistakeable. "Five or six months. More if it stays warm in Italy." Although he usually wouldn't go to Italy in the summer, the country seemed to be suffering the same prolonged cold spell the rest of England and Northern Europe were experiencing, the air filled with debris from several volcanoes that made the sunsets glorious and the sun less effective. There had even been reports of red snow falling in the mountains of northern Italy.

Marianne stared at her intended. "Will we go to the Colosseum?" she asked in awe.

"We can," he replied with a nod. "Once I've completed my search for mosaics on Sicily." Even though he didn't intend to spend more than a few days in the old city, it would be impossible to avoid the home of gladiators and the sight of circuses as they made their way north for sightseeing.

He had thought to spend most of the trip on the island of Sicily studying the ancient Roman city south of Girgenti, but with a wife on his arm, he realized he had an opportunity to show Marianne far more than a few sites of relics. They could visit Florence for the art and Venice for the glass. Eat rich foods and drink fine wines. Tour cathedrals.

Make love.

The thought of taking in the sights of Italy with Marianne on his arm had him looking forward to the trip far more than he had been just the week before.

"The Forum?" Marianne asked, her breath held in anticipation of his answer.

Jasper grinned. "Of course." He paused a moment. "I do hope you'll be able to *see* the places we visit."

Her body suddenly stiffening on the bench next to him, Marianne seemed to hold her breath once again before she finally responded. "I have a pair of spectacles," she admitted, her response a bit guarded.

"Then why aren't you wearing them now?" he countered as he negotiated the turn onto Rotten Row, pausing the horse so that a curricle could manage the turn from the other direction. "Do you have them with you?"

Marianne inhaled sharply, partly because she found she had to hold onto his arm or risk being tossed off the phaeton when he resumed their advance through the park. "I do," she replied as she indicated a reticule that hung from her other wrist.

"I should think you would wish to wear them," Jasper commented, rather liking the fact that Marianne had seen to gripping his arm as opposed to the front of the seat when the phaeton made the sharp turn. "Half the reason for coming to the park during the fashionable hour is to see everyone who comes out for the daily parade."

Blinking, Marianne considered his comment. "And the other half?" she queried.

"Why, to be seen, of course," Jasper replied with a teasing grin.

Marianne gave a start. "Which is why I will not be wearing the spectacles on this ride, my lord," she murmured. *Or anywhere else out-of-doors*, she nearly added.

Frowning, Jasper considered her words. "They cannot be that bad," he countered, turning to regard her when he was sure his horse had merged them safely into the line of equipage parading in Rotten Row.

"According to my aunt, they are hideous," she stated, trying her best to maintain a happy demeanor despite the subject of their conversation.

Jasper blinked. "Hideous?" he repeated. "That cannot be. Surely your beauty overcomes a pair of eyeglasses, no matter how bad they might be," he said lightly.

Marianne felt the heat of her blush even before she was sure her face displayed it. A combination of shock and awe and admiration for the man nearly robbed her of words just then. "You are very kind to say so," she managed. "But according to my aunt, I shouldn't wear them in polite Society. Or where anyone might actually see me."

A combination of shock and awe and disappointment in whichever aunt had put voice to such an instruction had Jasper holding his tongue just then. "To deprive a young lady of the ability to see more than a few feet in front of her face seems rather shortsighted," he said with no hint of humor. At Marianne's sudden grin and giggle, Jasper had to allow a grin of his own. "No pun was intended, my lady," he added.

After a few minutes of acknowledging greetings from a few riders on horseback as well as those who were walking along Rotten Row, Jasper regarded Marianne until she turned to face him. "What is it?" she asked, her face no longer partially hidden by her bonnet.

"If I were to take us to a place where no one can see, will you put on your spectacles? I wish to... to share a particularly beautiful sight, but I would like you to be able to *see* it."

Marianne dipped her head, realizing that if they married, he would eventually see her wearing the spectacles. Perhaps it was better he do so now. If it was apparent he was appalled—that he couldn't abide the sight of her wearing them—then she could break off the betrothal. Save him from having to marry her and her spectacles. Save him from spending a life with a woman he couldn't abide the sight of.

Especially if he didn't appreciate fleshy breasts.

And if he didn't seem bothered by the eyewear?

Well, then perhaps he could abide fleshy breasts, too.

Marianne had a thought that perhaps he couldn't see well, either. But if that were the case, Jasper wouldn't be able to drive them in the park, his command of the ribbons evident in how he managed to avoid so many collisions despite the close spacing of the equipage around and in front of them. Even without being able to see clearly, she could tell how close everyone else was to the phaeton.

Marianne allowed a sigh. "Very well," she replied to his query about putting on her spectacles. Her happy demeanor having been replaced with one of impending doom, Marianne hardly noticed when Jasper had the phaeton turning onto a side road. Under the shade of a maple planetree, Jasper pulled the horse to a halt and quickly jumped down to hobble it before coming around to help Marianne step down.

"Where are we?" she wondered, her limited vision revealing only a mass of greenery around them.

"Put on your spectacles so I can show you," he replied.

Her shoulders slumping, Marianne finally removed her reticule from her wrist and pulled apart the gathered opening. With a gloved hand, she reached in and plucked out the pair of eyeglasses. Mounted in a frame made of black tortoiseshell with hinged arms, the round lenses of the eyeglasses were thick but clear. Loops at the ends of the arms were threaded with ribbons.

Pausing a moment, Marianne gave Jasper a beseeching look before she placed the frame on her face so the slight wire arch between the discs rested on her nose. When she was about to tie the ribbons together at the back of her head, Jasper stepped around to stand behind her. "Allow me," he said as he took the ribbon ties from her gloved fingers and proceeded to tie them into a neat bow. "Is this tight enough?" he wondered.

"It's fine," she replied. She allowed a rather sad sigh as she slowly turned to face her escort and raised her face.

Angling his head first to one side and then to the other, Jasper's expression remained impassive. He allowed a shrug. "As I said, your beauty overcomes the spectacles."

Marianne's eyes blinked behind the thick lenses. "I could kiss you, my lord," she said, immediately embarrassed by her comment. "Oh! Oh, my! I cannot believe I just said that. Aloud," she added, her mortification apparent. "You must think me fast."

Grinning broadly, Jasper lowered his lips to hers and engaged her in a quick but thorough kiss. "I cannot either, truth be told, but they were very welcome words," he whispered. "When we are married, and we are alone as we are now, I hope you will always wish to kiss me."

Her eyes widening in surprise, Marianne allowed a nod. "So... you're not going to break off the betrothal?" she asked in a quiet voice. "Now that you've seen just how awful I look in these?"

Jasper blinked. "Of course not." He gave her a look filled with worry. "Were you... were *you* about to do so?" *Christ!* He had just purchased the marriage license earlier that afternoon! A detail he realized he hadn't yet shared with the young woman. "Because..." He reached into his topcoat pocket and withdrew the document he had obtained from the archdeacon's office. "I have already secured a marriage license. We can marry in five days without banns needing to be read."

Marianne's mouth opened, her astonishment apparent. "Not at all," she murmured, her head shaking from side-to-side. "Had you wished to, though, I was willing to suggest you allow me to do the *jilting*, since it would not reflect so badly upon me as it would you," she explained, her face screwing up to indicate her torn feelings on the matter.

Frowning, Jasper tried to decide if he should feel offended or not. He had every intention of marrying the woman.

Then Marianne stepped forward, the front of her body nearly pressed against his. "I didn't wish you to feel... *obligated* to marry me if you could not abide the sight of me in my spectacles, or the knowledge I will always be a burden because of my poor eyesight."

Closing his eyes, Jasper wrapped his arms around her shoulders and simply held her for a moment, reveling in how she didn't attempt to step away or seem scandalized by the close contact. "It is rather considerate of you, but please know that I had no intention of... of jilting *you*," he said quietly. He let go his hold on her and waved an arm to a small garden just off the crushed granite path. A collection of tulips and tiny white flowers were tucked into the intersection of the two hedgerows that hid them from the parkway. "But it reminds me that I never properly proposed."

Reaching into his waistcoat pocket, he withdrew a ring and held it between his thumb and forefinger. A lone sapphire—a rather impressive stone—topped the gold band. Marianne had never seen anything like it. Even her mother's wedding ring, with it's collection of tiny diamonds and her father's favorite garnet, wasn't as beautiful as the ring Jasper held for her.

"Will you wear it now? And forever more? As a symbol of my devotion to you?" Jasper asked in a quiet voice. "Will you be my wife?"

Marianne blinked as she struggled to remove the glove from her hand. "Oh yes. Yes, of course," she whispered, tears pricking the corners of her eyes. She wondered how she could have doubted him as she watched him slide the circlet of gold onto the fourth finger. Marianne sighed as he lowered his lips to the back of her hand. "Where are we? In the park, I mean?" she asked as she glanced around. The secluded area in which they stood appeared as private as any backyard garden, but she knew they still had to be in Hyde Park.

"Does it matter?" Jasper wondered, glancing about. He had brought her here because he knew there would be tulips. Tulips and enough hedgerows to provide a bit of privacy for his proposal.

Behind her hideous glasses, Marianne's eyes widened. "Of course it matters. I wish to know where to bring our children... our grandchildren... when I tell them of your most romantic proposal," she claimed, her body once again pressed against the front of his.

Jasper allowed a chuckle as he wrapped his arms around her shoulders and simply held her for a time. "I don't think it has a name," he replied finally. "But I will bring you here whenever you wish. When we're in the capital," he amended. He paused a moment. "Now. When do you suppose you would be amenable to becoming Viscountess Henley?" he asked with an arched brow. "We have to wait five days." Although he could have purchased a special license that would have allowed them to marry on the morrow, the twenty guineas it would have cost would be better spent on their trip.

At the mention of "Viscountess Henley," Marianne sighed in his hold. "When do we leave for Italy?"

He almost allowed a sigh of relief. "Friday. Late afternoon. The tide is scheduled to go out, and the captain of *The Fairweather* wants to go out with it." Jasper could feel Marianne's body tense a bit before she giggled.

"Aunt Cherice will be so vexed if we marry any sooner than that," she said with a huge grin. "Would Friday morning be agreeable? We can leave for the docks after the wedding breakfast."

Jasper considered the logistics before he finally nodded.

Earlier that day, he had arranged for an additional cabin for the trip to Italy, intending for Marianne and him to use it so his colleague, James Singleton, could use the smaller cabin he had originally reserved on their behalf. Marrying the day of their departure meant their first night together would be spent in a bed not much larger than a captain's bunk—that is, if he didn't arrange to bed her before that. Now that she had consented to marry him and he had Devonville's permission, she was essentially his to do with as he pleased.

He shook the thought from his head, wondering why he would even consider deflowering her before their wedding. Just because most men of his age had done so with their wives before their weddings didn't mean he had to resort to such behavior.

He could wait. And he would. Take her virtue on their wedding night on board *The Fairweather*.

For the next few nights, he could sleep in a chair or on the floor—if she was anything like Sophie, she wouldn't abide him sharing the bed.

"Oh, dear. You were hoping for an earlier date," Marianne said. "Any day is agreeable with me—"

Her words were cut off when Jasper's forefinger was suddenly pressed to her lips. He replaced it with his lips and gave her a kiss. "Friday morning is perfect," he said in a whisper. "My townhouse is in a shambles, what with packing for the trip, and I shouldn't want you to see it until it has been properly prepared for its new lady of the house."

Marianne gasped. "You... You have a townhouse? Here... in town?" she asked, obviously incredulous.

Jasper frowned at her implication. "Of course. In South Audley Street. Where else would I live?"

His affianced gave a shrug, although she appeared a bit chuffed. "Aunt Cherice feared you might only have bachelor quarters," she explained as she angled her head. "I wouldn't mind small quarters, truly. But she seems to think it necessary that I live in a townhouse. Close to the park, or to Grosvenor Square."

Feeling a bit of spite toward the Marchioness of Devonville, Jasper arched a brow. "You can inform Lady Devonville you will be living so close to the park, you will be able to *see* it from your bedchamber window." He didn't add that she would need to be wearing her spectacles, though.

Marianne's expression went from delight to one of quiet contemplation, which had Jasper angling his head. "What is it?" he asked carefully.

"You said, '*your* bedchamber window'," she repeated, the emphasis on "your."

"The window in the mistress suite, yes," Jasper replied, his manner guarded.

Marianne seemed to slump in his hold. "But where do *you* sleep?" she asked as her bespectacled eyes raised to meet his gaze.

Jasper allowed a teasing grin. "Wherever you are sleeping?" he guessed.

At the sight of her brilliant smile, Jasper realized Marianne Slater would be nothing like Sophie.

In fact, this marriage would be nothing like his first, he decided.

For better or for worse.

Chapter 7

UNDER THE GAZE OF A FATHER

The following Thursday night

The crowd at White's had thinned a bit just after seven o'clock when Jasper made his way through the black front door of the storied establishment in St. James Street. A footman saw to his hat and greatcoat as he surveyed the rooms beyond the vestibule. Those who were married had gone home to change for dinner. The Earl of Torrington was in his usual chair holding a glass of brandy and reading that day's issue of *The Tattler*. The shouts from the card room suggested a rather raucous crowd was enjoying a round of *vingt-et-tun*. And Alistair Comber stood regarding him with a knowing grin.

"I wondered if you would come," the second son of an earl remarked as he moved to shake Jasper's hand. "When Mother mentioned you were to be wed on the morrow, I thought she must be mistaken," he added with a grin. "But between you and me, she is the *Goddess of Gossip*."

Jasper matched his grin. Patience Comber, Countess of Aimsely, was a favorite in the *ton*, her tolerance of her misbehaving older son, Adam, at odds with her husband's stricter and more sober manner. How she had managed to stay wed to the Earl of Aimsley—without having taken a lover or moving into a separate household—was anyone's guess, but Jasper figured the two had a marriage built on affection rather than convenience. "It was good of you to meet me. The last time I was about to wed, Singleton saw to it I got thoroughly foxed," he said, referring to his fellow archaeologist who usually joined him on his expeditions.

"I'm happy to do the honors on this evening, but don't expect me to stay too late. I am a married man now, and I rather enjoy the company of my wife," Alistair replied, referring to the former Lady Julia Harrington. "Beside, I have to meet a client in the morning," he added.

"At Tattersall's?" Jasper half-asked. He knew Alistair was a consultant at the auction house featuring the very best in horseflesh.

"Indeed."

"I'm just glad you are not expecting me to visit Lucy Gibbon's brothel," Jasper said with an exaggerated shiver, his gaze taking in the current occupants of the club.

"Never," Alistair agreed, his distaste for the Covent Gardens brothel apparent in his expression. "So, name your poison and name your game."

Jasper was about to say, "Whisky," to the butler who approached from one side, but a voice featuring the slightest of Scottish burrs interrupted with, "Scotch. Your very best."

Both Jasper and Alistair turned to find William, Marquess of Devonville, and another gentleman regarding them with the most serious of expressions. "Devonville," Jasper managed as he gave the marquess a nod.

"I thought you might make an appearance here tonight," his future uncle-by-marriage said. "Your only stop, I presume?" he added with a bushy eyebrow that lifted in query.

"It is. And it will be an early night, given my friend is newly married," he said as he indicated Alistair. "Have you two met?" he asked, hoping his sudden nervousness wasn't apparent. Especially when he noticed how the man who stood next to Devonville looked almost exactly like Devonville. So much so, the two could be brothers. Which meant...

Alistair nodded and gave a bow. "Of course, I've had the pleasure. Devonville's daughter is a friend of my Julia's," he said proudly.

"Good to see you again, Comber. That Thoroughbred you recommended has become my favorite for this season's racing circuit," Devonville said before turning to the man who stood to his right. "I don't believe either one of you has met my brother, though. Lord Donald, I'd like you to meet Alistair Comber, an expert on horses," he said as he indicated Alistair, "And Jasper Henley. The man who is scheduled to make your daughter his wife on the morrow."

Eyes widened as three of the four gentlemen regarded one another. "It's an honor to meet you, sir," Jasper said as he held out his hand to his future father-in-law.

Donald Slater regarded Jasper for the briefest of moments before saying, "Good God! You're a bit long in the tooth. What ever does my daughter see in you?"

Jasper blinked, rather startled by the comment. "I am almost two-and-thirty, it's true," he acknowledged with a nod, any self-confidence he might have had quickly dissipating under the man's intense gaze. "And I'm not quite sure she has really seen me, my lord," he managed, not intending his comment to sound disrespectful of Marianne. "I cannot convince her to wear her spectacles when she is in my company."

There was a moment of stunned silence, as if his words had been heard by everyone in White's, and they were all waiting with baited breath to hear how Lord Donald would respond. Jasper was sure his heartbeat could be heard, it hammered so loud in his chest. He knew Alistair was equally stunned, for he heard his inhalation of breath and wondered if his friend would make his excuses and slink away to safety.

And then Lord Donald broke out into laughter, his loud guffaws causing Jasper to let out the breath he'd been holding. Alistair blinked and then allowed a tentative grin. "I suppose the better question would be, what did you see in my daughter that had you deciding you had to kiss her?"

The question sounded more like a challenge rather than a simple query, but it was one Jasper found easy to answer. "Her complete and undeniable appreciation for the things she can see, my lord," he stated. "It's rather charming."

The brothers sobered as they regarded him, their matching brows furrowing in the same way. "She is blind, you must know," Donald said in a quiet voice.

Jasper did his best to rein in the flash of anger he felt just then. "I believe she can see what she must, sir. With a good pair of spectacles, she'll be able to see everything else." He suddenly wished he had arranged for an oculist to make her a pair before they took their leave of London.

"Are you marrying her because you... you feel some sort of... *affection* for her," Lord Donald countered, just as the butler appeared with a tray of glasses.

"I am," Jasper admitted with a nod. "Or rather, I will, if I have your permission." After a half-second, he added, "Sir."

The glasses of scotch were distributed to the four gentlemen before Lord Donald said, "Well, then, I suppose you have my permission. My blessing, actually," he added with a nod. He held up his glass. "To my daughter," he said.

"To Marianne," Jasper agreed with a nod before he took a sip of the scotch. The liquor burned as it hit his throat, its heat fortifying him for what he was sure would be a long night in the company of Lord Donald.

The others drank their scotch before Lord Donald held up his glass to regard the remaining contents by the light of a nearby sconce. "Not bad," he said. "But not as good as mine." He turned to Jasper. "Has my brother served you my scotch?"

Jasper shook his head. "He has not."

"I have had the pleasure," Alistair offered. "My father stocks it in his study. I don't believe he drinks anything else."

"Ah. Aimsley knows what's best," Devonville agreed. He turned to his brother. "I rather imagine there will be a bottle or two of this making its way to Italy on the morrow, eh?"

Lord Donald gave a nod in Jasper's direction. "How long do you intend to keep my daughter away from me?"

Jasper swallowed. "I'm afraid our wedding trip will last at least six months. Perhaps more, if the weather cooperates on Sicily."

Devonville was about to say something before Donald stated. "Six bottles, then. Consider it a wedding gift."

Boggling at the offer, Jasper wasn't about to argue. Six bottles of scotch meant he had a universal currency for bribes, should he be required to arrange any. "That's very generous, my lord," he replied. "Thank you."

"I'll see to it part of her dowry is paid on the morrow, as well," Donald stated. "The rest... well, you'll have to come to Canobie to collect it," he added. "My way of ensuring you bring her home to visit before you're completely settled."

Jasper nodded. "Thank you for the invitation. I will be sure to bring her, of course."

"Started to think I was going to have to give it to *her*," Donald added, *sotto voce*.

"That's very kind of you, sir. The dowry, I mean. Under the circumstances, I... I wasn't expecting to collect a dowry."

Lord Donald's brows furrowed. "How many people saw you kiss my daughter?" he asked.

Instead of dropping his head in shame, Jasper lifted his chin. "Three, my lord," he stated with a nod in Devonville's direction. "Lord and Lady Devonville, and your sister, Lady Torrington."

Donald guffawed again. "Most of the family then. I wish *I* could have been there," he said when he finally sobered. "Well, Devonville, I do believe it's time we hit a gaming hell," he added as he turned to the marquess.

Devonville gave him a look of surprise. "You don't wish to see your daughter?" He turned to Jasper and Alistair. "He just arrived in town a couple of hours ago."

"I'll see her in the morning," Donald stated. "But first, I have to win some blunt for a dowry."

With that, the older gentlemen took their leave of White's while Alistair was left to regard Jasper with an amused expression. "I don't envy you one bit," he said.

His eyes still on the backs of his soon-to-be-wife's relatives, Jasper gave a shake of his head. "Perhaps I will have another drink."

Chapter 8

A WEDDING IS ALL A BLUR

The following morning
Devonville House, situated near the end of a series of mansions in Park Lane, was usually rather quiet and calm in the morning. Servants went about their daily routines well before the Devonvilles were out of their bedchambers. The housekeeper would be reviewing that night's dinner menu and writing up a shopping list for the cook's morning trip to market. The butler would be inspecting the silver and seeing to it a footman had the breakfast parlor ready for that day's morning meal.

Not so on this day.

Hatfield, the butler, had opened the back door no less than five times before the clock struck eight. Food, flowers, and even furniture paraded by as he stepped aside and did his best with directions. By nine o'clock, the front door had been answered even more often, given a modiste and her contingent of seamstresses were armed with what appeared to be a wardrobe for an entire Season. Why, he barely had a chance to see to it the dining room was properly set for that morning's wedding breakfast. He was about to do so when the lady of the house descended the stairs in a rush.

"Is the parlor ready?"

Doing his best to maintain an impassive expression despite his desire to growl, Hatfield gave her a bow. "I wasn't sure where you wished the florals to be placed, my lady," he replied, deciding it was safest to leave it in her hands. Had he directed the florist's men in that regard, he was sure Cherice, Marchioness of Devonville, would simply rearrange it all anyway.

"Of course not. I'll see to the flowers right away. What about the dining room?"

"I have a footman reviewing the place settings this very moment, my lady."

"What about the chairs?"

"There are forty in the dining room and ten in the parlor."

She sighed, as if she were disappointed at hearing the count for the number of chairs, despite them matching the very numbers she had requested not three days ago. "That will have to suffice, I suppose."

Hatfield knew this wasn't her ladyship's first wedding. She'd had two of her own before taking on the arrangements for her niece's nuptials, so he was rather surprised at her nervousness.

"I'm expecting the modiste at any moment," she suddenly stated.

"She has already arrived. I took her to Miss Slater's room almost an hour ago."

Cherice blinked. "Oh." Once again, a flash of disappointment crossed her face. "Well then, I suppose I shall see to the florals."

"Yes, my lady," Hatfield replied. He watched the small woman hurry off to the parlor, wondering at her strange mood. He thought she would be happy seeing to the wedding of her niece by marriage. How she had managed to secure a groom for the girl in such a short amount of time hadn't been as much of a surprise to him as it was to the other servants of Devonville House. When Cherice DuBois Winslow Slater put her mind to a task, it was always completed with efficiency. The marquess might have thought it was *his* idea to marry the widow—to be the first to court her on the very day she came out of mourning—but Hatfield knew better.

Cherice had probably decided she wanted to be the Marchioness of Devonville even before her husband died.

When the lion head knocker pounded at the front door, Hatfield straightened and answered it, prepared to direct the delivery to the back door. However, two men stood before him, and neither held anything but small items in their hands. He recognized Lord Henley immediately, having remembered the viscount from when he collected Miss Slater for their ride in the park. As for the other man...

"I am Vicar Cuthbert. Here to perform a marriage cere-mony," the shorter man said with a nod. "Not that it's really very proper to hold a wedding ceremony in a home, of course, but then I have been assured Devonville House is somewhat of a public place given anyone can tour it should they ask. Is that really true?"

Hatfield blinked. No one had ever come to Devonville House with such a request, but he couldn't imagine Lady Devonville turning anyone away. She would be happy to show off the house, he thought. She was a proud woman, after all. "It is, sir," he finally answered. He turned his gaze onto the viscount.

"Lord Henley. Here to... get married," the viscount stam-mered as he held out his calling card.

Hatfield stepped aside. "Lady Devonville is in the parlor," he replied, deciding he would simply escort the gentlemen there rather than interrupt her ladyship.

Once he delivered them to the parlor, a room that now featured a floral scent reminiscent of a perfumery, and to the direction of a rather relieved Lady Devonville—*did she think the groom wouldn't show up for the ceremony?*—Hatfield was about to pay a visit to the dining room when his attention was redirected to the top of the stairs.

The butler didn't try to hide his surprise at the sight of Marianne Slater as she stood in her wedding ensemble. He knew right away she couldn't see him—at least not clearly—for she remained at the top of the stairs for a moment more before finally taking one step down. The modiste, her head angled to one side and an expression that betrayed her pride in her creation, clapped her two hands together and caught his gaze for just a moment. "You're doing just fine, Miss Slater," he heard the woman say, her fake French accent sounding almost authentic. "Although I think you should wait for Lord Devonville. Seeing as how you cannot see very well."

Turning on his heal, the butler dared a glance back into the parlor. The vicar had taken a position at one end of the room, his attention on a small book that lay open in his hands. Viscount Henley stood at an angle, his attention suddenly on him. Hatfield gave a jerk of his head, and the viscount hurried over to him.

"I should think you would like to see this, my lord," Hatfield said as he nodded to the stairs. At seeing Lord Henley's reaction to his bride, the butler felt a sudden twinge in his chest. Until that moment, he had believed his master's niece was entering a marriage of convenience. Now, he knew without a doubt that Lord Henley truly wished to marry the girl who stood waiting for her uncle.

"Good morning, my sweeting," Lord Henley said as he moved to the bottom of the stairs. "Why, you look more gorgeous than you did the night I met you."

Marianne's inhalation of breath could be heard throughout the entire great hall, her blush of embarrassment pinking her face. "You bounder," she accused with a huge grin.

Lord Devonville was suddenly at her side. "Bounder or not, he's to be your groom," he said, his slight burr tinged with a hint of humor. He escorted his niece down the stairs and then let go of her arm when she was standing before the viscount. He disappeared into the parlor.

"Good morning," she said as she dipped a curtsy, the sarcenet overskirt of her gown shimmering in the morning light from the parlor.

Hatfield couldn't help but watch as the viscount bowed, and instead of taking her hand to kiss the back of it, he leaned over and kissed her on the cheek. He seemed about to say something more, but his attention was captured by the tall man who now stood at the top of the stairs. "I'll be waiting for you," he overheard Henley say.

For a moment, the bride seemed at a loss as to what to do, but she heard footsteps on the stairs and turned to discover her father hurrying down to join her.

"Father?" she said in disbelief. "When... where...?"

Lord Donald kissed his daughter's head and pulled her into a hug, ignoring the hiss the modiste allowed just then at seeing her creation crushed. "I arrived yesterday afternoon," Hatfield heard the man say. The rest of his words were too quiet to hear, but whatever he said seemed to please his daughter, for Marianne was soon smiling.

A moment later, and they entered the parlor.

Left in the suddenly quiet hall, Hatfield dared a glance into the room and paid witness to the beginning of the ceremony.

He would have watched the entire wedding, but the lion head knocker announced the arrival of the first of the breakfast guests, and he was forced to return to duty.

And to wipe away the tear that had collected in the corner of one eye.

Chapter 9

A BRIGHT AFTERNOON FOR
SETTING SAIL

Friday afternoon
While walking up the slanted wooden planks to board the sailing vessel, *The Fairweather*, Marianne couldn't help the combination of dread and excitement she felt. As much as she wanted to visit Italy—a trip she couldn't have hoped to make in her lifetime—she never imagined going there with someone she hardly knew.

On her wedding trip.

The ink was barely dry on the marriage certificate!

She hadn't even been in London a fortnight ago, and here she was, walking a gangplank onto a ship set to sail in an hour with a husband she had to marry because she had been caught kissing him in some aristocrat's garden.

Or because he had been caught kissing her.

Probably the latter, she thought, wondering if her uncle could have been disabused of the idea of her having to marry the viscount if she had just argued with him a bit. At the time, though, she hadn't *wanted* to argue.

For some reason, the idea of marrying Jasper Henley wasn't so daunting a week ago. Even yesterday, she had been so caught up in Aunt Cherice's excitement and the plans for the wedding and breakfast, Marianne hadn't paid much mind to those plans being for *her*.

Despite the lack of time, the Devonville cook had managed to create a feast for the forty guests who had invaded Devonville House earlier that day, just as she and Jasper repeated their vows in the flower-festooned parlor.

She barely recognized anyone at the breakfast, although she had been assured she had been introduced to most of them. Any others were members of the Royal Society, colleagues of Jasper's who had come to wish him merry and remind him of his primary reason for going to Sicily— archaeological research. They seemed in good humor as they did so, their elbows no doubt leaving bruises on his ribs.

Marianne had blushed at their implication, for what else could she do? But at no point had they said anything deliberately vulgar.

The biggest surprise had been the moment her father, Donald Slater, appeared at the top of the stairs. She rather wished she had been able to see him clearly, for she would have had a bit more warning before he gathered her into his arms and kissed her forehead.

She knew it was him just before that happened, though. The familiar smell of his cologne and the deep timber of his voice had her whirling around to find him regarding her with a mix of joy and sadness.

When she asked if she might introduce him to Jasper, he had given his head a shake and claimed to have spent an hour in the man's company only the night before. *I arrived in London yesterday afternoon, and sought out your viscount at White's after my brother told me everything*, he had explained. *I think I am most relieved you haven't ended up with a Gypsy.*

Not that she would have ever run off with any of the Lowland Gypsies that occasionally stayed next to the river near their village. She couldn't imagine the life of a nomad. Always on the move.

And then he had said the most important words of all.

I gave him my blessing, for he has promised to provide protection and affection for my favorite daughter. And then I gave him most of your dowry. The rest I have hidden in your bedchamber at home, so I have some assurance you will come visit me at least once more in this lifetime.

She had expected the protection, of course, but a promise of affection? They had only known one another a week.

Not even a week.

Six days.

As for his comment about her being his favorite daughter —she was his *only* daughter.

At least as far as she knew.

But his last comment? Despite Jasper's teasing question when they had ridden in the park—the one about her coming into her majority and guessing what she might have done with her inheritance—Marianne had told him that she hadn't taken possession of the fifteen-thousand pounds, but she hadn't mentioned that she or her husband, should she ever marry, would one day inherit a distillery. A rather lucrative distillery. If her father hadn't informed Jasper, then she figured she wouldn't, either. Better to allow some time to pass and to determine how well they suited before telling him what his future might hold.

Marianne watched as a porter saw to loading her trunks. Although one had been half-empty upon her arrival in London, her aunt had seen to it she had bride clothes to fill it and another they had purchased that week, claiming she would need a variety of gowns for where she was going.

Cherice was still grousing about Marianne's lack of a lady's maid, even after she was assured that Jasper would arrange one upon their arrival in Sicily. *I have a colleague who has arranged a villa for us and who can recommend someone*, he had assured her.

Marianne wasn't sure what she expected in the way of

accommodations on the vessel, but she was pleasantly surprised when a porter escorted them to a cabin with walls covered in mahogany and outfitted with rich furnishings. The room was small, to be sure, but every inch of space had been designed for optimal storage and comfort. There were even sconces mounted on the walls, their tiny flames bathing the room in a soft glow.

With the trunks delivered and the cabin's door shut and its bolt thrown, Marianne realized it would only be a matter of time before Jasper would bed her. She wondered if dinner would be served later, or if he had arranged for provisions to be delivered. Not having traveled on a ship before, she didn't yet know if she would suffer from seasickness.

"I hope you like it," Jasper whispered as he drew her into his arms. Although the quarters were larger than the cabin he had originally reserved, he didn't plan to spend much time in it given his discomfort in enclosed spaces. A frown creased his brow. "You can't even see all of it, can you?"

Marianne gave a shake of her head. She could see enough, although all the edges of the furnishings were blurry. "I can see that it's quite elegant," she countered, her gaze going to the settee. She realized right then that they would both be sharing the bed, for the settee wouldn't begin to accommodate either one of them.

"Would it be...?" He stopped and swallowed.

"Would it be...?" she repeated. His lips were suddenly on hers, his arms wrapping around her shoulders and waist so that he could pull her against the front of his body. When he ended the kiss, he left his forehead pressed against hers.

"I wish to make love to you."

Knowing she should have expected the request even before nightfall—Cherice had warned her he might wish to bed her even before the breakfast commenced—Marianne gave a nod. "It's your right, of course," she whispered as she pulled the drawstring of her reticule from around her wrist and tossed it onto the table. She followed it with her gloves, cursing at herself for how her fingers trembled.

Jasper took her hands into his and frowned. "If you don't wish to do it now, just say so, and I will wait." He nearly cursed himself for saying the words. He couldn't believe how his desire for her had bloomed since they had stepped into the cabin. For the first time since that moment in the park when he had formally proposed, they were alone.

Would he always feel this attraction to her? This *need* to hold her close? This lust? He couldn't remember his reaction to Sophie being this intense.

"That's very kind of you, but I think it best we do it now," Marianne replied, her words sounding so much more confident than she felt just then. "I haven't done this before," she murmured as she removed her pelisse and draped it over a chair. "Of course," she added, realizing how her comment would sound. She pulled her bonnet from her head.

"I shan't be long inside you," he murmured quietly. "I don't wish to cause you pain, but I fear—"

"I know," Marianne said as she regarded the small bunk. There was barely room for the two of them to lay side-by-side, but there wasn't another bed in the cabin. "Aunt Cherice told me."

Jasper bit back what first came to mind, wondering what the former Lady Winslow had told Marianne about the marriage bed. "I will pleasure you first, of course, and make you as ready as I can," he explained, his voice soft.

Merely nodding, Marianne turned her back to him and then comprehended his words about pleasuring her. A frisson shot through her body as she wondered how he intended to pleasure her when he also knew he would be causing her pain. "You'll have to help undress me," she said as she angled her head to one side. She swallowed, annoyed at how her body had begun to tremble, as if she feared what he would do to her. She didn't—not really—but she couldn't help the feeling of unease that gripped her. "Can you undo the buttons?"

About to lift his fingers to the nape of her neck, Jasper instead lowered his lips to the bit of skin that showed there. Despite her body's jerk, Jasper trailed a series of kisses along the top of her neckline and to the back of her ear. He heard her soft inhalation of breath as he wrapped an arm around her waist and gently pulled her against the front of his body.

With his free hand, he slowly undid the buttons, his fingers spreading apart the fabric of her gown until the ties of her stays were exposed. He pulled on the bow that held them in place around her bosom, closing his eyes when he felt the weight of her breasts settle onto his forearm through the fabric of her gown.

He burrowed the flat of his hand beneath the stays and over her chemise, sliding the fabric sideways until one sleeve fell from her shoulder. Trailing a series of kisses down the column of her neck and then along the top of her shoulder, he thrilled at hearing her soft gasps and barely audible moans.

He felt another thrill when he watched as one of her hands lifted to pull on the bow that held the neckline of her chemise in place. The ties loosened as his hand continued to slide down her back until it reached her petticoats, where his deft fingers undid the tapes.

When she shivered beneath his hold, Jasper lifted his lips back to her ear. "Are you cold?" he asked in a whisper.

Marianne's murmur of, "No," was a barely-there breath that changed when he switched arms and did the same with the other side of her chemise, and stays, and gown. He thought to slide the sleeves completely from her arms, but she was already doing so, her entire back suddenly bare. Jasper dropped a kiss between her shoulder blades as he lessened his hold on her so that the gown and chemise could fall unimpeded to the floor. The hand at the side of her waist slid up and under one breast, his palm slowly moving to cover it.

Jasper couldn't help but groan at feeling the weight of her, at realizing his hand could barely contain the soft orb. He also realized Marianne was holding her breath. "You need to breathe, my sweeting, or you shall faint," he whispered, not adding that he might faint as well.

He was stunned to find her breasts were larger than the palm of his hand.

One of Marianne's hands moved to his, the fingers of her small hand covering as much of his as possible. "They're too fleshy, I know, despite what Aunt—" Her words were cut off when he quickly turned her in his arms, his mouth coming down over hers, as much to quiet her as to counter her claim. His other hand had moved to her other breast, his hold not so gentle as he kneaded the soft mound. When he finally released her lips, he pressed his forehead against hers and whispered, "They are perfect, despite what anyone else may have told you."

Marianne inhaled sharply, pulling her head from his to regard him with a look of surprise. "You're not just saying that? Because... because you have to?" she asked. With her eyes wide open, she could make out every detail of his face, every lash framing his dark eyes, every bit of his lips, and his high cheekbones, and the length of his aristocratic nose. He was handsome, obviously a peer descended from some royal ancestor blessed with beauty and good bone structure. She couldn't help but lift a hand to his jaw, to use a finger to trace the line back to his neck.

Jasper had to resist chuckling at her question. "They are perfect," he repeated, his hand still kneading the one he held. An engorged nipple had settled between two of his knuckles, and he pressed them together to see how she might react.

He wasn't disappointed when she inhaled sharply. His mouth was over it in an instant, his tongue laving across the hardened bud before he suckled it with his lips. "So perfect," he murmured before kissing the nipple. He moved his mouth to the other side, but on the way, his gaze quickly took in her bare belly and nakedness below. Her gown and chemise had formed a silken puddle at her feet, and only her stockings and slippers remained on her body.

He could feel her breaths quickening beneath his hold, feel as her fingers speared his hair, as if she needed to hold onto something to remain standing. The scent of her changed then, a feminine muskiness that told him she was ready for something more. He pulled his lips from her breast and tried to straighten, cringing at how his arousal pressed against the placket of his breeches.

He would never last if he didn't keep himself under control.

Their eyes met for a moment before Marianne realized he was still clothed. She undid the knot at his neck, her fingers pulling apart the silk cravat until she could unwrap it from around his neck. She jerked at the tie at the top of his shirt before deftly undoing the buttons down his waistcoat and top coat. In the process of pushing the garments from his body, she gave a start when one of his hands delved between her thighs, the flat of his hand pressed against her most private place. Inhaling sharply, she stilled her movements and stared at him until he finally moved the hand. She gasped again, not sure what to do.

"Christ, I want you so badly," he whispered, nearly breathless as he pulled his hand from her and finished removing his top coat and waistcoat. He pulled his shirt from his body in a *whoosh* of fine lawn, which had Marianne's eyes widening at the sight of his bare chest. She could make out the details of it without even squinting, his dark chest hair sharp against a broad expanse of skin stretched over muscle and bone. Without even realizing it, one of her hands reached out to touch it before she quickly pulled it back, as if she had been shocked from the touch.

Jasper gripped her hand and placed it back onto his chest. "You can touch me where ever you'd like. When we're alone, of course," he managed to get out between gritted teeth. He struggled to undo the fastenings of his breeches and then realized he still wore his boots. He bit back a curse when he had to step away from Marianne—and away from her touch—in order to remove his footwear and stockings.

The coverage of his body suddenly gone, Marianne moved her arms to cross over her bosom, one hand dropping to hide her mons from his gaze. She dared a glance back at the small bunk, wanting desperately to climb under the white linens and hide.

Once again resisting the urge to chuckle at her modesty, Jasper lifted his gaze to her face and gave his head a quick shake. "Trust me when I tell you that you are a beautiful woman. You could have been a model for Michelangelo," he claimed as he pulled first one boot and then the other from his feet, barely able to keep his balance as he did so.

Marianne was about to counter his claim. None of Michaelangelo's statues featured fleshy women—at least as far she knew from the replicas that decorated some of the halls of the aristocrat's homes she had visited this past week. But something about the way he watched her as he removed one of his stockings had her slowly removing her arms from in front of her body. "I don't suppose you'll allow me to wear a nightrail tonight?"

Giving his head a quick shake, Jasper regarded her with a wan smile. "I would not forbid it, of course, but I really rather you didn't." He paused a moment as he removed his other stocking. "But you can tomorrow night."

Furrowing a brow, Marianne asked, "Why tomorrow night?"

Jasper finished undoing the fastening of his breeches and

paused before pushing them down. "I cannot expect to bed you again tomorrow night."

Marianne blinked. "But, why not?" she asked before she remembered Aunt Cherice's warning.

"I expect you'll be... too sore," he replied with a one-shouldered shrug. "I don't wish to cause you any more pain than you'll feel tonight."

Wondering at why she felt a combination of relief and disappointment, Marianne allowed a nod.

When Jasper pushed down his breeches, she couldn't help her slight gasp, for she realized then why it was she would be sore.

However in the world was he supposed to put *that* inside her? Down there?

Grimacing, Jasper kicked off the breeches and moved to put his arms around Marianne. "It's not as bad as it looks, I promise," he whispered, his words nearly breathless as he reveled in how his manhood pressed into her soft belly, a far more hospitable home than behind the placket of his wool breeches.

Startled by the heavy object that had come between them, Marianne finally nodded, even though she didn't believe him. She could practically feel how his manhood throbbed, how it seemed to have a life of its own. "I'm ready," she whispered, well aware of how her entire body trembled.

"I'll make you more so," he promised, his attention turning away from her. "Lie down, and I'll join you in a moment," he said before he disappeared from her view. He was back in a moment, a bath linen in one hand.

"What's that for?" she wondered as she watched him unfold the linen. She had stayed standing, not about to get onto the small bed just yet.

"Proof of your virtue, I suppose. And so we don't muss the bed linens too much," he added as he draped it over the sheets. When he straightened, he found Marianne regarding him with tears in the corners of her eyes and an expression that suggested she wasn't the least bit ready for what was about to happen.

He pulled her into his arms again and kissed her slowly, moved his hands over the soft skin of her back and her arms, moved his lips over her jaw, and down her neck, and across her collarbones, all the while his manhood begged for surcease and her body trembled.

He finally lifted her into his arms and placed her onto the small bunk, his body following hers down until he was settled beside and atop her. Having a hard time deciding which engorged nipple to nibble first, he used his nose to tickle both as the flat of one hand slid down her belly and over her mons. He felt her body stiffen beneath his, but she did his bidding when he coaxed her thighs apart and used the heel of his hand to press against her wet folds.

"Breathe, my sweeting," he whispered, as much a reminder for her as it was for him. Pulling his hand back a bit, he slipped a few fingers along the silken folds before sliding them sideways, circling and teasing until her womanhood finally emerged from the moistening folds.

Rubbing it gently as he continued to worry a nipple between his teeth, he felt a good deal of satisfaction when he heard her slight gasps. He had a mind to use his tongue and lips on her womanhood, but thought better of it. He could practice a Roman art when they were closer to their destination.

As her breathing quickened, Jasper rubbed a bit harder and then slid a finger into her tight haven. Expecting her reaction—to either pull away from him or to clench down to prevent his entry—he was surprised when she bent a knee and lifted it slightly. Her neck arched back into the pillow and a strangled cry sounded from her throat.

"Is it all right if I continue?" he asked in a hoarse whisper, his manhood throbbing against the side of her thigh. He knew it wanted to be doing what his middle finger was doing, but she was still far too tight to accommodate him.

Marianne nodded and murmured her consent, her breaths still a series of pants and gasps.

Spurred on by her body's movements and how her ambrosia dripped from his hold, Jasper slid a second finger into her as his thumb continued what his hand could no longer do. Circling and rubbing, his fingers pushing in and pulling out just a bit, he soon had her stretched as much as he could manage with just his fingers.

Rubbing her womanhood a bit harder, he thrilled when her entire body seemed to seize and his fingers seemed as if they were being sucked into her tight cocoon. The cry of his name sounded loud as he quickly repositioned his body and managed to press his manhood into her just as the last vestiges of her orgasm waved through her lower body.

He knew he had hurt her when he paid witness to her wince and quick inhalation of breath. He could feel how she clenched on her body's intruder, and it took everything he had not to simply allow his release just then.

Covering her mouth with his own, he managed a quick kiss before he stilled his body. Suspended over her, barely pushing into her a bit at a time and then pulling out slowly, he finally paused to take a labored breath.

"I'm so sorry this is hurting you," he whispered.

Marianne gave a quick shake of her head in the pillow. "It's not so bad, really," she managed, a tear rolling down her temple to her ear. She lifted her knees a bit, and gripped the sides of his thighs with them.

The movement had Jasper growling in response. "Yes!" he whispered hoarsely. Knowing he could no longer hold back, Jasper pulled his manhood almost all the way out of her body before thrusting once, twice, and a third time until he was as deep as he could go. His seed spilled into her as the spasm of pleasure, sharp and intense, had blinding flashes of lights exploding before his eyes.

Grimacing, he held himself suspended for a few seconds before his arms betrayed him, and he collapsed atop Marianne's soft body. He managed a kiss on the corner of her mouth before he passed out.

*N*ot sure what to do, Marianne slowly lowered her feet to the bed and allowed her breathing to return to normal. At some point, her hands had moved to his shoulders, as if she needed something to hang onto as Jasper took her body. She now moved them beneath his arms and around his back, wondering at how his body seemed to jerk a bit at her touch. Jerk at the same time he inhaled sharply.

Did her touch tickle him?

She smoothed a hand down his back as far as it would go, remembering how when he had done it to her, her skin had reacted in a series of pleasant frissons and tickles. She wasn't disappointed when she felt the same happening beneath his skin. Then she heard his breathing hitch and slow.

Whatever he had been doing *down there* had been uncomfortable at first, at least once he had his finger inside her. Uncomfortable mixed with a sharp pleasure that had her wanting more at the same time she wanted it to end. Then there had been the wash of warmth that seemed to spread through her lower body, a signal for his turn at the pleasure of sexual congress, she now realized.

Her body still trembled.

When would it stop?

She was no longer frightened, not that she had been too terribly scared by what had been about to happen. Except when she realized he was sliding two fingers between her honeyed folds. She had thought those two fingers too large to enter her, the assault stretching her until she thought she would burst. But then she remembered how large his manhood had appeared when it was released from his breeches, how heavy it felt pressed into her belly. Had he truly managed to get it entirely inside her?

He is still inside me, she realized just then. Filling her completely, pressed in so deep she didn't know where he stopped and she started. Even his torso, completely covering her own, was like a thick blanket of bone and muscle and warmth. Pressed skin to skin, his heartbeat apparent against one of her breasts, she didn't know where she stopped and he started.

Just thinking of what his thumb had been doing in her most private place had a frisson shooting through her entire body, a sensation accompanied by waves of pleasure. Jasper must have felt it, for his body quivered in response, and she heard his slight chuckle next to her ear before his lips left a kiss on her earlobe.

"I should move. I must be suffocating you," she heard him whisper, the words sounding loud so close to her ear.

"No. Stay," she replied, her fingertips tracing circles on his back, her drowsiness apparent in how far away her words sounded in her own ears.

If every night was like this—sans the painful pinch she had felt when he impaled her—she decided she would enjoy the marriage bed.

If all they ever did was hold one another like this, she would be satisfied. If all they ever did was kiss, well, she would be quite content.

Chapter 10

A DARK NIGHT FOR REFLECTION

*L*ater that night

The slight and constant sway of *The Fairweather* would have lulled Marianne to sleep had she not been so aware of her husband's body pressed against hers. Of the slight rise and fall of his chest, his warm breaths washing over one of her breasts. Of his pulse at his wrist where it rested under the other breast.

Warm and heavy, Jasper had finally moved from atop her, carefully pulling himself from her body before giving her a quick kiss and nearly collapsing at her side.

Trembling from a combination of arousal and uneasiness, Marianne felt a bit of relief when Jasper didn't remove himself entirely from the bed. Her aunt had warned her he might do so in some kind of misguided notion that she would desire privacy over staying close.

"May I stay?" he asked, his whisper sounding rather drowsy.

Marianne had to still herself, tempted to ask where he intended to go if she said "no."

She had no desire to be alone.

No desire to lose the pleasant warmth and weight that

kept her from floating away. "Please do," she replied in a matching whisper, one hand feeling about for the edge of the downturned bed linens. She pulled on the linens and blankets until both their bodies were covered.

"Thank you," he murmured, his voice so quiet Marianne had a hard time making out the simple words.

She allowed a grin, deciding she felt rather content just then. "You're most welcome." She couldn't complain of being sore, exactly, but something was different. Thrumming, almost as if she were cold despite the fact that she was blissfully warm, her body felt boneless.

"I think we shall suit one another."

The words sounded almost slurred and far away, delivered in a voice that betrayed its owner's drowsiness.

"Indeed," she replied with a grin.

Jasper opened one eye and yawned. "Good night, my bride." Within moments, he was sound asleep.

Good night?

They hadn't yet had dinner!

Marianne thought to get up. Find the pitcher and bowl of water and clean herself. Pull on a nightrail, despite Jasper's earlier words. What if someone should come into their cabin? She wasn't wearing a stitch!

Except Jasper had thrown the bolt when he shut the door. No one would be coming into the cabin. With that thought, she simply closed her eyes and finally dosed off.

*H*ungry, aroused, and well aware of the close confines of the cabin, Jasper rolled off the bed as quietly as he could manage. His breaths coming faster as his heart rate increased, he quickly pulled on the pair of breeches and the shirt he had shed earlier, his need to get outside growing more urgent by the moment. Although he didn't usually suffer from seasickness, he would be sick if he didn't get outside.

He hadn't intended to fall asleep after consummating his marriage. He had thought to request a tub of warm water be delivered to the cabin so that Marianne could bathe while he recovered up on deck. Then they would dress for the scheduled dinner with the captain at eight o'clock. After that, he didn't know what they might do—other than sleep—as he hadn't had a chance to think of anything other than to memorize the map of the Valley of the Temples on Sicily.

Daring one last glance at the bed and wincing at his primal reaction at seeing Marianne—her bare back and one arm were visible despite how the bed's counterpane covered most of her—Jasper took his leave of the cabin and raced for the companionway.

Reaching the deck, he took a deep breath, shocked by the bracing air and star-filled sky. He hadn't taken a glance at his chronometer before leaving the cabin, but he knew it had to be well after ten o'clock.

"Missed you at dinner, my lord."

Jasper whirled around, stunned at the sight of John St. John, the captain, regarding him from the door to the wheelhouse. The last time he had been on the sailing vessel, *The Fairweather*, St. John had been the first mate. "A situation for which I apologize profusely," he replied as he moved to shake the man's proffered hand. "Although..." He allowed the sentence to trail off, realizing he wouldn't have traded his late afternoon in bed with Marianne for dinner at the captain's table, no matter how hungry he was. He would have spent the entire meal in a state of extreme discomfort. Even now, the thought of his wife had him so aroused, he wondered how he was going to manage until a few nights from now.

"Rodney, my first mate, said I was transporting newly-weds. Am I to assume one of them is you?" St. John countered, a teasing grin apparent in the dim light from a nearby lantern.

Jasper regarded the captain with a nod. "Guilty as charged. But happily so," he added, hoping his arousal wasn't apparent.

"You must have had a long betrothal. I remember you mentioning you were engaged to be married whilst on your last trip to Italy."

Angling his head to one side, Jasper remembered his last sojourn to an area north of Rome had been a few years ago. The trip was far shorter than he had planned, but the change in itinerary couldn't be helped due to his impending wedding to Sophie.

He had managed to return in time to marry her on the promised day, her reaction to his tanned face and body not exactly welcoming. "Ah, my first marriage," he acknowledged with a nod. "Lady Henley died of influenza last year, though. My new wife is Miss Marianne Slater. Although she is from Scotland, she is an English miss through and through."

St. John's face displayed his surprise at the news. "I'm sorry for your loss," he commented. "But... is your new wife related to Devonville, perhaps?" he asked, his brows furrowed.

Showing his own surprise at the query—until he realized the sea captain would be familiar with the scotch from the Devonville distillery—Jasper replied, "Indeed. She is his niece."

The captain barked a laugh. "Got caught kissing her in the gardens, did you?"

Jasper dipped his head, a grin splitting his face. Did everyone on the planet know he got caught kissing young ladies in the gardens? "Indeed. Although I have no regrets. And what of you? Have you been enslaved by the shackles of marriage since last we met?"

The captain shook his head but dared a glance up at the

sails, the fabric filled with the night breeze that had them nearing the English Channel's intersection with the Celtic Sea's waters. "Only if you count this ship," he replied. "Now that she's mine to command, I rather doubt I shall ever take a wife. Wouldn't want to make her jealous."

Jasper nodded his understanding. "So... a girl in every port..."

"And port after dinner," St. John finished with a grin.

Sobering, Jasper remembered Marianne and the discomfort she might be suffering from her first experience with sexual congress. "I wondered who I might speak with about bath water for my viscountess?"

"I'll see to it a tub and water are delivered first thing in the morning," St. John assured him just as his first mate appeared from inside the wheelhouse.

"Already arranged, capt'n," Rodney said with a nod. "We'll be past Guernsey by then."

The captain nodded. "Let's hope these winds continue to favor us once we're past Brest," St. John commented, his brows rising with his comment. "I'm hoping we'll only have to make one stop. Port of Valencia. Get to Sicily in under two weeks." He turned his attention to the viscount. "I'm retiring for the night. Should you require anything, Rodney here can see to it," he said before he gave a bow and headed for the captain's quarters.

Jasper responded with a nod and watched as St. John disappeared into the darkness. He turned his attention back to the first mate. "Don't mind me. I just came up for some air."

Rodney gave a nod toward the companionway. "Seems you won't be alone," he whispered. "Good night, milord." He turned and made his way toward the wheelhouse.

Jasper followed the first mate's line of sight and was stunned to find Marianne at the top of the companionway. A dressing gown was wrapped about her body, her arms crossed over her chest as she glanced around, obviously in search of him.

He hurried to join her. "My lady, is something amiss?" he asked as he reached for her hand and brought it to his lips.

Marianne gave a start the moment he touched her. "I woke up, and you were gone," she whispered, relief evident in her voice. "Did something happen?"

Jasper sighed, realizing he probably should have woken her or left a note before taking his leave of the cabin. He had been in such a panic, though, he hadn't thought about what might happen should she wake up and find him missing. "I apologize, my sweeting. I... I needed air, and I didn't wish to wake you." He felt the tenseness leave her body, and he pulled her closer, nearly cursing when his manhood reacted.

"I wouldn't have minded," Marianne whispered. Her head tilted back as she attempted to survey the sails and skies above. "It's so dark," she murmured.

"Aren't the stars amazing? Like diamonds on black velvet," he said as he followed her line of sight, his gaze taking in the Milky Way that appeared to form a glittering cloud against the inky blackness.

Then he realized Marianne wasn't wearing her spectacles.

She probably can't even see the stars, he thought in despair. "I wish you could see the sky right now," he said as he wrapped an arm around her shoulders and dropped a kiss on the side of her head.

Marianne stiffened at his comment, but she lifted her other hand to reveal the eyeglasses she held. "Just in case I couldn't find you when I reached the top of the stairs," she whispered. "I figured you couldn't have gone far—it's not as if you could go to your men's club—but then I wasn't sure I would be able to locate the galley." She dipped her head. "You must be starving."

Jasper allowed a chuckle. "I admit to feeling hunger, but it is of the kind I dare not attempt to feed again. At least until the night after next," he added before he pulled her closer and led them away from the companionway. He didn't want her falling down the steep stairs.

Giving a start at his odd comment, Marianne stared at him until she felt the evidence of his arousal behind the placket of his breeches. Now that he was so close, she realized he was wearing his shirt, but the tie at the top was undone, and the neckline was open down to his sternum.

Reminded of what he had done to her earlier that afternoon, a frisson shot through her body as her breasts suddenly felt heavy. "Why the night after next?" she wondered as one of her hands reached out to touch his shirt. Her fingers splayed as she slid her palm over his chest, primal lust urging her to press her body against his.

Jasper covered her hand with one of his own as his head dipped to rest atop hers. "It would not be very gentlemanly of me to bed you again until you have... recovered," he stammered.

Marianne blinked. "Recovered?" she repeated, aware of how the space at the top of her thighs seemed to throb. She had cleaned the tender area with a cool cloth before making her way out of the cabin, relieved to discover she hadn't bled as much as she had been warned she might. Jasper's earlier ministrations had seen to that, she supposed. That and how careful he had been when he finally impaled her body with his heavy manhood.

Would he have known to do that if he had never been married before? His first wife had no doubt been a virgin, too.

"You must be... sore," he whispered, glancing about as if he just then realized they were out in the open where anyone might see their embrace or hear their intimate conversation. He was rather relieved to discover they were alone. Other than the sound of the water rushing past the hull of the ship and the occasional whip of the canvas sails, it was quiet on the deck.

"Are you... sore?" Marianne countered, her brows furrowed.

Jasper blinked. "No." He gave his head a shake. "I am... uncomfortable, but I'll be—"

His words were cut off when Marianne placed a finger against his lips. "Do you wish to bed me again? Tonight?" she asked, her breaths coming in short, barely-there gasps as desire gripped her body. Even if the pleasure was a mere fraction of what she had experienced earlier, she could abide a bit of discomfort.

"Of course," he answered, his hold on her tightening. "I thought once would be enough, but..." His lips settled onto hers, and he kissed her for a long time before he finally pulled away. "Oh, Marianne. Forgive me," he said as he reached down and placed his hands beneath the mounds of her bottom. He lifted her onto a wooden barrel and was about to use his hands to spread open her legs and her dressing gown when reason seemed to take hold. He paused and took a deep breath. "Jesus, I cannot believe what I was about to do," he whispered in dismay. "I apologize."

Marianne furrowed a brow, wondering what had happened to make him hesitate. One moment he seemed intent on taking her right then and there as she sat on the top of a whiskey barrel, and the next, he wasn't. "Were you about to make love to me?" she countered, her breaths still labored.

Jasper blinked. "I was, but we shouldn't... I shouldn't have... not like this," he stammered, his voice sounding rather strangled.

"Are we alone?"

Staring at his wife in disbelief, her simple question giving him pause, Jasper dared a glance behind him. He surveyed the entire deck from the shadowed area where a collection of barrels had been secured, realizing they, too, were in the shadows. "We are," he hedged. He felt her fingers undoing the fastenings of his breeches, the task made difficult given how his turgid manhood strained against the placket.

When the last button gave way, he gave a start as his engorged manhood sprung forth. Marianne's knees were suddenly on either side of his hips, her damp quim cradling his manhood. "Do I dare ask how it is you know how to do this?" he struggled to get out.

"There's a book in my uncle's library. My aunt encouraged me to read it, and to study the illustrations," she murmured. "She gave it to me the night after the ball."

Jasper blinked again, remembering how he had wanted to pay a call on her at three o'clock in the morning.

She was probably still awake, he realized. "Was it written in French?" he asked, wondering if the same book might be in his library.

Marianne nodded. "*Oui*. You're familiar with it?" she asked, her expression taking on a worrisome frown.

Recognizing her concern—*she probably thinks we'll be making love in some of those impossible positions*—he gave a shake of his head. "I am, but I assure you, we won't be doing most of what you saw in those color plates," he said quietly.

Allowing a nod of relief, Marianne moved a hand to where his manhood was pressed against her wet folds. She used a finger to touch the tip of it, jerking it away when Jasper's body reacted. He quickly captured the hand in his and brought it to his lips. "I want you, Marianne. Either here or in our cabin. It makes no difference," he whispered.

Marianne shifted a bit on the barrel, and she allowed a tentative grin at hearing his primal growl. A moment later, and she could feel him guiding his manhood into her, bit by bit and far more slowly than he had entered her earlier that day. The now-familiar sense of fullness had her holding her breath as she anticipated pain. Instead, his slow movements in and almost all the way out of her body were a balm to the soreness she felt from that afternoon's experience. Given how one of his arms held her, how his lips trailed down the column of her neck and to her collarbones, how one of his hand's teased an engorged nipple through the silk fabric of her dressing gown, Marianne could do nothing more than hold on and struggle for breath. She thought she should be doing something in return, but she couldn't recall just what it might be.

When his slow movements increased in speed and intensity, the delicious soreness gave way to a completely new sensation. A sensation that seemed to increase and subside with his every movement until it only increased in intensity. Until it seemed to consume her entire body. Until she could no longer breathe, perched just on the edge of an abyss her body seemed ready to tumble into.

She was barely aware of how Jasper ceased his movements, as if he, too, had crested a very tall cliff and was about to step over the edge. His sudden gasp, quiet curse, and final thrust sent them both over the brink.

How fortuitous for them that a sea bird happened to call out at the same time Marianne screamed.

As for Jasper's deep growl and guttural curse, they were silenced when he planted his face against one of her breasts and simply held onto her for dear life.

They remained like that for what seemed like hours, or perhaps it was only a few minutes—Jasper wasn't entirely sure and found he really didn't care—until he was aware of how Marianne trembled in his hold.

"You must be chilled to the bone," he whispered, about to lift his head from her breast and step out of her hold. Although they were sheltered from the worst of the winds that filled the sails, he could feel a cooling breeze on his back through the fabric of his shirt.

Marianne's arms tightened around his head and shoulders. "I am blissfully warm, in fact," she murmured.

"You're shivering."

"I know. And I don't know why," she replied with a shake of her head. Earlier that afternoon, she had experienced the same trembling through her entire body, as if it had been anticipating what was to come. As if it knew sexual congress would be unlike anything she had ever experienced. Her entire body thrummed, as if part of it had lain dormant and was suddenly awakened.

Jasper angled his head and allowed a long sigh. Perhaps she was frightened. Or excited. Aroused. "You did... feel pleasure?" he asked in a quiet whisper. She had to have come, for he was sure he felt his manhood drawn into her body with a series of undulating waves. Coupled with his own release and the position in which he had taken her, the experience had been entirely new to him.

Marianne wondered how much to admit. "I did, although I must say, I do not think the word adequate to describe the sensation."

Allowing a slight chuckle, Jasper tightened his hold on her. "If I don't get you down from this..." He paused as he pulled away a bit to determine on just what he had Marianne perched. "This *barrel*," he said with a hint of disbelief. "I fear we will be found sound asleep by a sailor in the morning. I cannot keep my eyes open much longer."

Reminded of one of the color plates in her uncle's book, Marianne was relieved her bright red blush wasn't apparent in the dark. "I thought you were hungry," she countered, the thought of food not so appetizing when she realized the ship's movements were becoming less smooth. The closer they were to leaving the Channel, the more choppy the waters below seemed to be.

"I can wait until morning," he said as he slowly pulled his manhood from her body, secretly thrilled when he heard her mewl of disappointment. He quickly buttoned the placket of his breeches. Moving his hands to her waist, he lifted her from the barrel and continued to hold onto her until he was sure her slippered feet could hold her up. "Can you? You must be starving," he murmured.

Marianne gave a shake of her head. "I'd rather not eat. At least... at least until I know if I get seasick or not," she whispered. "I've never been on a body of water larger than a river before."

Jasper hadn't even considered she might suffer from seasickness. He had been so concerned about his own inability to remain in the windowless cabin, he had forgotten to ask about her welfare. "Should you feel... queasy or nauseous, I can bring you up on deck. I should warn you, I prefer to be out-of-doors," he explained as he offered his arm. "So I spend most of the days on deck."

"Will they allow me up on the deck? During the day?" Marianne asked as she lowered a foot onto the first step of the companionway, thankful for Jasper's hold on her. In the dark, she couldn't make out steep steps, but then, she wasn't wearing her eyeglasses, either. Still clutched in one of her hands, she winced when she realized the lenses would have to be cleaned if she expected to see anything through them.

"Of course," Jasper whispered, kneeling so he could continue to hold onto Marianne's hand until she could find the railing. Once she was at the bottom of the stairs, he followed her down and then led them back to their cabin.

"Would it be agreeable with you if I wore a nightrail to bed?" Marianne asked in a whisper, just as Jasper opened the door to their cabin.

He allowed a chuckle. "Yes, I suppose you should, actually," he answered, just as Marianne froze in place and let out a sound of surprise.

Chapter 11

THE APPEARANCE OF A COLLEAGUE

*J*ames Singleton struggled to get up from the chair in which he was sitting and regarded the Viscount and Viscountess Henley with an arched brow. "Pardon me, my lord. I... I didn't know where I should wait for you," he said. When he was finally standing, his head came within mere inches of the cabin's ceiling. About to make his way toward Jasper, he paused and gave a slight bow. "Forgive me. I didn't realize you had... company."

Jasper had one arm gripped around Marianne's waist as if he intended to pull her out of the cabin, but at the sight of his colleague—and his partner on this expedition—he relaxed his hold and slipped past her into the cabin. "Singleton! I was beginning to think you had missed the boat," he countered as a brilliant smile lit his face.

Truth be told, he had completely forgotten the man was due to join them for the trip to Sicily. He silently cursed himself for having allowed the events of the day to render him so forgetful.

"I nearly did, my lord," Singleton replied, daring a glance to where Marianne stood near the door. She had closed it, but had her back pressed against the thick wood as she held the edges of her dressing gown together with clenched fists. "The mail coach from Cambridge arrived later than expected, and by the time I got to your townhouse with the last trunk and arranged a hackney, I nearly missed getting on board," he continued as he gave a nod. "I've brought the trunk you requested from the university, as well," he added as he pointed to a leather-clad traveling trunk. The scuffed surface betrayed its age and frequent use.

"It was rather sporting of you to make that trip on my behalf," Jasper said. "Dr. Jones' latest missive requested we bring it. He's been on site for a month already, and is apparently impressed with what he's found so far. Made mention of some Gypsy claiming it was about time he returned to the island."

James Singleton nodded. "Truth be told, I was beginning to think you'd gone overboard when you didn't make an appearance at dinner, my lord." He said this last as his gaze once again darted to the woman who still stood with her back against the door, her brilliant blue eyes wide and still filled with surprise.

Jasper dared a glance back at Marianne and failed at an attempt to hide his blush. He may as well have gone overboard when dinner was being served, seeing as how he was sound asleep at the time, the after-effects of his afternoon with Marianne having left him satiated and sleepy.

She was staring wide-eyed at the blond, blue-eyed intruder. At least she had her dressing gown firmly wrapped around her body, although the silhouettes of her nipples stood out in stark relief against the silk fabric. "Marianne, Viscountess Henley, may I introduce my colleague, James Singleton? He's become quite adept at clearing debris from tesserae, so he'll be joining me in my research whilst we're on the island of Sicily."

James' eyes widened before he gave a deep bow, a rather difficult maneuver given the cramped space in the cabin.

"Your servant, my lady," he said, before he aimed an expression of confusion in Jasper's direction.

"It's very good to meet you, Mr. Singleton," Marianne said with a nod, as she finally stepped farther into the cabin. "I've only just met a few of my husband's friends at breakfast this morning. May I be so bold as to ask how long you have known Lord Henley?"

"Just over ten years now, my lady. This will be my fifth expedition with his lordship."

Marianne blinked at hearing how long the two men had known one another. "Then my husband must find your company incomparable."

"Oh, I hope so, my lady."

At hearing Marianne's reference to him as "my husband," Jasper wondered at the slight tug he felt in his chest. Her words sounded almost as as if she were proud to be married to him. At no point during his marriage to Sophie had he ever heard her make such a claim without it sounding as if she was ashamed to be married to him.

"I apologize if I seem a bit... discombobulated, my lady," Singleton said. "I wasn't aware Lord Henley had taken a wife."

Jasper rolled his eyes when he realized he hadn't apprised his colleague about his marriage. The day before Lord Attenborough's ball, James had left London to secure a particular trunk in Cambridge—the traveling trunk in which he and Jasper had stored their research on the Roman mosaics they had uncovered north of Rome on their last expedition. Some of Dr. Jones' research from Italy was also in the trunk, as was a book detailing the history of Sicily. "Just this morning, in fact," he said, referring to his nuptials. He allowed a grin of embarrassment. "Lady Henley and I are on our wedding trip."

James' brows furrowed. "Oh, begging your pardon then,"

he said as he took a step toward the door. "I'll leave you to your... wedding night," he stammered.

"Thank you," Jasper replied with a nod. "I hope you find your accommodations acceptable?"

His colleague couldn't help the look of embarrassment that colored his face just then. "Very acceptable. I wasn't expecting I would have a cabin all to myself. It's the first door on the right—should you require my... assistance," James replied as he waggled his eyebrows.

"Oh, I nearly forgot. My father-in-law blessed me with some scotch," Jasper said, giving the man a quelling glance. He opened the trunk in which the bottles had been packed and pulled one out. He held it out to James.

"Well, I see you're well equipped for bribes," James commented before turning his attention to Marianne. "It's an honor to meet you, my lady," he added as he gave another bow and made his way to the door. "Best wishes to you both." He gave another nervous nod to Jasper and took his leave of the cabin.

When the door closed behind the other archaeologist, Jasper threw the bolt and turned around, his head shaking as if in disbelief.

"What is it?" Marianne wondered as she made her way to one of her trunks.

"In all the excitement of the day, I completely forgot about Singleton," he said with a sigh.

Marianne immediately understood his comment and nodded. "I thought you were being robbed when you opened that door."

Jasper gave her a sorrowful shake of his head. "I should have expected him," he murmured, as he watched Marianne pull a nightrail out of the trunk and shake it out.

"For a moment, I thought we were in the wrong cabin." She straightened and regarded Jasper for a moment before glancing about. There was no screen for dressing or for using a chamber pot. No privacy to speak of.

"I can help you with that," he offered as he moved to join her.

"Oh, I can manage," she said, rather uncomfortable with the lack of privacy. "Do you suppose you could... turn around?"

Jasper blinked, but he did her bidding. "I have seen you in all your gorgeous glory," he murmured, his head angling over one shoulder as he made the comment. He managed to see most of her as she pulled the nightrail over her head, but he quickly turned his head to face away from her before her head poked through the neckline of the gown.

Marianne sighed, not sure how to respond to his claim. She had been so anxious earlier that afternoon, she had barely paid any mind to the fact that he had completely undressed her. As for his claim that he had seen all of her, she rather doubted it. The bed wasn't large enough. Besides, she would prefer to use the coach pot without him watching. "Will there be someone to see to the laundry, and emptying the..."

"It's all arranged," Jasper said as he dared another glance over his shoulder, quickly turning back when he realized she was busy with a bourdaloue. Having never traveled with a woman, he hadn't considered the need for privacy—or a privy. "And I sent word ahead to have our hostess arrange a lady's maid to meet us at our villa on Sicily," he added, not about to mention his concern the woman might not speak any English. Between his Latin, limited Italian, and the bit of Greek he might remember from his days at Cambridge, he figured they could get by.

"That was very kind of you," Marianne murmured.

Jasper gave a start, realizing she had moved to stand almost behind him. He turned and took in the sight of her with her honey blonde hair down past her collar bones. Her virginal bright white nightrail was at odds with what they'd been doing only the hour before. But what struck him the hardest was how she gazed at him with her brilliant blue eyes. As if she adored him.

Sophie had never looked at him like that.

"It was the least I could do," he whispered. He would have reached out to pull her against him, but one of her hands touched his chest, her fingers smoothing over the lawn of his shirt until she had some of it gathered between her thumb and forefinger.

"Am I to act as your valet on this evening?" she whispered.

Jasper gave his head a shake. "I... maybe... would you mind terribly?" he whispered. "I was hoping you would help me," he stammered. He was so tired—hungry, too—he could barely stand up, so he was relieved when Marianne pulled his shirt over his head and pointed to the bed.

"Sit down before you fall down, and I shall do my best," she instructed, pretending not to notice his bare chest. It wasn't as if she'd never seen one before—she had paid witness to many a farmer threshing his fields sans a shirt. She had never been this close to one before, though.

Well, she had when they had made love, of course, but her attention was on other, more important considerations. Such as his lips and what they were doing to her breasts. His hands and how they traveled over her skin. His manhood and what it felt like buried inside her.

The thought of what he had done to her on this day— her wedding day—and how he had done it had Marianne realizing she was a rather lucky wife. He was a generous lover as well as considerate, minimizing her pain and seeing to her pleasure before taking his own. The least she could do was see to his comfort before he slept.

She had his boots and stockings pulled from his feet by the time he had unbuttoned his breeches. When he pushed them down, she was stunned to find his genitals looking very much like those on the Greek statues decorating her father's great hall.

"I really am exhausted," he commented, as if he could read her thoughts. A frown appeared on his face.

Marianne allowed a wan grin, ignoring the frisson that shot up her spine just then. For despite the desire that bloomed at the apex of her thighs, Jasper's exhaustion was evident.

He was asleep even before his head settled into the pillow, unaware of how Marianne studied his naked body before she turned down the wicks of the sconces and finally joined him on the bed.

Even if they never suited one another during the daylight hours, at least they suited one another in bed. Coupled with their mutual love of kissing, Marianne supposed that was enough.

Chapter 12

A CLEAR FORTNIGHT FOR SAILING

*T*he next day
During his last two trips to Italy—both occurring before his marriage to Sophie—Jasper had spent most of the voyages up on deck, reading books, or in his cabin, studying maps of archaeological sites related to his own specialty—Roman mosaics. Evenings were spent at the captain's table, enjoying spirited conversations about European politics, pirates, and ports of call. Later in the evening, he would read up on the deck until it was too dark to see the printed page. Back in his cabin, he studied the maps of known Roman ruins and planned his travels according to what he sought on behalf of his patrons.

Now that he had a wife to consider, he realized he would have to combine his research with sightseeing—not an impossible task considering where he planned to work. He wondered if Marianne had brought along any books in the two trunks that lined one wall of their cabin.

Jasper was thinking of all this and more before he finally opened his eyes. He turned his head, expecting to find his wife asleep next to him. Seeing only the mahogany paneling covering the wall across the room, he turned the other direction to discover he was the only one in the bed.

"Marianne?" he called out. He sat up in bed and glanced around, alarmed when he realized she wasn't in the cabin. His gaze immediately went to the table, remembering his comment about how he should have left a note. A square of white parchment, torn from a larger sheet, had been made into a tent. The note, a beautifully scripted missive, simply said she was up on deck.

Well, where else would she be? he wondered. Although he would have liked to hold her for a time before they got up and dressed for the day, he knew there would be other opportunities.

The pitcher of water had been refilled, the bowl emptied, and fresh bath linens delivered. A copper tub, its water still topped with a few bubbles, took up some of the available floor space. He dipped a hand in, stunned to discover it was still warm. *How did I sleep through the delivery of a tub?* And pails of steaming water? *Jesus, did I sleep through her bath?* he wondered, rather surprised at the disappointment he felt just then.

The idea of watching Marianne bathe had his cock hardening even more than his morning tumescence. Bathing with her... his squeezed his eyes shut in an effort to quell the thought.

He had never once watched Sophie bathe. He rather doubted he would have ever been welcomed in her bathing chamber.

Jasper stepped into the tub, deciding a quick bath would do him good. The feminine scent of the few bubbles that remained reminded him of Marianne. Inhaling deeply, he decided he needed to discover what had become of her. Perhaps she had already gone for some breakfast, although she wouldn't know where to go unless she asked one of the sailors.

That thought had him up and out of the tub in an instant, reaching for one of the bath linens at the very moment he heard a gasp from the doorway. He whirled around to find Marianne staring at him, her back pressed against the closed door and her fingers splayed out on either side of her mouth.

"I apologize. I should have knocked," she said, her eyes wide. One of her hands moved to the front of her body, a pose he recognized in women who were enceinte. *Could she already be with child?*

Jasper had to resist the urge to laugh at how she pretended not to stare at him. He wrapped the towel around his middle and moved to join her, bussing her on the cheek before he attempted to kiss her on the lips. She turned away before he could, though, which had him confused. "Thank you for leaving the note," he murmured. "Now, tell me what's wrong."

She regarded him through her lashes and allowed a nod. "I am sorry I had to leave you. I wasn't feeling well, you see. I felt rather ill, in fact, so I went up on deck and—"

"Did you make it to the railing?" he interrupted, his eyes closing as he imagined how hard it would have been for her —she wasn't wearing her spectacles, nor were they clutched in one of her hands.

"I did," she replied. "But I fear I left a bit of a mess down the side of the ship." Her expression suggested she was about to cry.

Jasper dropped his head to hers, unable to hide his humor. "It will wash off," he assured her. "Come. Have a drink of water. You'll feel better," he added, just then aware of how the ship seemed to be riding on rougher seas. "Are we past Brest, I wonder?"

"We are. The captain says the winds favored us last night. We'll make it to the Strait of Gibraltar before morning."

Blinking at this bit of news, Jasper wondered if he had missed breakfast. "What time is it?" he asked.

"Half-past eight, but breakfast will be served at nine, according to Captain St. John," Marianne replied. "He says I should eat something. That it might actually help, although I'm to avoid the fish." She sighed. "Do you need help dressing?"

Chuckling, Jasper gave a shake of his head. "I can manage, which has me wondering how you did. I didn't even hear the tub and water being delivered."

Marianne dipped her head. "I made sure the porters were very quiet," she admitted. "And I'm not completely dressed. Properly, I mean," she added, an eyetooth catching her lower lip.

"Oh?" he replied as he did a quick sweep down the front of her round gown. "You appear... dressed."

She lifted her skirts to reveal she wasn't wearing any stockings at the same moment Jasper realized she wasn't wearing any stays, either. The thought of peeling the gown from her body so he could help with her undergarments had him swallowing just then. He wanted desperately to bed her, but remembered he should wait, especially if she wasn't feeling well.

Gathering her into his arms, Jasper was relieved when Marianne didn't tense under his hold. She instead seemed to relax against the front of his half-naked body, her arms wrapping around his middle and her cheek coming to rest on his bare chest. She sighed. "Do you think we could do this every morning?"

Chuckling again, Jasper kissed the top of her head. "I look forward to it," he murmured. He tightened his hold before letting go. "However, I am starving, and you must be as well," he said as he moved to open his only clothes trunk. "Captain St. John will think I'm having my way with you if we miss breakfast."

Marianne blushed a bright red, and not just because Jasper had shed the bath linen in favor of pulling on a pair of smalls and his breeches. He didn't even ask her to turn around!

Just a few minutes ago, the captain had approached her, asking if he might introduce himself to the "other newly-wed." She had curtsied and held out her hand, intending to shake hands with St. John. He had instead taken her hand to his lips and kissed the back of it before saying, *You must be Lady Henley. Please excuse the impropriety, but since your husband is not here to introduce us, let me do the honors. I am John St. John, captain of this ship. I do hope you're finding your accommodations adequate?*

Marianne blinked. *Lady Henley.*

She hadn't thought of how she would be addressed now that she was married. Although her father was the son of a marquess and the younger brother of one, she had merely been a "miss."

It's very good to meet you, Captain St. John, she had replied with a curtsy. *The cabin is rather fine, thank you for asking, but I'm feeling a bit...* And it was at that point queasiness had her rushing to the railing and vomiting over the side. That the wind would be blowing such as it was to send what little had been left in her stomach onto the side of the ship was the least of her embarrassment. For when she straightened and attempted to take a cleansing breath, the captain was standing next to her, offering her his handkerchief.

I'm so sorry, she had said, tears pricking the corners of her eyes.

The man chuckled. *You needn't be, my lady. You are not the first—nor will you be the last—to decorate the side of my ship*, he said as he looked over the edge. *However, you may be the first to use a lifeboat as a chamber pot.*

Marianne's eyes widened before she took a look over the railing. *What?* She couldn't see a lifeboat, exactly, but if she squinted just so, she realized there was something hanging onto the side of the ship.

The captain regarded her for a moment. *The birds will see to it*, he had said with a shake of his head. He paused before continuing. *Do you usually wear spectacles, perhaps?* he then asked gently.

Swallowing, as much from an attempt to remove the taste of bile from the back of her tongue as to fight the sob she was sure was about to rob her of breath, she nodded. *I am in possession of a pair of eyeglasses*, she had admitted.

Wondering at how she reacted to his question, St. John allowed a sigh. *May I suggest you wear them whilst on deck? At least when you're alone? I would hate for you to become injured if you cannot see a boom swing 'round.*

Marianne nodded. *Of course.*

She had curtsied then and made her way back down the companionway, deciding she would simply spend the rest of the trip in the cabin.

"*Y*ou cannot spend the next two weeks in the cabin," Jasper said when she relayed the story, obviously amused by what had happened.

"I cannot face Captain St. John again," she countered.

Jasper sighed. "You can and you shall. Especially since we're to have breakfast with him at nine o'clock." He had to suppress the urge to grin at her look of embarrassment. "Now, let's get you properly dressed," he said as he buttoned up his waistcoat.

Marianne allowed a nod and turned around so Jasper could undo her buttons, well aware of how he sucked in a breath and seemed to struggle with his role as lady's maid.

Perhaps they would suit one another in the mornings as well as at night, she thought with a prim smile.

Chapter 13

A GLIMPSE OF GIRGENTI

*E*leven *days later at Marina di Girgenti*
Marianne peered through her spectacles, her gaze fixed on what appeared to be a cluster of white buildings atop a hill. As she slowly turned, she could make out the golden Doric columns of several Greek temples atop what appeared to be a long ridge halfway up the island. The canopy of leaves from a few gnarled almond trees hid some of the ruins from her vantage. Closer to the pier, a large, quadrangular tower rose from the beach. Two large swaths of cloth—sails, Marianne finally sorted—were held up with tent poles to form shaded areas under which men worked.

Before she could continue her visual sweep of the area known as the *Valle dei Templi*, Jasper's face suddenly filled her field of vision. She gave a start, about to step back but unable to do so when she realized he had an arm around the back of her waist.

"I didn't mean to startle you, my sweet," he said. "But we really must be going if we're to arrive at the villa before dark." He made a motion with one hand to indicate the general direction they would be heading—up a rising slope toward Girgenti. He then waved his hand to the west. "I cannot believe how gorgeous the sunsets have been on this trip," he added.

Marianne glanced in the direction he indicated, stunned at the colorful sky. In what seemed to be just beyond the edge of the island, a series of thin clouds reflected oranges and reds above the golden globe of the sun. Still well above the horizon, the sun seemed to shimmer as much as its reflection in the surface of the Mediterranean.

Her gaze swept back up to the city. "Are we going all the way up there?" she asked. Although she could do with a walk —her body felt as if it was still moving despite the fact that she was standing still—she didn't think her slippers would allow her to climb the road leading into Girgenti. She decided too late she should have worn her half-boots.

"If I'm to understand our guide, not quite," he said as he indicated a white-clad man standing next to a cart and two donkeys. Porters had just finished loading their trunks into the back of the cart, Singleton giving directions in Italian as they did so, and the guide was seeing to their pay. "Pietro says Signora Romano's villa is well before the city gate. Closer to the ruins, which means we may not require daily transportation to the site," he added hopefully. "We'll pay a visit to the temples tomorrow so that we can get the lay of the land. Pietro will help in that regard," he added as he nodded to their guide.

He dared another glance around the port town, wondering if Darius Jones was anywhere about. He was fairly sure the older archaeologist had taken a room here as opposed to one up in Girgenti, but if he had, Jasper didn't know where it might be. Given the fair weather, it was possible Darius was still up at the site of the old Greco-Roman town. From his latest missive, Jasper figured the man had hired some locals to assist with the excavation.

He would be relying on locals for nearly everything, including labor if his own expedition required considerable digging. Besides bringing Singleton along, Jasper had briefly considered employing a couple of students from Cambridge to assist him, but he didn't intend to return to British shores until well after they would be required to resume classes in the fall. As for how he would pay the help, he had already seen to changing some of his funds to the local currency of *Sicilian piastra*, a relatively new coin to the island.

"Pray tell, what is that building?" Marianne asked as she nodded toward the area's largest block-shaped building.

Jasper followed her line of sight. "Our guide says it's a storage building for grain. Carlo the Fifth had it built when he was in power."

Nodding her understanding, Marianne took her husband's proffered arm and allowed him to lead her to the cart. "There isn't room for both of us to sit up top," Jasper said as he assisted her. "So I'll ride on the back. I'll be right behind you," he added, when he saw her sudden expression of worry.

"But what of Mr. Singleton?" she asked, when she noticed the man was heading back toward the port.

Jasper pointed to a line of buildings that made up the central portion of the port city. "He has made arrangements to spend the evening here in town," he said, not adding that he wanted to have their villa to themselves for their first night on the large island. Once he had explained his changed circumstances with their hostess—he wasn't yet sure if she had received his letter mentioning his marriage—he would have James join them in their villa.

"He's expected for dinner with Dr. Jones." Jasper didn't add that he was fairly sure those arrangements included a prostitute. James had made mention of missing female company during their twelve days on board *The Fairweather*.

Jasper briefly wondered if the man employed a mistress in London. He was fairly sure James had a lover, but if so, he never spoke of it. "I sent him with another bottle of scotch to give to Dr. Jones. He has promised to come to the villa in the morning for breakfast."

Their guide joined her on the bench. "*Buon pomeriggio*, Lady Henley," Pietro said before he had the donkeys moving up the hill toward Girgenti.

"*Ciao*," Marianne replied, giving a quick glance over her shoulder to be sure Jasper was sitting on the back of the cart. Their trunks were lined up directly behind her, their bulk taking up most of the cart's space. Testing the bit of Italian she knew, Marianne turned to the guide. "*Quanto lontano?*" she asked. *How far?*

"About a mile," he replied in heavily-accented English. "You speak Italian."

Marianne blushed a bright pink. "No," she replied with a shake of her head. "Very little," she amended when she noticed his look of confusion.

"I speak English, as does the *Vedova* Romano," he replied. He turned his attention to the donkeys who trudged up the slope. "But it is kind of you to know even a little of our language."

Marianne wasn't about to tell him she had no choice— one of her governesses had insisted she know a bit of several languages. Although she was fluent in French, she couldn't claim the same for any of the other romance languages. "What is she like?"

Pietro gave a shrug. "She is like Atlas," he replied after a moment. He gave a quick glance in his passenger's direction, as if he wanted to be sure she understood his reference.

"She carries the world on her shoulders?" Marianne questioned, her attention suddenly going to the strange plants along the side of the road. She was sure they were a form of desert plant, but she had never seen anything looking so much like one of the pincushions in her sewing basket. Each plant looked as if it was made up of a dozen green pincushions stacked up in a haphazard array, sometimes forming an entire hedge.

"Her family, at least," Pietro said with a roll of his eyes, referring to Signora Romano. "She is mother to her own and mother to her brother's bambinos and anyone else who needs a mama," he added. When Marianne didn't ask another question, he added, "But she is a sad woman. Perhaps your visit will bring happiness."

Marianne wondered at the comment. He had said "*vedova*," which implied their hostess was a widow. At one time she'd had a husband. "Did *Signore* Romano die recently?" she asked, a thought that their arrival might be ill-timed.

What if her husband had just died?

Pietro's brows furrowed again. "Four years, I think," he replied after a time. "But she was sad even before Signore Romano's death. I used to say she lost a love long ago."

"Did she?" Marianne asked, giving another quick glance behind her to find Jasper's head turned, as if he, too, was listening to their guide.

"I no longer ask about such things, my lady. She..." He paused as if he was searching for the appropriate word. "Punched me." He frowned and turned in Marianne's direction, his open palm moving across his face in a pantomimed slap.

"Slapped you," Marianne corrected him. "I rather imagine she doesn't wish to discuss such a private matter."

The guide bounced his head from side to side. "Have you slapped him?" he asked, one thumb lifted to indicate her husband.

Marianne blinked. "I have not," she replied, a bit indignant, suddenly understanding why the Widow Romano had slapped the guide.

"You are new to wed?" Pietro countered.

Frowning at the man's impertinence, she finally said,

"*Sì.*" The word came out easily, as if she'd been using it all her life.

"Ah," he replied. "You will someday. All men are fools. Eventually, he will do something stupid, for which you will slap him."

"Hey!" Jasper finally spoke. "Speak for yourself. I have no intention of ever doing anything that has my beautiful bride reacting in such a violent manner."

Marianne grinned as she turned and gave him a wink. She realized after a moment that he may not have been able to see her wink, as she still wore her eyeglasses. About to remove them, she paused when she noticed Jasper's sudden look of awe, his gaze directed just beyond her shoulder. Turning to follow his line of sight, her mouth dropped open upon seeing the remains of a Greek temple just off the side of the road.

Bathed in the light of the setting sun, the honey-colored marble columns took on a reddish cast. Past the temple to their immediate right, the ruins of several more temples could be seen in the near distance. One appeared as if the sea would swallow it at any moment, although after a time, Marianne realized it actually sat atop a ridge well above the breaking water.

Pietro said, "*Templi dei Concordia* is the best preserved. Juno, not so much. Heracles has only the one column left standing." He paused until another opening in the trees allowed the ruins to show again. "The *Templi dei Zeus* is almost gone, although there is still a telamon there on the Olympian field," he explained as he pointed in the general direction of a fairly flat plane in the distance. Dotted with small palms and agave plants, it was difficult to imagine that columns—let alone a building—had at one time stood there. Giant honey-colored boulders and pieces of columns were strewn about as if they had been dice tossed by a Titan. "Many will say the Greeks never finished it, but if they had, and if it had withstood all the earthquakes, then it would have been magnificent," he claimed. "You already saw much of the rest of it," he added as he glanced back behind them. "It was used as a..." He struggled to find the right word. "Quarry. To build the marina."

Not sure why she felt sad at hearing the temple's marble stones had been repurposed, Marianne continued to study the temples she could see from their vantage. "Are there any Roman temples?" Marianne asked, her curiosity bringing a grin to Jasper's face.

"*Sì*," Pietro replied. "Norman, too." He pointed up to the city, where a square bell tower dominated the skyline. "Like the church in Girgenti."

Marianne glanced back at Jasper. "Will we have time to see all of them?" she asked, her voice hopeful.

Jasper smiled, partly because of how his wife looked wearing her spectacles and partly because of her enthusiasm. If he had any concerns she would be bored on this trip, he realized he had nothing about which to be worried. "Of course, my sweet."

Their guide lifted his head. "Ah. If he had said, 'no,' then you would have slapped him, no?"

Allowing a titter, Marianne shook her head. "I would have sneaked away while he was digging for Roman artifacts and seen the temples for myself."

Pietro's eyes widened. "You will only go in the company of Signora Romano," he warned.

A bit alarmed by his serious manner, Marianne's eyes widened. "Should I be worried for my safety?"

"Pietro is merely warning you that Sicilian men will find you as beautiful as I do, and they will attempt to capture your affections with words of adoration," Jasper said with an arched brow. "And capture *you* with offers of marriage."

Marianne considered this bit of information before saying, "That doesn't sound so awful."

"And your fortune," Jasper added, which had Pietro allowing a loud laugh.

At the mention of her fortune, Marianne wondered how much her father had given Jasper. She remembered his comment about having left some of it in her bedchamber at their home in Canobie, as if he had to bribe her to visit him. She had every intention of returning there, and hoped they might do so when they completed their tour of Italy.

"Your husband speaks the truth, my lady," Pietro said as he directed the donkeys to turn off on a well-worn path. "You will be... *proposte*," he warned. "They will wish to marry you, even if you are already wed."

The remains of a wall and chunks of marble marked where a gate and a wall surrounding the city had at one time stood. Almond trees lined one side of the lane, and more of the pincushion plants were scattered about the dry terrain. Small palms sprouted from around the base of rocks and boulders.

"What are those plants?" Marianne asked as she pointed with a gloved hand to one of the pincushion plants.

"Ah. *Fico d'India*," Pietro replied. "Indian fig. Prickly pear, I think is what the English call them. They are edible. If you are parched, you can..." He motioned breaking one open and sucking on the flesh. "Eat it," he finished.

Marianne frowned, deciding she would have to be very thirsty before she would try eating a cactus. "And those? What are they?" she asked as she pointed to a plant with a base featuring long, tongue-like leaves and a central stalk that sported a series of smaller tufts of leaves up high.

"Agave," Pietro replied. "The leaves are used to make..." He paused, as if he struggled to come up with the English word for the caning for chairs.

"Cord," Jasper offered. "But a bitter aloe to dose children is made from the flower at the top. Not a spirit I would recommend my lady trying," he said by way of warning.

Marianne made a mental note to ask Signora Romano if she had any of the aloe. She would have been satisfied with never having tried it, but Jasper's words had her curious.

"Where does this road go?" Jasper asked as he pointed to the one that headed down the hill at an angle and disappeared into a grove of almond trees.

"The old Roman city," Pietro replied as he turned the donkeys to go up the same road in the opposite direction. "Where you will wish to dig, if I understand your words," he added.

After only a hundred feet, he pulled the donkeys to a halt next to what appeared to be a stucco wall with a door. "This is the guest villa, and up there is Signora Romano's *casa*," he explained. "Come. I will introduce you," he said as he directed his attention to Jasper.

The viscount jumped off the back of the cart and came around to Marianne's side. He reached up and gripped the sides of her waist, lifting her from the cart. When Marianne had her feet beneath her and was gazing up at him in what appeared to be surprise, he grinned and said, "I shall never tire of doing that."

Marianne couldn't help the blush that colored her face. "I hope I shall never tire of you doing it," she replied, wondering if their ease with one another in the evenings would continue now that Jasper would be working. Although their nights on the ship had been spent making love, they had spent their days relatively apart from one another, Jasper conferring with Singleton and studying maps up on deck, or writing letters, whilst she read books or did needlework under the shade of the sails.

When they dined, she remained quiet unless someone asked her a question, preferring to listen as Jasper, Captain St. John and some of the other passengers discussed various topics. It was during their meals she realized she had married a man of some intelligence, a scholar who preferred the study of Roman history over Greek history and Roman mosaics over those of the Greeks, even if they were heavily influenced by Hellenistic styles.

If Marianne experienced any queasiness, she was quick to move to the side of the ship and stare out at the horizon. Although she didn't wear her spectacles very often, she kept them handy in the event the captain was on deck and able to see her, at which point she made sure to don the ugly eyewear. Now that she was no longer on the ship, she thought to only wear them when no one else was around.

"What are your first impressions?" Jasper asked, his gaze sweeping the tops of the almond trees to the Greek temples beyond.

"I feel as if I have stepped back in time thousands of years," Marianne replied, her bespectacled gaze following her husband's. She slowly surveyed her surroundings, as if she was memorizing them for future reference. Then she removed her spectacles and took Jasper's proffered arm.

Even before they reached the door leading into Signora Romano's courtyard, it swung open and a dark-haired beauty emerged to regard them with a brilliant smile. "Welcome to *Casa Romano*," she said as she dipped a curtsy, her sprigged muslin gown looking as if it had just been made by a modiste in Paris.

Jasper gave a leg as Marianne curtsied. "Thank you, my lady," he replied. "May I present my wife, Marianne Henley? And I am Jasper Henley."

Chiara Romano regarded her guests with a practiced grin as she gave a nod. "I am Signora Romano. Your villa is just there," she said as she waved to where their guide was helping a young man unload their trunks. The door to the villa's courtyard was already open, and a young woman stood beyond it, peeking about the edge as if she was spying on them. "Please forgive my niece. Angela will act as your lady's maid during your stay and is simply curious," she said to

Marianne. "Another of my nieces, Tamara, will be the house-maid during your stay. If she does her work correctly, you shouldn't notice her."

Allowing a tentative grin in the young woman's direction, Marianne was rather surprised to see her servant couldn't be more than fourteen or fifteen years old. From what Jasper had told her at the start of their trip, she expected her lady's maid to be a much older woman. "May we see it?" Marianne asked. The daylight was waning, and she feared it would be too dark to tour their villa without the use of candle lamps.

"But of course," Chiara replied. She led them to where her niece stood, the young woman curtsying before saying, "*Buonasera*, my lady, my lord."

"*Buonasera, Signorina* Angela," Marianne replied. "I am Marianne Henley, and this is my husband, Viscount Henley."

Angela's eyes widened, and it became apparent she was attempting to sort Marianne's words. "I am... honored to meet you, my lady." Although she struggled with the English pronunciations, it was apparent she had been learning the language.

The older woman gave the girl some instructions in Italian, and Marianne was able to understand something having to do with luggage.

"I was told you might require a valet on this trip, Lord Henley. My son, David, will be available, probably tomorrow should you need his services," the older woman said as she continued their tour. "He is on his way here from school."

"I appreciate the offer," Jasper replied, a bit uncertain as to how to bring up the matter of James. At the time the arrangements had been made for the villa, he and James were the only two in need of accommodations. Given Marianne was with him as well, they would require another bedchamber. "My colleague accompanied us on the trip. I was hoping there might be an extra room for him?" When Jasper noticed the older woman looking about, as if she was searching for someone, he added, "He is spending this evening down near the marina."

Chiara gave a shrug. "There are plenty of rooms, of course. I shall have Tamara see to fresh linens in the morning. Even though she is to be your maid, you will not see much of her as she is tending to a widow."

"That's very kind of you. Singleton is his name. James Singleton. He'll be joining us on the morrow for breakfast. Pietro said he would see to transportation for him."

Despite not wearing her eyeglasses, Marianne was able to see enough of the villa to know that Signora Romano was a proud property owner. The house was immaculate, the clear glass windows spotless, and the tile floors so clean, Marianne thought she could make out her reflection in their surface. "How is it your window panes are so large?" she asked in awe, when she realized there were only four mullions for each window when similar-sized windows in England required nine or more.

Their hostess angled her head. "Our glass makers are the finest in the world, my lady," she replied, her heavily-accented English easy to understand. "As well they should be, considering they were the first."

Jasper furrowed a brow at hearing the brag, and then remembered Captain St. John's comment about his spyglass being from Italy. He thought of some of his fellow colleagues at the Royal Society. The optics in Sir Elton's telescope were from Italy, as were the lenses in Lord Everly's microscope. "Is there someone in Girgenti who makes eyeglasses?" he asked, thinking he might employ someone to make a more attractive pair for Marianne. "And the frames for the lenses?" He ignored Marianne's sudden glare in his direction.

Chiara seemed to consider the question for a time before she finally gave a shake of her head. "I will discover an answer for you. In Venice, surely, and Florence, of course," she said, her attention on something in her mind's eye. "Even in Palermo. There are... I don't know the English word for the man who grinds the lenses," she started to say, one fist cupped by her other hand and moving about as if she were preparing for a fist fight.

"Oculist?" Jasper offered.

"Oculist!" she repeated with a grin. "They are found throughout Italy. They make eyeglasses for the old men who cannot read without them, and the young people who can only see clearly with them, and sunglasses for those who don't wish to be seen at all."

Jasper dared a quick glance in Marianne's direction. He couldn't help but notice how her face had taken on a reddish cast at the topic of their conversation. "I apologize, my sweet. We can speak of such things on another day. I am sure you wish to finish the tour."

Their hostess allowed a nod. "Follow me, and I shall show you to your rooms." Chiara turned and led the way through the sprawling *casa*, pointing out a high-ceilinged parlor and several small bedchambers as both Jasper and Marianne lifted their noses at the scents of baking bread and rich spices that filled the villa. "This room is for his lordship," Chiara said as she waved into a bedchamber decorated in rich reds and golds and dark, heavy furniture. Against the center of one wall stood a bed mounted on a high, stepped platform. "And this is for her ladyship," she added as she took a few more steps and opened the door to the mistress suite.

Despite her inability to see clearly, Marianne could make out that the room was decorated in deep purples and golds. "It's beautiful," she breathed, half-tempted to lift her eyeglasses to her face.

"*Grazie,*" Chiara replied. "My daughter, Signorina Aurora, will be your cook during your visit. She will see to your breakfast before you go to the temples and make dinner for when you return before dark."

Jasper sniffed the air. "Whatever she has made for dinner this evening smells delicious," he said.

"What about tea?" Marianne asked, thinking she could use a cup. It had been hours since their late breakfast.

"Are you ill?" Chiara countered.

Marianne blinked. "Not since I got off the boat," she replied, realizing she hadn't felt the least bit queasy since they pulled into port.

"Ah," Chiara said as if she suddenly remembered something. "We only drink tea when we are sick," she explained, "But we have excellent coffee for the afternoons."

Nodding her understanding, Marianne couldn't help the sense of disappointment that settled over her just then. Except for Angela's company as she dressed in the mornings, she would be alone whilst Jasper worked. Although she had spent years without the company of other women, she had grown to appreciate the afternoon teas to which her aunt had escorted her for the ten days prior to her wedding.

Even if she didn't participate in the gossip, Marianne found the hours with other women a diversion. Her concerns were no different than those experienced by other ladies of the *ton*. Her self-doubt was voiced by others, her fear of married life assuaged by claims of happy lives with children and the sense of purpose provided by overseeing servants and participation in charitable endeavors.

"That would be lovely," Marianne replied, realizing their hostess was waiting for her response.

"If you are amenable, I shall be happy to accompany you on your daily tour of the ruins, or to go to town while his lordship does his work," Chiara offered.

Marianne's eyes widened. Could the woman read her mind? "Oh, may I?" she asked as she turned her attention to her husband.

Jasper blinked. One moment he had thought Marianne was about to cry, and the next, her entire countenance had brightened with the prospect of spending time in the company of their hostess. "Of course," he replied. He turned his attention to Signora Romano. "But if she discovers any Roman artifacts, you will inform me," he ordered, his manner only half serious.

The woman allowed a wide smile. "So you can claim to have made the discovery? I think not, my lord," she teased.

Grinning, Jasper rolled his eyes. Then he suddenly sobered. "I suppose you have been host to many like me. Archaeologists who claim they only wish to study and then plunder your ruins."

Her chin rising a fraction, Chiara Romano's expression hardened. "Ever since the Duke of Serradifalco started his excavations, we have been visited by all manner of men."

Jasper couldn't help but hear the bitterness in her voice. Domenico Antonio Lo Faso Pietrasanta, Duke of Serradifalco, had hired a large team of laborers to assist in excavating and restoring some of the temples. He had ceased his work in 1812 though, although his efforts continued in other parts of Sicily. "I am not here to plunder," Jasper said with a shake of his head. "I am here to... to document. To study, and to write about my findings. But if I find a complete mosaic in danger of being lost to floods or to thieves, I shall do what I must to preserve it," he warned.

Their hostess considered his words for a moment. "Preserve it? Where?" she asked, obviously suspicious.

"Why, a museum, of course," Jasper replied. "I care not which one, as long as they promise to keep it safe." Realizing now would be a good time to gift a bottle of the scotch he had been given by Marianne's father, he held up a finger, hurried to one of the trunks, and fished a bottle from inside. "I wish to give you a token of our gratitude for allowing us to stay in your home." He held out the bottle to the rather startled hostess.

Chiara finally took it and allowed a nod. "*Grazie*. If I am asked as to the reason for your visit, that is what I shall say. Not that it will matter much. You will find you are welcomed by most on the island," she said. "Especially if you give away liquor like this," she added with a grin. "The British were well received here during the war. Better than the others who fought to control our island," she continued, just as a chime sounded from somewhere else in the villa. "Dinner is served, my lord, my lady."

Marianne's eyes widened. "But, I haven't changed for dinner," she protested.

"You needn't, my love," Jasper whispered. "It's just the two of us," he added with an arched brow.

Looking to their hostess as if she were seeking permission to forgo a change into dinner clothes, Marianne was relieved to see Signora Romano give a non-committal shrug. "If you're sure," she replied.

Jasper took her gloved hand and placed it on his arm. "I am." He turned his attention to their hostess. "Lead the way, my lady," he said with a grin.

Signora Romano did as she was told, and once she saw that they were seated in the elegant dining room, she took her leave of the villa with the promise that Angela would see to Marianne once they finished dinner.

Chapter 14

CONVERSATIONS CAN CLEAR
UP MISCONCEPTIONS

A few minutes later
For the first time since their wedding, Jasper and Marianne ate a meal without the company of others. Marianne continued her practice of remaining quiet during dinner. On the ship, she had only spoken when asked a question.

"This dish is excellent," Jasper commented, hoping to draw out his wife. Not having eaten a dinner with a lone woman since his first wife's death, he found he was at a loss as to what to say.

"Indeed. I've never eaten anything like it," Marianne replied, referring to the *caponata* the young lady named Aurora had delivered to the table when they took their seats. She could make out the main ingredient, eggplant, but couldn't identify the spices that made up the sweet and sour flavors. After a long pause, Marianne lifted her gaze to find Jasper regarding her. "What is it?" She set down her fork and straightened in her chair.

"Do you like it?"

Marianne blinked. "I do."

"The wine is made locally," Jasper said as he lifted his

crystal goblet, his expression changing when he noticed how clear the glass appeared. Not a single bubble marred the goblet.

"Have you met the vintner?"

Jasper blinked before giving his head a shake. "No. But then, I've not been to this part of Italy before." He couldn't help but notice she didn't say if she liked the wine or not. "Do you like it?"

"Very much," she replied, her relief obvious at the sight of their cook entering with a tray on which two steaming bowls were perched.

Aurora set the soup before them, dipping a curtsy before heading for the door. She turned around when Jasper asked, "*Mi scusi*. What is it called?"

The young woman gave a slight shake of her head, her gaze darting to Marianne. When Marianne realized she didn't understand the question, she repeated it in Italian.

Aurora nodded. "*Maccu*." She seemed to struggle for a moment before adding, "Fava beans."

Marianne said, "*Grazie*," before the raven-haired Aurora had a chance to escape to the kitchen. With her heart-shaped face, dark eyes, dark brows, full lips, and perfectly shaped nose, Aurora would be an exotic beauty should she ever appear in a London ballroom. "She's beautiful," Marianne whispered as she leaned forward a bit, as if she didn't want anyone else but Jasper to hear her comment.

The viscount blinked. "I hadn't noticed," he replied with a shrug, his attention on his soup.

Marianne allowed a sound of disbelief, which had Jasper grinning. "Yes, all right, she is... but she is not who I would be caught with kissing in the gardens."

Dimpling, Marianne felt an odd tug in her chest at hearing his comment. "She isn't married," she added, as if the tidbit of information was important.

"How do you know?"

"She was introduced as *Signorina* Aurora. Not *Signora*," Marianne replied. Her eyes widened. "Is Mr. Singleton married?"

Jasper's eyes darted to the side. "I'm quite sure he is not," he hedged. In fact, he had begun to suspect his colleague had no interest in women. At least, not in *that* way.

"Are you saying it like that because you married unexpectedly?" Marianne asked.

"I... I am," Jasper finally acknowledged, not about to suggest the real reason. "May I ask why you wondered?" he added, his brows furrowing as if in worry. Had Marianne developed a tendré for his colleague during their time on board ship?

Marianne dared a glance in the direction of the door to the kitchen. "No reason," she responded, "Other than he could do worse than an Italian wife who can cook."

Jasper dropped his spoon into his soup and stared at Marianne, a bit relieved at hearing her interest in Singleton's marital status had nothing to do with her. "Are you attempting to play matchmaker?" he asked, his face displaying a bit of shock and a lot of amusement. He suddenly angled his head. "Although... I could use a new cook in London. I shall have to pension Mr. Grimes soon. He's getting on in years, you see, and I can't say as I don't expect the kitchen to go up in flames at times."

Her eyes widening with her own shock, Marianne managed an, "Oh, dear," in response. She hadn't yet met any of the servants of his townhouse and now wondered if there would be one to go home to if Mr. Grimes really did set the kitchen afire.

Another long pause ensued before the two started to ask a question at the same time. They both dipped their heads and grinned. "You first," Jasper said.

Marianne sighed. "Will you have time to take me on a tour of the ruins before you begin your work with Dr. Jones?"

"I shall do so tomorrow," he assured her. "I wish to see them, too. But the day after, I really must begin my work at the old Roman city. It's not far from here, according to Pietro. Dr. Jones mentioned in his letters that the temperatures may grow too hot to work without benefit of a sun shade, at least in the afternoons. When the scirocco winds start..."

"Scirocco?" Marianne repeated, her brows furrowing with concern.

"Strong, hot winds that come here from Africa," he clarified.

Marianne's eyes widened. "Africa?" she repeated. "Isn't that far away?"

Jasper shook his head. "Only a hundred miles. Apparently, when the winds are blowing, the air grows much warmer here on Sicily. Then the almond harvest will start, and the hillsides will be covered with men shaking the trees and women picking up the shells from the ground. When that happens, I will have to give up any laborers Dr. Jones has hired for our dig, for they will be required for the harvest."

Marianne nodded her understanding. "What will we do then?"

"I'll take you to Rome."

Marianne's eyes widened. "What will you do there?"

Jasper grinned. "*We* will explore the city. See all the ruins. All the sights. And then possibly Florence or Venice, just as we discussed on the ship. If the weather holds, we'll return here, and I will continue to work until it's time to go back to London." When Marianne didn't immediately respond, he asked, "What is it?"

Allowing a grin, Marianne said, "I shall have to work on improving my Italian," she replied, just as Aurora appeared with their main course, a pasta with sardines.

Jasper matched her grin with one of his own. "Me as well."

When they had finished their dessert of *cassata*, a sponge cake layered with ricotta cheese and encased in marzipan, they sat for a time drinking wine and commenting on the villa's decor, the time their guide would reappear to the take them to the ruins in the morning, and on the pleasant weather. When Jasper paid witness to Marianne's attempt to suppress a yawn, he grinned. "Come. I think it's time we go to bed."

When they retired to their separate bedchambers, Marianne had the distinct impression she wouldn't be expected in Jasper's chambers this night. He hadn't said anything about the sleeping arrangements, which had her hesitant to invite him to her bedchamber.

Perhaps he wanted a night to sleep by himself.

The sound of running feet had her attention turning to the door. She called out, "Come," at the faint knock that sounded. Angela hurried in, a huge grin displaying her white teeth. "Lady Henley," she said as she came to a halt and dipped a curtsy.

"*Buonasera*," Marianne managed, the words for "good evening" coming to her after a moment.

"*Mio cugino vorrebbe incontrarti.*"

Marianne blinked, attempting to interpret the girl's comment. "Your cousin has returned, and he wishes to meet me?" she guessed.

Angela nodded. "*Sì. Lui è con* Lord Henley."

Rather surprised the young man would already be in her husband's chamber—especially if he had just arrived—Marianne allowed a smile. "I look forward to it. Who is your cousin?"

"David. He has returned from Palermo. He was..." Angela paused as she tried to sort the right word. "In school."

She allowed Angela to undress her and help her pull on a

nightrail. She watched her reflection in a mirror free of imperfections as the lady's maid brushed out her hair, her strokes tentative but thorough. And finally, Marianne dismissed the girl and crawled onto the bed.

Despite its comfort and the clean, bright white linens that covered the mattress, Marianne thought she had never felt so miserable.

So lonely.

*H*aving dismissed David Romano for the night —he had found the young man reading in a corner chair while he waited for them to finish dinner— Jasper regarded his bedchamber with a critical eye. He was determined to find something lacking or some evidence something had been missed when it was last cleaned.

He could find nothing wrong.

In fact, the room was clean to a fault. His trunk of clothes had been emptied, the clean clothes now perfectly folded and arranged in neat piles in the drawers of a tall chest. The clothes he had worn on the ship were collected into a canvas bag, apparently ready for a laundress to see to their cleaning. His cravats had been rolled into perfect cylinders rather than folded. His waistcoats and topcoats hung on pegs in the wardrobe, and his bed had been turned down to reveal white linens that appeared newly sewn.

He dared a glance in the direction of the door that probably connected to Marianne's, wondering when she would finish with her lady's maid and come join him. Climbing onto the raised dais on which the bed was displayed—almost as if it were an altar to Demeter, the goddess of fertility, or perhaps to Hypnos, the god of sleep—Jasper wondered if Marianne might be expecting him over in her bed.

They hadn't discussed which bed they would share, but after two weeks in the small bunk in their cabin on *The Fair-*

weather, two weeks of rather satisfying nights of shared pleasure and slumber, he couldn't imagine she wanted to sleep alone.

But perhaps she did.

Naked, he lay in the bed for a time, his gaze on the connecting door, willing it to open. After another half hour, he finally sighed and was rather stunned to realize he would have to join Marianne in her bed. He couldn't sleep without her body pressed against his, without her head in the small of his shoulder or her back pulled against the front of his body.

How odd that he had never had trouble sleeping alone when he was married to Sophie.

Not bothering with his dressing gown, Jasper made his way to the door, regarded it for a moment by the dim light from a candle lamp, and finally reached for the handle. Opening the door, he was about to make his way into the darkened mistress chamber when he collided with a soft body. He felt more than heard a startled gasp as his arm brushed against soft lawn. The body stepped backwards, leaving him disoriented in the darkness. For just a moment, he feared he might have walked into Marianne's lady's maid.

"Jasper?"

He allowed a sigh of relief. "Forgive me, my love, but I cannot sleep without you."

There was a moment of silence before Marianne had her body suddenly pressed against his, her arms wrapped around his waist. "And I cannot sleep without you," she replied, her words muffled given her lips were touching his chest.

Desire overwhelmed him. Desire and a deep need he knew had possessed him during the past two weeks. A need for her. For her body. For her hold on him.

As awkward as their days could be in each other's company, as stilted as their conversation could be when no one else was around, their nights more than made up for it.

"Your bed or mine?" he whispered just before he kissed her braided hair.

"Seeing as how you're not even wearing a dressing gown, then I think we should go to yours. I shouldn't want to scandalize Angela on her second day as my lady's maid when she finds you naked in my bed," Marianne whispered.

Jasper couldn't help but grin at the mental image her words brought forth. "Then I shall have to help you climb up to it," he replied before kissing her lips. "Damn thing is a veritable altar to a god."

Marianne nearly giggled, remembering how high the bed was compared to the rest of the furnishings in the master bedchamber. "You make it sound like Mount Olympus."

"Mount Vesuvius is more like it," he whispered, one eyebrow displayed in a wicked arch. "For I am quite sure I am about to erupt, and I wish to do so whilst inside you."

Any thoughts of having spent the last hour in misery flew from Marianne's head as Jasper helped her onto his bed. His hands and lips had her skin heated and her quim damp in only minutes. The evidence of his arousal was cradled by her soft belly before it soon found its home inside her. For a moment, he simply held himself still, his head resting next to hers on a pillow as he willed himself to slow down. But his body soon protested, and he began to move in the familiar pattern Marianne had come to learn during their near fortnight on board *The Fairweather*.

Her body certainly remembered. Remembered and welcomed the strange intruder that had become a regular visitor every night since their wedding.

It wasn't until the following morning when she realized Jasper hadn't even removed her nightrail. He had removed the ribbon tie from her braid, though, and although she thoroughly searched the bed linens, it was no where to be found.

thinking James Singleton had arrived to take breakfast with them. When she was dressed, she dismissed Angela and made her way into the master bedchamber through the connecting door, stunned to discover her husband wasn't there. Instead, a rather handsome, dark-haired man was busy shining a pair of Jasper's boots.

"Oh, *mi scusi*," she said as the young man stood and then bowed. She dipped a quick curtsy before she realized he was probably the valet Signora Romano had offered.

"*Mi scusi*," he replied and then gave a quick shake of his head. "I am David Romano," he said in English. "My mother asked me to act as Lord Henley and Mr. Singleton's valet while they are in residence."

Marianne blinked at hearing his perfect English. There was only a slight Italian accent to his words, which had her wondering if he had spent time in England.

"It's very good to meet you, Signore Romano." His black hair, cut short but long enough to display waves, framed a face featuring dark brows, dark blue eyes, and high cheekbones. His olive-skinned complexion was lighter than Aurora's and Angela's, but it was free of imperfections. A thought of how he could be a sculptor's model—he could *be* Michaelangelo's *David*—had a blush coloring her face. She knew just then why talk of Italian men had been so popular in the Mayfair parlors she had visited whilst in London. "I am... the viscount's wife," she managed, scolding herself for being so tongue-tied.

"Lady Henley," he acknowledged with another bow. "Lord Henley has gone to the dining room. My cousin is cooking breakfast."

"Signorina Aurora?" Marianne guessed.

He grinned. "*Sì*," he replied. He dared a glance around the room. "I must take his lordship's laundry to my other cousin, or she will make me do it," he said with a twinkle.

Marianne grinned. "Of course. I shan't keep you," she

Chapter 15

A CLEAR DAY FOR TOURING

L ater that morning
Angela stood back and regarded her mistress with a grin, rather pleased with the hairstyle she had managed to create given Marianne's unruly curls. Although her ladyship requested a bonnet, the young lady's maid instead produced a wide-brimmed hat from one of the traveling trunks. "The sun will be bright today," she warned in stilted English.

When she was packing, Marianne hadn't considered how the sun might shine more frequently on the island of Sicily than in England. She didn't even recognize the broad-brimmed hat that sported a mass of brightly-colored silk flowers on one side. "I shall take that into consideration," she said, as she decided Aunt Cherice had to have ordered the hat be packed. *She probably purchased it for me, too,* Marianne thought with a sigh.

Cherice had been determined Marianne leave London with a new wardrobe and accessories to match. The modiste she had employed didn't seem the least bit fazed by her requests, nor did she seem to mind the impossible deadline.

Male voices from the master bedchamber had Marianne

said with a nod. She left the room through the connecting door to the mistress suite, still a bit discombobulated by the young man's presence. Remembering his features—she had been close enough to see them—she realized he resembled his mother in many ways. The same nose, the same eyes— even their lips were similar—but David displayed an easy expression his mother didn't share. A happy demeanor, probably from lack of responsibility.

The weight of the world, she remembered Pietro saying.

Marianne made her way to the dining room to discover Jasper and his colleague already seated, a map spread out on the table between them. They stood up in unison when she appeared, bowing before she curtsied.

"You're up early," Jasper said, as if they hadn't spent that morning in the same bed together, making love and luxuriating in the soft linens.

"As were you," she replied, an arched brow replaced by a flush of color when she realized her double entendre.

James Singleton dared a glance between the two of them, his amusement barely hidden when Aurora appeared with a tray of coffee and orange juice. He stood up, as if he thought her the lady of the house, and gave a nod. "*Buongiorno, mia signora*," he murmured.

Aurora paused, her look of confusion going between Marianne and the blond, blue-eyed Adonis who stood before her. "*Mi scusi*," she managed as she set the tray on the table, well aware of how the man watched her every move.

That is, until Jasper nudged him. "*Signorina* Aurora is our cook," he said in a quiet voice. He turned to Marianne. "If it's agreeable with you, Singleton is going to join us for our meals."

"Of course," Marianne replied, rather surprised he thought he might think otherwise. They had dined with the man nearly every morning and every night on *The Fairweather*.

James shook himself out of his reverie, although he didn't seem to hear what Marianne and Jasper had said. "It's very good to meet you, signorina," he said as he continued to stare at Aurora. "I am James."

Jasper and Marianne exchanged glances before Marianne allowed a grin. "How is your Italian, Mr. Singleton?"

The younger man finally pulled his gaze from Aurora and turned it on Marianne. "Fairly good, I should think."

"You'll need to speak to her in Italian. I don't think she knows much English."

"Ah," he replied. He turned his attention back to the cook, but Aurora was already heading for the kitchen. "*Mi scusi*," he said as he followed the woman out of the dining rom.

Jasper and Marianne stared after him, once again exchanging glances. "Do you suppose he finds her beautiful?" Marianne asked, not quite sure about the man's strange reaction to the cook.

"Yes," was all Jasper could manage before he grinned.

Marianne remembered their conversation from the night before and arched a brow. "I may not have to play matchmaker at all."

Jasper rolled his eyes before he glanced toward the door to the kitchen. "I do hope he isn't in there taking advantage..."

But before he could finish the sentence, James reappeared carrying a tray on which several plates were arranged, their contents sending up curls of steam, as he ignored what sounded like protests from Aurora. He lowered the tray so Aurora could remove each plate and set it before them, holding onto the last plate until James reluctantly gave up the tray and sat down. He spoke in a stream of Italian Marianne could barely follow before Aurora sniffed, turned on her heel, and left the room.

"What was that all about?" she asked in alarm.

James gave a shrug. "I think she likes me," he said with a huge grin. "At least, I think that was the gist of it," he added in a whisper.

Marianne exchanged a quick glance with Jasper, deciding she would have to wait until she could ask if Aurora had anything to fear from his colleague's attentions.

After a breakfast of coffee, brioche, sausage, and eggs, Jasper, Marianne, and James joined their guide in a very different conveyance from the one they had ridden on the day before. The carriage, an ancient barouche pulled by two horses that weren't much younger, looked as if it might collapse at any moment. The barouche rumbled along the dirt path as Pietro managed the reins.

"Our accommodations are excellent," Jasper said when James asked about them. "David said he would see to your things, by the way, and act as valet for us both. There's a room for you on the other side of the villa."

The mention of the young man had James angling his head. "Black hair, blue eyes, and far too handsome to be a servant?" he queried.

Jasper blinked. "That would be him. I take it you two have met?"

James shook his head. "I only saw him briefly. Outside, when Pietro dropped me off. He was seeing to my trunk." The reminder of his first sight of the young man had James tamping down a sudden arousal. He couldn't remember being so awestruck by the sight of another man before. "Signora Romano didn't mind learning there would be another guest?" he asked, his voice kept low. He knew the original arrangements had been for Jasper and him to share the villa. With Jasper married and his wife with him, their need for an additional bedchamber might have proven difficult for their hostess.

"I believe Signora Romano is pleased, actually. She has a younger niece she is anxious to teach, so my wife has a lady's maid, and I, of course, will be paying her more rent," Jasper explained. "I'm still not sure how Dr. Jones knew of her, though. How did you find the old man?"

James gave a shrug. "Lord Darius seemed in rather good spirits last night," he commented. "He was where you said he would be. Dressed in his usual garb, I took him for a local until I heard him speak." At Jasper's look of disbelief, he added, "Remember, I haven't seen him since I was up at Hadrian's Wall. Four, five years ago."

Jasper allowed a grin, remembering the older archaeologist eschewed topcoats and sometimes even waistcoats when he was directing a dig. His casual mode of dress—breeches, boots, and a white shirt—was also a reminder that it would be warm working on the island. Jasper was about to ask James something else, but he noticed Marianne staring at him with what looked like surprise. "What is it?"

"I... I didn't realize *Lord Darius* would be working with you and Mr. Singleton," she said in disbelief. "When you said, 'Dr. Jones,' I didn't make the connection."

Jasper gave a shake of his head, realizing just then that his wife must have known the older man—and met him as the brother of a duke rather than in his preferred guise as an archaeologist. "Is he a friend of your father's?"

Marianne allowed a shrug. "An acquaintance, really. He's come for the scotch."

Allowing a bark of laughter, Jasper could imagine Dr. Jones imbibing in Lord Donald's liquor. "Dr. Jones' interests lie elsewhere, but he is digging in the same ancient city in which we will be working," he explained. "And the fact that he recommended Signora Romano's villa has me wondering why he isn't staying there," he added in a quiet voice.

"May I be so bold as to ask how you found Signora Romano?" James asked.

Jasper and Marianne exchanged glances before Jasper gave a shrug. "Efficient," he stated. "Not friendly, exactly."

Marianne's eyes widened, as if she didn't agree. "She is as our guide says. Like Atlas. And proud of her property, as she should be. It's a beautiful house, and her nieces are proving to be very adept in their duties." After a pause, she added, "Aurora is her niece."

James arched a brow at this bit of information. His attention was directed toward *Casa Romano*, as if he was willing its owner to appear from behind the closed door to the courtyard. "The weight of the world, eh?" he murmured. He sighed as Pietro directed the horses down the hill and to the path that would take them to their daily destination for their excavation work.

Jasper pulled a folded map from a leather satchel and opened it. The detailed drawing appeared to be old, its charcoal and pencil marks smeared at the edges where fingers had gripped the paper. "The old Greco-Roman quarter has been partially excavated by Serradifalco's men," he said as he used his fingertip to indicate a grid on the paper. "It's laid out in a square, with its streets parallel and perpendicular to one another. Dr. Jones wrote that there is evidence of an aqueduct system—that's what he is concentrating on, of course—and foundations for some rather impressive villas. Those are where I expect we'll find the most impressive tile floors."

Jasper compared his map with the scene that appeared before them as the barouche made its way. "Christ, it's huge," he remarked as he scanned what appeared to be ordered rubble directly ahead of them. He didn't even realize he had cursed until James cleared his throat. "Oh, forgive me, my love," Jasper said as he placed a gloved hand over one of Marianne's.

But his wife's attention was on what appeared beyond the knee-high ruins of the old city. She was holding up her spectacles like a lorgnette and was staring at the honey-colored columns of a well-preserved Greek temple. Its Doric columns still stood in support of a mostly intact entablature and pediment. "Is that the Temple of Concordia?" she asked in awe.

"Hold up, Pietro," Jasper ordered. "Yes. How did you know?

"Angela told me about it last night. She said it was a basilica until the last century, and that's why it's still in such good condition. May we go there?"

James stood up so he could take in the entire *Valle dei Templi*, its series of colonnaded temples strung out along a ridge. Although Jasper and Marianne had seen some of them the night before as they made their way to *Casa Romano*, their vantage was from the east edge of the ruins and hampered somewhat by trees. "We'll see all of them today," Jasper assured her. "I promise.

"Where will we go first?"

Jasper dared a glance at their guide, hoping Pietro would chime in with a suggestion. "Ladies first," the man said with a grin. "We go to Juno Lucina." One gnarled finger pointed to the temple at the east end of the island.

When he noticed Marianne's quizzical expression, James said, "We call that a peripteros temple," as he took his seat, referring to the fact that the original Doric building was surrounded by a colonnade. "Although it's missing most of three sides, it has the traditional arrangement of six columns on the ends and thirteen columns on the long sides." He gave a whistle of what sounded like approval as they neared the ruins.

"The columns are almost all there," Jasper said in surprise.

"Because some of the columns have been restored," Pietro said as he pulled the barouche to a halt. "Serradifalco's men reconstructed some of this when they were here five years ago."

Marianne allowed Jasper to remove her from the barouche, barely noticing when he set her down. She had fished her spectacles from her reticule and pulled them on as they neared the structure, and she hadn't taken her eyes off of it since. "It's so majestic," she murmured.

Jasper afforded the temple a critical eye, impressed at how it was difficult to tell where the restoration efforts had taken place. "Anastylosis," he murmured to James, referring to the technique of restoring a ruin using the original materials as much as possible.

"Indeed," his colleague agreed. He glanced around the grounds, figuring that with the marina so far away, any marble from this temple would have been ignored in favor of ruins closer to the marina. "There was enough left here for them to do the restoration using the original pieces." He turned to find Jasper leading Marianne to the intact steps of the temple, and watched as the two passed between two columns and made their way to what was left of an altar. He hurried to join them, glancing about in search of pieces of friezes or the naos—the walls that would have made up the inner temple—and wasn't disappointed to see a few of the ruins scattered about.

"It burned around four-hundred BC," Jasper said when Marianne asked about its color, the stone a far darker golden brown than the honey-colored columns of the Temple of Concordia. "And the Romans substituted clay tiles for the marble tiles." He stood in front of a column and examined it closely, marveling at how it seemed to bulge about a third of the way up before beginning a slight tapering to the top.

"They're not as tall as they seem," Marianne remarked, her head tilted back as she surveyed the tops of the columns where they met the entablature.

"It's an illusion created by their shape," Jasper explained, secretly pleased by Marianne's interest. He watched as she turned her attention to the sea, grinning as she hurried off to the other end of the temple. He was about to follow, but James pointed to some marble blocks, and soon the two were engaged in a spirited discussion about the Roman reconstruction. Neither noticed as Marianne continued off the end of the temple and headed to the edge of the ridge.

"Where did she go?" Jasper said suddenly, turning around and scanning the horizon. He noticed Pietro at the barouche, the man's attention toward the east. He followed his line of sight and spotted Marianne looking over the edge of the ridge. He broke into a run, dodging marble blocks and clay tiles on his way to where Marianne stood, her slippers at the very edge of the ridge. "Marianne," he said as he struggled for breath. "You cannot go running off like that," he admonished her. But his gaze fell to the river below, where it led to the remains of another building.

"Why is it so small?" she asked in a whisper, oblivious to Jasper's worry.

Jasper sighed as he realized she referred to the Sanctuary of Asclepius. Situated on the edge of the river San Biagio, the structure had once been a place for healing. "It was a sort of hospital," he replied, placing one of her hands on his sleeve, as if he expected her to go running down the embankment if he didn't hold onto her.

An olive tree hid one corner of the ruins from their view, and several prickly pears were scattered about the grounds. The two columns that they could see were actually built into one of the partial walls that still stood, although the amount of rubble at the base of the structure was a testament to the earthquake that had destroyed it.

"There is some question as to its validity as a sanctuary of Asclepius," James offered, his hands going to his hips as he surveyed the ruin below. Jasper gave a start, unaware that James had joined them. "I read about it last night. This structure is not exactly where Polybius said it would be, but there isn't another that matches his description," James explained, referring to the Greek historian that had documented the area.

"Do you wish to see it up close?" Jasper asked, his attention on Marianne.

She shook her head. "Not today. We should be going. There are so many others to see," she said as she turned to find Pietro driving the barouche to the east end of the temple, shortening their walk. Within minutes, they were on their way to the Temple of Concordia.

The best preserved of all the temples near Girgenti, Concordia dominated the skyline as they made their way west. Farm fields seemed to extend right up to the temple steps—at least from the two sides they could see—and a number of livestock dotted the land around it.

"Serradifalco's team must have spent a couple of years on this one," Jasper murmured, as he pulled a dog-eared drawing from a pile of papers. James held up the drawing and compared what they saw now to what had been drawn the century before. "They reconstructed the ends of the pediments," James acknowledged. "But all the columns were intact, as were the architraves and most of the triglyphs and metopes." When he noticed Marianne's furrowed brow, he pointed to the top of the temple and added, "The recessed rectangles above the columns are the metopes, and the set of three vertical channels in between are the triglyphs. We only find them on the entablatures of Doric structures."

Marianne nodded her understanding. "And if there were no metopes or triglyphs?"

Jasper shrugged. "It wouldn't be Doric but rather..." He shrugged.

"Tuscan," James offered, his knowledge of ancient architecture a bit better than Jasper's.

"I knew there was a reason I had you come along," Jasper teased, before he noticed Marianne was counting the columns. "The peristatis is six by thirteen," he offered, referring to the number of columns on each side.

"Just like the last one," Marianne half-asked.

"Indeed. Most of them are. The notes here mention the tympana was intact, too," Jasper said with some awe. "So they only had to reconstruct the outer edges of the pediments."

James grinned at how Marianne's eyes widened. "The tympana is that triangle above the entrance," he explained.

"Yes, but where are the carvings? Aren't there supposed to be... religious figures on it?" she asked. She had slid to the front of her seat and seemed ready to bolt from the conveyance.

Both James and Jasper dared a glance up at the end of temple, just as Pietro halted the horses. "Not likely on this one, but it's true that tympana usually have them."

They stepped down from the barouche and climbed the steps into the temple. Marianne would have raced ahead, but Jasper kept her hand on his arm. "Unfortunately, the interior is not going to be as the Greeks built it," Jasper said with a sigh.

"Because it was used as a church?" Marianne asked, remembering what Angela had told her.

"Indeed. The rear wall of the cella was destroyed to make an entrance, and those arches were carved out to make a nave," he explained as he pointed to where the stones of the interior walls of the cella had been cut to create twelve arches. From the sound of disappointment in his voice, Marianne knew he wasn't pleased with the alterations.

"The original altar was destroyed," James remarked as he stood before the one that had been put in its place. His gaze swept the rest of the remodeled interior as he gave a shake of his head, as if he, too, were disappointed.

Marianne was staring up at a series of holes in the entablature's interior. "That's where the wooden beams for the ceiling were," Jasper said, when he noticed what had her attention. He turned and pointed to pylons where stairs would have allowed someone to reach the roof. "And there would have been stairs all the way to the top."

Staring out toward the Mediterranean, Marianne was struck by what any church goer of generations past would have seen from this vantage. With almond and olive trees framing the scene, the view was magnificent. She was still regarding the reflection of the noon-day sun on the calm water when Jasper dipped his head a bit and managed to kiss her cheek beneath her broad-brimmed hat. "Jasper!" she exclaimed in a hoarse whisper, shocked he would do such a thing, and in a temple no less.

"I could not help myself. And besides, no one is about," he replied in a quiet voice. "Are you ready to see more?"

"How did the Duke of Serradifalco make the repairs?" she asked, turning to gaze up at her husband.

Jasper blinked, rather surprised she was so interested in the restoration efforts. "Well, his team used the broken stonework that was on the ground, and mortared it back into place."

"But it's so high. However did they get up there?"

Jasper gave an, "Ah," and said, "They built scaffolding and used ladders to climb up. I have a drawing of it in the barouche."

Marianne's eyes widened. "Oh, may I see it?"

Tempted to kiss her—despite how ridiculous her spectacles made her appear—Jasper gave a nod. "Of course." He turned and found James already back at the barouche. "I'll show you on the way to the next temple."

Pietro had them on a path to a tall, rectangular structure as Marianne studied the print of the drawing Jasper mentioned. The artist had done it during the reconstruction of the Temple of Concordia, the detailed illustration showing a number of men atop what appeared to be rather rickety scaffolding that had been built on the south side of the temple. Other men down below were on horseback or inside a tent that had been erected adjacent to the tomb.

"More Roman than Greek, wouldn't you say?" James commented as he stood regarding the edifice before them. A cornfield extended right up to the huge stone base.

"The Tomb of Theron," Jasper announced when Marianne finally lifted her gaze from the drawing and stared at the giant block and two short walls adjacent to it.

James had already made his way to the base of the pyramid-like structure, a hand pressed against the large stone blocks that made up the base. "Tuff," he said when Jasper and Marianne joined him.

"Tuff?" Marianne repeated.

"It's a kind of rock made from the ash of a volcano. From Mount Etna," Jasper explained as he made his way to another side of the *naiskos* sepulcher. Positioned above the large base was a secondary rectangular structure with ionic columns built into the corners and topped by an entablature. There were no pediments, though, but each side appeared to have a door carved into it. Plants had obviously grown on the roof, for their leaves could be seen along the top edge.

"Who was Theron?" Marianne asked as she pressed a gloved hand against the stone.

"A Greek tyrant who once ruled the ancient city of Acragas," James said as he pointed in the direction of Girgenti. "With some help from another tyrant, he was able to defeat the Carthaginians. That helped Acragas to become one of the most important cities in Sicily at the time."

"So he is buried here?" Marianne asked as she moved around the corner to regard another side of the tomb. She frowned at the strange, stone walls, wondering at their position. They weren't attached to the structure, but they seemed intact. Just beyond them, the corn grew to half their height.

"One of the gates to the ancient city," Jasper said from behind her. "Walls completely surrounded it at one time," he added as he examined the one he stood nearest. "This one would have been important, given it's so close to the sea."

Just as Marianne rounded the next corner, she came to a halt and let out a loud gasp.

"What is it?" Jasper called out as he hurried to join her, jerking to a stop for the same reason as Marianne. A goat stood staring at them, the front half of his body poking out of a doorway at the base of the tomb.

"I think I shall not go in there," Marianne whispered.

"I wouldn't allow you to," Jasper countered, just as James rounded the corner and let out a laugh. "So much for respecting the dead," he said under his breath.

"Is Theron buried here?" she asked again.

"Probably not," Jasper replied. "According to the notes I brought along, it was built as a monument to the Roman soldiers who died fighting the War Against Hannibal," he explained. "One of the deadliest wars of ancient times."

Marianne gave a shake of her head. "Why have I not heard of it?" she whispered.

The two men turned to stare at her, rather surprised to learn she had heard of any wars, other than the one that had just ended.

"Perhaps you have heard of the Second Punic War, my lady," James offered. "Your husband refers to it as the Romans do."

Marianne nodded. "Indeed," she murmured, her attention on a single column that appeared between some trees atop a hill just to the north. "What is that?"

Pietro, who had stayed with the barouche but was close enough to overhear their conversation, followed her line of sight and said, "That, my lady, is what is left of the Temple of Erocle."

"Hercules," Jasper whispered.

"Our next stop," Pietro stated.

"We can walk if you'd like," Jasper suggested, noticing

Marianne wore a pair of half-boots. Although he had expected it to be far too warm to be outdoors at this hour of the day, it wasn't as hot as Dr. Jones had warned it might be.

"I would like that," she said as she allowed Jasper to lead her along a well-worn path up to the rubble-strewn base of the temple. James followed, and Pietro saw to it the barouche was moved by way of the ancient road up to the same level as the temple.

Although the climb wasn't too steep, the rubble made it hard to get to the single column that jutted up from the remains. "I take it Serradifalco's team didn't work on this one," Jasper said as he surveyed the field. He could tell from what was left of the base that the temple would have been larger than Concordia and its columns broader.

"There are enough pieces here to have done so, though," James remarked. "This one would have been six by fifteen columns," he added as he regarded the single column that still stood. "And tall," he added when he saw how broad the capitals left on the ground were.

"Why is it so ruined compared to the others?" Marianne asked in dismay.

"According to the history book I've been reading, there was an earthquake in fourteen-oh-one that destroyed most of the temples on the island," Jasper explained.

James arched a brow. "Who wrote it?" he asked, his curiosity evident.

"A Dominican friar. Tommeso Fazello. Damn thing's in Latin, though, so I admit it's taken me longer to get through it than I expected. From what I can tell of the title page, it was written sometime in the fifteen-hundreds," Jasper said with a shake of his head.

"I should like to read that," James said. "When you're finished, of course."

"You're welcome to it." Jasper glanced around, his attention on another set of columns to the west. "Is that our next stop?"

Their guide nodded. "Either that one, which is dedicated to Castor and Pollux, or the Olympian field and the remains of the Temple of Zeus are to the north."

"We'll save Zeus for last," Jasper said as he led the way west to the Dioscuri's temple. Not that Zeus' temple was the best any longer—Dr. Jones' last letter had warned him the temple lay in ruins—but they would be traveling in the right direction to return to the villa. Their canteen was nearly empty, and he was growing thirsty.

Chapter 16

AN INSIGHT INTO A GODDESS

*W*hen the barouche departed from the ruins of the Temple of Vulcan—or Hephaestus, Pietro reminded them—the heat from the mid-afternoon sun had Marianne silently thanking Angela for insisting she wear the broad-brimmed hat. The top hats that Jasper and James wore barely provided any protection from the sun, and she could see they would both be sunburned if they didn't find shade.

Located at the tip of the spur on which most of the temples had been built near Girgenti, the God of Fire's temple had at one time been the most impressive temple on Sicily.

Only two columns remained of the structure, and both of those were badly eroded, giving one a phallic appearance. Surrounded on three sides by almond and olive trees and a huge collection of prickly pear, its *crepidoma*—the multilevel platform of rectangular stones on which the structure had been built—was too high to allow Marianne to climb atop it. James clambered up from the opposite side, where some of the steps to the temple were still in place. She watched as his practiced eye surveyed the remains.

"What do you suppose happened?" she asked as she

removed her hat, sadness coloring her voice.

"Earthquakes, probably from when Mount Etna erupted," James replied simply. "And that was after the Carthaginians invaded." He glanced around the semi-secluded spot, glad for the shade. "It seems a shame the temple for the God of Volcanoes and Fire would succumb to the effects of one."

"But where are the broken columns? The entablature? Surely they would be here somewhere?"

Jasper gave his wife an approving glance, realizing she had probably learned the term that day. "Most of the larger rubble was used for the buildings at the marina. Some of the smaller pieces have been taken to museums. Some are no doubt in private collections," he added with a sigh. "But I do believe this one suffered the most from erosion," he murmured as he studied one of the columns.

They had just come from an open plain on which a two-level circular altar made of wedge-shaped stones was surrounded by a haphazard array of other blocks and foundations. "The Sanctuary of the Chthonic Deities," Pietro announced, before he turned and pointed to four nearby columns. "And the Temple of the Dioscuri. Castor and Pollux," he added when he noted Mariannes quizzical expression. The four columns were topped by an entablature, and even a pediment was on display. Marianne thought the ruins there were in excellent shape until Pietro explained that Serradifalco's restoration efforts had recreated the northwest corner of the otherwise flattened temple from pieces obtained from the ruins of other temples.

The reconstruction was impressive simply because it wasn't hidden by trees but rather stood out from its landscape of what appeared to be strewn boulders. As for the circular sanctuary, James made mention of Demeter and Persephone. "Do you know the details of the myth, my lady?" he asked when he saw how Marianne studied the circular structure.

"I do," she replied. "Father has always been fond of Greek mythology."

"Then tell me, because I only know the Roman tale," Jasper said as he stood up from examining a square floor of rectangular blocks.

Marianne wondered if she was being tested. "When Demeter, the goddess of the harvest, learned her daughter, Persephone, had been captured by Hades, she became so angry, she caused the crops to wither and die. Famine spread over the earth, so Zeus commanded Hades to give up Persephone," she explained.

"Did he?" Jaspers asked.

"Indeed. Hades allowed her to leave the underworld, but he tricked her into eating some pomegranate seeds, knowing that if she ate anything from the land of the dead, she would have to return to him for at least part of the year."

Jasper frowned. "Which is why we have growing seasons?" he guessed.

"Because every time Persephone returns to Hades, Demeter mourns, and the plants wither and die." She regarded her husband for a moment, wondering why he gazed at her the way he did.

"Women have such power over men," he murmured with a shake of his head. "Remind me never to cross you."

Marianne blinked behind her spectacles, rather stunned by his comment. For a moment, she thought him angry, but a grin suddenly split his face, and he leaned down and kissed her on the cheek. His hat nearly had hers upended from her head, but she angled her cheek so he could reach it easier. "I shall if need be," she replied in a whisper.

"I believe we're ready for the next temple," James said, his comment directed to Pietro. The guide stood next to the barouche with a huge grin on his face, obviously a witness to what had happened between the aristocrat and his viscountess.

Chapter 17

A PASSING GLANCE INTO
THE PAST

*B*y the time the barouche departed from the ruins of the Temple of Vulcan, a pink and orange array had formed in the western sky, portending another colorful sunset. The longer light cast a golden veil onto the Olympian field, where a telamon lay amongst ruins that were scattered far and wide.

Marianne gasped as she hurried up to it, stunned at the size the recreated atlas. "Is this the only one?" she asked as a gloved hand smoothed over one of the many stones that made up the huge figure. He was at least twenty feet long. His arms were folded above his head, and a piece of the entablature he had been supporting was still attached to his forearms.

"The only one Serradifalco's men put back together," Pietro replied.

"The Temple of Zeus would have had, what? Twenty-four of them?" Jasper asked of his colleague.

James nodded. "At least that many. Each one mounted about halfway up and between each column." He glanced around, obviously dismayed by the amount of damage—and the number of missing columns. He couldn't even tell how tall the temple would have been. "Where is it all?"

Jasper pointed in the direction of the marina, rather surprised when he saw *The Fairweather* had already departed for its final leg to Venice before it would make its way back to England. "You were spending the night in it, no doubt," he said with a hint of disappointment. "According to Pietro, it was the quarry for the port."

James rolled his eyes. "I should have known. There are pieces of columns everywhere down there," he complained. His hands on his hips, he allowed his gaze to sweep the field. "Surely, *somewhere* around here there must be a Roman temple," he groused.

Pietro brightened. "There is!" he said with some excitement. "I'll take you there on the way back to Vedova Romano's villa."

Jasper and James exchanged questioning glances. "Is it in the Greco-Roman quarter?" Jasper guessed.

"Near there, just before San Nicola," Pietro replied as they climbed back into the barouche. "Close," he added.

Recognizing the remains of the Temple of Hercules as they made their way northeast, Marianne marveled at how the late day sun colored the columns in a deep gold and cast long shadows over the plain. She still wasn't sure exactly where Jasper would be doing his excavation work, but she rather hoped it would be close to the villa. Although she didn't intend to go with him everyday—she didn't think she would be welcome—she found she liked being near him.

They hadn't quite cleared the field of debris when James suddenly straightened in the barouche. "There it is!" he said with some excitement.

Marianne followed his line of sight, frowning when she realized he referred to a small, blocky building. Dark golden red in the waning light, it featured an arched opening on one side. "What is it?" she asked, thinking from the shape that it might be a tomb.

"The Oratory of Phalarus," Jasper replied. "It might have been a tomb, but it was more likely a religious building of some sort."

"It's definitely Roman, wouldn't you agree?" James said, as the barouche stopped across from the structure.

Jasper stepped out of the conveyance and turned to assist Marianne. Once her feet were on the ground, he rushed over to the building and walked around it. "There's an apse here on the east side," he commented.

"The Christians have used it," Jasper said from the west side, his hands on his hips.

"Was it Doric?" Marianne asked, noting how the entablature was eroded and may have supported far more than what was left.

"Possibly," James replied with a nod. He gave a sigh of frustration. "The Normans may have made some changes." He gave a glance to his right, noting how close the Church of San Nicola was to the small temple before him. "This is the entrance to Girgenti," he commented as his gaze traveled up the hill, following the road that led to the sprawling city.

Jasper reappeared from the east side of the building and gave his head a shake. "If only," he said with a sigh.

"What is it?" Marianne asked as she moved to join him.

He gave a shrug. "If only the Normans hadn't altered it, or the Christians modified the entrance..." He pointed to how the arch had been changed so it was more pointed. "Or time hadn't had its say in the matter, it would be a true Roman relic."

Marianne dipped her head. "Perhaps you will find the ruins better in the Greco-Roman quarter," she said in a quiet voice.

Jasper allowed a grin. "I shall, if what Dr. Jones wrote is

LINDA RAE SANDE

true," he agreed. He reached for her, his arm snaking around her waist so he could pull her close. "I do hope you'll be amenable to my working every day," he whispered.

Angling her head so her hat brim lifted, Marianne allowed a grin of her own. "I wouldn't think of complaining," she answered. "Do you suppose I might join you on occasion? I won't interfere, of course," she added quickly. "I just think it will be interesting to... to watch you work. To pay witness to history being uncovered."

Jasper blinked, rather touched by her sentiment. "I shouldn't want you to be bored," he warned, managing to land a kiss on her cheek when he was sure no one was looking. "But I wouldn't object to your sitting nearby as you... read, or... sightsee." The sound of a throat clearing had Jasper straightening.

"I should be getting you back to the villa, my lord," Pietro said as he pointed to the west. The sun was already touching the sea, and the peach and gold clouds were darkening by the minute. "Signorina Aurora will have your dinner ready soon."

"Of course," Jasper replied, his gaze turning to discover James regarding the arch in the temple with a practiced eye. "We'll give it a closer look on another day," he called out. He turned to study the horizon, as if he were looking for something.

"The Temple of Demeter?" James asked as he pointed to a honey-colored building to the northeast. Set against a steep slope, it appeared part of the structure had been taken over by a church. "It's the last of the temples around here."

Marianne dared a glance to the west before turning her attention to the next temple. Hungry and thirsty, she gave her head a shake. "Perhaps another day," she said to Jasper.

"Perhaps," he agreed.

James straightened and hurried over to the barouche.

"Not sure it will be worth the effort," he said with a sigh of frustration.

They climbed into the barouche, and Pietro took them back to the guest villa.

Chapter 18

REFLECTING ON BOLLE

*L*ater that night

Marianne watched as Chiara Romano and her niece, Angela, approached her from across the road, affording her a tentative smile as they carried pails of hot water. David followed, smiling despite the larger pails suspended from his hands. "It's very good to see you again, Signora Romano, Signorina Angela, Signore David," she said, hoping a bath was in her immediate future.

"Please, call me 'Chiara,' my lady," the woman said as she dipped a curtsy.

"Chiara?" Marianne countered, trying out the traditional Italian name for the first time. The request for informality was a bit of surprise given the woman was probably old enough to be her mother.

"Very good," Chiara replied. "Have you met my son, David?"

"Yes. It's good to see you again, Signore David," Marianne said as she afforded them a curtsy. "May I ask how is it you speak English so well, my lady?" she asked as they made their way into the guest villa. Even though she knew some

Italian, she was relieved she wouldn't need to speak it in the company of the widow.

"My father taught me, my lady," Chiara replied, as they made their way to the mistress suite. "Said I would need to know it some day, and he was right, as fathers usually are." A wan smile appeared. "I was asked by his lordship if Signorina Angela might see to a bath for you." She pointed to the younger girl who dipped a curtsy. "How do you prefer your water?"

Rather relieved at hearing the comment about the bath, Marianne heaved a sigh. When she had left the villa that morning, she hadn't thought to make arrangements for a bath. After a day spent sightseeing—meandering through dusty ruins and feeling a bit overheated from the sun, she was ready for one. Jasper must have known, bless his heart.

Or perhaps he preferred his wife take frequent baths.

"Not too hot. And I've brought bubbles," she replied as she moved to open one of the traveling trunks. The thought of the citrus-scented bubbles reminded her of the first morning she had been on the ship. The first morning after her wedding day. How welcome those airy orbs of delight had felt when she stepped into the warm water.

Chiara was a step ahead, though, opening the trunk as she said, "Angela will see to it, my lady," she said. "She learns quickly."

Marianne stepped aside and listened as Chiara instructed the girl and David on what to do in Italian. Although she understood some of what she heard, Marianne was left wondering about the rest.

"What is *bolle?*" she asked in a whisper.

"Bubbles," Chiara replied with a grin. "Angela isn't familiar with them, so I expect she will be a bit surprised when they appear atop the water."

From the sound of giggles and male laughter coming from the bathing chamber, Marianne realized Angela was paying witness to the bubbles as they formed atop the bath water. David, armed with the empty pails, gave her a bow before he departed the villa.

"Angela will see to the rest," Chiara said as she gave the girl some instructions in Italian.

"Your husband must have been a very handsome man," Marianne said in a whisper.

Chiara furrowed a brow. "Not too handsome," she hedged, a look of confusion crossing her face. "Antony was... Sicilian," she said with a shrug.

"Your son is..." Marianne paused, realizing she was speaking as if she were in a Park Lane parlor, gossiping about a young buck at the last ball. "Very polite and handsome," she said carefully. "You must be proud of him."

An odd expression crossed Chiara's face before she allowed a nod. "Thank you," she said. "I am proud. He is a good boy, and educated, too," she added. "He studies architecture. But I fear there is not a girl on this island who is worthy of him."

Marianne recognized the comment, for she had heard similar words spoken by the mothers of young men in London, mothers married to aristocrats and convinced their sons deserved better than the current crop of *demoiselles*. "What about in the rest of Italy?"

Chiara allowed a grin. "Perhaps in Palermo. Or Roma," she replied. "Tomorrow, if you would like, I shall come for you, and take you to town. I have shopping I must do."

Marianne's eyes widened. "I would like that very much."

"Your men will wish to leave early. So they can work before the sun is too high," Chiara said, as if she had hosted archaeologists in the past.

"Then I shall be up early, as well," Marianne replied. At Chiara's look of disbelief, she added, "So I can have breakfast with them before they go."

Her words were obviously a surprise to Chiara, for the

woman finally shook her head and said, "They will be gone before Aurora has begun cooking. She has seen to some cheese and bread for them to take."

Marianne furrowed a brow. "Then perhaps we can deliver a late breakfast to them. Like a picnic," she countered, which had Chiara giving an agreeable shrug.

"I will see you in the morning."

With that, the hostess took her leave and Marianne allowed Angela to help her undress for her bath.

A few minutes later, Marianne luxuriated in the sensations created by Angela's fingers as the lady's maid washed her hair.

Marianne decided she rather liked having Angela as a lady's maid. The young woman was obsessed with details, seeing to it everything was folded precisely, the bed made perfectly, hair dressed to its best advantage, and gowns wrinkle-free. Lulled almost to sleep and deep in thought, Marianne was entirely unaware of the bathing chamber door opening until Angela suddenly inhaled and stood up.

"What...?"

"I didn't mean to startle you, my lady," Jasper said as he stood leaning in the doorway, his arms crossed as he regarded her with a grin.

Marianne pulled her knees to her chest, the move made instinctively, causing water to slosh over the edge of the tub. "My lord!" she admonished him. Her expression of surprise soon turned to a grin when she noticed how Angela seemed unsure of what to do. "You may go," she said in Italian, "And I will see you in the morning."

Angela gave a quick curtsy before she disappeared from the bathing chamber, leaving Marianne with her arms still wrapped around her bent knees.

"I didn't mean to interrupt your bath. Truly," Jasper said in a quiet voice.

Marianne gave a shrug. "I don't mind. Truly."

Jasper straightened from where he had been leaning against the door jamb. "Does that mean... could I...? Join you?" he stammered.

A jolt of something rather pleasant shot down Marianne's spine as her breath quickened. Her gaze darted to the tub in an effort to determine if there was enough room for the two of them. "I think so. If we..." She let out a gasp as Jasper was suddenly next to the tub, unwinding the cravat from around his neck and unbuttoning his waistcoat and trying to remove his boots all at the same time.

"Isn't that what David is supposed to be doing?" she asked as her hands moved to grip the edge of the tub.

"Usually. Except I told him I could manage tonight and to see to Singleton."

"Where is Mr. Singleton?" she asked in a whisper.

Jasper frowned. "He's still in the dining room. He's studying a map Darius gave him last night," he said, some of his words muffled when his shirt went over his head. He had his breeches unfastened and was about to push them down when he noticed Marianne averting her eyes. "What is it?"

"What is what?"

Jasper blinked. "Why did you look away?"

Marianne blinked, her gaze back on him. All of him. "I thought you might want a bit of... privacy," she managed, her eyes widening when she realized how his face displayed more color than usual. And not from a blush.

His top hat hadn't begun to shade his face from the rays of the sun. She wondered if the sunburn hurt.

Sighing, Jasper finished undressing and dipped a hand into the water, his sigh of satisfaction at odds with his thought at hearing her words. "You have seen all of me. I have seen all of you," he replied patiently. "Unless..." He paused, a frown settling on his face after he was halfway into the water, crouched and bent much like she was. "Does the sight of my body... offend you?"

Marianne shook her head. "I can't really see it that well," she reminded him, although this close up, she could make it out in great detail.

All of it.

Aware she hadn't really answered his question, she added, "No. It does not. I'm just... I'm still getting use to *this*," she whispered, waving her hand to indicate their situation in general. Why they could be so comfortable together in bed—making love and ending up in each other's arms was easy—but struggle with nakedness at other times had her perplexed. "By the way, you're a bit sunburned," she murmured. "Does it hurt?"

Jasper shook his head. "I put some aloe on it after dinner. Not the first time I've been sunburned," he added with an arched brow. "Which is why I'll be wearing a different hat on the morrow." He settled deeper into the tub and frowned. "There must be a more comfortable way in which to bathe together," he said with a sigh.

"I suppose," she hedged. "Perhaps if you put your legs on either side of mine..." she started to say. "And I straighten mine..." She gave a start when she heard his "Oomph," and felt his hand grab her foot.

"Careful, my sweet. Those are the twiddle-diddles, and it's rather painful when they're kicked. I do wish to get a child or two on you."

Marianne's eyes widened. "Oh, I apologize," she said as she quickly bent her legs and wrapped her arms around them, making herself into a tight ball and causing a wave of water to wash almost over the top of the tub.

Jasper couldn't help his chuckle. "I think we would both be more comfortable if you turn around and back up."

Furrowing a brow, as if she was trying to determine if she

could so such a thing, Marianne decided to give it a try. Keeping her knees bent, she slowly turned around. Well aware of Jasper's legs—his knees broke the water's surface— she slowly straightened her legs and slid backwards until Jasper had his arms wrapped around her waist. "I'm not... hurting anything, am I?" she asked in a whisper.

Jasper placed his head alongside hers. "Not at all," he replied in a quiet voice. He kissed her hair. "Before you wonder too much, I have never done this before." He couldn't imagine Sophie allowing him anywhere near her bath.

Marianne frowned. "What do you mean?"

"I've never invaded a lady's bath," he said as one of his hands smoothed up and over one of her breasts. "I do hope you don't mind. I find it rather pleasant. Never bathed with bubbles before."

"*Bolle*," she replied with a sigh, remembering Chiara's word for bubbles. "I need to learn more Italian so I can converse with Angela."

"Is she going to be an acceptable lady's maid?"

Sighing, Marianne was suddenly aware of how his other hand had moved to cup her other breast beneath the water. "I think so. She's eager to please."

Jasper leaned back, gently pulling her back so her head ended up on his chest. "I fear Singleton and I dominated the conversation at dinner this evening, what with all our talk of the temples."

"Oh, but it was such an interesting conversation," Marianne assured him, turning her head to the side, her cheek pressed against his chest. "Until I was able to see all those temples up close today, I wasn't aware of how majestic they really are."

"So, you won't mind spending several months here while I dig up Roman mosaics?" he half-asked, not sure what he would do if she claimed she would mind.

"I won't mind," she replied. "Chiara said she will accompany me if I wish to see any of them again. She said there are many more ruins and old buildings up in Girgenti."

"Chiara?" he repeated, rather surprised to hear her use their hostess' given name.

"She told me to call her that, so I told her to call me Marianne."

Jasper arched a brow. "Hmm. Perhaps you can discover why it was Dr. Jones recommended this villa," he replied. "And why he's staying down by the marina and not here. There are certainly enough rooms." He supposed there would be more prostitutes near the port than in Girgenti, but he couldn't imagine the archaeologist with a different doxy every night. There had been times on other expeditions when he thought the man a monk until he learned Lord Darius was married. Estranged from his wife for many years before she died, the man preferred to keep a household near Hexham while his wife and son lived in London.

"I will ask when next I'm in her company. Tomorrow morning, in fact. She's taking me to Girgenti. Do you still plan to begin your work in the Greco-Roman quarter?"

"Indeed. The weather should be fine." He suddenly yawned. "As much as I like sharing your bath, I fear I may fall asleep, my lady."

Marianne allowed a sigh. "The *bolle* have all gone," she murmured. She slid forward and turned her head to regard her husband from over her shoulder. Angela had left a bath linen just behind where he leaned against the end of the tub. "Could you... hand me the linen?" she asked as she pointed over his shoulder.

Jasper allowed a mischievous grin. "Will you promise not to put it on until you're out of the water?"

Marianne blinked, realizing she would be forced to emerge from the water with him watching whether he helped with the linen or not. "Will you promise to close your eyes?"

His look of disappointment had Marianne giggling as she stood up and stepped out of the tub, making sure to slosh water onto Jasper's face as she did so. "Hey, that's not fair," he cried out. By the time he had the water wiped from his eyes and could see again, Marianne had the linen wrapped about her body. "Is there a linen for me to use?" he asked as his gaze darted about the small room.

Marianne found the stash in a cupboard and held it just beyond his reach. "Promise you won't splash me when you get out?"

Jasper's mischievous grin was back. He was up and out of the tub and pressed against her in a split second, the linen between them suddenly drenched. "I promise," he said before he kissed her thoroughly.

Despite his weariness, they made it to his bedchamber, climbed onto Mount Olympus, and worshipped one another until sleep took them both.

Chapter 19

HINDSIGHT PROVES
HEARTBREAKING

eanwhile, across the lane
        Chiara returned to her villa, her arms crossed over her chest as if she were cold. She was sure her guests would have included a different man from the one called Singleton, or perhaps an additional archaeologist, but it was obvious the three people who had let the villa for the next six months were all that were coming.

She supposed she should have felt relief at learning *he* wasn't among those she was hosting.

But if it wasn't him, then who had been asking about the identities of every 'Chiara' in Girgenti?

Gossip traveled quickly in a town like Girgenti, the old women left with nothing better to do than to speculate on who she might marry next—even if she had said she had no plans to remarry. Widowhood suited her just fine. Since she was seeing to her three nieces—Aurora, Tamara, and Angela —she had quite enough to keep her occupied.

When Antony Romano had been alive, everyone in Girgenti treated her as if she was an aristocrat's wife. Given his wealth and the lands that even now were being tended by farmers, she supposed the regard was to be expected. Very few in this part of Sicily were wealthy.

As Antony's only son, David had inherited most of the property, including the villa in which her guests were staying. Antony had seen to it Chiara would keep the villa in which she was now wandering about, deep in thought.

So learning that someone down in Marina di Girgenti had been asking about women named 'Chiara' had her curious.

Curious and a bit concerned. As far as she knew, there were only five women in Girgenti that shared her given name.

What if someone had learned the truth?

What if the person was there to make trouble for her?

Or perhaps she wasn't the Chiara they were looking for at all, and she had no need to be worried.

The problem with considering the "what-if"s was where the questions led, which had her remembering just why she feared the person was seeking information about her in the first place.

David wasn't her late husband's son.

Oh, he had been born after she married Antony. He was legitimate in the all ways necessary to be considered Antony's son. But David's father had loved her and left her.

They had spent his last day in Rome visiting all the important historic sites. They had crossed the Tiber River on the *Pons Aelius*—the Bridge of Hadrian. Tossed a *piastra* into the Trevi Fountain, where he explained that the water was from the Aqua Vergine, which was a fifteenth century restoration of the Aqua Virgo aqueduct. He had pointed out the architrave dating to 46 AD, which told of how Claudius had to rebuild a portion of the aqueduct before Caligula had the stone removed to build an amphitheater. *They were always stealing stones from one thing to build another,* she remembered him saying in disgust.

There had been the stop at the Pantheon, Hadrian's temple to all Roman gods, where he claimed the roof was made of the largest concrete span in all the world. Inside, they had studied the Egyptian obelisk dedicated to Ramses II. *There are more Egyptian obelisks in Rome than in all of Egypt, because they were taken as trophies by Roman emperors*, he explained.

When it was too hot to be out of doors, they had gone into the tunnels under the *Thermae Antoninianae*—the Baths of Caracalla—and wandered along the imperial bath's high walls.

When they toured the world's oldest public museum, *Musei Capitoline*, he explained how the *Palazzo dei Conservatori* had been built on the Temple of Jupiter. *Michelangelo did the plans, and it was the first piazza in Rome*, he claimed with the exuberance of a child.

She had merely smiled and nodded, as if she hadn't been to the museum at least a dozen times with her father.

The walk by the Colosseum had been followed by the slow stroll to the end of the *Via Sacra* and onto the steps of the Forum. She remembered that moment as if it had just happened—the way her heart had clenched at seeing the pain in his face.

His parting words had been filled with sorrow and regret. She even remembered how his voice broke, and how he seemed to have trouble breathing before he gave her one last kiss, placed a *piastra* in one of her palms with instructions to take a hackney to her home, and suddenly turned and took his leave of her.

Antony had found her crying on the steps of the Forum, alone and heartsick. Perhaps he had felt sorry for her, or perhaps he had been attracted to her—she had been a beautiful young woman back then—but no matter the reason, he had offered to drive her to her home.

As they made their way in his town coach, a conveyance

pulled by a matched set of four black horses, he asked simple questions and answered some of hers, so that her tears were soon dry and the hiccups from her sobs finally ceased. Having met the man in her father's home—he was a patron of the archaeological expeditions her father helped arrange— she knew he was from a family of means.

When dusk deepened the shadows around them and the coach-and-four had arrived in front of her *familia's* large villa, she was about to beg forgiveness and take her leave of the coach when she was kissed for the second time that day.

Antony proposed later that night, angering his parents with his impulsiveness. But when he announced only two months later that Chiara was expecting their first child, his father suddenly welcomed her into their *familia*. By the time David was born, she had become their second daughter and could do no wrong.

As for David's real father, she never saw him again after that day. *Good riddance*, she remembered thinking after she and Antony had repeated their vows in the cathedral.

So why had she thought of him nearly every day since?

Chapter 20

A DAY OF VISUAL DISCOVERIES

he following day
"Where do you suppose he is?" Jasper asked as he surveyed the ruins of the area known as the Greco-Roman quarter.

"It's a bit early for his lordship," James replied, referring to Dr. Darius Jones. His gaze took in the early morning sunrise, and he marveled at how the rays of the sun illuminated the honey-colored bits of columns and foundation blocks in a golden glow.

The ancient city, located just southeast of the current city of Girgenti, appeared to have been laid out in a traditional grid pattern. From the series of foundations that poked above the level of the surrounding grounds, it was apparent the Duke of Serradifalco's team had begun some excavation work. A few areas had been freed of dirt and debris, and the floors of some of the buildings were exposed, while others remained hidden beneath the earth.

"Did he say where he would be working?" Jasper asked as he led them along the east perimeter, his shadow cast on the foundations that appeared above the ground. Although the morning was cool, he knew the sun might make it too warm to work in the midday. He hoped they could locate the place they had found on the map to start their work.

"He's been concentrating on the aqueducts over by the southwest corner," James said as he pointed across the field of ruins. "Said he's uncovered a stash of Roman coins and evidence of the military, but that area was most likely a gate into the city back in the day, so it was probably heavily guarded."

Stopping to consult the map they had studied the night before, Jasper compared it to what he was seeing. "I think we're here," he said as he pointed to the barely visible foundations of what was most likely a Roman villa near the edge of the city.

James hoisted his satchel and placed it atop the remains of an ancient wall. He pulled several wood stakes from it and went about marking the perimeter of the area in which they would work while Jasper extracted several tools from his bag. He wished they could have brought the entire trunk, but Pietro had been unavailable to provide transportation, so they brought what they could carry.

"Do you wish to draw this before we begin?" James asked.

Jasper shook his head as he unrolled a crude drawing of the area. Although it included a far larger area than the one they would begin excavating on this day, their particular foundation was easy to discern from the rest. "No need," he said as he moved to one of the foundation walls and settled onto the dry ground next to it. Although he was tempted to start in the middle of the nearly square area, he had learned long ago that walls were the best places to start when searching for the best preserved floors of villas. The middles tended to remain exposed to the elements—and to scavengers and looters—far longer and were usually in poor condition as a result. The floors nearest the walls were usually sealed with enough dirt and debris to keep them preserved.

Using a small hand shovel, and soon joined by James, Jasper made quick work of digging down the side of a wall until he was sure he had reached the original floor of the villa. The bucket in which he dumped the dirt was nearly full despite the small perimeter of the hole he had created.

"It's not too deep," James commented as his gaze swept to the west in an effort to determine how deep they might have to dig there.

"It's not," Jasper agreed. *Could it really be this easy?* he wondered as he widened his hole. When the bucket was full, James saw to its replacement and took care of depositing the contents of the full pail on the eastern edge of the city. When he returned, he let out a whistle when he noticed Jasper had already exposed several small tiles. Although they appeared stained by dirt, they had obviously been nearly white at one time. "I see you're not wasting any time," he commented, lifting the already full second bucket and putting down the one he had just emptied.

"The ground isn't as hard as I expected, although I think it will be later into the summer," Jasper replied, his small shovel breaking up the dirt to reveal the rich, dark volcanic soil that made up most of the island.

When James returned from having emptied the second bucket, he boggled at what Jasper had already uncovered— row upon row of the cream-colored tiles and a single row of black tiles. "We need another bucket," James said as his hands went to his hips.

"Let me take a turn at emptying pails," Jasper replied. "Let you have a bit of fun." He scrambled to his feet and hurried off with the full pail, amazed at the display of the Temples of Concordia and Juno Lucina in the early morning sun. Farmers were already tending their fields around the temples, and goat herders watched their animals as the beasts cleared the land of vegetation.

When he returned, he found that James had merely loosened the dirt along the wall and toward the center of the room. He began scooping it into the empty pails as Jasper continued to clear away the debris from the developing scene. "There are rust-colored tiles," he said in awe.

"It's Roman, then, right?" James asked hopefully. He lifted both pails and took off to empty them.

"We'll know soon enough," the viscount replied as he continued his work.

Another hour passed before Jasper stood up to regard what he had uncovered—a piece of what he thought was a hunting scene featuring what appeared to be a jaguar and at least one huntsmen, possibly with a bow and arrows. He hadn't yet uncovered enough of the scene to be sure, nor had he discovered the signature that might reveal just who had created the detailed art.

He was about to settle back down onto the dirt when he realized he wasn't alone.

"I brought you some breakfast," Marianne said as she motioned to a basket that dangled from one arm. "Signorina Aurora said you left before she could make it this morning." She turned her attention to the mosaic that was still only partially revealed. "It's beautiful," she added as she leaned over to get a closer look, her spectacles held in one hand as she pulled them close to her face.

Blinking, Jasper turned to regard her and Signora Romano with surprise. "You are a welcome sight, my lady," he said. "And not just because you come bearing food." He could swear she blushed in the morning light. With her broad-brimmed hat mounted at a jaunty angle, he had a flash of a memory of how she had looked when he made love to her the night before, their still-wet-from-the-bath bodies mounted atop his tall bed, engaged in mutual worship.

Marianne's attention was on the tiles he had unearthed. "Did you just uncover this today?" she asked in awe.

"Indeed. With any luck, I'll have the entire scene exposed

before the sun gets too hot." He dared a glance at Signora Romano, noting how she stared at the mosaic. "Have you seen anything like this before, my lady?" he asked, directing his query to her.

Chiara angled her head. "Similar. In Palermo," she murmured.

"I would be interested in seeing it," he replied, just as James returned with the empty buckets. "Have you seen Dr. Jones this morning?"

Chiara and Marianne exchanged quick glances. "We haven't seen anyone but the farmers this morning," Marianne said with a shrug, her gaze darting to Chiara again. The older woman shook her head.

"I don't believe I know this Dr. Jones," Chiara said.

Jasper furrowed a brow. "How can that be? It was Dr. Jones who recommended you. Wrote to let me know about your guest villa."

The older woman gave a shake of her head. "He must have learned of it from someone else," she said with a shrug, although it was apparent she was bothered by the comment.

"Hmm. Well, I could certainly do with some breakfast," he said as he removed his gloves. "We'll have to make do with these foundation walls for seating. You will stay and eat with us?" he asked.

"I'll sit with you, but Signorina Aurora has already seen to our breakfasts," Marianne said as she allowed him to help her take a seat.

When Jasper moved to assist Chiara, the woman hesitated before taking his hand. Even before she was settled, Marianne had a blanket spread over the ground adjacent to the dig site and was pulling sliced sausage, olives, cheese, bread and a bottle of wine from the basket. "What do you two have planned for the day?" he asked as he motioned for James to join them.

"Chiara is taking me to town."

"Ah, shopping then," Jasper said. "Which means you need some money." He pulled a purse from a pocket and extracted several *piastras*. "These are the latest coins for the kingdom," he said as he passed them to Marianne. "So they should be valid currency."

She studied first the fronts and then the backs, turning to Chiara to ask as to their value.

"Are you planning to buy out all the shops?" Chiara teased, her eyes widening at seeing the *piastras*.

Suppressing the urge to grin, Jasper dared a glance in James' direction. His colleague gave him a questioning look. "How much did you give her?"

"Probably enough to buy out all the shops," Jasper replied in a hoarse whisper, wondering how much she would spend.

And on what.

Chapter 21

A LADY SEES HER COMPANION IN A NEW LIGHT

A few minutes later
When the women left the men to their excavation, each with an empty basket dangling from one hand, they made their way up the road to the city. They spoke of London and Rome, of fathers and mothers, and finally of why Marianne found herself married to Jasper Henley.

"I do not think you regret what happened," Chiara said when Marianne finished her tale of how she became a viscountess.

"Oh, I don't," Marianne agreed. "Not at all. My father gave him his blessing and most of my dowry." At Chiara's look of confusion, she added, "We have to pay a call on him in Canobie—just north of England—in order for Henley to collect the remainder."

Chiara allowed a brilliant smile that displayed her white teeth and youthened her by a decade. "Bribery!" she said with glee. "It works every time with children."

Marianne allowed a giggle before they came to a shop fronted with baskets of nuts and fruits. The clerk bade them welcome, and Chiara motioned for Marianne to follow her in. The respite from the bright sun had Marianne pulling a fan from her reticule and batting the air with it as she perused the shelves of dried spices, pastas, and beans.

"I don't recognize any of these," she commented as she examined various jars. The dried spices looked nothing like their fresh counterparts, so when Chiara pointed to each in turn and said the name and what dish it was used in, Marianne was rather stunned. "Why don't you grow them in a kitchen garden?"

"Not all the spices can grow here," Chiara explained. "It's too hot in the summer. They wither and die." She pulled a small parchment from her basket, her eyes scanning the writing for a moment before she pulled several jars from the shelves. "Aurora's list," she said when she noticed Marianne's interest. "She has planned menus for the next month of your stay."

"She's an excellent cook," Marianne said. "I admit to being surprised that she isn't married. Is she... betrothed?"

Chiara shook her head. "There is no man worthy of her, so I am glad she is not yet, but..." She allowed the sentence to trail off before sighing. "She will have to wed sometime."

Marianne dipped her head. "Mr. Singleton is sweet on her, I think."

Blinking, Chiara furrowed her brows. "Sweet on her?" she repeated. "What is this?"

Rolling her eyes, Marianne realized the expression didn't translate. "He likes her. He... *flirts* with her."

Chiara huffed. "And she allows this?" Her manner was suddenly one of annoyance.

Realizing she shouldn't have said anything, Marianne shook her head. "No. No. She... *avoids* him." She lifted a palm up and pantomimed pushing. "Pushes him away. My husband said he is no longer allowed in the kitchen. In fact, Aurora threatened him with a knife when he tried to help her serve the meat course last night." Marianne didn't add that James seemed more amused by the exchange than put off by it, as if the woman had merely challenged him to continue his pursuit of her.

When she asked Jasper about it, he shook his head and said something about James chasing her until she caught him.

At the memory of his words, Marianne's eyes suddenly widened.

Was James really serious about courting Aurora?

She was about to ask Chiara if Aurora had said anything about James, but thought better of it.

She didn't want the man impaled by a kitchen knife.

Chiara was regarding her with a frown but finally seemed satisfied with her explanation. "She has a temper, that one," she murmured, "Which may prove a challenge to any suitor."

Marianne wasn't about to mention that James seemed ready for the challenge—kitchen knife not withstanding.

"Come, I have more shopping to do," the older woman said as she paid for her purchases.

"Do you keep a garden?" Marianne asked, stooping a bit so she could better see the rows of fresh produce displayed in front of the next shop. Some of the items she recognized while others were a puzzle.

"Not for several years, but Aurora does," Chiara replied. "She has more patience than I do. Better knees." After she selected several ears of corn and two onions, examining each before adding them to her basket, she asked, "Do you?"

Marianne had only ever looked after a small flower garden in front of her father's house. A gardener saw to the lawn and trees on the estate. "I haven't yet seen Henley's townhouse, so I don't know if there is a garden there or not," she murmured.

Chiara stared at her. "You haven't been to your house?"

Marianne shook her head. "Not yet. Henley and I were married the same day we left to come here," she replied. "He said it's a townhouse. And I expect from its proximity to

Hyde Park that it's a rather fashionable home, with servants and a cook, although apparently the cook is getting on in years, and my husband says he needs to hire a new one."

A glimmer of interest seemed to flash in Chiara's eyes before it was suddenly gone. "How long have your known your Lord Henley?"

Marianne dipped her head. "Not even a month," she replied.

Chiara whirled to regard her. "That explains much," she said with a grin.

Her eyes widening, Marianne wondered at the older woman's words.

"It's nothing bad, I assure you. I only mean that you two seem... *tentative*, I think the word is... with one another. As if you are afraid what you say might... irritate him, and he is unsure of what to say to you. Although he adores you."

"He does?" Marianne boggled at the comment.

Chiara continued to grin. "He shows his affection out in the open. My first love did so..." She suddenly stopped and sobered.

"Your first love?" Marianne prompted, wondering how long ago that might have been. Her gaze followed Chiara's until she noticed an old woman who was staring at them. "Is she a Gypsy?" she asked in a whisper.

"*Sì*," Chiara replied, rather surprised the younger woman would be familiar with Gypsies. "How did you know?" She hadn't even realized the woman was a Gypsy until Marianne's query.

"We have them where I am from. The Lowland Gypsies. They set up camp and stay for a few weeks near the river. Near the border with England. Then they pack up and move on."

"Causing trouble, no doubt," Chiara said with a huff.

Marianne frowned. "Not at all. They sometimes put on a play—a comedy, usually—to make a bit of money, but for the most part, they keep to themselves. Except for the one time when one of the young men in the village decided to marry one of them."

"Let me guess. She married him, took all his money, and left without him," Chiara said in disgust.

"Oh, no. He left with them. He always suffered from wanderlust, so it was probably best he ended up with a wife who was a traveler."

When Marianne turned to look in the direction where the Gypsy had been regarding them, she found the woman had disappeared. "Now, you mentioned your first love. Forgive my impertinence, but you really must tell me about him," she pleaded.

Allowing an audible sigh before she stepped into a butcher's shop, Chiara whispered, "A long time ago, I, too, had a man who kissed me out where anyone could see. I was young and... stupid. I allowed him the impropriety because I was foolish enough to believe he would offer for my hand."

Marianne blinked. "He didn't?" She couldn't imagine a man being so free with his affections, with no intention of marriage. Even Jasper had kissed her thinking their only witness was a statue of Cupid.

Or had he known we would have an audience? He hadn't seemed the least bit surprised at discovering the identity of their interlopers that night.

"He did not," Chiara replied. "I discovered later why he could not, and..." She paused, as if she were having trouble catching her breath. "Let us just say my heart was broken... *hardened* by what happened. When I married my late husband, Antony, I did so for practical reasons. Besides, he was rich," she said with a grin.

"You didn't feel affection for him?" Marianne asked, not realizing how inappropriate her query was just then.

"Did you feel affection for your Lord Henley?"

Marianne blinked. No one had asked her *that* before.

Not even Cherice. "I don't think I knew him well enough to know one way or the other," she finally whispered. She turned when she realized a rather large, burley man with hairy arms and a bloody apron was regarding them from the other side of a wide counter. He held a meat cleaver in one hand and displayed a wide grin featuring a missing tooth or two.

"My *bella*, Vedova Romano!" he greeted Chiara. "And who might this lovely creature be?" he asked in Italian. "If you will not marry me, perhaps she will?"

Chiara indicated Marianne with a wave of her hand. "*Lady* Henley," she replied, emphasizing the 'lady'. "And she is not interested in marriage to you. Or your son."

Marianne did her best to interpret the words, wondering if the butcher was asking as to her suitability as a wife for him.

"She knows not what she is missing!" the butcher countered, his meat cleaver suddenly doing a somersault in the air before them. Marianne stepped back. She might not have been able to see it clearly, but she knew exactly what it was capable of doing.

"Signor Garcia's family has lived in Girgenti for many generations," Chiara explained in English. "All butchers, and very proud about it," she added.

Nodding to the man, Marianne said, "*Buon pomeriggio*, Signor Garcia."

Chiara placed her order while Marianne moved to study the various carcasses that hung from hooks in the front of the shop. Although she recognized most of the animals and fowl, she was glad she had never had to prepare one for a meal. Her status as an aristocrat's daughter had sheltered her from having to learn how to shop for food and prepare it.

When they took their leave of the butcher's shop, Marianne had to stifle a grin at hearing Signor Garcia's parting proposal of marriage. "Was he asking you or me?" she queried.

Chiara gave her a quelling glance. "He is a widower. He misses having a woman in his bed at night is all," she said, which had Marianne blushing.

"He seems friendly," Marianne replied, wondering if Chiara had ever considered the butcher to be her second husband.

Chiara grinned. "He is, but he is a... friend. Not a lover," she replied. "He wouldn't feel affection for me as your Lord Henley feels affection for you," she explained before she led them across the street and into a shop featuring fabric and threads.

Unsure of how to respond to the woman's surprising comment, Marianne instead wondered at how Chiara could know such a thing. They had barely been in her company! "How can you be so sure?"

Chiara allowed a shrug as she examined a length of fabric. "I am old. I know these things." After examining some white muslin, she glanced over at the young woman to find Marianne on the verge of tears. She frowned. "You don't wish him to feel affection for you?" she asked as she moved to wrap an arm around Marianne's shoulder.

"Oh, I do. Very much," Marianne whispered. "I just... how can you be so sure when I... I cannot see it for myself?"

Chiara blinked. "Perhaps because you are blind, my lady," she replied. "How often does he visit your bed?"

It was Marianne's turn to blink, and not just because a tear was about to escape one eye. "He has not," she answered with a sniffle. At Chiara's look of disbelief, she added, "He... We sleep in *his* bed."

"Ah," the older woman said with appreciation. "High up, where he is king," she teased.

Marianne blinked again. "He called it Mount Olympus."

Chiara furrowed a brow for a moment before her face lit

up in delight. "Where he can worship you as a goddess, no doubt," she whispered. Then she chuckled.

"Signora Romano!" Marianne scolded, glancing about in a failed attempt at learning if anyone could hear their inappropriate conversation.

Chiara was worse than her Aunt Cherice!

"Forgive me. I am... I am merely remembering what it was like to be in love," she said in a quiet voice. "A man once worshiped me like that. Several nights a week for three months. Took my virginity, but gave me..." She stopped and inhaled sharply.

"What is it?" Marianne asked, her brows furrowing in worry. "Gave you...?"

Chiara turned away and pulled a length of folded fabric from the stack next to where she stood. She carried it to the shopkeeper and recited a litany of instructions in Italian that Marianne couldn't begin to follow.

What had the woman been about to say? She obviously had mixed feelings about her first love. One minute she was remembering him fondly, and the next, she seemed about to curse him.

Will I have such conflicted feelings about Jasper one day? Marianne wondered as she watched Chiara interact with the shopkeeper. A hand absently went to her belly. If she did, she hoped it would be long after she had borne a child or two.

Preferably never.

Chapter 22

BRINGING MOSAICS INTO
THE LIGHT

*M*eanwhile, back in the Greco-Roman quarter
Dr. Darius Jones regarded Viscount
Henley from where he stood on the other side of an ancient
stub of a column and gave a shake of his head. Prepared to
chide the younger man for his poor skills in the field, he
watched as the viscount did exactly what he would have done
upon revealing a possible artifact. "Well, I'll be damned,"
Darius murmured, crossing his arms and leaning against the
honey-color marble as he continued to watch Jasper clean
away dirt from whatever he had discovered using a
soft brush.

The younger son of a duke and the current heir to the
Westhaven dukedom, Darius Jones had been an archaeologist
well before his studies at Cambridge cemented his avocation
in the minds of the members of the Royal Society.

His older brother, Dr. Alexander Jones, currently held the
title of duke, but was frequently away from England on expeditions to study Greek antiquities. His Grace, Duke of Westhaven, had so far only fathered a daughter, so it was possible
Darius might one day inherit. Otherwise, the dukedom
would go to his son, Carter Jones, a ne'er-do-well dandy who

frequently gambled and ran with a crowd of young bucks intent on spending their inheritances before they turned thirty.

Darius knew his lack of presence in his London household was part of the reason Carter was so reckless. Carter's late mother had indulged the boy from the time he was born, spoiling him with expensive gifts and seeing to it he was dressed in the finest clothes. At least the boy had learned how to ride and could manage the ribbons of a phaeton; otherwise, Darius was sure Carter would expect to be driven about in the capital in a town coach with four matched greys and an army of grooms.

Shaking thoughts of his son from his mind, he returned his attention to what his colleagues were uncovering.

*H*is leather gloves damp from perspiration, Jasper shed them before he pulled a bare hand through the loosened dirt uncovering another portion of the mosaic he had been revealing since early that morning. His eyes widened as the black and dark rust-color tiles appeared.

He nearly had a complete corner of the hunting scene uncovered when a sharp, stinging pain had him jerking one hand from the soil. "Christ!" he hissed, hoping James couldn't hear his curse. He wiped the ancient Roman dirt from his hand and stared at the tip of his index finger, grimacing as he realized the cause of his discomfort.

"What is it?" James asked as he paused in his own work at the other end of the mosaic floor. Now that they had most of the excess soil removed from inside the foundation walls, they had each taken a pail and begun to work on removing the last layer of dirt from the tiles.

"Just a hangnail," Jasper replied, shaking his hand. His attention was captured by what appeared before him, though, and he gave a shout.

James was up from his work and crouched next to Jasper in only a moment, his gaze following an area his colleague had just exposed. "Is that the signature?" he asked in a whisper.

"Part of it, I think," Jasper said as he used his forearm to push away a swath of black soil. Given how dry the earth was toward the middle of the ancient room—the soil nearest the walls remained moist from rainwater washing down the foundation walls—chunks of dirt stubbornly clung to the tiles. "And there's the rest," he said in awe. He glanced around and behind him. "There must have been at least... four rooms in this house," he commented, which meant some of the mosaics they had uncovered were probably not part of the hunting scene before him.

"Probably more, which means every room had a tile floor," James said, his own gaze taking in the rest of the space inside the foundation walls. He pulled a thin, folded parchment from a pocket along with a charcoal. Placing the paper over the signature, he traced the shape as best he could, leaving voids where tiles were missing or the cursive shapes were incomplete. When he was finished, he held it up to the afternoon sun, his eyes squinting in the Mediterranean glare.

"Do you recognize it?" Jasper asked, one of his brows furrowing as he studied the signature in silhouette. He suddenly cursed. "Shite! It's *Greek*," he complained.

Angling his head and then the parchment, James shook his head. "Not necessarily," he replied as he held out a staying hand. "This may be a Roman copy of a Greek mosaic. You said the Romans were notorious for copying designs created by others," he reminded him. "What's to say they didn't copy the signature as well?"

Jasper regarded his colleague with new-found appreciation. "You have the right of it, of course."

"Which means the colors will tell us if it's Greek or Roman," James said with a nod. Roman mosaics were almost always white with black and red or rust-colored tiles. It was rare if other colors were found in the intricate artwork.

"Or something else."

James and Jasper lifted their heads in unison to find Dr. Darius Jones regarding them with an amused expression. "Where have you been?" Jasper asked as he scrambled to his feet and held out his right hand.

Darius straightened at the same time he angled his head. He shook the proffered hand and noted how his counterpart's face was newly tanned from the harsh Mediterranean sun. "Down there," he said with a nod in the direction of the marina. "Found an engraved triglyph decorating a tavern at the end of the widest street."

"Greek?" Jasper guessed.

"Roman," Darius countered with an arched brow. "Offered the proprietor some *piastras*, but he says it is not for sale. Probably because it's holding up his roof," he added in feigned disgust.

Jasper couldn't help the hiss that escaped his lips. The triglyph was probably from either Erocle's or Zeus' temple, given their proximity to the port town. "Well, it's good of you to join us, Dr. Jones. Rather fortuitous that our schedules are so closely matched this season."

"Indeed. You have accomplished much today," Darius commented as his gaze swept the area they had unburied. "Looks like a sweep with a corn husk broom will be your next step."

"Indeed. It was faster work to dig near the foundation walls, but the middle wasn't as deeply buried as I expected it might be," Jasper explained. Now that he was standing and surveying their work from a higher perspective, he understood what Darius meant by using a broom. In most places, only a thin layer of dirt hid the mosaics from view.

"The strong summer winds keep the middles of all of these foundations fairly clear," Darius agreed as he glanced at an adjacent foundation. "Did you have help?" he asked as he looked around, as if he expected to see some locals with shovels and pails.

James shook his head. "No need. At least, not today." He gave a glance toward the southwest corner of the Greco-Roman quarter. "How is your work progressing?"

Darius gave shake of his head. "Found the base of the aqueduct. Found some Roman coins. A piece of what I think might be a relief of Minerva," he said, referring to a Roman goddess. "Still have some digging to do at one end, but it's better preserved than I expected. Damned earthquakes really did some damage to these areas, though."

"How many men do you employ?" Jasper asked.

"Depends on the day and how many wish to work. Usually two or three. I have to keep a close eye on them, though, or they do more damage than the earthquakes did," he complained.

"Can you join us for dinner this evening? I'm sure our cook won't mind too much," Jasper asked as he wiped his forehead with a sleeve-covered arm. "It's been an age since we shared notes."

"Depends. Who is your cook?"

James finished collecting his tools and stood up. "A Sicilian goddess whom I shall be making my wife," he said in jest.

"If she doesn't impale him with a kitchen knife first," Jasper said, *sotto voce.*

"I heard that," James countered.

Darius angled his head. "Aurora Romano?" he guessed, one hand going to a hip as his attention was drawn to the road that led up the hillside where their guest villa was located.

"Indeed. Have you had the pleasure?" Jasper asked, lifting his satchel to his shoulder.

"Of her, or her cooking?" Darius replied as he waggled

his eyebrows. At the murderous look James cast in his direction, he sobered. "I have not. But the local butcher seems to think his son will take her as his wife."

James blinked. Jasper rolled his eyes, wondering if the butcher's son was in any kind of danger.

And not just from a kitchen knife.

"Are they betrothed?" Jasper asked, before James could.

Darius straightened, amusement apparent on his features. "They are not. Yet. But rumor has it, Signorina Aurora is not of a mind to marry a local boy, so I doubt there is a marriage to a butcher's son in her future."

James stepped forward. "Does she have a suitor from somewhere else?"

Realizing James was more serious about his interest in Aurora than he originally thought, Darius gave his head a shake. "No. But she has a severe case of wanderlust."

It was James' turn to blink. "Are you saying she wishes to travel?" he asked, a hint of hope in his words.

"She doesn't want to remain in Girgenti, and that is all I'm going to say on the subject," Darius replied, not about to admit he hadn't heard much more on the topic of Vedova Romano's oldest niece. "When is dinner?"

"Seven o'clock, we think," Jasper replied, remembering the telling of time was quite different on the island. He was sure the woman had said one o'clock, but that really meant an hour after sunset. "My understanding of Italian isn't as good as I remember."

"I'll hurry then. 'Bout time I took a bath and dressed for dinner," Darius said with a nod. He bade farewell and headed back in the direction of the road, where a donkey and cart were waiting.

Jasper allowed his gaze to sweep the horizon, just then noticing the bright blue of the sea beyond the island. If it hadn't been for the slight breeze that ruffled his hair when he removed his hat, he was sure they would have had to quit their work for the day when the sun reached its zenith. He guessed it was probably past three o'clock, which accounted for why perspiration trickled down his temples and the middle of his back.

"We should be getting back to the villa," James said suddenly. When Jasper gave him a look of surprise—they had just uncovered a major find, given the signature his colleague had traced—he saw James was holding their canteen upside down. No water dripped from it.

Jasper's gaze darted to the remains of the picnic Marianne had brought. The wine in the flask was also gone. He did a sweep of the area they had worked on that day, rather impressed at how much they had accomplished on their first day. "I think we've done enough," he said as he brushed the dirt from his trousers and retrieved his gloves from the ground. "See if we can't borrow a broom for tomorrow."

Gathering up their tools, the two took one last look at what they had uncovered—partial scenes of much larger images—and made their way toward the villa.

Chapter 23

IMAGINING A COURTSHIP

A few minutes later
Jasper regarded James as they made their way back to the villa. "Are you truly serious about courting Signorina Aurora?" he asked, his query almost too quiet given the late afternoon breeze that warmed the air.

"I am," James replied after a moment. "It was a bit of a lark at first—my flirting with her—but now that I know she wishes to travel, I am intrigued. I am not getting any younger. You're already married for a second time. And I think it's past time I take a wife."

"What has you changing your mind?" Jasper asked. "You once mentioned you never intended to marry." He thought he knew why, but he didn't think it best to bring it up just then.

Allowing a sigh, James Singleton pondered how to reply. "Until that night you introduced Lady Henley in your cabin, I didn't," he said quietly. When he noted Jasper's angry expression, he quickly added, "The idea of having my own woman to warm my bed every night was suddenly... a welcome thought. Although variety can be... diverting, I find I don't like the idea of sharing a lover."

"But is Signorina Aurora really the best choice for you?" Jasper countered. Although James wasn't expected to inherit a family business—his older brother would do that—or marry into the aristocracy, he was still from well-to-do stock.

"I don't want an English miss," James said with a shake of his head. "I want... *passion*. I want a lover who... challenges me. Excites me."

"Who might throw a knife at you," Jasper teased. He sobered when he realized James could be describing Marianne. At least, at night. During the daylight hours, Marianne was as meek and mild as any gently bred English miss, probably more so given her inability to see well without her spectacles. But at night... He had to erase the image of how she had met his every thrust with one of her own the night before. Of how she had spurred him to a release so intense, he had been reminded of his times at *The Elegant Courtesan*. Of his nights with Miss Ann.

Who would have ever thought a nearsighted daughter of the *ton* could have him looking forward to going to bed? They hadn't been married for three weeks, and yet she was already a perfect bedmate for him.

He finally regarded his colleague with a furrowed brow. "Forgive me for my impertinence, but I cannot believe my ears," he said in a quiet voice. "I didn't think you would ever want to take a *wife*."

The unspoken implication hung in the air before James finally gave Jasper a sideways glance. "How long... how long have you known?"

Swallowing, Jasper wondered how much to admit. There had only been the one time he had seen his colleague in the company of another man in a manner that might have suggested Singleton was a homosexual. He knew the younger man's claims as to how frequently he visited brothels seemed forced. "I didn't," he replied finally.

James hissed and allowed a quiet curse. "What happens now?"

Jasper frowned. "Well, I would hope you would cease your pursuit of Miss Aurora. Or, at least, not propose marriage."

Boggling at Jasper's comment, James stopped in his tracks. "That's it?" he questioned.

Dipping his head, Jasper allowed another sigh. "Well, I'm certainly not going to... to *report* you, if that's what you're thinking." The man was his colleague. They had spent months every year working on various projects together. If Singleton was discovered, the backlash might taint him as well.

When James still looked uncertain, Jasper gave his head a shake. "Christ, Singleton. We spent our university days studying the famous ancient Greeks who were homosexuals. What kind of hypocrite would I be if I decided to fire you from this project for that reason?"

"I didn't know I was *employed*," James replied, his comment meant to lighten the conversation. "If that's the case, then I suppose I should ask when I might be paid."

"You know what I mean," Jasper countered. "Just... be careful. For your sake, use discretion."

"About that...," Jasper said under his breath.

James stopped in his tracks and turned to regard the younger man. "What?"

"The valet."

Jasper blinked. "What about the valet?" *Good God!* Was he talking about David Romano? About Chiara Romano's son?

One hand going to his hip as he readjusted his satchel, James said, "I think he... he knows."

"Knows... what, exactly?"

Giving Jasper a quelling glance, James said, "Never mind."

"What?" Jasper insisted.

"Does his gaze linger on you when he dresses you?"

Jasper blinked. "No," he hedged.

"Does he make comments about your clothes?"

Jasper shook his head.

"When he was helping me dress for dinner, he commented on..." James stopped and rolled his eyes. "My cravat, my boots, my haircut. The way he looked at me—"

"Was he speaking in Italian?"

"English. Rather damn good English, in fact."

"Dammit, Singleton. His mother is acting as a companion for my wife. Should she discover—"

"She won't find out, I promise," James insisted. "I don't intend to do anything to... embarrass you. To compromise our work here," he insisted. He paused a moment before allowing a long sigh. "But he is... beautiful."

Although he had been attracted to others—James had spent his recent night in Cambridge with a lover from his university days—he had never been so affected—so haunted—as he was by thoughts of David Romano. "I often wonder if I shall go through life never being able to love another," he murmured.

"I don't blame you," Jasper said in a quiet voice. "I admit to being rather... lucky in that regard." He squeezed his eyes shut, wishing they had never had this conversation. "I believe I am in love with my wife," he said as a means to change the subject.

James cleared his throat. "A situation made most apparent during the eleven days we sailed here," he said, *sotto voce*. At Jasper's sudden frown, he added, "My cabin was adjacent to yours. The walls were... thin," he said as his attention went to two women who were climbing the road just up ahead. "Speak of the devil. Or rather, his temptress," he said with a grin.

His gaze going to his wife—at least, the back of her—

Jasper had to tamp down the arousal he felt at the sight of Marianne just then. Her hips swayed with every step as she climbed the inclined lane up to their villa. She and Chiara were calling out farewells to one another before Marianne suddenly turned in their direction and waved. "You would be wise to restrain from referring to my wife in such terms," Jasper warned.

"Consider it done," James replied. "I... I apologize. I promise, I do not covet her. Only the idea of a willing bedmate," he explained in a quiet voice, as if he feared Marianne would overhear his words.

But Jasper was already hurrying on ahead, his grin wide when he finally reached Marianne and gave her a kiss on the cheek. "You are a welcome sight for sore eyes," he whispered.

Marianne grinned. "As are you," she replied. Her brows suddenly furrowed. "Well, most of you, I suppose," she said as she noticed how dirty his clothes were.

"I shall bathe before dinner," he promised in a whisper, before hurrying over to Vedova Romano's villa. "Perhaps you would be willing to share your *bolle*?" he hinted before he disappeared behind the courtyard door.

Marianne suppressed a giggle and made her way into the guest villa alongside James. "Did you make any discoveries today?" she asked, wondering at his pensive expression.

"Indeed. Not the least of which is that I am severely underpaid," he joked.

Her eyes widening in concern, she asked, "Oh. Are you in need of funds? Lord Henley gave me far too much money this morning," she said as she moved to open her reticule.

"No, my lady," he answered quickly. When he glanced into the basket that hung from her arm, he realized why she had so much money left over—there was only a length of ribbon and a spool of silk thread lining the bottom of the basket. *So much for buying out all the shops in Girgenti.* "The ribbon is rather beautiful," he commented.

Marianne angled her head as they entered the house. "Thank you. It seems I have lost the ribbon for my braid," she commented before giving him a curtsy. "I will see you later at dinner, Mr. Singleton."

Chapter 24

A GYPSY SEES A WIDOW'S FUTURE

eanwhile, inside Chiesa di San Nicola
Chiara crossed herself as she entered the *Chiesa di San Nicola*, murmuring in Italian before moving to light a candle in the narthex. About to kneel to pray, she had the oddest sensation, as if she were being watched. Reminded of what had happened earlier that afternoon, she turned to discover a black-robed nun regarding her from the other side of the nave.

"*Buon pomeriggio, sorella,*" she whispered, giving the old woman a nod. Having come to San Nicola nearly every day to light a candle in honor of her late husband, Chiara was quite sure she didn't recognize the nun.

The black-garbed woman stepped forward, glancing about as if she were worried about being discovered in the narthex. "Do not tell anyone I am here," she whispered.

Chiara frowned. "Why ever not?" Besides, who would she tell? There was no one else in the church at the moment.

"I am a Gypsy."

Inhaling a deep breath, Chiara glanced around the church before returning her attention to the nun. "What kind of Gypsy?" she countered, recognizing the woman wearing a black habit with a black and white coif. The woman had been watching her and Marianne as they shopped earlier that day.

"The kind that knows what is best. The kind that recognizes a lonely soul and knows of another that will provide it comfort. I have come to you because it is time."

Chiara frowned at the implication. "I am not lonely," she argued.

The nun shook her head. "For twenty years, you have pined for someone other than the man you promised fidelity," she countered. "But that man—that someone—is now within your reach. Do not choose the path of a fool, for that leads to more loneliness. Choose the path of love and devotion. For that path promises a life of fulfillment. A path of eternal happiness. A life blessed."

Chiara blinked, and not just because a tear had formed in the corner of one eye. She turned to stare at the candle she had just lit. "Who do you mean?" she finally asked, the quiet narthex causing her words to sound loud in her ears. But when she turned around to face the nun, she frowned.

No one was there. In fact, the entire church was empty.

A chill had her entire body shivering just then. A chill and a rather stunning thought.

The Gypsy had been referring to her son's father, she was sure.

Lord Darius.

Who else could she have meant with her words?

Chiara Romano crossed herself before rising to her feet.

Lord Darius?

I would sooner hang myself, she thought in dismay.

Chapter 25

A SIGHT FOR SORE EYES

*I**n the early evening*

Bathed and dressed for dinner, Jasper dismissed David and made his way to the dining room in search of Marianne. A quick glance into several rooms proved she wasn't in the villa, so he made his way back to the kitchen to ask about her when David appeared carrying two large pails of steaming water. *For James, no doubt*, Jasper thought. He couldn't help but notice how David grinned as he carried the bathwater to the younger archaeologist's bedchamber.

He was informed by their cook that his wife had taken her leave of the villa with a book. A bit alarmed—he wasn't yet sure just how safe Marianne would be outside of the compound—Jasper made his way out of the villa's enclosed courtyard and glanced up and down the dirt lane. Just off the path that led to the Greco-Roman quarter, he spotted his wife. Perched on what had probably been the base of a column, Marianne was reading a book while Angela leaned against the marble stone and sewed in the shade of an almond tree.

Deciding the two were in no danger, he was about to head back into the villa when he noticed a mule-drawn cart on its way up the lane. He recognized Lord Darius right away, but his appearance was nothing like how the Duke of Westhaven's brother usually looked when working in the field. Hurrying down the lane to meet the cart, Jasper called out a greeting.

"Ah, I see you have decided to dress as well," Darius said as he paused the cart so Jasper could jump on.

"I intend to keep up appearances as much as possible," Jasper claimed as he took a seat next to the older archaeologist.

Darius tore his attention from Jasper and squinted his eyes in an attempt to make out the identity of a young woman who was over a hundred feet away and apparently enjoying a good book.

"I didn't take you for one to acquire live artifacts as part of your excavations," Darius remarked, his head nodding toward where Marianne sat reading atop a broken column base. "Your latest mistress?"

Jasper followed his line of sight and lifted a brow. "Why, I've a mind to knock you on your bum for that comment," he countered. "That, sir, is my wife."

Frowning, Darius gave him a look of disbelief. "Forgive me, but I was sure I heard your Sophie died. Just last year, wasn't it? Influenza, or some such?"

Jasper nodded, rather surprised when the familiar wave of sadness didn't leave him nearly robbed of breath. "She did. I remarried the day I left England to come here," he explained.

Darius, a widower himself, regarded Jasper with a furrowed brow. "I wasn't aware you were courting anyone," he replied. "Dr. Curzon would have said something if he knew," he added, referring to one of their fellow members of the Royal Society who had a reputation as the organization's most notorious gossip. There were those who claimed the explorer was a contributor to *The Tattler*, London's premiere gossip rag, but given the man's extended absences from the capital, it seemed rather unlikely.

When Darius halted the mule just before the villas, Jasper jumped down from the cart, realizing he wasn't going to be able to bamboozle Darius Jones with a variation of the truth as it related to Marianne. The older archaeologist might have spent most of his time researching Roman ruins around Hadrian's Wall, but the man did have access to newspapers, and a mail coach went through Hexham on a regular basis.

"Until a week before I left London, I wasn't courting anyone," Jasper stated, his chin rising a bit, as if he expected a pithy response.

He got what he expected.

"Got caught kissing in the gardens again, did you?" Darius accused with a huge grin.

Jasper cleared his throat and gave a curt nod. "I did."

Darius blinked. And blinked again. "You're... you're not joking," he half-asked.

Realizing he may as well tell his colleague the whole truth, Jasper directed his gaze towards his wife. "Marianne Slater. Lord Donald Slater's daughter," he said as he returned his attention back to Darius. Of course the older man would know of Slater's distillery just north of the border in Canobie. Darius had probably paid a personal visit to the distillery a time or two. He and Slater shared the distinction of being the lone younger brothers to peers.

"Miss Slater?" Darius asked in disbelief. "But... she's *blind*," he said with a shake of her head. "What were you thinking?" he asked in disbelief. He gave his head another shake. "You weren't, of course, or else you were letting your cock do your thinking—"

"She's not blind," Jasper countered, annoyance evident on his tanned features. "I met her at Lord Attenborough's ball last month, and I escorted her to the gardens—"

"—Without the benefit of a chaperone."

"Lady Devonville was dancing with her husband at the time, and not in the ballroom, if you catch my meaning," Jasper said in a low voice, one brow arched up.

"Talk about a man being led by his cock," Darius murmured. "As soon as Winslow was buried, Devonville had his eye on Lady Winslow. Told everyone in Parliament that none of them were to go near her, or it would be pistols at dawn."

Although Jasper had been attending Parliament that Season, he wasn't aware of that particular edict. "Careful there, old man. You're speaking of my... my uncle-in-law," Jasper warned. After a pause, he added, "I knew what I was doing when I took her to the gardens." He didn't really, but Darius didn't need to know that. He was still trying to figure what had him deciding it was a good idea—nay, a necessity —to take Marianne Slater on a tour of the gardens. Although given what they had been doing the night before—and every night since their wedding—he realized he had merely trusted his instincts.

Furrowing a bushy eyebrow, Darius dared another glance in the direction of Jasper's new viscountess. "Did she?"

Jasper held his breath a moment. Truth be told, he had never learned from her if she was glad or not that they had been forced to marry. She could have called it off, though. Devonville had said as much. If not him, then Cherice had most likely explained to the young woman that she could end the betrothal. Young ladies were allowed to end engagements.

Men were not.

"Probably not at the time," Jasper admitted. "We both just wanted to get out of the crush of the ball."

"Ah, your fear of crowded spaces got you again, did it?"

Jasper inhaled sharply before he nodded. "With the very best result, though. I have no regrets," he claimed, almost daring Darius to say otherwise. He suddenly frowned. "Well, except for the fact that she won't always wear her spectacles. It's true, she cannot see well without them." He dared another glance in her direction and was pleasantly surprised to see she was wearing her spectacles, her attention on a small animal that appeared to be begging for food near where she sat. Although Angela had been with her, the young woman was now missing.

"Well, she's got them on now. Jesus, Henley, you could at least see to it she's got somethin' better than those portholes, though. Poor girl looks like Everly when we put kohl on the eyepiece of his microscope, right before he did that presentation for the Society," Darius said as a huge grin lit his tanned face.

Jasper rolled his own eyes as he recalled the incident. Harold Tennison, Earl of Everly, had just returned from a trip to India and was giving a lecture on tropical fish at the Royal Society when the incident occurred. Rather unprofessional of Everly's colleagues, who had thought it funny when the man pressed his face against the eyepiece just before he announced his discovery of a new fish. Half the audience had gasped in fear, thinking he had been somehow infected by whatever was under the microscope's eyeglass, and the other half did their best not to laugh out loud at the black ring that encircled the man's right eye. "I welcome any suggestions at what I might do," Jasper replied, rather hoping Darius would know of someone in Sicily who could arrange an examination of Marianne's eyes as well as the grinding and mounting of lenses better suited to her station as a viscountess.

"Are you planning a trip up to Palermo?" Darius wondered as he secured the reins.

"I am considering it, seeing as how I may have an artifact for their museum," Jasper replied, referring to one of the mosaics he was unearthing. "Although I haven't yet arranged it," Jasper replied, his brow furrowing in thought.

When he originally made plans to excavate on Sicily, he

hadn't considered going to the mainland. Once he realized he would be married, though, he had thought to take Marianne to Rome when the heat grew too harsh to work in Sicily and then return to the island to continue his work in the fall. If he uncovered any mosaic floors and could determine their origin—Greek or Roman—he intended to do what he must to see to their preservation. He planned to take smaller designs with him to London while leaving the larger examples in a museum on Sicily—if not in Girgenti, then somewhere else on the island. Somewhere like Palermo.

As for other cities on the mainland, he had already spent a month in Pompeii and helped to excavate some ruins there. Another earlier trip had him directing the excavation of an area just north of Rome, a working class community that had at one time been a port city.

The island of Sardinia offered a plethora of ruins, and even though most were Greek, there was a treasure trove of Roman ruins if one merely studied some of the inland towns and villages. He had half a mind to simply relocate to Italy and spend the rest of his life uncovering mosaics, but he had responsibilities in England. And there was the expense of living abroad to consider.

"There is a man who has a shop with nothing but spectacles in Palermo. Ricardo Ricciardini. Gets his glass from Venice. I rather imagine he's capable of grinding lenses to suit any kind of eyesight," Darius said with a shrug. "If he cannot, or will not, he will know of someone who can. Venetian glass is the best on the entire planet," he claimed as he waved his beefy hands in front of his large body.

"What does the glass matter if it's to be ground down to make a lens?" Jasper asked in annoyance.

Darius blinked. "The very best lenses start with the very best glass," he explained, reaching out with one hand to rest it on the younger man's shoulder as the other lifted in a gesture familiar among Italians. Jasper expected he might even kiss his fingertips, but the archaeologist merely dropped his hand when he finished his proclamation. "No bubbles. No *bolle*. No imperfections."

"And the..." Jasper paused to use a finger to circle one eye. "Wires?"

The older man allowed a grin. "They have that specialty as well." He paused a moment and leaned in closer. "The Italians invented eyeglasses. Back in the thirteenth century. They are the best at it. The best at all of it. Why, they'll have your viscountess looking like the wisest woman in all of Europe," he said as he turned his attention back to where Marianne had been seated. "And looking as beautiful, as well."

Except Marianne was no longer seated—and no longer wearing her spectacles—but extending her arms to an older woman who had appeared from somewhere beyond the almond orchards. A younger woman walked by her side.

Darius blinked but continued to stare, watching as Lady Henley greeted the woman, an Italian whose dark hair was nearly black. Despite her age, the woman wasn't as plump as most of the women who lived in Girgenti, nor did she display a dour expression, as if everyone in her family had somehow disappointed her. This woman was smiling, and in doing so, displaying white teeth and sparkling eyes he suddenly wanted aimed in his direction.

Jasper noted his colleague's stare, a grin forming as he realized Darius Jones was experiencing the same sort of attraction Jasper had felt that night at Lord Attenborough's ball, when he had the strange feeling of being watched. Of feeling lust. Well, not lust, exactly, but a combination of desire and curiosity.

"Who is she?" Darius asked, his eyes still on the Italian woman who now walked arm-in-arm with Marianne toward the lane. The younger girl trailed behind them.

"My wife's companion and our hostess," Jasper said as he finally turned his attention back to Darius. "She owns this villa you recommended, in fact." From the way Darius stared at the woman, Jasper wondered if he had ever met her in person. "I thought you knew her."

But Darius didn't seem to recognize her despite his open appreciation. "By God, the Gypsy was right," he murmured, *sotto voce*.

"Gypsy?" Jasper repeated. When Darius didn't respond, he added, "Would you like an introduction?" He gave a start when he realized Darius hadn't heard a word he said. The man simply stared at Chiara as if he was transfixed. "Look who's being led by his cock now," Jasper said with a hint of humor.

The comment was lost on Darius, though, for the man continued to watch the three women as they made their way up the lane.

"She speaks English," Jasper said as he leaned towards the older archaeologist.

"I can speak Italian," Darius claimed. A moment passed before he added, "Well enough."

"Would you like an introduction?"

Darius finally tore his eyes from Chiara. "Eventually. Maybe. No," he finally replied with a shake of his head, as if he was suddenly brought back to his senses. He turned his attention to the ground below. "So, what has Signorina Aurora made us for dinner?" he asked, as if the past twenty minutes hadn't happened.

Blinking at the man's change in behavior, Jasper gave a shrug and admitted that he had absolutely no idea.

Despite Darius' attempt to seem unaffected by Chiara, Jasper knew the man was astonished. *Happens to the best of us*, he thought as he dared another glance in Marianne's direction, at the exact same time she lifted her gaze to meet his. He gave a wave and allowed a smile, rather glad she had done the same to him that night at Lord Attenborough's ball.

"Ladies," he said as he reached for Marianne's gloved hand. "Dr. Jones will be joining us for dinner this evening."

Darius gave a start as he stared at Marianne. "Miss Slater!" he said in a voice that suggested disbelief, his gaze going between her and Jasper. "Forgive me. I... I haven't seen you in an age..." He reached for her gloved hand and brushed his lips over the back of it. His attention went to Jasper. "How is it you two met?" he asked, the twinkle in his eye suggesting he was going to once again tease Jasper.

"At Lord Attenborough's ball," Marianne replied, a grin forming when she recognized Darius. It had been several years since the last time she had seen the older man in the company of her father.

Darius' face suddenly took on a look of delight. "He got caught kissing you in the gardens, didn't he?" he asked happily.

"Deliberately, I might add," Jasper stated with a nod, knowing full well the duke's brother simply wanted to embarrass him. He ignored the slight inhalation of breath Marianne allowed just then, and he rather wished he could have seen her expression.

This news had Darius' brows furrowing. "Wait. How long have you been married?"

Jasper and Marianne exchanged quick glances. "What time is it?" she asked, her gaze going to Darius' waistcoat.

Darius pulled a chronometer from his waistcoat pocket. "It's nearly half-past-six," he said before snapping the lid shut and stuffing it back into his pocket.

"Then.... just about fifteen and a half days," Jasper said, rather stunned to think of all they had accomplished since they had exchanged vows in the parlor of Devonville House. He turned to Marianne. "Seems longer than that, don't you think?"

"I would have said sixteen days," she agreed, her expression so deadpan, Jasper wondered whether she was teasing or not.

Blinking several times, the older man allowed a huge grin. "Oh, well then, it's no wonder you look as if you've been tumbled three ways to Thursday," he said, his comment directed to Jasper. He suddenly sobered. "Beggin' your pardon, Miss Slater," he added as his ears took on a decidedly reddish cast. "Or rather, Lady Henley," he corrected with a nod.

"If you're to be doing archaeological research with my husband, then I should like you to call me 'Marianne'," she said. "Especially since it seems we'll be away from London for a time."

"Well, then, it's good to see you again, Marianne," Darius said with nod. He took Marianne's gloved hand so he could brush his lips over the back of her knuckles once again. "I cannot believe you took such an old man to be your husband," he chided.

Marianne blinked. "But..."

"I am not an old man," Jasper said with a sigh. "I am one-and-thirty," he added, his gaze going briefly to Signora Romano. Her cheeks seemed bright red, and he wondered if she had been in the sun too long.

"Now, now, no need to have your first marital spat over age," Darius commented with a good deal of humor. "Although I am reminded of my own wife, God rest her soul. She was older than me, and I didn't discover the fact until we'd been wed for nearly ten years." He frowned then. "We could hardly abide one another's company, which is why she stayed in London whilst I decided my place was at Hadrian's Wall."

Although he words were aimed at Jasper, he seemed intent on learning how they were received by Marianne's companion.

Marianne was sure the duke's brother was flirting with

Chiara despite his odd words about his late wife. She dared a quick glance in her husband's direction, hoping they would never come to such a state in their marriage. After what had happened in the course of just a fortnight, she had decided they suited one another very well. Why, if all they ever did together was engage in sexual congress, she would be a happy wife.

"Where is your son these days, Dr. Jones?" Marianne asked, remembering he had one with his late wife. Her father had at one time hinted she might receive an offer from the young man. They had met Carter Jones whilst visiting one of the sites of an old Roman fort Darius was excavating near the remnants of Hadrian's Wall. Marianne remembered the boy, who was forced to spend time with his father as Darius did his research. None too pleased with the arrangement, Carter's protestations were as annoying as they were childish.

She wanted nothing to do with him.

"London. Spoiled brat claims he's ready to take the Westhaven dukedom whenever my brother, Alexander, drowns in the Aegean Sea. As if he forgets *I* have to die as well for that to happen," he added in disgust. "I keep hoping Alexander's wife will bear him a proper heir."

Not familiar with the Westhaven dukedom—other than knowing that Alexander, Duke of Westhaven, had only a daughter a few years younger than she—Marianne didn't respond.

"Don't lose faith, old man," Jasper teased. He allowed a sigh before he suddenly realized Darius hadn't been introduced to the woman whose villa he had recommended for their stay on Sicily. "I apologize, Signora Romano. I haven't introduced you to Dr. Jones. He is the man who told me of your guest villa."

Chiara's eyes widened a fraction, betraying her surprise at hearing Jasper's claim again. "I am honored to meet you, Dr. Jones," she said as she dipped a curtsy.

Darius gave a bow and took her hand in his. "The honor is all mine, my lady." He lowered his lips to the back of her gloved hand.

Jasper couldn't help but notice how Darius lingered over Chiara's hand. "Thank you for recommending her villa," Jasper said as he continued to glance between Chiara and the archaeologist.

"I did not catch your name, milady," Darius murmured, holding Chiara's white-gloved hand between his beefy thumb and forefingers.

Chiara blinked before she dared a glance at Marianne, almost as if she were seeking permission to respond. "I am Chiara Maria Valentina Ferraro Romano," she stated, straightening until she was nearly the archaeologist's height. When he removed his hat and she could see his entire face, her eyes suddenly widened with recognition.

"It's very good to meet you, Signora Romano," Darius said as he once again lowered his lips to her knuckles. "You are from Rome, no?"

Her eyes widening again in surprise, Chiara dipped her head a bit. "I am," she acknowledged, her olive skin displaying the tell-tale signs of a blush.

Darius looked as if he intended to simply lift Chiara from where she stood and carry her off to his cave or his den or wherever he was spending his nights. "Where are you stay-ing, Dr. Jones?" Marianne asked, realizing someone needed to take the man's attention off her companion or she would no longer have one.

The archaeologist finally tore his gaze from Chiara. "I took a room at the Villa Vigata down near the marina," he answered.

Marianna blinked and gave a quick glance at Jasper, wondering if he knew what was going on. When he simply gave a shake of his head, Marianne turned her attention back to Chiara. "I think it's time to change for dinner. Forgive me, Lord Darius, Lord Henley," she added as she dipped a curtsy.

Chiara curtsied at the same time before stepping back while Jasper gave a bow. "I'll see you at dinner, my love," he murmured.

Marianne allowed a grin and hurried into their villa while Chiara disappeared into her own.

Neither looked back at the two men who stood staring at their retreating backs.

Chapter 26

EXPOSING A PUZZLE TO
THE LIGHT

*T*he next day
"Ah, more progress," Darius said when he appeared at the edge of the foundation in which several mosaics were on the verge of seeing their first daylight in possibly thousands of years. Since the harsh light of the sun washed out the colors of the tiles, James and Jasper had erected a makeshift sunshade of a thin fabric that allowed light to pass through but helped them see the details of the exposed tesserae.

The toe of one of his Hessian boots knocked away the dirt surrounding a series of stones at his feet. "What have you determined?" Darius asked as his gaze swept their dig site. James was off in the opposite corner of their site, using a broom and a small shovel to remove the last layer of dried dirt from the hunting scene they had partially uncovered the day before.

"At first, I thought this was all Greek, because instead of traditional tiles, you can see these tiles appear as tiny pebbles," Jasper said as he brushed away the soil that Darius had just dislodged. A faint pattern began to emerge from what Jasper had originally thought of as a mosaic tile floor—

an *opus tessellatum*—but farther out from his initial discovery, the colored stones were indeed more square. "Now that I'm seeing these more square tiles, I'm beginning to think I just started at a spot where the tiles were more damaged. Closer to the surface. The edges worn away by erosion."

Frowning as he angled his head, Darius tried to imagine what the entire pattern might reveal. There just weren't enough black and white tiles exposed, yet, though. "Given the shape of the columns and the foundation that have been dug up, this has to be Roman," Darius claimed as he waved a hand at the rest of what had been excavated.

"I'll know for certain when I reveal more of the pattern," Jasper replied. "But I agree. The entire site seems Roman." Just the day before, he had felt a good deal of disappointment at the thought that the mosaic might be Greek. He had nearly arranged to head for Rome a few weeks earlier than planned, ready to write a letter to a Greek researcher to let him know the location of the excavation site. With today's findings and Darius' assurances, Jasper decided he should continue his work.

"I still don't know how you can tell the difference," Darius murmured, pulling out a stiff brush and joining Jasper in removing the loose dirt from over the tiles. "The last three I saw up in Pompeii looked Hellenistic in every aspect. Subject, tile colors. One was even signed with a Greek name."

"Roman copies of Greek originals," Jasper acknowledged. "Especially if they were colorful. Took the Romans some time to develop their own style. In this area, I would expect to find only black and white tesserae, maybe with some red, and motifs featuring sea creatures," he explained. "On my last trip to Rome, almost every mosaic I uncovered was made up of black and white tiles in a sea horse pattern."

Darius nodded. "I read your book on those ruins. Roman baths, weren't they?"

"Indeed," Jasper replied. "What I didn't include in the book was any mention of the mosaics I discovered in one corner of the bath house," he teased as he moved sideways a few inches and used a tool to scrape away a layer of hard ground from the artwork below. "I think it must have been a changing room, or a steam room, perhaps."

Intrigued, Darius brushed away the newly loosened dirt. "Something too salacious for a book?" he guessed, a low whistle following his question when several rows of tiles were suddenly exposed.

"There were sixteen sets of mosaics, all different positions of sexual congress. Some featured more than two participants," Jasper claimed, once again using a small ax to break away the stubborn ground. "Only a few tiles were missing, and they appeared to have been deliberately removed from strategic locations, if you catch my meaning."

"You uncovered a Roman orgy!" Darius said with a huge grin. The grin disappeared when the sun that lit this part of their workspace was suddenly cast in shadow.

Jasper glanced up to find Marianne and Chiara regarding him with looks of shock, their faces framed by the open parasol his wife carried. Or perhaps their gaze was directed at the older archaeologist, who seemed oblivious to their presence. Scrambling to his feet, and followed a moment later by Darius, Jasper gave a bow.

"We didn't mean to interrupt," Marianne said as she dipped a curtsy. "I was just curious as to what you may have uncovered today."

Jasper bowed. "We're still uncovering the entire scene," he replied as he waved to where James was working. "That one over there is definitely a hunting scene. Three hunters and a jaguar. Are you on your way to town?" he asked.

Marianne shook her head. "No. Just sightseeing," she replied. She indicated a basket hung over one arm. "And bringing your luncheon. Where shall I put it?"

James hurried up to take it from her. "Signorina Aurora is most kind," he said as he took the basket from Marianne. "Always seeing to our stomachs," he said with a nod in Chiara's direction. "I've a mind to marry her."

Chiara Romano narrowed her eyes. "You and every other man of your age in Sicily," she said with a grin, her gaze avoiding Dr. Jones.

"We will leave you gentlemen to your mosaics," Marianne said. Although her attention was directed at the tesserae that had been completely exposed, she wasn't wearing her spectacles and couldn't make out any of the details of the mosaics. She curtsied, as did Chiara, and the two took their leave of the dig site.

"*Y*ou looked as if you had seen a ghost when you met Dr. Jones last night," Marianne said with a quick glance back at where the men were once again crouched down under their makeshift shade. "When did you first meet him?" she asked when she was sure they were out of the men's earshot. She had watched in fascination as the two older people stared at one another, as if they couldn't believe their eyes.

They had obviously met before, and not just the night before.

Chiara allowed a sigh. "A long time ago. Before I was married," she said. "Twenty years, maybe more?"

"Here?" Marianne queried, rather surprised by Chiara's words.

"Rome, actually. I was still living with my family," Chiara replied. "I only came to Sicily because Antony brought me here. After we married. His *familia* is here, you see. Or, rather they are in Palermo now. It is why David and I have two houses to manage instead of just the one."

Marianne nodded, realizing the sprawling villa in which

they were staying had belonged to her husband's family. David had probably inherited it upon his father's death. "How did you come to meet him?"

Chiara allowed a grin. "My husband?" she clarified. At Marianne's nod, she sighed. "Antony found me. On the steps of the Forum. Crying my eyes out of my head."

Blinking at the odd comment, Marianne suddenly understood what she meant. "What had you so upset?"

Inhaling, Chiara seemed to think about how to respond before she finally let out the breath in a hiss. "A man, of course." She let out a humorless laugh. "I was young. I was in love. I was sure..." Here she stopped and sighed again. "But I was wrong. He left, you see, and my heart was broke. We had spent that day wandering the streets of Rome, visiting all the ancient sites..." She suddenly rolled her eyes, blinking as if she had to stave off tears.

"Why?" Marianne prompted.

"They were the places he took delight in visiting. He had such a... *reverence*, I think is the right word, no? For the old. For the ancient. So I went to all those places with him again, but I didn't know why."

Angling her head, Marianne realized Chiara referred to the man who had broken her heart. "What happened then?"

"Antony found me."

Marianne blinked. "Your husband?"

"*Sì*. He escorted me home in his town coach and kissed me."

"Just like that?"

Chiara displayed a brilliant smile. "I didn't even tell him why I was crying." She suddenly sobered. "I couldn't tell him everything, of course. I never did."

"You couldn't tell him about the man who broke your heart?"

"Oh, I told him just a bit about him, *sì*, but not all of it."

They walked in silence for a time, the midday sun finally

becoming warm enough so Marianne paused to remove her pelisse. "This man who broke your heart... do you think he loved you?"

Chiara turned her gaze out toward the water and then scanned the horizon until she returned her attention to Marianne. "He said so. Many times. But if he truly loved me, he would not have left me in Rome, no?"

Having read many a tale of women who had been left heartbroken by men—men who went off to war or who left to find employment—Marianne finally shook her head. "I suppose it depends on why he left."

"To go back to his country." At Marianne's look of confusion, Chiara added, "He was not Italian."

Furrowing a brow as she considered the older woman's earlier words, she said, "But he had reverence for old Roman places."

"Just as your husband does." Chiara grinned at seeing Marianne's reaction to her comment. She added, "Maybe more."

Strolling in silence for a time, Marianne wondered how different life for Chiara would have been if she had ended up with her first love. "Would you have gone with him?" Marianne asked. "If he had proposed marriage?"

"If?" Chiara repeated, one eyebrow arching up.

"Did he propose marriage? Because in England, if a man proposes marriage and then changes his mind and breaks off the betrothal, the woman is left ruined," Marianne explained in a hoarse whisper.

Chiara shook her head. "Because she has given up her virginity?"

Marianne's eyes widened. "Possibly," she hedged. "Although..." She paused, just then remembering Jasper hadn't attempted to take her virtue before their wedding. She supposed he could have. "My husband didn't even try," she murmured, disappointment suddenly apparent in her voice.

"Did yours?" She covered her mouth with a gloved hand. "I apologize," she said. "I cannot believe I even put voice to such a question!"

Chiara threw her head back and laughed. "English ladies are so proper," she said with a giggle. After a moment, she leaned her head toward Marianne. "I fear you will think the worst of me should I tell you what happened," she murmured.

Marianne paused and moved to stand in front of Chiara, stunned by her words. "I rather doubt there is anything you could say that would change my good opinion of you," she replied with a shake of her head.

Straightening, Chiara nodded. "I was *enceinte* the day Antony found me at the Forum." She quickly waved a hand and added, "I didn't know it at the time, of course, but my son was already growing inside me. A good thing, too, for Antony could never get another child on me. He loved that boy, though. I never told Antony the truth—and he never asked—but I often wondered if he knew."

Trying her best to hide her shock at Chiara's confession, Marianne wondered if David's real father knew he had a son in Sicily. "David? My husband's valet?" she asked quietly.

"*Sì*. He's a good boy. Twenty years old already," she said proudly. "Until today, when your husband introduced me to Lord Darius, I had not given his father a thought in a very long time."

Marianne frowned, remembering how her husband had introduced Darius Jones.

Dr. Jones.

He hadn't mentioned Darius' other title.

"How did you know...?" Marianne shivered as a chill suddenly ran up her spine. She inhaled slowly as she regarded the older woman, her eyes widening. "*He* was your first love," she said in a whisper, her mouth left open as she considered the ramifications.

Chiara took a deep breath and finally allowed a nod. "It's very kind of you to call him that. *First love*," she repeated with a wan smile.

Marianne nodded. What other words would she use? Chiara had said them first. "Does he know? About David?"

Shaking her head, her manner dismissive, Chiara said, "No." She rolled her eyes and displayed a grimace. "I wasn't sure at first, and then Antony was so happy to be a father. So I left the dogs to lie sleeping. Is that how you say it?"

Furrowing a brow, Marianne realized what she meant. "Let sleeping dogs lie," she replied. Glancing back to where the men continued to work under their makeshift shade, she asked, "Will you tell him? I promise I will keep your secret, of course, but..."

Chiara crossed her arms over her chest and followed Marianne's gaze. "What is your Shakespeare's phrase about bygones?"

Marianne blinked. "Let bygones be bygones?"

"That one, *sì*. In answer to your earlier question, no, he did not propose marriage," she said with a shake of her head. "He did ask me to go to England with him, though," Chiara murmured, her voice sounding far away. "But I do not think he intended for us to be married there," she added with an arched brow. "I am Catholic, you see, and he is not."

The woman's implication was clear. Darius Jones had offered her *carte blanche* to go with him when he returned to England all those years ago, and Chiara had refused him. Which was just as well, Marianne decided, for she remembered something Dr. Jones' had said just the night before.

His legitimate son, Carter, was one-and-twenty.

The archaeologist was already married when he had his *affaire* with Chiara.

Chapter 27

A FIRST LOVE'S LIGHT

*L*ater than day
Chiara saw Marianne to the door of the guest villa and was about to say her farewell when the viscountess placed a hand on her arm. "I cannot help but believe Dr. Jones still holds you in high regard. From the way he reacted when he saw you today. Perhaps...," she started to say something about second chances when she realized Chiara's manner had suddenly cooled.

Straightening, Chiara allowed a sigh. "The Lord Darius I met a long time ago was very different from that fat man back there," she replied, a note of bitterness in her voice. "Twenty years different. As am I," she added with another sigh. "I admit to some surprise that he would have recommended me to your viscount, since I would not have expected him to remember me," she explained. "Seeing him was... a shock, I think is the word."

Marianne nodded. "I suppose it would be if it's been... if it's been so long," she agreed.

"We were both much younger then. Younger and... let us say more beautiful."

Her eyes widening at the claim, Marianne said, "Oh, but I am sure you are more beautiful now."

The older woman allowed a self-deprecating grin. "You are kind to say it." She gave a glance up the lane toward the villa in which she lived before she turned her attention back to Marianne. "I will send Angela to you right away."

"Oh, there's no hurry," Marianne assured her. "I will change for dinner, of course, but otherwise there is just the laundry to be done."

"If she followed my instructions, she would have finished it this afternoon," Chiara replied. "I am determined to have her ready to manage her own household when she is old enough to marry. My brother is a solider in Palermo. With the unrest there, he does not want Angela to live with him, so that is why she is with me."

Marianne nodded her understanding. Ever since Napoleon's defeat the year before, the Kingdom of the Two Sicilies seemed determined to declare its independence. At least Ferdinand I of Spain had seen to it the Bourbons no longer ruled over the island. "It's good of you to act as her mother."

"Thank the gods my son likes her company," Chiara countered. "He spends more time with her than I do."

Marianne blinked, realizing the woman referred to Lord Darius' son. "He sounds like a good son. An obedient son," she said. Almost immediately, she realized she had said something wrong, for a flash of... something... seemed to cloud Chiara's eyes. "I apologize... it's none of my concern, of course," she added quickly.

Chiara shook her head. "He's my only child. The light of my life," she claimed. "And far more honorable than his father. But then, I raised him to be. Now if only he could find a suitable woman to be his wife," she added, almost as if she doubted he would ever marry.

One brow furrowing, Marianne gave her head a shake.

She would never have thought of Lord Darius as dishonorable, but obviously Chiara didn't hold her first love in high regard these days. "David is lucky to have you as his mother, then," she replied, just then aware they were being watched. She turned, and despite her poor vision, she knew it was Angela who stood watching them from the entrance to the guest villa's courtyard. "As is Angela," she said before giving Chiara a curtsy. "Seems my lady's maid awaits."

Chiara returned the curtsy before crossing her arms. "She can wait." She disappeared behind the door to her courtyard, not even giving a wave to her younger niece.

"What have you been doing today?" Marianne asked as she joined Angela.

"The laundry," Angela said with what sounded like pride.

Marianne nodded her understanding as they moved to her bedchamber. Stacks of folded clothes were arranged on the bed. "Dry already?"

"*Sì*," Angela replied. "Which gown will you wear tonight?"

Despite what the Sicilians claimed was a cool summer, the afternoons had been windy and warm since their arrival. Had she remained in Canobie, Marianne knew the weather wouldn't be nearly as fine, though. "The blue watered silk, I should think." She remembered how Jasper had looked, his trousers caked with dirt and his shirt sleeves rolled up to his elbows. He had eschewed a cravat in favor of a handkerchief wrapped about his neck, so with his broad-brimmed hat and waistcoat, he looked like a farmer.

Farming for mosaics.

Such an odd occupation. But having watched his careful work, the way his tightly-gloved hands worried away the dirt and debris to reveal the treasures beneath, Marianne could understand why he did it.

The thrill of discovery.

She was contemplating how much longer he might stay

235

at the site when she realized Angela was staring at her. "What is it?"

Angela's eyes darted to one side before she asked, "Are you blind, milady?"

Rather alarmed by the question—had someone mentioned her poor eyesight? Or had the girl noticed her careful steps up the road to get to the villa?—Marianne shook her head. "No. Why do you ask?"

The young girl's shoulders sagged a bit. She seemed to consider how to say her response in English before she said, "The other visitors who come from England always speak of the beautiful things they see. The temples and the night sky. But you do not. I thought maybe because you couldn't see them."

Marianne blinked, realizing Angela had sorted her situation. "It's true, I don't see very well," she acknowledged. She pulled the eyeglasses from her reticule. "But I dislike wearing these so much, I almost prefer not seeing."

Angela angled her head as she regarded the eyeglasses. She held out a hand. "May I clean them for you? Perhaps you will like wearing them if you can see through them."

Giving a chuckle, Marianne said, "Of course," as she handed them over. "Do be careful not to scratch the glass," she warned as Angela took her leave of the room. She wondered what the girl planned to use on the lenses as she examined the clean clothes. She marveled at how white the cotton and lawn fabrics appeared. Although the lady's maid she shared with her aunt in Canobie saw to their laundry, she rarely had the clothes looking so white.

When Angela returned, she proudly held out the spectacles. Marianne lifted the lenses up and dared a glance through each one, impressed at how clear the glass appeared. "What did you use?"

Angela gave a shrug as she saw to putting away the laundry. "Lemon and water. It is what Tamara uses to clean the window panes." She closed the dresser drawers and then asked, "Will you put them on? To be sure they are clean?"

Marianne hesitated, not sure she wanted the girl to see her wearing the eyeglasses. "Promise you won't laugh?"

This had Angela frowning. "I promise."

Sighing, Marianne pulled the spectacles onto her face, bending the hinged bows around to the back of her head. She didn't tie the ribbons, but merely held the loops in place at the back of her head. "I despise them," she said as she gazed down at Angela. Blinking, she gave a glance around the room, rather surprised as how much clearer everything appeared, although there was a hint of distortion at the edges of her vision.

"But can you see better?" Angela asked, a look of concern aging her appearance.

"Oh, yes. They make the edges of everything... crisp. Clear. Except for a strange curling up at the edges of my vision," she tried to explain as she slowly scanned the room.

"If I was nearly blind, I would wear them all the time," Angela said, her comment almost wistful. "I shouldn't want to miss anything. Well, except for *Signor* Loren," she amended.

Forgetting she wore the spectacles, Marianne regarded Angela for a moment. "And, who, pray tell, is Mister Loren?"

The girl rolled her eyes. "An old man who wishes me to be his *moglie*."

Marianne blinked. "Wife?" she questioned. Angela nodded before visibly shivering in disgust. "Aren't you a bit young to be... *sposato?*"

"*Sì!*" And then Angela giggled before she suddenly sobered. "My aunt married when she was but seventeen. She had her son the next year. I don't want to be a *madre* so soon."

Thinking she could be a mother within a year—it was possible she was already with child—Marianne realized she was nearly twelve years older than Angela. "Twelve years ago, I did not want to be a mother, either. But now... now I *want* a child," she said in a quiet voice.

"Then you must spend your nights *fare l'amore*," Angela said with a grin. "I will get your gown, and we will make you *irresistibile*."

Marianne couldn't help the blush that colored her face just then. A fourteen-year old girl was telling her she had to spend her nights making love.

As if she wasn't already.

An hour later, after Angela had her dressed in the blue watered silk and pinned up her hair in a riot of curls, a long look in the dressing table mirror had her realizing what Angela meant. Even wearing her spectacles, she looked irresistible.

She hoped Jasper would think so, too.

Chapter 28

THE ROMAN ARTS REVEALED

*I*n the middle of the night
         The feather light touch brought Jasper out of a dream he had been desperate to leave. One in which an ancient monster seemed intent on taking his life. And that of Marianne's. Instead of opening his eyes, though, he concentrated on what was touching him.

Finger tips.

Traveling over the crisp curls on his chest, they sent tiny shockwaves beneath his skin, shockwaves that soon had his entire body giving a shudder.

The touch was gone then, and he finally opened his eyes to find Marianne staring at his chest. "Good morning, Viscountess," he murmured, a grin forming as he took in her sleep-tousled hair and bright blue eyes.

She turned those eyes on him then, their expression betraying shock, as if she'd been caught doing something she shouldn't have been. "Good morning, my lord," she whispered. Her attempt at rolling away from him was preempted by the arm that had wrapped around her shoulders to hold her in place.

"You can call me Jasper, my sweeting," he whispered before he bestowed a kiss on her nose.

Marianne allowed a tentative grin before she suddenly sobered. "I didn't mean to wake you."

"I'm rather glad you did," Jasper replied, kissing her cheek. "I'm afraid my last dream was more of a nightmare."

Her brows furrowing, Marianne simply stared at him a moment, finally realizing that if she were to learn what terrors his nightmare featured, she would have to ask. "Was I in it?"

Jasper inhaled slowly, not sure he wanted to capture the last tendrils of the scene in which a fire-breathing dragon had singed his backside. "I think so, although I don't remember much more than the dragon."

Her eyes widening, Marianne regarded him a moment. "Did you escape?"

"I did," he replied with a nod. He kissed her on the mouth then, rather pleased at how she seemed both surprised and pleased by the intimacy. The feel of her body so thoroughly pressed against his reminded him of the night before, and desire slammed into him. He was already aroused, but then he usually was when he awoke. "You saved me. You were wearing that blue gown you were wearing last night," he added before moving his kisses down her cheek and to her ear. He captured the plump earlobe between his teeth and gently nibbled, grinning when her entire body stiffened and she inhaled sharply. "And then you captured me."

Marianne sighed when he finally lifted his body over hers and entered her, his movements slow. Within a few minutes though, her release took them both into ecstasy, and then she fell back asleep.

*W*hen Chiara appeared at the guest villa door only a few hours later, Marianne was dressed and ready for another walk about the ruins.

"I am glad you are not wearing your best," Chiara said when she noticed Marianne wore a simple round gown, the handle of a basket filled with luncheon items threaded over one arm.

"Oh?" The younger woman held out the edge of her skirt, realizing it was one of her old gowns—one from before she was married. "What are we doing today?"

"I think I have accidentally discovered what your viscount searches for," Chiara replied as they made their way down the lane toward the Greco-Roman quarter.

"A mosaic?" Marianne asked, her excitement evident. "A complete one?"

Chiara shrugged. She carried with her a basket with a small whisk broom made from corn husks and two gardening shovels. "Just a hint of one. I have walked by it every day for years on my way to San Nicola," she explained as they made their way along the familiar path. "But yesterday, I finally looked at it with… new eyes, I think is the expression."

She stopped quite suddenly after they turned toward the church, the well-worn dirt path passing by a flattened area near where Marianne had been seated when she read her book only the week before. "You saw tiles?" Marianne asked.

"Indeed. Right here," Chiara said as she pointed to the ground. A row of cream-colored tiles were visible in the dark dirt, as if a channel of water had eroded away the top layers of soil. "Shall we see if we can do better than the men?"

Marianne gave her a brilliant smile, helped herself to a small shovel, and lowered herself to her knees.

The two worked in companionable silence for the rest of the morning, loosening dirt and brushing it away to reveal a series of small designs. By the time the sun was overhead,

Marianne remembered she still had the basket for the men's lunch. "I should take this to my husband," she said, as she struggled to get to her feet. She had leaned on one leg so long while she worked, it had nearly fallen asleep. The pins and needles sensation had her wincing almost as much as she did when she saw what they had uncovered. "Oh, my," she breathed.

Despite her age, Chiara was on her feet far more quickly, her head angling this way and that as she attempted to determine which way was "up" in the mosaic designs. She allowed a laugh at the mosaics below. "I think we found the floor of a brothel," she said with a giggle. "Or a horny man's bedchamber."

Marianne furrowed her brows. "What are they depicting?" she asked. She stepped around to the other side, blushing when she realized the four designs were all positions of sexual congress. None of these had been depicted in the French book her aunt had loaned her, though. These had several people engaged in... well, she wasn't really sure what they were doing as the designs weren't terribly intricate, and some tiles were missing, and one of the men wasn't really where she would expect him to be with respect to the woman who was beneath him, and there was another man doing something with the first man. "What is this?" she asked in a whisper.

"An orgy," Chiara said with amusement, before she finally sobered. "Probably one of the reasons Rome fell," she added as she shook out her skirts. "Come, let us deliver your basket to the men. They will be wondering what's become of you and their food."

Marianne gave one last look at the mosaics before lifting the basket and joining Chiara on the path to the temple floor. "Was that common, do you suppose?" she asked. "To have more than just a husband engaged thus?"

Chiara allowed a shrug. "Some men have insatiable

appetites. Why have just one woman when they can have two or more pleasuring them at the same time?"

"I thought there were two men and only one woman," Marianne countered, wondering if she had completely misinterpreted the designs.

Laughing again, Chiara allowed a shrug. "What is good for the goose is good for the gander, no?"

Marianne couldn't begin to think of a suitable response, so she was relieved when they were suddenly at the edge of her husband's most recent excavation. A large swath of ground had been removed to reveal a giant mosaic, one that Jasper and James were both studying from where they stood off to one side. They appeared to be arguing until they noticed the women's arrival.

"Finally!" Jasper said as he hurried up to Marianne and bussed her on the cheek. He gave a bow to the ladies. "We're famished, and we have good reason to be." He held out an arm and swept it through the air. "Look what we've uncovered today." He helped himself to the basket as James joined them, bowing to the ladies before he angled his head.

"Did you have an accident?" James asked when he noticed their dirt-stained gowns.

Marianne gave a start and used a gloved hand to swipe at the ground-in dirt staining her skirts. "We've been doing some excavating of our own," she replied, her gaze taking in the patterns in the mosaics the men had been working to reveal. "Is that Poseidon?" she asked. She noted that all the smaller mosaics surrounding a trident-carrying man were of sea creatures and shells. The tiles were all cream, black or rust in color.

"Neptune," Jasper replied, rather impressed his wife had been able to visualize the god of the sea, especially since so many of the small tesserae were missing from the overall design. "It's most definitely Roman," he announced proudly. After a pause, he regarded the two women with a furrowed brow. "Were you planting a garden?" he asked then, noting the tools in Chiara's basket.

Marianne exchanged glances with Chiara. "We uncovered some mosaics up by the path to San Nicola," she replied. She dipped her head. "Chiara saw what looked like what you have been cleaning, so we started to do the same as you were doing. The dirt brushed away easily. I had several tiles uncovered in only a few minutes."

"You did?" Incredulous, Jasper furrowed a brow. "Where? Were they... intact?"

Dipping her head again, Marianne gave a shrug. "Just up by the path to the church. On the other side of that row of olive trees," she said as she pointed up the hill.

Jasper frowned. "How...?"

"I noticed some tiles in the ground next to the path. Your wife was kind enough to help me expose them," Chiara explained, thinking Jasper was about to chide his wife for attempting to do what he was there to accomplish. "As I expected, they are not from a wealthy villa or a temple."

James paused in his perusal of the food basket, a wedge of cheese gripped in one hand. "Could you make out the design?" he asked, his curiosity apparent. "Was there a signature?"

The two women exchanged glances. "I'm quite sure I didn't see a signature, but they are not large like this one," Marianne replied. "Rather small, really, and of no consequence."

Continuing to frown, Jasper wondered why his wife seemed so hesitant. "Will you show me?" he asked, ready to leave his own discovery to determine what had her so nervous.

Allowing a sigh, Marianne finally said, "Of course." She placed a hand on Jasper's proffered arm and dared a glance back at James and Chiara, surprised to find them directly behind them.

"I'm just as curious," James said then. "Why, from the way you're blushing, I'm of a mind to think you've discovered the site of an old brothel," he accused with a hint of humor.

"You have the right of it," Chiara said as she walked next to the younger archaeologist.

"I do?" James replied, obviously surprised he had guessed correctly.

Jasper dared a glance over at Marianne, understanding why she seemed so embarrassed. And then they were suddenly standing next to the find, the four distinct patterns clearly depicting people engaged in the "Roman arts."

Many people.

He glanced around the area, rather surprised to discover there was only one hint of a foundation block—the stone on which Marianne had been sitting to read a book—and a faint flatness to the land around them compared to the adjacent path that led to the church. A row of olive trees lined one side of the flat area. "I admit to a bit of shock that a brothel could be found so close to a church," he managed to get out as he placed his hands on his hips and studied the surrounding land.

"Indeed," James said as he walked what he thought might have been the perimeter of the building. "Ah, here's some of the foundation," he said as he discovered the tops of some stone blocks barely visible in the ground. He continued to walk, backtracking a bit when he realized he had missed a turn. "And some more," he announced triumphantly before he made another turn. The single stone block turned out to be a corner stone. "Now the question is, how do we preserve it?"

"Cover it over," Jasper said with a shrug.

At James' look of disbelief, Jasper pointed toward the

church. "Do you really think it's wise to leave these exposed? So close to the church?" he asked.

"We're going to document them before we do so," James argued. "This is an important find! And it's Roman."

Jasper finally nodded. "Agreed. But any further work will have to wait until we're finished with the other one," he reminded his colleague. "Let's hope no one is scandalized in the meantime."

He was quite sure his wife was already scandalized.

As for Chiara, she merely seemed amused by it all.

Chapter 29

A FORMER LOVER FOCUSES
ON THE FUTURE

*L*ater that afternoon
       The sun dipped behind behind the trees as Chiara made her way back to her villa from the church, her strides long through the deepening shadows. She was nearly to the entrance to her villa's courtyard when she realized someone walked behind her. A thought that Angela might have already been dismissed by Lady Henley was soon replaced with the realization that the steps were far too loud and too far apart to be those of the girl.

Chiara dared a glance over one shoulder, a bit concerned when she didn't see anyone behind her. She turned in the other direction and nearly let out a yelp.

"Don't scream, I beg you."

She took a step back, rather stunned to find Darius Jones regarding her from only a few feet away. A quick glance down the lane proved they were the only ones about. "I should make you give me a reason," she replied, annoyed the archaeologist would follow her to her home.

"I wished to a have word," Darius said as he gave a bow. He was about to reach for her hand, but Chiara took another step back.

"There is nothing to say," she replied in a voice tinged with anger.

Darius recoiled as if he had been hit. "Then would you allow me to simply look upon you? I have an appreciation for beautiful things, you see..."

He later realized he really should have taken Chiara at her word. Should have bowed and taken his leave of her. But Darius was determined to renew his acquaintance with the woman from his past.

The best part of his last trip to Italy. The reason he had agreed to join Lord Henley this season.

He didn't notice how her right arm straightened, nor how her hand closed into a tight fist, or how her body tensed until that arm suddenly swung around and her fist impacted his cheek with a force he hadn't felt since his last bare-knuckle match at Cambridge. A force that sent him sprawling to the dirt below.

Chiara's hands were suddenly covering her mouth as she stared at Darius' prone body. "Oh!" she gasped, daring a glance toward the villa and another down the hill to determine if anyone had paid witness to what she had done. A lone figure was on the road, but she couldn't make out who it might be. Shaking out her right hand, Chiara felt annoyance at the pain that radiated up her arm.

"Ow!"

The delayed complaint had her turning her attention back to Darius. He placed a hand against the side of his face, grimacing as he raised his eyes to regard her in shock.

"Ow," he said again, blinking before he displayed a huge grin. He winced in the middle of it though. "How is it you are still so *bellissimo?*" he asked in a quiet voice.

Chiara blinked as she stared down at him. Despite his sweat-soaked dirty clothes and the twenty years of what appeared to be days spent out-of-doors and nights spent carousing, her belly did a flip. A memory of nights long ago had her breasts growing heavy. A frisson passed through her entire body, and she cursed in Italian as her hands went to her hips. "Damn you, Darius Jones," she cursed.

From where he lay on the ground looking up at his first and only love, Darius allowed a sigh. "God, I've missed you."

Frowning, Chiara continued to glare at him for a moment. "I thought to knock some sense into you, but I see I have only made you worse," she said in response. She held out a hand and Darius eyed it, as if he expected it might strike him again. He finally gripped it and struggled to stand as she jerked on it.

"*Grazie*," he said as he straightened. He regarded her for a moment before saying, "I deserved that. I will always regret having left you all those years ago."

Blinking at the unexpected words, Chiara frowned before her chin lifted in defiance. "Then, why did you?"

Darius dipped his head and then glanced toward her villa. "May I tell you over a glass of wine?" he asked hopefully.

"No," Chiara replied before she turned and disappeared behind the door to the villa. The sound of a bolt being thrown made its way to Darius, and he knew his opportunity to make amends was not to be.

At least, not on this night.

*U*pon seeing Jasper Henley make his way up the hill from the Greco-Roman quarter, David hurried to the kitchen in the *familia* villa. A kitchen maid armed David with one of the ever-present pails of hot water from the stove. Despite the protests of the household laundress, he helped himself to a stack of newly-washed bath linens and made his way out of the villa.

He was nearly to the courtyard door when he heard a man's voice beyond. A voice he didn't recognize, speaking in English. *Then would you allow me to simply look upon you? I have an appreciation for beautiful things, you see.* David winced and sucked air through his teeth even before he heard the resulting commotion and the man's loud "ow!"

His mother would never allow a man to speak to her using such flowery language. She rarely allowed men to speak with her at all, except perhaps the butcher, and then only because she needed his meat for their dinner table.

Daring a peek through the space between the gate and the courtyard wall, he watched as his mother lifted her hands to her hips and cursed the culprit.

David blinked when he recognized the older man lying in the dirt. Dr. Jones, he was sure, an archaeologist who was employing some of his boyhood friends to excavate the ancient aqueduct in the Greco-Roman quarter.

Despite having knocked the man to the ground, his mother helped him to his feet before shaking out her injured hand. Quiet words were exchanged—he could only make out *I deserved that. I will always regret having left you all those years ago*—but he could tell from his mother's stance that she was angry with the archaeologist.

There was a moment when he thought Dr. Jones was going to kiss his mother, and she almost looked as if she would allow him to do so. But at his query about a glass of wine, she was suddenly at the gate.

Stepping back to avoid being hit by the heavy wooden door, David held his breath as his mother flung open the gate, passed through the opening, slammed it shut, and threw the bolt before stalking into the house. In her anger and haste, she didn't even seem to notice him standing beyond the hinges.

*H*is shoulders slumping, Darius turned and started to make his way back down the hill when he realized Jasper Henley was watching him from the entrance to the guest villa. "The show is over," he called out.

Jasper shook his head. "Then why does it appear as if it's only just beginning?" he countered with an arched brow.

Darius allowed a sigh when he was abreast of the viscount. "Because it is a long story?" he offered.

Nodding, Jasper waved to the courtyard door of the guest villa. "One you could share with me over dinner," he said by way of invitation. He had paid witness to his wife's companion walloping the man and wondered what Darius had said to deserve such a response. Having paid witness to how the two reacted to one another the first day they saw each other, and then when they were introduced the night before, he sorted they must have known each other in the past.

And not just socially.

Considering his colleague's words for a moment, Darius finally allowed a nod of his own. "As long as I'm allowed to clean up. I forgot how filthy I get here in the Mediterranean," he complained.

"Agreed," Jasper said with a chuckle, his head ducking to take in his own dirt-smudged trousers and sweat-streaked shirtsleeves. "Come. My valet can see to some hot water and a change of clothes."

The two made their way into the guest villa, their noses lifting into the air as the scents of roasting meat and garlic assaulted them. "Oh, how I've missed this," Darius said as they made their way to the master suite. "I've a mind to take this cook back to Hexham with me."

Not having let a house with a cook the last time he was in Italy—he had simply taken a room at an inn—Jasper wondered at how many times Darius had done so. "Where did you stay before? When you were in Rome?" he asked as he made his way to the pitcher and bowl of water.

Since Signora Romano claimed no knowledge of Dr. Jones, he had wondered how the older archaeologist knew to recommend her villa. Now that it was apparent they had known one another—Darius had mentioned Rome to the woman the day before—Jasper was beginning to piece together their past.

"With *whom*, would be a better question," Darius replied, pulling his shirt from his body.

David appeared with a stack of bath linens and a pail of water, his gaze darting between Jasper and Darius. Having paid witness to his mother's assault on the larger man through the edge of the wooden gate, and having heard Dr. Jones' odd response, he hoped the two would simply ignore him so that he might learn more of his mother's past with the man.

Darius angled his head. "*Il tuo tempismo è perfetto,*" he said. *Your timing is perfect.* He helped himself to a bath linen and scrubbed the sweat from his chest and arms.

Giving the older man a nod, David murmured in Italian, "I'll see to another bowl of water."

He made his way into the bathing chamber and listened as Dr. Jones said, "There was a reason I recommended Signora Romano's guest villa."

When David reappeared with another bowl of water, Darius leaned over the bowl and splashed water on his face. He took another linen from the valet and wiped his face. "*Grazie.*"

"And I believe she was ever so grateful for the opportunity," Jasper replied in a teasing voice. "Let me guess. You loved her, and you left her," he accused as he finished his ablutions and moved to the chest of drawers. He cursed under his breath, just then remembering David was in the room.

In the room and able to understand English.

He tossed a clean shirt to Darius and sighed when he figured David was probably listening to their every word. He couldn't blame the young man, though. His ears had probably perked up at hearing the mention of his mother.

Darius pulled on the shirt and gave a nod to David. "*Lasciaci, per favore*," he said. *Leave us, please.*

Hiding his disappointment, David gave a nod and left the bedchamber.

Jasper collected more fresh clothes from his trunk and stood up. "You just dismissed my valet," he complained. "That's her son, David, by the way."

"You can dress yourself," Darius said, his brows furrowing as he glanced back at the door, as if he regretted having sent the servant away. "I can't believe you thought to hire a valet whilst you're on a dig."

About to add to his complaint—Darius was dripping water all over the bedchamber's tiled floor—Jasper regarded his guest for a moment before he nodded. "I felt the need to keep up appearances, given I've brought my wife along," he explained. "She's never been away from British shores, and I shouldn't want her to think I've brought her to a land of savages." He paused a moment. "Besides, Signora Romano offered to be her companion."

Darius gave a snort. "Sicilians are hardly savages," he countered. "More civilized than half of those in London," he added as he held up his filthy shirt. "What else did she offer?"

Frowning at the odd query, Jasper gave a shrug. "David as my valet. Here," he added as he tossed Darius a cravat from the chest of drawers. "I expect to get it back." He reached for another and shook it out. "I suppose if you're familiar with Signora Romano, you're familiar with the other servants here as well?"

Pulling the shirt over his head, Darius disappeared from view for a moment. When his head popped through the neckline, he shook it. "No. I just... when I got here a couple of months ago, I asked someone I knew down at the marina about her. He told me she had an empty villa—her late husband owned half the hillside—so that's when I wrote to you. I had mentioned to some of the locals that one of my colleagues would be in need of a place to stay. It's been over twenty years since I was in Rome, remember, and I was only here on Sicily for a few weeks. Just to see what work there might be to do."

Furrowing a brow, Jasper regarded Darius as he continued to dress. "So... it's been over twenty years since you last saw her?"

Darius allowed a shrug as he regarded his waistcoat. Jasper tossed him one, but Darius tossed it back. "Indeed, and I haven't been able to wear anything that small since I was last in Italy," he said with a nod to the embroidered waistcoat that had landed in a heap on the bed.

"I don't have any others," Jasper replied as he reached out and took the waistcoat for himself.

"I'll make do," Darius said, turning to regard his reflection in the room's only looking glass. He gave a start at what he saw, nearly cursing. *No wonder Chiara reacted like she did. I look terrible!* he thought. His hair was plastered to his scalp from having worn a wide-brimmed hat all day. A five o'clock shadow darkened his jawline. The barest suggestion of a belly showed behind his shirt.

Chiara probably thought me a rogue! he pondered in dismay. The way her body had jerked just a bit as she glared down at him was probably a sign of disgust. The way she had inhaled and held her breath was probably because she couldn't stand the stench of him. And the moment her entire body seemed to shiver despite the late afternoon warmth? *Probably revulsion*, he thought in despair.

"You look as if you've lost your best friend," Jasper commented, forcing Darius from his reverie.

"I certainly feel as if I have," the older man replied. He tore his gaze from the looking glass and regarded Jasper for a moment, rather surprised to find him fully dressed for dinner. Even his cravat was already tied in a simple knot, although it hadn't yet been decorated with a pin. "Don't ever leave the woman you love, Henley. Not for duty. Not for king or country. And certainly not for another woman," Darius stated in no uncertain terms. "Even if she is your wife."

Jasper regarded Darius for a long while, rather stunned at hearing the man's words. What the hell had happened in Darius' past to have him saying such a thing? *Even if she's your wife* implied Darius was already married when he met the love of his life.

Given how close he and Marianne had become in their short marriage, at least at night, Jasper couldn't fathom ever leaving her. Although he had left Sophie for a time—about a month while he was in Bath to study some mosaics at the Roman baths there—he had given her the option of traveling with him. She had declined in favor of staying in Kent.

"Thank you for the advice," Jasper finally said, almost making it a question. "Now, to be sure my wife doesn't leave *me*, we really need to be making our way to the dining room."

Darius gave a nod and quickly finished dressing.

*O*n the other side of the dressing room door, Marianne wondered at the words she had just overheard. She had been about to knock, thinking her husband was with his valet when she realized the other voice she heard belonged to Lord Darius. *Even if she is your wife* had been followed by Jasper's *thank you for the advice*.

What had the older man been saying about her? *Even if she is your wife* implied her husband should be doing something contrary. Was he suggesting Jasper take a mistress? Go to a brothel? She was quite sure the older man had been doing just that every night since his arrival on the island.

A bit heartsick, Marianne made her way to the dining room and did her best to hide her renewed insecurities.

Chapter 30

A NEW LOVER FOCUSES ON
THE PAST

M eanwhile
      "Forgive me. I did not mean to startle you," David said with a bow when James appeared at his bedchamber door. He had brought the rest of the bath linens to James' room and was folding the man's newly-ironed laundry.

James gave a shake of his head and closed the door. "You didn't," he countered. His gaze went to the laundry, and a grin appeared. "I appreciate you seeing to my clothes. I haven't had the benefit of a valet in a very long time," he added.

"There is hot water for you," David said as he indicated the pail near the pitcher and bowl. "I can bring more, and a tub, should you wish to bathe."

His gaze intent on how David held his clothes, on how he carefully folded each piece, on how he placed each item just so in the wooden drawers, James fought the urge to touch the younger man. "I would like that, but... later. After dinner. Will that be too late?"

David gave a shake of his head. "Not at all." He finished putting away the clothes and straightened. He couldn't help but notice that the archaeologist hadn't yet moved to wash or remove his sweat-soaked shirt. "Would you like help with your buttons?"

Inhaling slowly, James nodded his head. "I... I would." He let the breath out and struggled to keep his hands from reaching for the younger man as David stepped up to undo the waistcoat buttons. "Have you already seen to Lord Henley this evening?"

David nodded as he pulled the waistcoat from James' arms. "Dr. Jones dismissed me before I could assist the viscount."

James frowned. "Why would he do such a thing?"

Undoing the crushed cravat from around James' neck, David considered how to answer. "They were speaking of my mother, and I believe he wanted to do so without me hearing what he had to say." The words were said without emotion as he continued to unwind the length of lawn until it came free.

Remembering Lord Darius' reaction to Signora Romano's appearance earlier that day, James lifted a brow. "Dr. Jones is the one who recommended this villa to Lord Henley," James said with a shake of his head. "How long has he known Signora Romano?" he asked as he pulled the shirt from his body. He moved to the bed and sat down. When he lifted a foot to remove the boot, David was quick to kneel before him and take over the task.

"For more than twenty years, if what he said is true," David replied, his brows suddenly furrowing. "Back when my mother lived in Rome." He managed to get the boot off and began pulling off the other, his eyes darting to the bare chest level with his gaze.

"Twenty years?" James repeated, just as the second boot came free. David had his stockings peeled off his feet a few seconds later. "She must have been very young."

David sat back on his haunches, staring at James with a combination of awe and confusion. "She is eight-and-thirty, I think," he managed, as he admired the man's chest. A dusting of blond curls was barely visible against the pale skin.

James gave a shrug. "So she married rather young," he commented. "Seventeen? Eighteen? How old are you?"

"Twenty."

Blinking, James regarded the younger man a moment, wondering why he suddenly looked so stricken. All he could think about was taking him into his arms. Holding him. Providing comfort. For he was sure David was on the verge of tears.

"What is it?" he asked in a whisper. He lowered himself from the bed and knelt on the floor in front of David, his arms wrapping around the young man's shoulders until David's face was pressed against a bare shoulder. A moment later, and David's arms were around James' back. "Pray tell, what is wrong?"

David shook with a sob as he fought back tears. "I do not believe I am my father's son," he whispered.

Frowning at the implication of his words, James countered with, "But, you're not a bastard." He felt David's head give a slight shake against his shoulder, his silken hair tickling his bare skin.

"Worse," David said, his hoarse whisper barely understandable.

James moved a hand to the back of David's head, his fingers spearing the black waves as he pulled the younger man closer. "What could be worse than being a bastard?" he whispered.

David stiffened before he finally gave into James' hold. "I think Dr. Jones is my father."

Holding his breath a moment, as if he couldn't believe what he had just heard, James wondered how to respond and found he couldn't.

What could he say?

He couldn't deny the possibility, nor could he confirm

the younger man's suspicion. So he simply held David for a time. When the younger man finally pulled away, his eyes were red.

"I apologize, Mr. Singleton," David started to say. But James held a staying finger against the valet's lips and then replaced it with his own. The kiss, barely there and lasting but a second, confirmed what he had suspected but dared not speak of.

Their foreheads left pressed against one another, they finally lifted their gazes until they were staring at one another. James was the first to break the silence. "I have to get dressed. They'll wonder where I am if I don't join them for dinner," he said quietly. "Come to me tonight, when you have finished with Lord Henley," he murmured. "That is, if you'll allow me to hold you for a time."

David nodded. "I will come. With the tub and water," he replied. "But first, I will dress you."

Rising to his feet, James offered a hand and helped David to his feet. Fifteen minutes later, James joined Lord and Lady Henley and Lord Darius in the dining room.

It was the longest dinner of his entire life.

Chapter 31

SIGHTSEEING NEARLY LEADS
TO A FALL

a *week later*
     "Do you suppose I could come with you today?"

About to pull on a pair of trousers, Jasper turned around. He was surprised to see Marianne sitting up, her sleep tousled curls wild about her face. He was sure he hadn't disturbed her from her slumber when he left the bed. "Of course. If you're sure you won't be too bored," he replied before moving to the pitcher and bowl. He smeared shaving soap over his cheeks and chin and lifted a straight razor from the dressing table.

"What will happen to all the mosaics?" Marianne asked as she speared her fingers through her hair in an attempt to smooth her curls. When the men had all the dirt swept away, four distinct mosaics made themselves evident, although only three were mostly intact, their tesserae still in place.

"The one of the hunting scene and the small one of the seashell have already been removed to a flat crate for transport to Palermo," Jasper said with a hint of sadness. "As for the two smaller ones..." He had to grin at the thought of the two simple seashells outlined in rust tiles. "I think I shall see to them myself. Take one of them back to England for the museum."

Marianne grinned as well. The pair of matching mosaics had probably been part of the floor of a bathing chamber, although James had first thought their shape something entirely different from what finally emerged. "So you will start a new house today?"

Jasper shook his head, his gaze on his reflection in a mirror as he shaved. "Singleton said he'll be going into town. Our valet has agreed to give him a tour. Since we're finished with the first excavation, he wants to see the ruins up there before we start work on another."

The two younger men had become fast friends since the week before, David's interest in James' studies leading to long nights spent discussing a variety of topics in the villa's drawing room. Despite his role as valet to Signora Romano's guests, David was at least as educated as Singleton, his barely accented English occasionally drifting to her bedchamber whilst Angela helped her undress for bed. Although she had pretended not to notice, Marianne was quite sure she had seen them holding hands whilst they discussed the architecture of a cathedral in one of Singleton's books that lay open across their laps.

"I'll bring a book and my sewing basket," Marianne said to Jasper, as she moved to get down from the bed.

The appearance of her nude body in the dim light of a single candle lamp forced Jasper to tamp down his morning tumescence. "If you come with me this morning, who will bring me my late breakfast?" he teased in a quiet voice as he set aside the razor and rubbed his face with a linen.

"I will. Aurora made up a basket for me last night," she whispered.

The odd tug in his chest was suddenly evident, and Jasper gathered Marianne into his arms. "That was kind of her," he said as he bussed her on the cheek. "And rather kind of you, as well. Tell me, how did I get so lucky to marry such a good wife?"

Marianne blinked, her gaze searching his for evidence he was teasing. "I suppose if you kiss enough women in the presence of Cupid, you're bound to get lucky with one of them," she said, her words spoken in a manner far too serious just then.

Jasper blinked. "You were only the second, I promise," he said, his brows furrowing. "And the last, I hope."

Marianne inhaled sharply, reminded of his conversation with Lord Darius the week before. The one she had overhead from the other side of the door. "The other night—when Lord Darius was here—what did he mean when he said, 'even if she is your wife'?"

Straightening, his hold on her suddenly gone, Jasper gave a shake of his head. He then realized why she had been so distant that evening during dinner. Why she had been especially cool towards the older archaeologist despite the warm greeting she had afforded him the first day he made his presence known. She had only spoken when asked a question, and then she spent most of the dinner lost in thought. Later, it had taken him longer than usual to coax her into readiness for his manhood. Longer for her to succumb to his ministrations and even longer to join him in ecstasy.

"He was warning me that I should never leave the woman I love for another," he whispered, well aware Marianne was ready to bolt from the room. "Even if she is my wife." He wrapped an arm around the small of her back, effectively preventing her from escaping. Given her sudden start beneath his hold, he was glad he had anticipated what she was about to do. "Apparently, he did so, and has regretted it ever since. But since I am in love with my wife, I have no intention of ever leaving her," he said as he pulled her closer.

His lips were on hers before she could respond, the kiss as punishing as it was passionate. When he finally pulled away, mostly because he had to take a breath, he touched his forehead to hers. "I do not for a moment regret what happened to make you my viscountess. In fact, I am rather hoping to discover a heretofore unknown statue of Cupid I might take home and display in the back gardens, so I can kiss you in his presence whenever I am so moved."

"You're in love with me?" Marianne asked in a whisper, ignoring the comment about Cupid.

Jasper blinked. "You needn't make it sound as if you're surprised," he countered. "Surely, you..." He paused, his shoulders slumping. "Had some idea," he finished with a sigh.

Marianne was suddenly pressed hard against the front of his body, her arms wrapped around his shoulders and her lips on his. When she pulled away, she struggled to catch her breath before saying, "I hoped, of course, but you never..." She let out a yelp of surprise when she was suddenly being carried to the bed.

"Said it?" he finished for her. "Are words really necessary given my nightly worship of your most beautiful body?" he murmured before he settled her onto the mussed bed linens.

"Well..." she started to respond, the rest of her response swallowed by another kiss as one finger traced his clean-shaven jawline.

"I apologize if it seems as if I haven't done enough to convince you, my sweeting," he said in a quiet voice, just before he impaled her in a single thrust. His growl filled the bedchamber when ecstasy overwhelmed him, his body slumping atop hers after only a few moments.

As Marianne lay mewling beneath him, tears pricking the corners of her eyes in a combination of relief and happiness, she still wondered at Lord Darius' words. For if he hadn't been discussing *her* when he said them, who was he talking about?

*J*asper considered spending the day indoors—spending it in bed with Marianne—but curiosity about the floor of a ruined temple had him finally departing their nest of mussed linens and counterpane. Although he expected Marianne would stay abed, she soon made her way to her bedchamber to get dressed. When she returned, she presented her back to him and asked if he might do up her buttons.

His lips took purchase on her neck before his fingers fumbled with the fastenings. "I'll be exploring a different site today. Lord Darius says he is quite sure there are the remains of a temple with a tiled floor in an area near the ridge. A bit farther walk for us, but—"

"I don't mind," Marianne said as she turned to face him. "Perhaps Singleton will share what he discovers in town at dinner tonight. Although Chiara showed me around a bit, we didn't begin to see everything."

Jasper angled his head. "Or we might go exploring another day and find out for ourselves," he suggested.

"Is everything... all right between the two of you?" she asked carefully.

"I think so," he replied, despite the twinge of annoyance he felt at not having been invited by Singleton to join him and David on their sojourn to Girgenti. "I do think he's had a bit too much sun." He wasn't about to add that he was fairly sure James had taken a lover. Jasper had never seen the man more content. Happy, even.

As for whom he had taken as a lover, Jasper sorted it had to be someone close, because he was sure James wasn't spending his nights down at the marina or up in Girgenti. He was also fairly sure he knew who it was. He just hoped the young man was truly willing and of a similar mind, and not because he was being paid to warm Singleton's bed.

a few hours later
Jasper studied the odd carving, frowning when he realized the stone he had lifted from the volcanic soil had suffered a break at some point. Digging a bit deeper, he was about to pull out what he hoped was the adjacent piece when he noticed movement from the corner of his eye.

Lifting his head, he allowed a grin as he watched Marianne gaze out toward the sea. Her parasol cast her head in shadow, but her yellow muslin gown appeared almost white in the harsh sunlight. About to return his attention to the carved stone, he realized she was strolling far too close to the cliff's edge.

Then he remembered she had refused to wear her spectacles that day, tucking them into her pocket when he started his excavation project. She seemed oblivious to the ground beneath her.

The lack of ground only inches away.

Panic gripped Jasper, but he had his feet beneath him and was launching himself from the ground just as one of Marianne's half-booted feet was about to step over the edge. He had an arm around her waist just as a rock gave way and bounced down the rocky slope. About to stumble, she let out a squeak before she was suddenly thrown sideways and down to the ground by the force of his arm. The parasol tumbled down alongside her, it's handle still attached to her wrist by a leather strap. Jasper landed next to her, although he quickly pulled her atop him in an effort to get her away from the cliff's edge.

Marianne blinked as she stared down at him, her bonnet toppling from her head. "Oh!" she managed, her breath held despite her astonishment. And then her brow furrowed as she realized his face displayed anger.

Aimed at her.

"Christ, Marianne! You could have been killed!" he

shouted as he placed his hands at her waist and lifted her from atop him. Her legs akimbo and her gown nearly up to her knees, Marianne struggled to sit up. "What were you thinking?" he asked as he finally regained his feet, wincing when he realized he had skinned an elbow. His shirt sleeve had torn, and blood from the wound was already staining the fabric.

Marianne gave a start at hearing his curse and jerked again when she was close enough to make out that he was bleeding. Glancing around where she had been dumped from atop his body, she struggled to understand just why he had pushed her to the ground.

"What...what happened?" she managed to get out, wincing when she noticed a tear in the fabric of her gown. Her face screwed up when she heard his curse again. Tears pricked the corners of her eyes as she attempted to look in his direction, pain radiating from her arm from where she had landed on the hard ground. Her limited vision coupled with the glare of the sun made it appear as if he was a silhouette bobbing about against a sea of blue.

"Put on your spectacles right this minute, dammit," he shouted.

His hands were suddenly at her waist again, lifting her from the ground until she barely had her feet beneath her. Trembling in fear, she felt for the pair of eyeglasses and pulled them from her pocket, wincing in pain when she realized she had hurt the back of her gloved hand when she was thrown to the ground. The parasol still dangled from her wrist, and she struggled to get the strap off so that she could open the folded spectacles.

Jasper pulled them from her grasp, opening them and then placing them onto her face in a less than gentle manner. He had his hands at her waist again, forcibly turning her body until she faced the cliff's edge where she had been walking.

One side of her body ended up pressed against the front of his, and through his light shirt, she could tell his body quaked, could feel his racing pulse, and hear his ragged breaths. Given his curse and how he held her and the expression she could make out in great detail, she thought him angry. Very angry.

Suddenly fearful, she attempted to leave his hold—until one of his arms lifted parallel to the ground and he pointed out to the sea. "You nearly walked over the edge of the cliff," he yelled. "Jesus, Marianne, you would have *died*," he added, his voice still raised.

Tears poured from Marianne's eyes, the droplets collecting in the bottom edge of her lenses so that she could barely see anything. Her fright, as much to do with his yelling at her as from having been thrown to the ground, had her entire body shivering. And then she was suddenly facing him, pulled hard against the front of his body, his arms like steel bands wrapped around her shoulders and waist.

"Oh, Christ. I apologize, my sweeting," he murmured as he struggled to breathe. "I didn't mean to curse at you. Jesus, I just... I was so *frightened*," he whispered, his lips coming down to press hard against the top of her hair. "I could not bear losing you, my sweeting," he added. "I would be bereft for the rest of my..." He allowed the sentence to trail off.

Tears still streaming from her eyes, Marianne sobbed and finally relaxed into his hold. "I'm sorry I frightened you," she said between attempts to breathe. "But, you merely had to call out to me," she replied finally. "Warn me."

"I barely saw you as it was," he countered, pulling her away so that he could direct his attention to her. He wanted her to see his frustration—nay, his anger—at what had just happened, but he had to stifle the sudden urge to grin. Her tears made the lenses of her spectacles appear as if they were partly under water. He lifted them from her face and silently cleaned them using the fabric of his shirt. He aimed them in the direction of the sea and glanced through them, as if to confirm they were clear before he turned and settled them back onto her face. "I had just made a discovery and was concentrating on it. I don't even know what had me looking in your direction," he murmured. "You must have an angel watching over you."

Marianne sniffled before reaching into the pocket of her gown for a hanky. Wiping the tears with the linen, she sniffled and finally allowed a nod. "I shall be more careful," she promised, dipping her head. "I feared this would happen. I... I have become a burden to you..." Her words were cut off when her lips were suddenly covered by his. It dawned on her then that every time she tried to put voice to a complaint, or a suggestion she return to England, or apologize for her poor eyesight, Jasper silenced her with a kiss.

Well, there are worse ways to be silenced, she considered, one hand moving to his shoulder as he continued to kiss her. Worse ways to be treated when she expected he truly wanted to throttle her.

When Jasper finally ended the kiss, he left his head bent so his forehead rested on hers. "You are not a burden," he murmured. "You are stubborn, though," he stated, ignoring her gasp of shock. "I would not have believed you capable of allowing vanity to override good sense."

Marianne's eyes widening even more, she gave a huff. "Vanity has nothing to do with this," she countered, angered by his comment and struggling to swallow a sob.

"Then why? *Why?* When I have assured you at every turn that you are a beautiful woman, why are you so damned stubborn about not wearing your spectacles?"

Daring another glance at the expanse of blue, Marianne felt a bit disoriented by the wavy image at the edge of the lenses. Her gaze then lowered to the cliff's edge. From her vantage, it appeared as if the ground simply stopped and the water began.

She was sure it wasn't supposed to look like this. But how could she explain it to Jasper? Explain that the spectacles might have provided a clearer image, but not necessarily a truer image?

Marianne stared at her husband, momentarily forgetting she wore the awful spectacles. She had seen her husband's reaction when he had forced them onto her face—even he was appalled at how they made her appear. At least he hadn't said anything right then, though. She was quite sure she would have jumped off the cliff if he had.

Well, perhaps not. She did have that fear of heights.

She hadn't even realized she had such a fear until they had been on the ship. When she had worn the spectacles and gazed out on the sea, and then made the mistake of looking down from where she stood at the railing. She could see the surface of the water so far below, with its churning whitecaps and swirling eddies as the ship made its way toward the Strait of Gibraltar.

Perhaps it wasn't really so far down—she wasn't really so high—but her glasses had made it seem as if the water was far away. The disorientation led to a wave of nausea, which had her stepping back from the railing. Had her removing the spectacles even as she struggled to keep her feet beneath her.

She hadn't ever been that high up before, she was sure. Even when her aunt took her to the top floor of the British Museum, she wasn't as high above... well, above the surface as she was then.

"What is it?" Jasper asked, his attention going from the Mediterranean Sea to Marianne and back again.

"I cannot believe what I see when I am wearing these," she replied, her manner still defensive.

Jasper frowned. "Cannot believe because... because it's a sight you've never seen before? Because it's vast, and so blue—?"

"No," Marianne replied with a shake of her head. "No. It's... distorted, I think is the word. When I look there," she lifted a finger to point at where the beach met the water's edge. "I see there are rocks, but their edges tip up," she claimed as her other hand joined the first. She used her fore fingers to illustrate what she meant by drawing arcs in the air. "...When I know they do not, because when I look to the right just a bit, the rocks straighten out but the other side tips up." She motioned with the flat of her hand. "Now, if I do this..." She slowly scanned the horizon, her body giving a start as if she thought she were falling to one side. "Then it appears that the entire horizon is... wavering." One of her gloved hands reached out and formed a wavy pattern in the air.

Frowning, Jasper carefully lifted the spectacles from her face and held them up. He pulled them toward his face until the bridge between the lenses was settled on his nose, his eyes darting about as he attempted to replicate what she was describing. He jerked them off his face after a moment, squeezing his eyes shut before opening them again.

He held the spectacles aways from his face a ways and slowly brought them toward him again until they were nearly mounted on his nose. "I think... I think I see what you mean," he murmured. He screwed up his face in annoyance, unable to force his eyes to see the horizon clearly. When the lenses were a few inches from his face, he was suddenly able to replicate what Marianne had described. "Is this how *everything* looks to you? All curved down in the middle and turned up at the edges?" He was about to imagine how *he* might look through her lenses, and decided he didn't want to know.

Marianne felt a hint of excitement when she realized Jasper understood her dilemma. "Mostly things far away. It's not so bad for objects that are closer," she explained. "You do see what I see then?" she asked then, wondering if she could make him understand just how frustrating it was to wear the eyeglasses.

Jasper gave a half-chuckle. "I rather doubt I'm seeing exactly what you're seeing, but I think I have a pretty good idea," he replied. He allowed a sigh. "The thing is, they do make what you see far more clear, do they not?"

Allowing a shrug, Marianne had to agree. "As long as I look through the middle of the lens, and what I'm looking at is directly in front of me."

He gave a nod. "So, you can make out the cliff's edge?"

Marianne glanced at where she had nearly stepped off the cliff, the area evident in how the ground had been marred when Jasper knocked her down. "Yes," she hedged.

Jasper placed a hand against the side of her face and turned it toward him. "Then I must require you to wear your spectacles. I cannot abide the thought of losing you." When tears once again filled her eyes, Jasper gave his head a shake. "Why are you crying?"

"I feel as if I'm being punished again for having poor eyesight."

"Again?" he countered, wondering what she meant.

"Having to wear spectacles, of course. They're... they're *hideous*," she spat out.

She hadn't thought about them in that respect back home. The first time her father had placed them on her face —back when she was only eight or nine—her entire world seemed to come into focus. Suddenly, everything had crisp edges when before, only the things she was standing closest to had those edges, especially when she squinted. Books were the best, though, for she could see the print clearly without using the spectacles and without having to squint. Later, when her mother taught her how to embroider, she found she could master the stitches without having to wear the eyeglasses.

Jasper sighed. He had to agree with her assessment of the

eyewear, at least when it came to the pair she was wearing. If they'd had the time in London, he would have arranged for her to see Wather-Wallen and would have had lenses made to be mounted in a more stylish pair of gold wire frames.

"I think we shall make our way north the day after tomorrow," he announced.

"North?" she repeated, her gaze going to the map he had spread out on the ground next to where he had dug a hole.

"Palermo," he said with a nod. "Dr. Jones says there is an oculist there who gets his glass from Venice."

Marianna angled her head. "Glass? For what?"

Jasper shrugged. "Everything, but our interest is for a new pair of spectacles for you. See if we can't find the oculist Dr. Jones mentioned. The man who can grind a pair of lenses perfectly suited to your vision and mount them in a beautiful gold wire frame."

"Gold?" Marianne repeated. "Like the ones Lady Evangeline wears?"

His brows rising in surprise, Jasper wondered when she'd had an opportunity to meet the bluestocking who was Lord Everly's sister. Marianne had only been in the capital a few days before they had met at the ball. "Yes, like hers," he said with a nod. "Where—?"

"Aunt Cherice introduced me to her when we were in *The Temple of the Muses*," Marianne replied. "She was... reading the end of a book," she whispered, one brow arching up as if she were sharing gossip.

"Ah, skipping to the end, was she?" he teased.

"And then to the beginning," Marianne countered. "That's when Cherice... Lady Devonville... asked if she might introduce me. Lady Evangeline was wearing the most dainty pair of eyeglasses, and she didn't seem the least bit embarrassed at having been caught wearing them in the bookshop."

Probably because she doesn't have a chaperone admonishing her for wearing them, Jasper nearly replied, remembering

Lady Evangeline was under the protection of her older brother, Harold Tennison, Earl of Everly. And he was usually off on some expedition searching for some rare flower or bird.

Or fish.

Jasper still hadn't paid a visit to the man's library, where apparently a collection of tropical fish were housed in a large, glass tank.

"If we find the oculist in Palermo, we'll see what he can do for you," Jasper explained. "I know one in London who has some special lenses he uses to determine how one's sight can be improved, but I do not wish to wait until our return to British shores before arranging new eyeglasses for you."

Marianne finally nodded, deciding the sooner she had a better pair of lenses, the better Sicily would look.

Chapter 32

A FEAR IN PLAIN SIGHT

The next day
        When Singleton claimed he was sun sick and unable to join Jasper at the ruined temple, Jasper allowed a sigh of frustration. Before the incident with Marianne, he had managed to locate the small flags Dr. Jones had used to mark what he was sure was the location of a small temple's floor near the edge of the ridge.

Jasper had surveyed the site from four vantage points, finally understanding his colleague's claim. The area featured an evenly flattened rectangle, as if a giant had pressed a large block onto the ground and then removed it. Knowing that other Roman temples featured mosaic tile floors, Dr. Jones was sure Jasper would find the same beneath the volcanic soil that covered most of the island.

Working closer to the ridge meant he was more exposed to the wind than he had been in the Greco-Roman quarter, but the breeze was cool. Jasper erected the sunshade he and Singleton had used at the other site, glad for respite from the bright sun.

Although he had worked inward from one edge of the temple ruin the day before, he had only exposed a small fraction of a mosaic design. He had hoped to finish uncovering the entire mosaic—the soil covering it was only a few inches thick—but without Singleton's help, it might take a day or two longer. If he took Marianne to Palermo on the morrow, it would take even longer.

The younger archaeologist's face had been rather red when he appeared in Jasper's bedchamber, and he looked as miserable as he sounded when he made his apologies and headed back to his own bedchamber.

"I will see to some aloe for his face and neck," David offered, once he was finished seeing to Jasper's morning shave. "And lots of water. I fear Signore Singleton did not abide my warnings yesterday," he said by way of apology.

"I expected you two would spend most of the time inside important buildings," Jasper commented.

David's eyes widened. "Oh, we did, my lord. But we spent the rest of the time out of doors, walking from place to place. If I hadn't warned him of my cousin's wrath if he missed dinner, Signore Singleton might still be in Girgenti."

Jasper suppressed the grin he was tempted to display, quite sure his colleague wouldn't want to anger the woman he flirted with every night during dinner. "I plan to take my viscountess to Palermo on the morrow. I am in need of an oculist. Do you suppose Pietro can drive us?"

David blinked. "Are you quite sure? It is a long journey—eighty miles."

"I expect we'll need to spend a few nights. Do you know of a coaching inn, or... a hotel along the way?" Jasper asked. "And one in Palermo?

"There are hotels, of course. A good one near the port," David replied. "Would you like me to come with you?"

Jasper considered the question, realizing the valet was offering to go. "I would like that," he agreed. "We could use a guide."

"Very good. I will pack for you."

Rather surprised at the young man's enthusiasm, Jasper finally nodded. "If you're sure—"

"Very," David replied. "As for an oculist, I only know of one gentleman who makes eyeglasses in the capital. Ricardo Ricciardini. He has a shop there," he said with some excitement.

Ricardo Ricciardini. Darius Jones had mentioned the same man just last week.

"Will Signore Singleton be joining you?" David asked, his query sounding a bit guarded.

"If he is of a mind to do so, and if he is recovered from his sunburn, then I suppose so," Jasper replied carefully. He watched as David's face seem to indicate relief.

Jasper noted the change in the man's demeanor and wondered if perhaps David was the reason James seemed so much happier the past few days. Had the two merely become good friends? Or was there more to their relationship?

*J*asper was thinking of his earlier conversation with David as he used his arm to push dirt away from a series of white and cream tiles, their pattern suggesting at least two people were featured in the mosaic floor.

Readjusting his position, he was about to use the same arm to reveal more of the mosaic when he noticed Marianne had taken a seat on a marble block, her attention on a book.

She wasn't wearing her spectacles.

Frowning, Jasper scrambled to his feet and stalked over to his wife. "Where are your eyeglasses?" he asked, barely reining in his anger.

Marianne blinked. "In my reticule," she replied, as she held up the fabric purse that she had nestled against one hip. "I really don't need to wear them whilst I'm reading," she started to say, but Jasper's expression had her dipping her head.

"If you're going to be out here, you need to wear them," he countered, his impatience with her apparent.

Struggling to open the gathers at the top of her reticule, Marianne gave a start when her book slid to the ground, creating a puff of dust when it landed in a heap.

"Oh!" she let out, one of her gloved hands going to her mouth.

Jasper bent down and retrieved the book, wiping it against his trousers. When Marianne reached for it, he shook his head. "Not until your spectacles are on your face," he said sternly.

Marianne's brows furrowed, and her entire body seemed to rock in place. "Please, don't make me—"

"We talked about this yesterday. I thought I made it clear—"

"You did," she replied as her rocking became more pronounced. "I'll just go back up to the villa—"

"Not by yourself, you won't," Jasper countered, his ire increasing.

Marianne lifted her gaze to meet his, tears falling freely from her eyes.

Oh, Christ! Tears! he thought as he chided himself for having upset her so. "There's no reason to cry..." he started to say. "Marianne—"

"Please, don't make me," she said as she held the spectacles by their hinged bows.

Hands going to his hips, Jasper allowed a sigh of exasperation. "What are you so afraid of?" Jasper asked, his face taking on a look of confusion.

Or was that anger?

Marianne realized just then that until the day before, he had never before displayed anger—or even dismay—during their brief marriage.

She allowed a quick glance to where the ground on which he stood seemed to stop and water started, ending only where it met the sky. From her perspective and without her eyeglasses, she couldn't see anything below the cliff—not even the beach.

"I'm afraid you'll find my appearance so abhorrent, you won't be able to be in the same room with me. That every time you look at me, you'll see..." she waved her hand over her face after she put the spectacles into place..."This, even when I'm not wearing them. That you'll take a mistress because you didn't say a vow of fidelity during our wedding. That you'll fall in love with an Italian beauty and get a child on her.

"And it seems I'm terribly afraid of heights."

Jasper blinked three time as he stared at his wife, stunned at hearing her list of fears. He knew full well tears would be collecting behind her spectacles if they weren't already. He also knew she was shaking so hard, her knees were about to give out and she would land in a heap at his feet. He stepped forward and wrapped his arms around her shoulders, pulling her hard against the front of his body. He dropped his lips to the top of her bonnet and took two breaths before he remembered exactly what she'd said.

"I do not find your appearance abhorrent," he stated firmly. "Ever." He felt her sob and wondered how he was going to make her understand her beliefs were unfounded. "In fact, I find I look forward to the sight of you so much, I like to wake up and watch you whilst you sleep," he added, rather gratified when she suddenly stilled in his hold.

What else had she said? *Something about the wedding vows.*

"Since I recall being rather nervous when I was repeating the wedding vows, I cannot remember if I said anything about forsaking all others or not. If I did not, it was entirely the fault of the vicar, because I am, and I do, and I shall for the rest of my days forsake all others, which means I won't be getting a child on... on an Italian beauty, and..." He paused to stare down at her. "Where does that idea even come from?" he asked suddenly.

Marianne sniffled in his hold, rather comforted at how he held her so close. At how his arms had wrapped around her shoulders and her waist. At how his chin rested atop her head. "It happened to Chiara," she managed to get out between sobs.

Jasper frowned. "What?"

For a moment, Marianne forgot about the promise she had made to Chiara. That she wouldn't say anything. "An archaeologist fell in love with her. Got a child on her, and then left to go back to England. To his *wife!*"

Tightening his hold on Marianne, Jasper wondered who would have done such a thing. "I swear to you, Marianne, I never did that," he said, thinking she was accusing *him* of being the archaeologist guilty of such an act. He was far too young to have gotten a child on Chiara! She was probably in her forties.

He suddenly straightened.

"Oh, Jesus," he breathed, just then sorting who *was* old enough to have done such a thing.

Who had been in Rome twenty years ago.

Who had highly recommended he consider Chiara's guest villa for his stay on the island.

Jasper loosened his hold on Marianne and stepped back. "Darius?" he whispered. He allowed his mind's eye to remember the moment the older archaeologist had spied Chiara as she strolled with Marianne near the edge of the dig site.

The moment they had been introduced the night before that, in front of their villa.

There was recognition there, to be sure, but then he

would have expected it. Darius had been the one to recommend the woman's guest villa.

Did Darius know he had left the woman with child though? Darius had never mentioned having another son. Never mentioned having left a lover behind. And given the political situation in Sicily for the past two decades, Jasper knew Darius wouldn't have been able to come back to the Mediterranean's largest island to excavate the site on which they stood.

Jasper realized Marianne was regarding him through teary eyes. Teary but filled with relief. Even behind the spectacles, he could see she had heard his claims and comprehended their meaning. "I promise to forsake all others," he whispered, his eyes darkening as he leaned down. "And if I haven't already, I will get a child on you. Perhaps when we're in Palermo. We're going there tomorrow."

His lips were suddenly on hers, the kiss hungry and hard. Stunned, Marianne finally returned the kiss, well aware of how quickly his manhood hardened, the bulge pressing into her belly.

A frisson shot through Marianne as he deepened the kiss. If they hadn't been out in the open, she was sure he would have lifted her skirts right then and there and driven himself into her. The thought had her aware of the dampness at the top of her thighs, of how her breasts felt heavy despite how they were crushed against his chest, of how much she wanted him to be inside her.

Her feet suddenly left the ground as Jasper changed his hold on her, one of his arms behind her knees as he carried her to the nearest foundation block between two broken marble columns.

"What are you doing?" she asked when he lowered her feet to the ground.

He sat on the marble block, unbuttoning his breeches as he did so. "Proving myself," he murmured as he pressed his back against the cool stone of a column. He pulled her atop him so she straddled him, her skirts and petticoats rucked up between their bodies. His hands splayed over the globes of her bare bottom as he guided her over his turgid manhood.

Marianne gasped as he impaled her and gasped again when his hands lifted her from his body until he was almost out of her. She gripped his shoulders, well aware he was about to drop her so his cock would drive deeper into her. When he did, she whimpered, stunned when his lips suddenly covered hers. Once she realized her feet touched the ground on either side of the marble block, she found she could leverage her movements. Jasper held her hips down for a moment though, at the same time his own hips thrust up so his crisp curls ground into her quim. One of his hands moved to a breast, cupping as much of the fabric-covered orb as he could manage.

The move was so unexpected, Marianne nearly cried out. Through the lenses of her spectacles, she could clearly see how the cords of his neck strained as his body stiffened. She did cry out when his hand slid from her bottom and his thumb was suddenly where their bodies met. He pressed it against her swollen womanhood. Pressed it and rubbed until she screamed his name. Although he paused his movements for just a moment, he continued them until she once again reacted. Even before she cried out again, he was aware of her orgasm when his manhood was suddenly gripped and drawn deeper into her.

Although Jasper had intended to bring her to ecstasy at least one more time, he found his body had other ideas.

Caught in his own spasm of pleasure, Jasper could only watch as Marianne's body stiffened and arched. He moved his other hand behind her back and pulled her hard against the front of his body, needing to hold onto something. He knew when the wash of warmth filled her lower body, for Marianne whimpered and finally relaxed into his hold. Her head fell to his shoulder as her body continued to quake and shiver for another moment.

Drowsy and thoroughly sated, Jasper gazed out toward the sea before rolling his head around to the other side. The dig site was abandoned, almond and olive trees hiding them from most vantages. He lifted his head to ensure no one else was about when he realized his wife's lower legs were on display.

What the hell did I just do? he suddenly wondered. He had treated his wife no better than a whore, having his way with her right out in the open, where anyone might have seen them.

The scene from the mosaic he had uncovered the day before came to mind, though, and he grinned.

"What is it?" Marianne asked in a whisper, one of her fingers reaching up to caress his jawline.

Sure he wasn't yet ready to move, Jasper redirected his gaze to her, rather surprised to find she still wore her spectacles. "I wonder how it is I can simply have my way with you out where anyone can see us, and I'm reminded of what I uncovered yesterday."

Marianne straightened, although she didn't pull her body from his. "The one of the couple in a garden?" Although the tiles were somewhat faded and the overall image was missing an entire corner, the design was intact enough to identify what it depicted.

Jasper nodded. "I wonder if they might have been making love here," he murmured. Just beyond the marble foundation of the structure, the yellow, pink and bright white blooms of oleanders would have covered the grounds to the edge of the cliff during the spring. The air would have been scented with orange blossoms. Now the purples and scarlets of bougainvillea and hibiscus decorated the surrounding grounds. "And then been caught," he added with a quirked lip.

A dimple appeared in one of Marianne's cheeks, and she suddenly blushed. "And forced to marry."

Jasper frowned and shook his head. "*Allowed* to marry because that's what they wanted."

Marianne's head returned to rest on his shoulder. "I wonder how long they had to remain in that position," she murmured. At his furrowed brow, she added, "To model for the artist who made the mosaic."

Chuckling, Jasper returned his gaze to his wife. Despite the dark rings of her spectacle frames, she was a lovely woman. "I'm quite sure they didn't mind a bit," he whispered. He kissed her then, rather impressed she hadn't yet remembered she wore her eyeglasses. He was sure she would have torn them from her face if she did.

After he ended the kiss, he took a deep breath and let it out slowly, stunned when he smelled the floral scent he had just been imagining. "Come. Let's get back to the villa and have some dinner," he said as he lifted her body from his and buttoned up his breeches.

Marianne shook out her skirts and straightened, her gaze sweeping the horizon before it settled back on Jasper. Then she blinked and removed the spectacles. "I cannot believe you... allowed me to wear these... all that time," she stammered.

Grinning, Jasper took the spectacles from her and put them back on her face. "I wanted you to be able to see me. To see everything around us," he said in a whisper. He leaned over and kissed her nose. "Especially if we got caught."

Chapter 33

A VISIT TO PALERMO

The following day
Marianne wasn't sure what to expect by way of transportation for their trip to Palermo, so she was rather impressed when a glossy black traveling coach pulled by four black mules appeared outside the villa gates just after six o'clock in the morning. Despite the early hour, the sky had already begun to lighten with a red glow in the east. "Who do you suppose it belongs to?" she asked in wonder.

Jasper pulled her hand onto his arm. "Signora Romano, of course," he said in a whisper. "I'm beginning to believe her husband was quite well-to-do."

David was already seeing to their valises and a small trunk. Seeing as how they planned to be away for less than a week, Marianne assured Chiara she wouldn't require Angela's services. She did so only after being assured by Jasper that he would see to her buttons and baths.

Pietro had agreed to man the ribbons for the trip, and he greeted them from where he was perched on the driver's seat. Once David had their luggage loaded, as well as the preserved mosaics from Jasper's first dig site, Marianne, Jasper, and James stepped into the coach and made themselves comfortable in the light velvet squabs. David climbed up to sit with Pietro on the box. Although he had been invited, Lord Darius had deferred with the excuse that a trip through the mountains would leave him a cripple.

"Will we be stopping anywhere?" Marianne asked in a whisper.

"At least a few times, I should think," Jasper replied. "Palermo is a good eighty miles away." After a pause, he asked, "You did bring your spectacles, I hope?" At Marianne's motion of lifting her reticule, he had his answer.

Her eyes widened. "Will we get there today?"

Across from her, James straightened in the squabs. "Our valet says it can be a slow trip due to the mountains. I am told we'll be spending the night in a coaching inn."

Although the trip was slow going—the road was barely passable in spots, torrents of rainwater having carved out deep channels in the soil. When James leaned his head out of the coach to determine just how deep one such trench was, he allowed a low whistle and claimed it was at least twenty feet to the bottom.

The coach was forced to move to the side of the road several times to allow *leticas* to pass, the conveyances reminding Jasper of sedan chairs, but these were supported on the sides by two mules. Their occupants would wave and call out greetings, which delighted Marianne since she had begun the trip with a fear they might encounter highwaymen.

Indian figs—the prickly pear Marianne had asked about during their first day on the island—grew in huge hedgerows, making it impossible to see beyond the road in some spots.

"It's a good thing they're edible, or they would probably overrun the entire island," James commented when Marianne actually put on her spectacles to better see the vegetation.

Instead of removing them, she left them on and admired the view from her side of the coach.

"What do you think of it?" Jasper asked as he leaned his head over her shoulder and followed her line of sight. He spent most of the trip with his face at the other window in an attempt to quell his panic at being in such close confines. The open windows helped a bit in that regard. Still, there were several times he almost requested to trade places with David.

"It's rather romantic, in a... a savage sort of way," she murmured. Fields of grain stretched out to the horizon in some spots, but it was apparent they suffered from poor farming techniques.

"It's no wonder painters come here from all over the world to practice their art," James commented. "A rather beautiful setting." As the sun rose higher, the light colored the grain in different shades of gold until it was nearly white.

The village in which they stayed the night seemed to exist for the sole purpose of housing travelers. The inn, at one time purported to be a "miserable lodging" had apparently been modernized since Pietro's last encounter, for Marianne claimed the bed was acceptable—and not just because Jasper was in it—and the macaronis and salads were more than edible. Jasper was relieved there were rooms available for the night. He was about to claim he could have slept outdoors if circumstances had required it—he had done it before while on expeditions—but the thought of sleeping without Marianne in his arms kept him quiet.

The following day, the coach made it to the great road to Palermo, and the scenery changed to prosperous vineyards surrounded by Indian fig hedges. Peasants returning from market made their way to small houses that dotted the countryside. In the area between the mountains and the sea, the domes of several buildings appeared where several valleys joined together.

"There's the capital," Jasper said as he pointed toward the domes.

"This is all so charming. The boats on the water, the vineyards," Marianne enthused. "Why, if I could paint landscapes, I should want to do it from here."

Once they were in Palermo, her expression changed from adoration to worry. Although the architecture of churches and palaces was rather grand, there were equal numbers of ugly buildings that marred the scenery. In the Via Toledo, a street whose tradesmen seemed dedicated to the fashion trades, the first floors of the palaces belonging to nobles had been converted to coffee houses and shops. Those who practiced trades did so out in the open, including shoemakers and even tailors. Nearly ever corner of every street featured a vendor cart overflowing with Indian figs.

From the crowds of people they passed, it was evident most who lived in Palermo did so in poverty. Occupation by the French and Bourbons had done them no favors.

"What is that building?" Marianne asked, indicating what appeared to be the finest in all of the city. The steps leading up to it were solid blocks of marble.

"The College of the Jesuits," James replied. He knew only because David had told him the night before, the younger man's descriptions of Palermo's architecture vivid in detail. *It is my field of study*, he had reminded James.

"Where will we be staying?" Marianne asked, her worry evident. Given the crowds of people, she couldn't imagine there were enough houses and apartments for all those they had passed as they made their way.

"Pietro has a hotel in mind," Jasper replied. "On one of the piazzas. Perhaps this one," he added when he spied an open square near the port on his side of the coach.

Before Marianne could ask anything else, the coach stopped in front of a stone building festooned with wrought iron. At least four stories high, the smooth stuccoed structure appeared in far better shape than most of the buildings they had passed that day.

A slight jerk indicated David had stepped down from the driver's seat, and a second told them Pietro had as well. Marianne was quick to depart, happy to stretch her legs and take in the historic buildings that surrounded the square. The familiar odor of the sea drifted past her on the breeze from the port.

"*Mi scusi*, but I should tell you of the time," David said when James and Jasper had stepped out of the coach. "One o'clock is one hour after sunset." He pointed west. The sun hadn't yet touched the horizon but would do so in a few minutes. Then he pointed to a large public clock in the piazza that displayed the hours in a most peculiar fashion. "It's nearly noon here," he said.

James rolled his eyes, remembering the odd manner in which Sicilians kept track of time. "Which is our eighteenth hour," he said.

"Six o'clock?" Marianne guessed, not exactly sure she understood

Grinning, Jasper gave her a nod. "Indeed. Let us get to our rooms and see if we can't arrange a dinner."

"You mean supper," James reminded him.

Jasper frowned, realizing Signora Romano and her family had been keeping regular time on their behalf, rather than forcing them to rearrange the way in which they kept time and ate their usual meals.

Given most on the island didn't even eat a breakfast but instead drank coffee and sometimes had bread, he had been happy when Aurora saw to cooking a decent meal for them before they made their way to their dig site every morning. Dinners on Sicily were supposed to be when a Brit would normally eat a luncheon, and suppers were served later. "Supper it is," he agreed.

"Do you suppose there will be beef served here in

Palermo?" Marianne asked as they made their way into the hotel. Aurora had only served a beef dish once since their arrival.

"There is beef, my lady, but it can be very expensive," David warned when Jasper looked in his direction. "There are many British here now, so there are more cows."

Marianne stopped short upon entering the hotel. She wasn't sure why she was so surprised by the opulence on display. Large paintings lined the walls, and the furnishings were covered in beautiful fabrics. On the small tables, ancient Greek and Roman artifacts were displayed as if they had been purchased in a local decor shop.

"I think we shall be far more comfortable here than where we were last night," Jasper whispered in awe.

David hurried up to the clerk and made the request for rooms. When he rejoined them, he mentioned the price for two nights, wincing as he did so.

"Does that include a room for Pietro?"

"A small one, yes," David replied. "A small breakfast in the morning, and space in the stable for the mules."

"Very good," Jasper replied as he fished some *piastras* from his purse. "Could you ask if he knows the location of an oculist's shop? Ricardo Ricciardini is the man's name. And the museum?"

Nodding, David returned to the clerk and made the arrangements, returning with keys to three rooms and a paper on which two addresses were written. "We passed the museum on the way here, but they are closed for the day. He said the oculist's shop is not far, but then nothing in Palermo is."

"The entire city is but four miles," James said when Jasper displayed a quizzical expression.

"Well, then we may not require the coach after we drop off the mosaics."

"I've also requested water for bathing. He assures me it

will be delivered within the hour," David said. "I will see to the luggage."

Marianne and Jasper made their way to their room, murmuring their appreciation of the finery on display. But when Jasper opened the door to their suite, the two burst out laughing.

The bed was as tall as the one in Jasper's bedchamber.

Chapter 34

A REUNION IS CLEARLY REQUIRED

*M*eanwhile, back in Girgenti

When her late husband's coach disappeared in a cloud of dust, Chiara Romano allowed a sigh. She knew with Pietro at the reins and her son armed with a small pistol, the coach would make it to its destination.

Chiara wondered at the sense of loss she felt just then, though. Despite the difference in their ages and in their cultural backgrounds, she and Marianne Henley had become fast friends. The viscountess never put on airs or acted as if associating with Chiara was beneath her station. Perhaps the grandness of the villa, nestled into the hills with its shady trees and vantage of the sea helped in that regard.

Her concern that Marianne's blurry vision might prevent the woman from enjoying the sights Chiara was intent on sharing with her was quickly replaced with appreciation for how the young woman reacted to everything she could see— as if her entire world was everything up-close, viewed in great detail and appreciated for the same reason.

David had only returned from Palermo a few weeks ago, so the household was back to the way it was when he was away at school—just she and Aurora, Tamara, and Angela.

Chiara allowed a grin at the thought of how noisy her household could be with the addition of a single young man who teased his cousins mercilessly. Now that David was gone again, the three girls had left for the other villa with the intention of cleaning and doing the laundry.

Chiara had promised to inspect their work later that day.

At some point, marriages would have to be arranged for her nieces, but she bristled at the thought of any of them ending up with the available young men in Girgenti.

She couldn't even imagine Aurora betrothed to the butcher's son, and he probably had the best prospects of anyone in the town. Remembering again the comment Lord Henley had made about his cook in London, Chiara made a mental note to ask the viscount if he might hire Aurora for the position. Her prospects at finding a husband in England's largest city—a good husband—were far better than on Sicily.

Struck by the sudden quiet, she wandered aimlessly from room to room, her mind's eye replaying scenes of her life with Antony, of her son and how he played with his cousins when they visited, or played by himself when they weren't there. She remembered how homesick she had been when she had first come to Sicily with her husband, and then how shocked she had felt when she learned she had married a man of more fortune than she had originally thought.

And she remembered why it was she had agreed to marry Antony.

As if her memories had conjured him into existence, Lord Darius appeared at her door, a cluster of pink oleanders clutched in one hand and a bottle of scotch in the other.

A bottle of scotch that looked ever so familiar. She almost said something about it, but her attention was drawn to other, more important details. Such as how he was dressed.

She had never seen him look so formal.

Lord Darius was dressed far better than he had been at any time since his arrival on the island, his Nankeen breeches, red waistcoat, navy topcoat, and white shirt making him appear as aristocratic as he should, given he was the younger brother of a duke. She hadn't heard a conveyance, but noted from the dust on his boots that he had probably walked at least part of the way from where he was staying.

Thinking she was frowning because of his dirty boots, Darius was quick to employ the boot brush next to the door.

"*Buongiorno, mia signora*," he said as he afforded her a bow.

Why, he even looked handsome, although every year of the intervening twenty years was displayed in great detail on a face. Having worked outdoors for most of his career as an archaeologist, his coloring was closer to that of the natives of Sicily. Had she seen him dressed as he usually was down by the marina, she would have thought him a pirate.

Chiara angled her head, deciding she would at least hear what he had to say. She could always yell and curse and slap him across the face if he said something stupid.

Besides, she was intrigued by the bottle of scotch.

"Good morning, Lord Darius," she replied in English, stepping aside. "Or should I address you as Dr. Jones?" The query came with an arched eyebrow, as if she was a bit miffed at having learned of his other moniker.

Darius was relieved and pleasantly surprised at her unspoken invitation to enter. It hadn't been that long ago since she had punched him in the face, illustrating her displeasure with him in an unexpected manner. As a result, he had half-expected shouting, cursing, and perhaps—maybe —a slap across the face.

Wasn't a slap across the face supposed to a be sign that a woman secretly loved the victim of her slap? He was sure he had heard of it at some point during his brief visits to London.

"Just Darius will do," he replied, almost tempted to

remind her of the endearment she used to use when they had known each other when they were in Rome.

Il mio uomo. My man.

Well, he had always been hers—from the moment he caught her watching him from the steps of the Forum and ignored protocol by introducing himself. As the son of a duke, he tended to ignore protocol when he traveled abroad. Back then, he hadn't completed his studies at Cambridge. Hadn't earned his title as a doctor of archaeology. But he had come to the attention of her father, a man who insisted the history of their culture would be lost unless those who dug up the past could help preserve it as well interpret their findings. And so Darius accepted Samuele Ferraro's invitation to an archaeological conference in Rome, intending to stay for no more than a month to attend the conference and survey the sites Signore Ferraro claimed were in danger of destruction.

He stayed for over ten months.

Ten months that had him making friends with like-minded historians and wealthy patrons, like Antony Romano. Ten months that had him falling in love with Ferraro's oldest daughter. Six months that proved his passion for Roman history and three months for Chiara Ferraro.

*D*arius glanced around the vestibule, realizing he had underestimated just how well the widow was living despite her husband having been dead for nearly four years. He wondered how Antony had died, but thought better than to ask just then. "I was hoping we could go for a walk. To talk," he managed. He held out the oleanders, just then remembering he held them. "These are for you."

Still suspicious of his motives, Chiara took the flowers, rather stunned by how many were in the cluster he offered. Why, he had probably picked all the blooms from two or three bushes. "*Grazie*. I should put these in water," she said as she dipped a curtsy, her gaze going to the bottle. Had he brought it for courage? Or was it a gift? "Come. Join me. I shall only be a moment."

Glancing about the plaster-walled central hall of the villa, Darius was impressed by the lavishness on display. Paintings framed in gilt were guarded by life-size statues, some probably originals from the nearby temples. Rich furnishings, some obviously antiques, gleamed as if they had been made yesterday. The painted ceiling reminded him of cathedrals in other parts of Italy. Antony Romano had continued to do well for himself, it seemed, despite the wars.

Darius was staring at a marble bust of a Roman general, fairly sure he had been the one to unearth it, when he realized Chiara had made her way to another room toward the back of the house.

Hurrying after her, he wondered at the quiet. At no point had he seen any servants, nor did he hear the three young women he knew had been living with her. "Where is everyone?" he asked as he followed her into the kitchen. She was filling a crystal vase with water from a pitcher next to a deep marble sink when she gave him a quelling glance, as if she thought he knew damn well where everyone was. Otherwise, why would he have come on this particular day? At this particular hour?

"My servants are on holiday, my nieces are seeing to the cleaning of the other villa, and my son has gone back to Palermo with my guests."

"Cleaning?" he repeated. "I would think your servants could see to that," he murmured.

Chiara gave him a quelling glance. "I am teaching them what they must know to be a good wife. They may not end up married to wealthy men." Probably wouldn't, given the economic status of so many on the island. The wars and the changing of the monarchies laying claim to the island had left most in a state of near-poverty.

Dipping his head, Darius chided himself for asking about the nieces. Having been on the island for a month, and in Rome for nearly a month before that, he had seen first-hand how things had changed in twenty years. "Did your son go to school in Palermo?" He knew Antony Romano would demand the best for his son.

"*Sì,* but he has finished his studies. In architecture. Probably not what Antony would have wanted, but a good second choice."

Darius nodded. "Is there work for him in Palermo?"

Chiara gave a shrug. "Probably, but he did not go there for that. At least, not on this day. He is escorting my guests."

If he hadn't been invited to join them, Darius would have felt a bit left out, but learning his colleagues intended to be gone for a few days allowed him to arrange some time alone with their hostess, and so he had declined. "Did Lord Henley take one of the mosaics with him?" He had noticed the empty floor in the Greco-Roman ruin they had been excavating, the perfect rectangle of tiles dug out, transferred onto a large wooden sheet, and crated for transport.

"A few, I think. But I believe they are seeing to a pair of spectacles for the viscountess. Is there a reason you are not with them?"

Darius was about to tease her, thinking she hadn't realized she had put voice to a pun. But her brilliant smile suddenly appeared, and he knew she had been intentional with her words. "I was invited," he replied. "But I declined. That trip is bad in the best of conditions."

Chiara's nonchalant expression faltered a bit. "I made sure David had Antony's gun," she said, thinking he was referring to highwaymen rather than the poor road.

"Hopefully he won't have to use it," Darius replied, his gaze taking in the airy kitchen. Unlike most of the kitchens in townhouses in London, this one was large and bright, with marble counters that extended around to where a massive stove and oven filled half the adjacent wall. Everything was so clean, he had a thought it was never used. But he knew better. He knew how Italian women prided themselves on their spotless households. "Do you like the quiet?" he asked.

Not expecting the question, Chiara angled her head to one side as she made her way out of the kitchen and to the front parlor. She set the vase on the low table in front of a settee. "Sometimes," she finally replied. "Do you always carry a bottle of scotch with you?"

Giving a start—he had forgotten he still carried the bottle from Slater's distillery—Darius held it out to her. "It's for you," he said. "A... a peace offering, if it helps," he added when she didn't immediately reach for it. "Lady Henley's father made it."

Chiara remembered Marianne's mention of her father's avocation and just then realized the young woman had come from a wealthier background than she had first thought. "I haven't yet had my morning coffee. Would you like a cup?" She took the bottle, an eyebrow arching when she saw that it really was the same scotch Lord Henley had given her the day of his arrival.

Relieved he wasn't about to be forced out of the villa, Darius allowed a grin. "I would."

"Then, I am going back to the kitchen. Have a seat, if—"

"I'll join you," he replied, offering an arm.

Chiara ignored it and made her way back the way she had come, her healed slippers tapping on the tiled floors, Darius directly behind her. Halfway to the kitchen, she suddenly whirled around. "Are you...?"

She was about to ask if he was watching her bottom as she walked when Darius said, "I have always admired the way you walk. You sway so perfectly," he said, making sure there wasn't a hint of a grin on his face. He caught her hand before it impacted his cheek, moving it to his lips so he could kiss her knuckles. "You always have."

Staring at him for a moment, Chiara struggled with how to respond. She was still angry with him—she probably would be for the rest of her life—but because of him, she had been blessed with a son. A son and memories of being in love. "You would do well to keep your eyes in their sockets," she said, wincing when she realized her choice of words might have him laughing at her.

But he didn't laugh. Instead, he pulled on her hand, forcing her closer to him. Then his arms wrapped around her shoulders and he pulled her hard against his body. He buried his nose in her hair, inhaling deeply at the slight scent of gardenia. When she didn't relax into his hold, he allowed a sigh of frustration. "I have missed you so much," he said in a whisper. "Every day. Every day since I had to leave you in Rome. I go to sleep thinking of you, and I wake up thinking of you. I think of you when I am digging in the Roman forts by Hadrian's Wall, and I think of you when I'm berating myself for having left you all those years ago."

Chiara stepped back from his hold and regarded him with a furrowed brow. "Yet you wait until *today* to say these things?" she replied, obviously incensed.

"I wasn't sure of where you were," he argued. "Who you were... I mean, who you had become. Who you married." He always hoped his bit of meddling would result in her becoming Antony Romano's wife. If she couldn't be his, then at least he wanted to be sure she ended up with an honorable man who could provide a life of privilege.

Frowning at the odd comment, Chiara's hands went to her hips. "Then how did you find me *here?*" She had never written to him after his disappearance from her life. She didn't have many dealings with other archaeologists who might know him. For a few years, she barely gave him a thought.

Until David canted his head just so, or displayed certain expressions, or his eyes caught hers in secret understanding. Then memories of Darius haunted her dreams, sometimes for weeks.

Darius rolled his eyes and allowed a sigh. "My letters to you in Rome were returned, but the last one I sent was returned with a note that said you had married and moved to Sicily. To Girgenti."

Chiara took a step back, as if she had been the one who was slapped. "Who wrote that?" she asked in surprise. She hadn't received any letters from Darius. Not a single one. Which is why she had willingly agreed to move to Sicily with her new husband. A man who had worshipped her from the day he found her sitting on the Forum steps in Rome, tears dripping from her eyes.

"A friend," Darius replied. "It was written on the outside of the letter. In a masculine hand, if I remember correctly."

He remembered quite well, actually. Remembered the way his heart had pained him when he read the words, as if a fist was clenching it. But at least he knew where she had gone. Knew she was married, although he didn't know to whom at that point.

Finding a 'Chiara' in Girgenti was far easier than finding one in Rome. He rather wished he had begun the quest a long time ago, but having a wife and a baby boy required he spend time with them in London, at least until he could make his excuses and return to his life as an archaeologist.

Then the wars had worsened, Napoleon conquered Naples, and travel to Sicily was suddenly impossible. Years of conflict coupled with the changing guard on Sicily didn't help matters. So he had moved to Hexham and immersed himself in the legends surrounding Hadrian's Wall.

a friend.

Probably my brother, Chiara thought, remembering how Lucian and Darius had become good friends back when Darius was using Rome as a base from which he took trips to several archaeological sites in central Italy at her father's request.

"So... what took you so long to find me? Pietro tells me you have been in the marina for a month," she accused before she suddenly adopted a manner of boredom. She didn't want him knowing Pietro had come to her with news of a British archaeologist who was in search of a woman named 'Chiara' the day after Darius had stepped off a sailing vessel from England.

Darius was about to tease her. At least she was a tiny bit interested in his quest to find her. "According to the men I spoke with in a *taverna* in the marina, there are at least five women in Girgenti who are named 'Chiara,'" he replied. "I paid a visit to the first, who was happy to make my acquaintance and would have been happier to take me to her bedchamber, but she was at least eighty years old—"

"Signora Garcia!" Chiara said, her eyes bright with humor. "She's a hundred-and-two." After she blinked and sobered, she asked, "Did you...?"

Darius gave her a quelling glance. "She fell asleep before we got that far," he said, trying to seem serious but failing in his attempt. "Thank the gods." He allowed a sigh. "The next one was far too young, but she already had five bambinos clinging to her legs and was about to go into confinement with another."

"Signora DiCarlo. She was twelve when she married a widower twice her age," Chiara said with a roll of her eyes. "Poor thing."

"Pietro pointed out the other two when he took me into Girgenti so I could visit the Norman church."

"They're both unmarried," Chiara remarked, one shoulder going up in a sort of shrug. "A war widow and an old maid."

Darius gave her a quelling glance. "But neither one was you," he said in a quiet voice. "That day I received that letter was the worse day of my life. Knowing someone else had captured your heart—"

"Oh, you bastard," she hissed as she turned and made her way back into the kitchen.

Darius frowned and paused before following her. If Antony Romano did what he had promised Darius he would do, then Chiara would have been under his protection from the moment after Darius left her on the steps of the Forum all those years ago.

He stopped at the threshold, deciding he could at least prevent her from leaving the kitchen if he said something that angered her. "Are you saying Signore Romano *didn't* capture your heart?"

Chiara blinked, not about to admit Antony hadn't. He had merely been a means to an end. A way to move on without the love of her life. A means to give her son a name and legitimacy. "I respected him," she said in a whisper. "I liked him. Father was pleased, I think because Antony was a patron of his projects." She busied herself with the large pitcher of water and a glass urn before saying, "How did you discover where I live? I suppose Pietro told you—"

"My brother has been here. A couple of times, with the Duke of Serradifalco. I asked if he might have met you, and he said he had. At a reception of some sort."

Chiara's eyes widened before she remembered the night in question. Her husband had hosted the duke and his colleagues when Serradifalco had been in Girgenti to do the restoration work on the temples. "The Duke of Westhaven," she said with a nod. "His wife was Greek. I remember," she said with a nod. "A very beautiful woman."

"She's dying," Darius said, realizing just then why his brother spent so much time on his wife's home island of Mykonos and avoided England as much as he could. Dr. Alexander Jones loved his wife. Loved the culture from which she had been delivered into the world. The same culture that accepted his daughter and him when London would not accept his daughter and wife. "She told me of how she met you," he said in a whisper.

"I am sorry to hear she is dying," Chiara said as she returned her attention to the urn set before her. "But you must be disappointed at what you see now," she said as she waved a hand to indicate her face and body before turning to resume making the coffee.

"I am not," he argued. "In fact, I find you far more beautiful now," he claimed. He leaned against the arched opening into the kitchen, wondering if perhaps she might throw a knife at him. "Look, I know I'm certainly not as handsome as I used to be—"

"On that we can both agree," she said as she measured ground coffee into a small, long-handled cup. She held it over the top of the urn and poured boiling water from a pot on the stove over the cup.

"But I... I still... I still care for you. Which is why I came here to excavate this season." Darius frowned as he watched what she was doing, imagining his cup of coffee would be filled with the bitter grounds. But then he noticed the water didn't flow over the cup, taking the grounds with it, but rather through a hole in the bottom of it when she pressed a large spoon over the top.

"Do you like it strong?" she asked, reaching for another glass urn. She acted as if she hadn't heard his words.

"Do I?"

Chiara gave a start, remembering just then how much he had enjoyed the beverage when they were in Rome. "If you haven't changed, then I shall make it the way you used to like it." She held the cup of grounds over the empty urn and poured the first urn's contents onto the used grounds, steam clouding the air above the second urn. "I don't have the lever machine, though, like they use in the *caffès*." The spoon had to act in its stead, her steady fingers pressing the spoon into the grounds as the coffee flowed in a steady stream. When she finished, she poured the coffee into two cups and offered him one.

He took an experimental sip and closed his eyes in appreciation. "Perfect," he murmured.

"*Sì*," she agreed after she took a drink. "So, why have you come on this day?"

Darius regarded her from over the rim of his cup. She hadn't invited him into the parlor—they still stood in the bright kitchen, although he was quite happy to remain there. Chiara was in her favorite room of the house, and he just wanted to be wherever she was. "I wish to court you."

Chiara blinked, pulling her cup from her lips. "Court me?" she repeated, as if she didn't understand the English words.

"With the intention of marrying you. As I should have done twenty years ago."

A cloud passed over her eyes. "You were already married. You made an adulteress out of me," she countered in an angry whisper. "Do you have any idea what my father would have done to you if—?"

"I do," Darius interrupted. "I did." He sighed. "I was part of an arranged married—one my father insisted on—and neither of us wanted anything to do with the—"

"Oh! That gave you the right to woo me into your bed?" she countered, her ire increasing by the moment.

"I woo'd you because I fell in love with you," he countered, his attempt to keep his voice low failing. He half expected she would toss the remains of her coffee on him at any moment. He almost wished she would, for he was fairly sure she would regret it and beg forgiveness and end up in his arms.

He suddenly straightened.

"How did you know I was *married?*" Back then, he hadn't said anything about his wife. About the impending birth of his son. His three letters to her had never been answered, nor had two of them been returned—just the one on which Lucian had written the few sentences that mentioned Chiara had married and moved to Girgenti.

"The Duke of Westhaven said so," she replied with an arched brow. "After I asked if he knew of another archaeologist from England who went by the name, 'Lord Darius'."

Darius blinked.

"Imagine my surprise when he said you were his *brother*," she added before taking a long drink of her coffee. She set the cup down on the counter, afraid if she didn't, she would throw it at Darius, and she didn't want the fine porcelain to shatter.

"I had hoped you had read my letters. I explained everything," Darius claimed in his defense. "Christ, no wonder you were so angry at seeing me," he murmured.

Chiara allowed a shrug. "We're both older. Wiser, I hope," she said before she finished her coffee.

"Wise enough to know we have a second chance?" Darius asked in a quiet voice. "My feelings for you have not changed," he added with a shake of his head. She was still the headstrong, opinionated girl he had fallen in love with in Rome.

The very opposite of an English miss.

Regarding him with an elegantly arched brow, Chiara was about to argue that she *had* changed. That she was no longer that naive girl who had fallen in love with a mysterious young man from another country. A rather handsome man who spoke the language her father had been teaching her since she was old enough to speak. Whose golden brown eyes, a bit downturned at the outer edges, seemed to see right into her soul. Back then, he had been nearly as pale as every other Brit who visited Rome on their Grand Tours. Now he displayed a complexion as dark as any Sicilian who worked in the fields, but his eyes were still the same.

Then she wondered if he knew about David. If he knew David was his son. But how could he? She hadn't told anyone. Not even Antony.

Chiara thought to keep the information from him—keep her secret even from David—but a fit of spite had her deciding to tell him. His reaction would provide the answer she sought just then.

"Antony did not give me a child," she said, her chin lifting.

Darius frowned, his attention on the bottom of his empty cup. "But, you have a son..." he started to say. He closed his eyes and allowed a long sigh. "The valet," he said in a whisper.

"He is a student of architecture," she argued. "He is only a valet because I have guests who cannot always dress themselves, and I knew of no other who could..." She stopped speaking when she saw how one of his palms lifted as if to stop her.

"I have met your David," he said with a nod. His eyes widened. "Jesus. I dismissed him from Lord Henley's bedchamber," he added before he rolled his eyes. "Are you saying...?" He suddenly frowned. "Are you saying *I* have a son?" he murmured, his eyes widening until they were no longer downturned at the edges.

"Carter. Isn't that his name?" Chiara asked in a quiet voice, deciding she wasn't ready to admit anything just yet.

"Only because I cannot disown him," Darius replied, placing his coffee cup on the marble counter. "Is David my son?"

Chiara was tempted to deny him the truth. To claim

David belonged to another. But the look on Darius' face had her breath catching. A look that seemed to plead for her to claim that David was his. As if he truly hoped he had fathered a young man more honorable than the one who had his name.

"He is your son," she finally admitted in a quiet voice.

The words were barely out of her mouth before his lips were suddenly on hers, his arms wrapped around her back like steel bands, pulling her hard against the front of his body.

Chiara considered pushing him away. Considered biting the lips that crushed hers in a kiss so filled with passion, she was reminded of a day long ago, a day when he had taken her to every Roman site of importance and shared his enthusiasm with her.

His last day in Rome.

His last day as her lover.

It would be easy to deny him, she thought at first. Easy to push him away and tell him to leave Sicily and her life as a widow.

But why?

She had no one else. Nothing else but her son and her nieces. They had been enough. At least, they had been enough until they had grown old enough to see to their own lives.

Despite Darius' good looks having changed to something more mature, something older, something suggesting too much sun, and too much drink, and too many late nights, Chiara couldn't help how her body responded to his.

Recognition was a powerful force, it seemed.

"I love you," Darius whispered when his lips barely let go of hers, only to recapture them and worship them as if his very life depended on them.

She pulled away with a gasp, her large golden eyes

blinking before her gaze returned to his lips. "But for how long?" she challenged.

"The rest of my life." He sucked in a breath. "Marry me, Chiara. Marry me so I can prove it to you," he demanded.

Chiara didn't have a chance to respond, for a collective sigh sounded from the arched doorway into the kitchen.

Darius and Chiara turned in unison to find Aurora, Tamara, and Angela staring at them, their mouths open in astonishment and their hands clasped together as if in prayer.

"Well?" Aurora finally spoke. "Aren't you going to tell him you say '*Sì*'?" she asked in Italian.

"Oh, do say, 'yes'," Angela agreed, the words said in English.

Tamara merely stared at her aunt, obviously a bit befuddled by what was happening.

Chiara regarded Darius for a long time before she said, "Perhaps we should go for that walk," she suggested.

Darius allowed a grin. "Your wish is my command."

"It will be that way for the rest of your life," she countered with an arched brow.

"Promise?"

The collective sigh could once again be heard from the doorway.

Chiara frowned as she turned and regarded her nieces. "*Da quando capisci l'inglese?*" she asked. *Since when do you understand English?*

The young women merely giggled in response.

Chapter 35

A VISION IN THE DARK

*L*ater that night

As Jasper stared out the hotel room's only window, he wondered at his wife's stubbornness. The moment they had stepped out of the hotel in search of a place to eat dinner, Marianne had stuffed her spectacles into her reticule. *How can Marianne go about without wearing her spectacles in such a breathtaking city?* he wondered. How could she be happy in such a place when she couldn't see all it had to offer? When she had the means to see clearly but not the will to employ them?

Before they took another step, he had stopped and made her put them back on, ignoring how tears brightened her eyes at the order.

This is Palermo, he thought with some despair. A feast for the eyes as well as for the stomach. Except Marianne had barely eaten anything that night. She hadn't even tried the wine or the rich dessert, a cheese-filled confection called *cannoli*, Jasper had offered her. Perhaps the heat from the afternoon had her listless, or she was merely tired from their two days of traveling.

Or perhaps she was upset at his insistence that she wear

her eyeglasses, at least until the two of them were safely back in their hotel room.

Having seen her wear them on the few occasions she had done so, he understood her complaint that they were unattractive.

They were actually rather hideous.

The frames were definitely like those of a pair of Martin's Margins, the round, thick black frames surrounding each lens, their black bows hugging her head to where they bent in the back and then were fastened together with a ribbon. When she wore her hair down, as she had done for their trip from Girgenti, she admitted it was to hide the back half of her spectacles from anyone who might see her from behind.

Why hadn't Lord Devonville seen to a more modern pair of eyeglasses for his niece when she first arrived in London? Jasper wondered. There were a number of oculists in the capital, surgeons who specialized in problems of the eyes. Two were even fellow members of the Royal Society. If they hadn't left London when they did, Jasper realized they could have had Dr. Wathen-Waller see to a proper fitting and to a better looking pair of spectacles.

Although they still wouldn't be fashionable—at no point were spectacles seen as anything other than a sign of old age or a clergyman—at least they would look better than her Martin's Margins.

Given they were in Italy now—the birthplace of eyeglasses—and after what had happened at his dig site— Jasper was determined to find a pair of spectacles Marianne would be willing to wear during every waking hour. If he couldn't find something here in Palermo, he knew he would somewhere on the mainland. In Florence or Venice. Surely the capital of glass would have suitable eyeglasses.

Having settled on a plan and knowing the directions to an oculist's shop in town, Jasper took a deep breath and was about to go back to the high bed when he realized Marianne was standing next to the chair. He hadn't even heard her get out of bed, nor approach the window. "I didn't mean to wake you," he whispered, quickly coming to his feet. Unable to sleep, he had pulled on a pair of breeches and his shirt for his moment of contemplation by the window.

"What's wrong?" Marianne whispered in reply, one of her hands reaching out to touch his shirt.

Jasper knew she could probably make out the white lawn fabric despite the dark. He gently wrapped one of his hands around hers and raised it to his lips. "I couldn't sleep, is all," he replied, just before he kissed her knuckles. In the dim light from the window, he could make out the glisten of a tear rolling down her cheek. "It seems I am the one who should ask what's wrong?" he asked in alarm. He reached out and wiped away the tear with a thumb.

"I've become a terrible burden to you," she managed to get out before a sob interrupted her breath. "I know it was never your intention to marry me. I wondered if perhaps...?"

His arms were suddenly around her, pulling her hard against him. "No, no, no," he murmured, his lips kissing the top of her head.

"...There might be a way I can go back to England?" she continued, as if she couldn't hear his response. "Or... home to... Canobie? I understand your need to stay, of course."

Jasper gave a start, stunned to hear her words. "Marianne," he breathed, disappointment—nay, sorrow—evident in his voice. He had a mind to simply lift her into his arms and put her back in the bed, follow her down and cover her body with his own. If he kissed her to distraction, made love to her until she pleaded for him to stop, perhaps she would want to stay. Instead, he sat back down in the lounging chair and pulled her down atop him.

He half-expected she would resist his attempt to hold her, so he was gratified when she finally relaxed into his hold, her bent legs resting on the lounging chair as he pressed his back into the high side of the chair. "You are not a burden, my sweet. The opposite, in fact. I rather adore having you with me," he stated, his voice sounding loud in the quiet room. Even though there were people in the piazza below—there would soon be more as businesses closed for the night—their voices didn't reach them up here. "In fact, I cannot imagine what my life might be like without you," he added.

How had she managed to endear herself to him in only a month's time? To make him forget his life with Sophie and his brief stint as a widower, where he wondered from day to day where he might eat and where he might take tea? Where he would spend his evenings and where he might have a cup of chocolate or coffee? Where he might find solace in the arms of someone just as lonely as he was?

"You see, I am quite smitten with you," he said then, well aware of how her body jerked in response to his soft words. "I cannot imagine having to spend any night without your company," he added. "Without your body next to mine."

"And yet you left the bed, and came to this..." She allowed the sentence to trail off when she was forced to sniffle.

"I just needed to think a moment," he countered. "When I'm wide awake and lying next to you, I find I am too distracted to think straight, you see."

Marianne sniffled again. "Distracted?" she repeated.

"Oh, yes. I want nothing more than to make love to you. All the time. I thought by now... I thought by now I might have become used to having such a beautiful woman sharing my bed. Become used to seeing your beautiful smile in the morning. Used to watching you as you sleep. But I am not. I never will be, for I can never get enough of you."

Marianne frowned, her unseeing gaze going to the window. "How can you say such a thing when I look so hideous in those awful spectacles?" she countered.

Jasper sighed, realizing her desire to return to England had nothing to do with him and everything to do with her eyewear. "Your beauty transcends ugly eyeglasses. I don't even notice the damned things," he claimed with a shrug. "I only see you."

Marianne continued to frown at him. "You're a bounder," she accused, her head lowering to his shoulder despite her words.

Finally allowing a grin, Jasper managed a snort. "I must admit, until you, I have never in my life been accused of being a bounder," he claimed, just before his lips found hers. He kissed her then. Lightly at first, and then more thoroughly when she finally turned in his hold so her breasts pressed into his chest. When he eventually pulled away, he struggled to catch his breath. "May I take you to bed? I still wish to make love to you," he murmured, his lips barely touching the column of her throat.

"I think not," Marianne replied, suddenly moving her body so she faced him, straddling him and the lounging chair.

He had the placket of his breeches undone in a second and was pushing them down when he realized he was suddenly inside Marianne. She hadn't waited for him to remove the offending garment but had simply moved her body so she could capture his member.

Hot and slick and ready for his turgid manhood, she allowed a hiss and a murmur of 'yes' as he buried himself into her wet haven. Her hands were at his neck, her lips pressed against his forehead as he thrust himself deeper into her body.

"It's like you're a daughter of Jupiter," he whispered hoarsely, "I have my very own goddess of love to worship."

Marianne paused in her movements, rather shocked at hearing his words. "Are you my slave, then?" she wondered in a harsh whisper.

"I am," he replied just before he stripped her of her nightrail and took one of her nipples in his mouth.

"To do as I might command?"

Jasper was about to agree when he sensed a trap. He rested his forehead against one of her collarbones, feigning an attempt to catch his breath. Not difficult to manage given he was rather breathless just then.

"What would you have me do?" he asked, deciding he best hear her request before agreeing to it.

Marianne's fingers speared his hair, her fingernails scraping his scalp as she lifted his head and gazed down at him. "Don't require me to wear the spectacles," she whispered.

Already expecting the condition, Jasper couldn't help but frown. He was about to remove her from atop him, about to set her aside and leave the room, about to join the revelers down in the piazza and yell his frustration with her at the top of his lungs.

Couldn't she understand the danger she was in by not being able to see? How she was missing out by not being able to see the wonders of the world? How she was only able to see a fraction of anything she did see because she had to stand so close to it?

Jasper finally sighed and lifted his eyes to meet hers. "I will agree on one condition," he said in a hoarse whisper. He could feel how her body jerked in his hold, as if she didn't expect he would be the least bit amenable to her request. "If I think you are in any sort of danger—mortal or otherwise— you will put them on and leave them on until the danger has passed."

Marianne allowed a sound of protest. "You will merely claim I am *always* in danger," she argued, straightening her legs so that his manhood was no longer inside her.

"That's not true," Jasper managed, his wince apparent when she pulled her body from his. "But I cannot bear the thought of losing you," Jasper claimed, his arms tightening their hold around her body so she couldn't remove herself completely from the lounging chair. "So, I promise I will only require you wear them if I think you will be in danger of falling off a cliff, or being crushed in a crowd, or hurt by a falling statue."

Marianne stared down at him, finally allowing a sigh of reluctance. "Very well. I agree," she finally whispered, although it was apparent she wasn't the least bit happy with the arrangement.

The moment of intimacy having passed—Jasper was sure they had been about to make love as they did the morning after their wedding—he realized he didn't want to give up his hold on her. Not the way he had her settled atop his body, her bare breasts still only inches from his lips. At least she hadn't attempted to leave his hold completely. "Is there some deed my goddess wishes me to do?" he asked in a whisper, the back of one finger brushing against the side of her breast.

Marianne sucked in a breath at the slight touch. Despite her momentary anger and frustration with Jasper, she couldn't help the surprise she had felt at hearing his declaration.

I cannot bear the thought of losing you.

Does he feel more affection for me than he did for his first wife? she wondered. Marianne was never sure of his feelings for his late wife. Sometimes he spoke of her fondly, and then caught himself, as if he thought she didn't wish to hear about Sophie. Other times, a mention of her would be accompanied by a strange expression, as if he detested the woman.

Marianne had to admit to a bit of curiosity about Sophie. Like her, she had to marry the viscount because they had been caught kissing by the fountain in Lord Attenborough's garden. The idea that it was all Cupid's fault was never brought up, although she had believed it for that brief moment when they had been kissing. There were some nights, when they made love and for the few minutes after, when she believed it.

I cannot bear the thought of losing you.

Does that mean he loves me? she wondered as she settled her head onto his shoulder, gratified when one of his arms slid up her back and tightened its hold on her.

Do I love him?

There were times she was certain she was *in love* with him. The moments of ecstasy, when he was deep in her body and the waves of pleasure and the wash of warmth filled her near to bursting. The moments when his fingers barely touched her skin, as if he wanted to remind her he was there, perhaps because he thought she couldn't see him.

Like now, because there were no antiquities or relics to keep him occupied. His attention was entirely on her, his lips kissing the top of her hair between murmurs about worshipping his goddess. His finger once against brushed the side of her breast, and she sucked in a breath between her teeth. Desire overwhelmed her. Desire and wanton lust. And, mayhap, love.

Marianne didn't wait for Jasper to make another move. "If you truly wish to worship me, then you shall do so whilst in that bed," she whispered as she pointed in the general direction of the largest piece of furniture in the room, never mind that her finger was really directed toward the fireplace. "You will take me to that bed right this moment, and then you shall..." She gave a yelp when she was suddenly off of his lap and into his arms.

"Yes, my goddess," Jasper managed before he carried her to the bed. He settled her onto the middle of the mattress and followed her down, his lips nipping at her breasts and belly as he made his way down the front of her body, his hands smoothing over her thighs as he pushed them apart.

Realizing what he was about to do—she remembered the mosaics depicting an orgy—Marianne was ready to pull her legs together when his tongue touched the space just below her mons. She allowed another audible gasp when his hands were suddenly beneath the globes of her bottom, lifting them while his thumbs caressed the tender flesh. When his tongue flicked across her womanhood, she cried out. A second later, and his tongue was circling the swollen bud, the motion at once a great tease as well as the perfect foreplay, for she was sure he would simply end the exquisite torture by impaling her with his manhood.

But he didn't.

Instead, his tongue suddenly delved into her wet haven. She nearly screamed at the sensations his rough-textured tongue created, nearly pulled herself from his hold at the extreme pleasure his ministrations manifested. About to cry out from the intensity of it all, Marianne swallowed the exclamation when his assault changed again, his lips capturing her womanhood to suckle it. Her body bucked and jerked beneath his hold until her cry of his name had Jasper finally pulling away a bit.

Once Marianne seemed to relax a bit—as if her body had been wrung out—he flicked his tongue across her woman-hood one last time and felt a good deal of satisfaction at hearing her inhalation of breath and soft whimper of, "No more."

He had half a mind to bury himself in her then and there, but decided instead to allow her a few moments to recover so that he could simply do what he had just done all over again. Although his manhood begged for respite—he had been aroused since their time on the lounging chair—Jasper ignored his need and concentrated on providing more pleasure for his wife.

He used his nose to caress the inside of her thighs, his fingers to barely touch the back of her knees, his short-cropped hair to tickle her belly, all the while delighting in how she whimpered, how she softly gasped and sighed.

When he was sure she had recovered, he repeated the entire process. This time, he was gratified when her thighs seemed to spread wider for him, when her womanhood seemed easier to coax from its honeyed folds. Ecstasy had her crying his name, her hands moving to either side of his head until he finally pulled away.

On his way up the front of her body, he left a trail of kisses that had her murmuring words he couldn't make out. Her legs, suddenly bent, trapped his thighs and had his manhood pressed against her mons. He wondered how she had the strength to lift her knees—he'd been quite sure she was satiated and relaxed to the point of being boneless.

"What would you have me do now?" he whispered just before his lips captured hers for a quick kiss. "You seem to have me..." He gave a start when he realized one of her hands had taken possession of his manhood, guiding it to her wet folds. "At your advantage," he managed as he slowly entered her. He had to suppress the urge to chuckle at the same time he had to resist the urge to simply thrust himself into her and allow his release.

She was ready for him. She had been ready for him since before he had brought her to ecstasy the first time.

"Give me a child," Marianne whispered in reply, one of her hands going to the side of his face so her fingers caressed the slight stubble of his beard.

Jasper held his breath a moment, as much to control what he wanted to do just then as to be able to hear her command. "I'll do my very best, my goddess," he murmured in awe.

He was expecting some kind of plea that he simply make love to her. Her command that he get a child on her was completely unexpected.

Unexpected, but not unwelcome. It was past time he start a nursery. What better place to conceive a child than in Palermo?

And so he made love to her. Slowly at first, and then a bit faster when her body seemed to demand it. When he finally allowed his release, it was because he could no longer hold on. Her hands had moved from his sides to his buttocks, and then one of her fingers had touched his sac and stroked the base of his manhood as he pulled himself from her to begin another thrust.

The white hot stars and intense pleasure had him blinded and bewildered, for it seemed as if he had somehow left his body and was hovering above, watching Marianne as her head pushed into her pillow and her neck and chest arched up to meet him. Her expression had him pausing in his descent, for he was about to end up falling onto the front of her body in exhaustion. Instead, his elbows managed to hold him up as he paid witness to her heavy-lidded eyes and the look of adoration she bestowed on him. He kissed her then, a quick but thorough kiss between gasps for air.

Overcome in too many ways, Jasper finally settled his head into the space above her shoulder and fell asleep.

*F*eeling as boneless as Jasper apparently was at that moment, Marianne wasn't surprised when he seemed to pass out atop her. His manhood was still tucked inside her, a situation she found rather satisfying. Despite how his head had fallen next to hers, most of his torso rested on hers. She found she didn't mind the weight. The warmth of their coupling soon dissipated, and she struggled to pull a blanket over their bodies before she finally allowed a long sigh and closed her eyes.

Back in London, she had read in great detail about almost everything he had done to her tonight. Cherice had shown her the book in Devonville's library the night before her wedding. *Don't be too terribly scandalized. You'll find you'll enjoy the marriage bed if you just allow it. If you don't think you can, drink a glass or two of wine before bed. You'll do fine.*

Marianne hadn't been frightened of the marriage bed—curious was probably a better word to describe it—but she had appreciated her aunt's words of encouragement.

She also appreciated the graphic descriptions in the book even more, wondering if her desire to learn more and to experience some of the activities first-hand made her a wanton.

All except one, that is. For having seen it in the form of one of the mosaics she and Chiara had dug up had her wondering. Had Jasper done something on this night that was entirely inappropriate for a wife to experience?

The longer she thought about it, the more uncomfortable she was with it.

She always intended to leave the more scandalous activities to the courtesans and mistresses to perform. But what about what had been done to her?

Earlier that evening, she had felt lust, she was sure. At least, once she had Jasper's assurance that he hadn't left their bed over something she might have done wrong.

Well, besides almost falling over the cliff.

He had been frightened for her.

I cannot abide the thought of losing you.

He had been so close when he said the words, she could make out his face, even in the dim light. Make out his eyes as he seemed to stare into her very soul. He had said the words with such conviction, she was sure he must have felt affection for her. And now that he had made love to her the way he had on this night—to within an inch of her life, she was sure —Marianne found she felt more than simple affection for him.

As to whether or not it would be enough—enough to warrant wearing the damned eyeglasses—she didn't yet know.

Chapter 36

A WALK LEADS TO
ENLIGHTENMENT

*E*arlier *that afternoon, in Girgenti*

As Darius walked alongside Chiara, their path down the lane that led to the Greco-Roman quarter, he thought of all the things he had wanted to say the last day he had been in Rome.

None of them seemed appropriate now.

"Was he good to you? Romano, I mean," Darius asked just as they reached the path that led to San Nicola. At Chiara's gentle urging, they turned onto it.

"He was," she replied. "You knew him, didn't you?"

Darius nodded. "I did. I knew he... he was in love with you."

Chiara nearly stopped at hearing his words. "How did you know such a thing?"

He managed a chuckle. "I would have had to be blind not to notice," he claimed. "When we were at those receptions and dinners your father hosted, I saw how he looked at you. He looked at you the same way I did. I have to admit, I was jealous of him back then—I knew he was rich, and I knew your father liked him. But when I saw that he hadn't made his intentions known to your father, I figured I could have you. At least for a time."

Bristling at the last comment, Chiara stepped farther from him. "For a time?" she repeated, obviously incensed.

"I regretted having married long before I left London for Rome," he said, his jaw clenched at the memory of his arranged marriage to a spoiled daughter of a duke. "I didn't want to have anything to do with my wife, especially after she made it clear she didn't want to have anything to do with me," he added. "So going to Rome without her seemed the perfect solution."

"Not for me," Chiara whispered.

"I am sorry about that, but at the same time, I don't regret it," Darius replied. "I went to Rome because I wanted to immerse myself in the work. I wanted to dig up treasures and learn about the ancient Romans. I wanted to make discoveries," he said in a quiet voice, realizing just then his goals hadn't changed a bit in the intervening years.

"Did you? Make discoveries?" she asked in a quiet voice.

"I did. I discovered you." At the way her face displayed one changing emotion after another, he added, "Of all the places I went, and of all the treasures I found, you meant the most, Chiara. You were the most valuable."

She stared at him for several seconds before replying. "And yet you left me on the steps of the Forum."

Darius nodded. "The hardest thing I've ever had to do," he said. "Even though I had already arranged for Antony to find you—I knew he would come for you because I knew he was already in love with you—it was probably the worst thing I've ever had to do. Watching him take you down those steps and into his coach. Driving off to spend the rest of his life with you.

"That is what happened, isn't it?"

Chiara gasped. "You saw that?" she asked, one hand going to her chest.

"Of course! I wasn't going to just leave you there without making sure you had an escort home," he replied, a bit indignant.

"As soon as we arrived back at my father's *casa*, he asked father's permission to marry me," she said, remembering the day as if it were only yesterday. "He proposed that night."

"Lucian said as much in his note to me," Darius admitted. "He wrote it on the last letter I sent, and saw to its return in the post. But that didn't make it any easier."

Having arrived at San Nicola, Chiara gave him a glance before she said, "I come here every day to light a candle for Antony," she said.

"And you will continue to do so for the rest of your life," Darius said, half-hoping she would deny the words.

"Perhaps not every day," she countered. She turned and entered the church, moving to the display of candles in the nave. Kneeling, Chiara picked up a tapered wood lighting stick and lit the end from an existing flame. She then lit another candle. Setting the votive in place, she said her usual prayer.

The sensation of being watched had her turning her head to see the Gypsy nun regarding her from the other side of the nave, a knowing grin lighting the woman's face. Chiara slowly got to her feet and was about to join the Gypsy when she saw Darius approach the old woman. She stopped and watched as Darius regarded the nun for a moment. He finally gave her a nod. "*Grazie*," he said with a sigh.

Chiara moved to stand next to him. "Do you know this man?" she asked of the Gypsy.

The old woman gave her a slight grin. "Only that he was a lonely soul," she said in Italian. "But he is no longer."

Giving the woman a curtsy, Chiara placed a hand on Darius' arm, and the two took their leave of the church.

They made their way back toward the villa in companionable silence, although Darius stopped at the cornerstone of the brothel ruins. He glanced around, noting how a rare cloud obscured the sun and cast a giant, cooling shadow over the area. "Now you have to marry me," he said with a hint of amusement. At Chiara's look of surprise, he added. "I shouldn't want a Gypsy to curse you."

Chiara arched an elegant eyebrow. "Hasn't she already?"

The smile that appeared in response reminded her of the Darius she had known twenty years ago, and she allowed a grin to match.

Chapter 37

CLEARING UP A MISCONCEPTION

*L*ater that night

    Jasper awoke with a start, his heart beating a tattoo so loud he was sure Marianne could hear it. Reaching out, he was stunned to find her gone, the bed linens cold where he was sure she had lain when he had collapsed only moments ago.

Or had it been hours ago?

He sat up and stared into the darkness, allowing his eyes to adjust before he moved to get off the bed. Before he could put voice to a query, he heard a sniffle and directed his gaze toward the hotel room's only window.

Marianne sat in the velvet lounging chair staring at the blackness beyond the window. He had moved the chair there earlier that night, thinking Marianne might enjoy the vantage should she deign to wear her eyeglasses and gaze out on the spectacle of a Sicilian city rich in history and beautiful buildings.

A huge fountain sat in the center of the piazza below, the coins at the bottom glittering when the sun was directly over-head. The building directly across from the hotel featured architecture from the twelfth century and rich marble floors

LINDA RAE SANDE

and mosaic tiles within. To the left, a fourteenth-century cathedral loomed, its gothic windows reflecting the morning light and its mass preventing the rays of the afternoon sun from baking the piazza and its visitors.

Marianne was barely silhouetted in what little light came from the piazza below, her white nightrail appearing almost ghostly. The revelers had long since dispersed into the night, and the quiet in the room was almost deafening.

"What's wrong?" Jasper whispered when he attempted to take her into his arms. She stiffened at his touch, her body rigid despite his effort to provide comfort.

"You must think me no better than a... than a *whore*," she whispered.

Jasper furrowed his brows, wondering at the odd comment. He reached up with a thumb and brushed away a trail of tears from one of her cheeks. "I assure you, I have never thought of you in that way," he murmured, wondering what had her so upset. Then he replayed the words in his mind. *No better than a whore.* "Why ever would you say such a thing?"

Marianne attempted to catch her breath, sobs interrupting her response. "What you did to me."

Blinking, Jasper had to take a moment to remember just what he had done to her that was any different from what he usually did with her. To her.

The memory of his earlier method of foreplay came to mind, and he tightened his hold on her. "Are you referring to how I pleasured you? Before we made love?" he asked in a whisper. He thought to ask it in a teasing voice, but realized she was in no mood to be teased.

"I should not have... reacted as I did," she whispered, tears once again streaming down her cheeks.

"Why ever not? Your reaction was... completely expected. Rather appreciated. It was perfect, really," he replied, remembering how her body writhed beneath his hold, how she

326

whimpered, and mewled, and finally screamed his name during that moment he had suckled her swollen womanhood with his lips and laved it with his tongue before slipping it into her honeyed haven.

He had never tasted her before. He had wanted to, of course. He had thought to try it their first night together, but realized it would be best to ease her into the pleasures of the marriage bed. She had been a virgin. She had no experience with sexual congress. Other than the few kisses they had shared, she had no experience with foreplay.

Every night since their departure from London—except for the night when they arrived in Girgenti too late and were exhausted from their travels—they had enjoyed a round of simple foreplay before engaging in rather tame intercourse. Despite the fact that he knew Marianne was at least some-what familiar with other positions—it was obvious she had seen illustrations in a book, or her aunt had described them —he had thought to simply wait until the time or place was right to try something different. He had no intention of attempting the more scandalous acts—with her or anyone else. He had decided long ago never to subject his wife to sexual positions not suitable for a lady of quality.

Unless it was her idea.

He wasn't even thinking of the brothel mosaics when he engaged in one of the Roman arts. He had never employed it on Sophie, of course—she would never have allowed it—and he hadn't tried it on anyone since Miss Ann at *The Elegant Courtesan*. Marianne was a far more accommodating lover. Far more eager in the marriage bed. Perhaps her aunt had helped in that regard, or perhaps she had merely learned enough from an illustrated book.

Jasper felt Marianne's body finally give in to his hold, and he kissed the top of her head. "Now, tell me what's really wrong," he encouraged.

Marianne lifted her head and stared at her husband. "I

never wish to be part of an... of an *orgy*," she whispered hoarsely.

Jasper blinked. And blinked again. "I should hope not!" he countered, his voice no longer quiet. *What the hell?* "Which begs the question. Why would you feel compelled to say such a thing?" he asked as he held her away from his body so he could see her face.

"Isn't that... isn't that what you were doing?" she asked, her manner rather timid.

At first confused by her implication, Jasper finally allowed a sigh. "I was performing *cunnilingus*," he said quietly. "A way of providing pleasure. Men have been doing it for women for centuries," he added before asking, "Pray tell, why would you think I expected you to engage in an *orgy?*"

It was Marianne's turn to blink. "The mosaics. The ones that Chiara and I uncovered," she finally said.

Jasper inhaled, wondering what those mosaics had to do with what he had done to her. They were now covered with a canvas sail to protect them from the weather as well as from prying eyes. At some point, he knew they would be unveiled for anyone to see, but he didn't want that to happen until he had them completely documented. If there was any chance to remove them to some sort of protection—a museum or a private collector with the means to display them properly—he would make the arrangements before leaving for Rome.

"What about them has you so upset?"

"There were two I could not sort at first, but Chiara said they were depictions of... of orgies. You saw them. The men had their heads... down there—" She pointed to the apex of her thighs. "And one of the women had her head down there. On a man," she struggled to get out. "While a different man was behind her and..." She stopped, apparently robbed of breath by a sob.

Jasper could practically feel the heat from her blush. He

cleared his throat before deciding how to explain what she had seen. "Orgies are where multiple men engage in sexual intercourse—and other... sexual practices—with multiple women," he said quietly. "You have not been a participant in an orgy, I assure you," he added carefully. He suddenly frowned. "How do you even know the word?"

Angling her head to one side, Marianne sighed. "Chiara said the word when we uncovered the mosaics. She said it was the reason Rome fell."

Resisting the urge to chuckle at hearing the companion's assessment, Jasper sighed. "Orgies were not the reason Rome fell, although they may have been a contributing factor," he replied, deciding he really didn't want to get into a discussion of ancient Rome's politics just then. "They were more of a... an indicator of how their civilization was becoming less civil." He paused and indicated the bed. "Let's continue this conversation lying down, shall we?" he asked gently.

Marianne gave him an uncertain glance before she allowed him to lead her to the bed. She regarded it a moment, almost as if she were frightened of it, before finally settling herself onto the mattress.

Jasper thought to go around to the other side before joining her, but instead he simply followed her down, one arm moving beneath her shoulders to pull her almost atop him. Although she resisted his hold at first, she soon sighed and dropped her head onto his chest.

"I thought you liked what I did to you earlier," he said softly, his manhood coming to attention when it realized its favorite place to be was only inches away.

"I must have looked just like one of those women in the mosaics," Marianne whispered.

"How do you mean?"

There was a long moment of silence where Jasper thought his wife might have fallen asleep, but she finally spoke. "I was making sounds, and begging, and my body was—"

"You were doing what I would hoped you would do," Jasper whispered. "What I wanted you do to. Moan, mewl, beg, plead, scream. Otherwise, how would I know if I was pleasuring you properly? Doing it right for you?"

Marianne considered his words. "Right for *me?*" she repeated, her body once again stiffening in his hold. "Was it different for Sophie?"

Jasper gave a jerk beneath her, stunned by her question.

How could he explain Sophie's dislike of the marriage bed?

Despite his attempts to pleasure his first wife—and he knew he had on many occasions—Sophie seemed to think his ministrations were more to benefit him than her. That sexual congress was a duty to be endured rather than enjoyed. That finding pleasure with him would negate the feelings she had for the man she had truly wanted to marry. "It was different," he finally replied. "Very different. She was... embarrassed by what we did in the marriage bed. She claimed she didn't like making love, but I know I gave her pleasure." He was silent a moment. "She just wanted the one providing the pleasure to be a different man."

Marianne lifted her head and regarded her husband for a very long time. "Then she was a fool," she whispered.

Jasper frowned. "Was she now?"

The subsequent quiet in the room unnerved Jasper until Marianne finally replied. "I did feel pleasure at what you were doing to me. More than I have ever felt before, in fact," she whispered. "But I also felt as if I was no longer the one moving my body. That someone else took it over and made me say naughty things, and move in ways that made me seem... wanton. Lustful."

"Ah," Jasper said on a sigh. "Then I coaxed the tigress from her hiding place," he teased gently.

Marianne inhaled sharply. "The tigress?" she repeated.

"Or lioness, or whatever erotic creature you become

when you are aroused," he countered. Pausing a moment, he drew a finger down her arm and placed a kiss on her forehead. "It's all right to let her out when you're with me."

Marianne considered his words a moment. "Is it?" she murmured. "You wouldn't think me... lustful?"

He kissed her again, this time on the lips. "I want you to be lustful. But just with me. Not with anyone else," he added quickly.

Before he quite knew what was happening, Marianne had her legs straddling him, her bottom resting on his thighs, her arms lifted above her head to pull the nightrail from her body. When the fabric cleared her head and was tossed aside, and the waves of honey-blonde hair settled past her shoulders, Jasper finally took a strangled breath. His cock pressed against her mons as she regarded him from above. "She was a fool," Marianne affirmed with a nod before she lifted her hips and guided his turgid manhood into her body.

Stunned by what she was attempting to do, Jasper stared up at her for a moment before allowing a huge grin. "Let me guess. You saw this depicted in one of the mosaics you uncovered," he accused.

Marianne placed her hands on either side of his shoulders as she shook her head, secretly pleased with how the ends of her hair barely touched his chest and had his body trembling with frissons. "I saw it in a book. I think it was called, 'riding St. George'," she whispered as one eyebrow arched up.

Jasper blinked as another frisson passed through his body. "You're welcome to ride me whenever you would like, my... my *dragoness*," he managed before his hands gripped her hips and helped her on her way. "Just don't breathe any fire on me," he added before she clenched on him and sent him into ecstasy.

Chapter 38

THE GIFT OF SIGHT

*T*he following morning
              Despite having spent part of the night wide awake, Marianne opened her eyes to a room lit with oranges and golds from the early morning sunrise. Jasper was watching her, his head supported by a bent elbow.

"I do adore watching you sleep," he whispered.

Marianne gave a start, her eyes blinking several times before they focused on him. "How long have you been awake?"

Jasper shook his head, not about to admit he had just then opened his eyes. He had passed out in the middle of the night—after she'd had her way with him. *Riding St. George, indeed.* "Not long." He leaned over and kissed her on the temple. "Are you anxious?" he asked in a whisper.

Blinking again, Marianne turned her attention to him. "About what?"

He gave her a quelling glance. "About seeing the oculist. I'm taking you to Dr. Ricciardini's office today," he said. "James and David gave me directions. As it happens, it's not far at all. We actually passed it on the way here to the hotel."

"If you insist," she finally replied. Truth be told, she

didn't hold much hope that the oculist would be able to help her. She expected she would end up with spectacles much like she currently wore, but maybe in a more attractive frame. That thought alone had her suddenly brightening, though. "When do we leave?"

Grinning, Jasper maneuvered his body over hers and began kissing her sleep-warm skin. "After I worship my goddess, of course," he whispered.

For just a moment, Marianne thought to push him away, to resist his attempt to make love to her. But why? He had put her mind at ease with his words. With the way he held her. And should he elect to practice a Roman art on her, she decided she would allow it. Why deny herself the pleasure of his tongue?

*D*avid and James left the hotel at the same time as Jasper and Marianne, the four making their way in the Via Toledo while Jasper kept an eye out for a particular shingle. When he found it, he was stunned to discover the space beneath it wasn't simply a hole-in-the-wall hovel, but a brightly-lit shop with a large glass window. The stories above no doubt belonged to a duke or marquis who had fallen on hard times. A few pairs of eyeglasses rested on marble blocks in the display window. Sunglasses were also on display, their dark lenses and large frames favored by those who didn't wish to be recognized.

Jasper conferred with James before sending him and David on their way, their valet anxious to share his favorite coffee shop with James. Although Jasper would have liked a *caffè*, he figured he would indulge after he and Marianne had seen the oculist. Like in London, there seemed to be coffee shops on every corner, although Italian coffee was a much stronger beverage.

A bespectacled man greeted them before they had even

made it through the door. Having put on her own spectacles before they entered the shop, Marianne curtsied and returned the greeting.

Jasper gave a short bow and attempted to explain why they were there. His enunciated English nearly had Marianne giggling, so at the oculist's blank look, Marianne stepped up and spoke in Italian. She introduced herself, pointed to her spectacles, and explained that she was in need of a new pair.

The man's demeanor entirely changed, his look of curiosity replaced with understanding. He introduced himself as Dr. Ricciardini, pointed to a chair for Jasper, and waved Marianne into a back room.

Alarmed—he had no intention of allowing Marianne to be alone with the doctor—Jasper followed and watched from the arched doorway as Dr. Ricciardini led Marianne to a wooden chair that faced a contraption the likes of which Jasper had never seen.

Dozens of round lenses were mounted on hinged metal arms that were in turn attached to a huge frame. Once Marianne was seated, the oculist took her existing spectacles, made sounds of disgust, waved his free hand as if to reinforce his displeasure, and gave instructions Jasper couldn't make out. Marianne seemed to understand, though, for she straightened on the seat before leaning forward to rest her chin on a small platform.

Dr. Ricciardini held up a small printed card in one hand, a series of drawings and letters scattered about the surface.

Then the lenses began moving as the oculist touched their hinges, one from the left joining one from the right side of the frame to fall in front of her line of sight. "*Meglio? Peggio?*" he asked. *Better? Worse?*

Marianne seemed familiar with the equipment, her gaze steady as the different lenses popped into place in front of her, sometimes two or three deep before Dr. Ricciardini said, "*Meglio? Peggio?*" She answered in Italian, but sometimes pointed to the left or right. He would remove one lens and repeat the question. Add another lens and repeat the question. And on it went for nearly fifteen minutes until the oculist suddenly straightened. He moved to a counter and extracted several oval lenses from pasteboard boxes, holding them up to a gas light one by one, before setting aside two of them.

Then he moved to the contraption, loaded the lenses into two hinged arms. He placed the lenses in front of Marianne's eyes and then motioned for her to rest her chin on the small platform. Holding the card farther back from where he had originally held it while he was flipping the lenses, he waited as Marianne's eyes widened in delight. She recited the Italian numbers displayed on the card, adding, "Prickly pear" and "Tree" when his finger pointed to the drawings. "The images are so clear!" she said in an excited whisper. When the oculist queried her, she said, "*Sì*," and the man retrieved the lenses from the frame. When he disappeared into another room for a moment, her gaze lifted to where she knew Jasper was watching. Although she couldn't see him clearly, she allowed a grin and then winked at him.

"Did you just wink at me?" he asked in a whisper that gave away his amusement.

Marianne was about to do it again, but the oculist returned with a handful of metal frames. He held them close to her face, knowing she couldn't see them clearly. "*Argento? o oro?*" Silver or gold?

"*Oro*," she replied, and then watched as he set aside several pairs of frames. He offered her a gold frame and pointed to a looking glass to her right.

Marianne carefully put the simple hinged eyeglass frames onto her face, resting the bridge on her nose. Unlike her black pair, these featured bows that curved slightly at the ends and rested atop her ears. There was no need for the additional hinged piece that would normally wrap around the back of her head and tie with a ribbon.

Jasper straightened from where he had been leaning against the doorway, stunned at how different she appeared wearing the gold wire frames. He wasn't given a chance to make a comment before the oculist frowned and gave her another pair to try.

Daring a glance at the looking glass, her reflection clear in the flawless mirror, Marianne's eyes widened and she grinned.

This time, Dr. Ricciardini allowed a nod before he removed the frames and offered yet another pair. Marianne said, "*Sì, Sì!*" as she she nearly bounced in her chair.

Jasper couldn't help but grin as he watched her excitement. He supposed she was experiencing something much like a blind man suddenly given the gift of sight. "Third pair is the charm?" he half-asked from where he stood.

"Indeed," Marianne said, giving up the empty frames when the oculist held out his hand.

At the stream of Italian the man said, Marianne gave a shake of her head. "I'm not sure."

"What is it?" Jasper asked, his brows furrowing in concern.

Dr. Ricciardini regarded him before he said, "*Quanti?*"

"*Due*," Jasper answered quickly, understanding the man's query. Should something happen to her glasses, he wanted to be sure she had a second pair.

"*Sì,*" the oculist replied. "*Due ore,*" he said, holding up two fingers. "*Può essere uno.*"

Jasper frowned and glanced over at Marianne.

"He'll have them ready in two hours," she said. "Maybe one." She settled back in the chair, as if she was prepared to wait right there until they were ready, and moved to open her reticule.

"Do I pay him now?" Jasper asked as he reached for his purse.

But Marianne had already pulled apart the gathers of her reticule and extracted the coins he had given her the day she went shopping with Chiara. She held them out to the oculist, and he took two of them with a nod. "*Uno ore*," he said, apparently pleased he was to be paid right then.

Marianne dimpled.

Although Jasper thought to take her to a coffee shop to wait until the lenses could be mounted into the frames, he realized she had every intention of waiting until at least one pair was ready. So he joined her in the examination room and held her hand as Dr. Ricciardini assembled her eyeglasses from the lenses he had pulled from the pasteboard box.

When she put on the first finished pair, Jasper was quite sure he hadn't seen a happier human being in his entire life.

Within moments, her infectious enthusiasm for everything she could see had him just as happy.

Chapter 39

ENVISIONING THE FUTURE

Five days later

When Jasper Henley stepped down from the town coach, wincing at the sight of how dusty the glossy black exterior had become over their two-day trip back to Girgenti, he knew something was different.

All three of Chiara's nieces stood shoulder to shoulder, much like the servants of an English home would do when their master returned from a trip. They curtsied in unison and smiled as if they were truly glad to see him.

Then he remembered that David sat up on the driver's seat with Pietro.

He turned and offered his hand to Marianne, who was beaming with delight and looking as beautiful as the day he had married her. Her new spectacles, oval lenses framed in gold wire, were barely noticeable, and a glow suffused her face. He thought at first she might have stayed in the sun too long—they had spent a few days sightseeing in Palermo and visiting the nearby Greek ruins—but her skin didn't appear any darker then when they had left.

Marianne dipped a curtsy to the young women who smiled at her and allowed one of her own. "It's good to be back," she said as her gaze swept the lane on which the villas were located. She took a few steps until she was beyond the trees surrounding the villa, her view taking in the red and gold sunset beyond the hill.

Jasper was standing to her side when he said, "Gorgeous, isn't it?"

"Indeed. I've never seen it so clearly before," Marianne whispered.

When David stepped down from the coach, his cousins surrounded him much as they had done the month before, greeting him with hugs and speaking all at once. Watching from where he still sat in the town coach, James wondered at the bit of jealousy he felt.

Their four days in Palermo had been an eye-opening experience.

Learning that David was the owner of the villa in which he was staying had him seeing the young man in a different light. David was a landowner, his holdings including much of the cultivated farmland below and to the east of the villa.

He was also a man who had inherited a good deal of wealth. His late father had managed to hide his money before the various usurpers of Sicily and southern Italy took their turns claiming ownership. As a result, Chiara was a rich woman, and her only son was even richer.

He already knew David was educated. Their late nights discussing ancient architecture and Roman history was a testament to it. But learning his so-called valet was actually in a class higher than his own was a humbling lesson.

Even more humbling was David's dismissal of his concerns, and his proposal for how they might continue their relationship. *Must you go back to England?* David had asked the night before, when they were staying at the coaching inn in the mountain village.

James had been asking himself that very same question. As the second son, he didn't stand to inherit the family business. He wasn't betrothed to a young lady. He didn't even have regular employment, but rather a stipend that allowed him to participate in archaeological expeditions. *I don't have to go back*, he had finally answered.

Then you shall stay in my villa and continue your research. And I shall oversee my farmers and those of my mother.

The arrangement seemed far too simple, but then he supposed the best arrangements were.

Despite having spent most of the day inside the town coach—for a time, he had sat up on the driver's seat with David—he hadn't yet mentioned the plans to Jasper.

When James finally stepped out of the coach, he gave a nod to the women, ignoring how Aurora glared at him—perhaps a kitchen knife was still in his future—and made his way down the lane to where Marianne and Jasper were standing. "What has captured your attention so...?" He stopped in his tracks at seeing not only the brilliant sunset, now rich with golds and peach and dark yellows, but a couple caught in a passionate embrace on the path that led to San Nicola.

Standing next to the large canvas sail that covered the Roman mosaics Marianne and Chiara had unearthed were Darius and Chiara. She had no doubt just come from the church, where she lit a candle for her late husband every afternoon. As for Dr. Jones, James wasn't sure if the archaeologist had lain in wait for her, or if he had escorted her, but it was obvious much had happened during the week they had been gone.

"They loved one another a long time ago," Marianne whispered.

Remembering what she had said that night when she imagined him leaving her for a gorgeous Italian woman, Jasper took her hand in his and lifted it to his lips. "I would venture to say they never stopped loving one another," he murmured, before kissing her gloved hand.

"Do you suppose Dr. Jones will stay on Sicily?" James

asked, not sure he welcomed the thought of Darius Jones living across the lane from where he would be staying for the rest of his life. "Or will she join him in England?"

"Both, perhaps," Marianne replied with a sigh.

"Summers in Hexham, winters here?" Jasper guessed.

"I do hope she'll be amenable to allowing Angela and Aurora to join us in London," Marianne said then. "Tamara, too, although that may be asking too much."

James' eyebrows arched in surprise. "What is this? You're taking my Aurora with you?" he asked in mock shock. "Don't I have a say in the matter?"

Marianne gave a shrug. "Jasper says he has to pension his cook, so, *sì*, we wish to take Aurora with us when we return to London," she explained.

The older couple had finally separated a bit, but were now arm in arm as they made their way up the path to the lane where Jasper, Marianne, and James stood watching.

As they approached, Marianne noticed how they were dressed. Chiara wore a gold silk gown with vertical rows of embroidered flowers, the laced, scooped neck displaying her décolletage. A small veil was attached to her pinned up hair, and earbobs decorated the sides of her neck. Darius, dressed in a topcoat of superfine, Nankeen breeches, a gold embroidered waistcoat, and polished boots, actually had the appearance of an aristocrat.

"Hello," Jasper called out when the couple were within earshot.

"Ah, the wayward travelers have returned," Darius replied when they were a bit closer.

"I think they've just *married*," Marianne said in a whisper. She had never seen Lord Darius so finely dressed, and Chiara looked like a... "She will be *duchess* one day," she added with a sigh.

James frowned. "But.. it's too late in the day to get married, isn't it?" he argued.

"It's not yet noon," Jasper countered, the query reminding him of Sicilian time.

"Then it is perfect timing," David said from where he stood next to James. "Twenty years too late."

The other three turned to stare at him, not having noticed his arrival. "What are you saying?" Jasper asked in confusion.

"They are my mother and father," David said with a shrug, before he broke away from them and hurried down to greet the couple.

Marianne watched as the younger man first shook hands with Lord Darius and then embraced his mother. But before he could break away, Lord Darius had them both in his hold. She was sure she hadn't felt such happiness—and relief—in a very long time. Stubbornness, it seemed, could be overcome.

When Jasper glanced over at Marianne, he found she had tears streaming down her face. "Oh, my sweeting. What is it?" he asked in a whisper.

She turned her face to gaze up at him, her lips quivering. "I have no idea. I am just so... overcome."

"Happiness then?" he asked as he angled his head. His brows furrowed then, as if he was deep in thought.

Marianne nodded. "I suppose so."

Jasper's eyes widened then. "Well, I suppose it's to be expected when you're... expecting," he said in a hopeful whisper.

Her eyes widening to match his own, Marianne realized he spoke the truth. She hadn't had her monthly courses since leaving England. "Oh!" she managed before Jasper's lips were suddenly on hers.

Rolling his eyes and feeling just a bit left out, James Singleton made his way down the hill to congratulate the couple.

EPILOGUE

A year later in Mayfair
Lady Marianne Henley surveyed the dining room one last time, carefully counting every place setting at the long table. Tamara appeared with a plate of aspic and a basket of rolls, her grin widening at the sight of her mistress with the viscount's heir in the crook of one arm, her gold spectacles firmly in place.

"Are they here yet?" Tamara asked in her halting English.

"Their coach has just pulled up," Marianne replied with a grin, wondering at her nervousness. Angela had finished pinning up her hair only moments ago, and a quick check of Aurora in the kitchen assured her everything was in place for their first family dinner since leaving Sicily.

Their first family dinner to include Lord Darius and Lady Chiara, Lord and Lady Devonville, Lady Torrington, and her father. Even David and James had sailed from Sicily for a visit to the capital.

Jasper stopped in the doorway. "There you are," he said as he kissed her on the cheek. "Looking lovely as usual," he added before he turned his attention to the sleeping infant. "Our little Cupid seems unimpressed by all this. I don't know why I'm so nervous, but I am," he added with a shrug. "It's not as if I haven't met these people before."

Marianne dimpled at the comment. "You are not alone. I still wish Aurora had allowed us to hire a cook for the evening. It's not fair she's had to do all the cooking," she said with some concern.

"I believe it's a matter of pride with her. When I suggested we could hire another kitchen maid to help, she threatened me with a knife. Besides, what other cook in London is going to know how to make the Sicilian food we've come to know and love?" he countered.

He started counting the chairs at the table, and Marianne gave him a quelling glance. "Tamara knows how to count," she chided him. "Come. Let us greet our guests."

The butler had already opened the front door, and the first of their dinner guests—and guests for the next few weeks—filed into the vestibule.

"I wish to hold the bambino," Chiara called out even before she was out of her mantle. She was through the vestibule and approaching Marianne and Jasper with open arms, her gown giving away her own post-pregnant state. "I cannot get enough of holding my own," she said as she took the babe from Marianne and carefully moved it into the crook of her arm. "Oh, he looks just like Cupid." With his head of golden blond curls and cherubic face, the babe did bear a resemblance to the statue Jasper had acquired and had placed in the back garden.

"What have you done with yours?" Marianne asked in alarm, when she saw the woman wasn't carrying her own newborn. Chiara Jones had given birth to a boy only a month after Marianne had Marcus William Henley, the heir to the Henley viscountcy.

"His father has him. Holds him all the time. I have to send him to go digging so I can have my turn," Chiara complained.

Darius appeared in the great hall, a swaddled baby held up to a shoulder as he allowed a huge grin. Behind him, a rather tanned James Singleton stood smiling with David Romano at his side.

"Which way to the kitchens?" James asked after he had kissed the back of Marianne's hand.

Marianne waved in the general direction. "Be careful, you two, or I fear you'll be stabbed with a kitchen knife," she warned as the two hurried off to give their regards to David's cousin, Aurora.

Kisses and handshakes followed, the cacophony of voices drawing the three nieces into the fray. Marianne managed to get most of them to move into the parlor, but not before the door knocker sounded again. Given the noise and general merriment, the butler was the only one who heard it.

William and Cherice, Marquess and Marchioness of Devonville, entered the vestibule followed by Adele, Countess of Torrington, and then Lord Donald.

"Must I go to the nursery to see my grandson?" Donald called out, his query eliciting a gasp from Cherice.

"I'm sure Marianne will have a nurse bring him down for you to see," Adele said in a scolding voice.

But Marianne was already on her way out of the parlor, hurrying into her father's arms. Curious to meet the young woman's family, Chiara had followed, still holding The Honorable Marcus Henley as if he was her own grandson.

She curtsied to the newcomers, her smile wide as Marianne made the introductions. The babe made it into Donald's arms even before Marianne was finished, her father making sounds she was quite sure she had never heard him make before. Assured her son was safe in her father's arms, she turned and watched with interest as her uncle and Chiara regarded one another with recognition.

"Have I met you? In Rome, perhaps?" William asked. "A reception, I believe it was." He had visited the country as part of his grand tour, a few years after he had married his first wife but before the wars prevented such travel.

"*Sì*," Chiara replied. "My father was Samuele Romano."

"He was in charge of archaeological matters, by chance?" William ventured.

"*Sì*," she replied with a nod, her smile tentative.

"That's why I remember you," the marquess said, one of his fingers still bouncing in the air. "And if I remember correctly, Lord Darius was at that same reception. Do you remember him?"

Marianne allowed a giggle. "She married him, Uncle," she said as she led them to the parlor.

Rather surprised by this bit of news, William was about to argue that it was impossible the two were married, but Cherice and Adele soon had him surrounded and on the way to the parlor. "Your spectacles are rather attractive," Cherice commented on the way. "Where ever did you find such a stylish pair?"

"Yes, do tell," Adele said.

"In Palermo," Marianne replied, rather relieved at hearing her aunt's compliment.

"Is that a shop in New Bond Street, perhaps?" Cherice asked before she disappeared into the middle of the fray in the parlor.

Once everyone was in the parlor—everyone but Aurora —Marianne stood with Jasper in the threshold and surveyed the scene before them. "What have you done with our son?" Jasper asked in a whisper.

"Father has him. You may have to bargain to get him back," she warned.

"Not if Marcus wets his sleeve first," Jasper said, *sotto voce*. He lifted a hand to her shoulder and turned her slightly. "Thank you for suggesting this dinner. This reunion," he said with a nod. "I don't believe I've seen such a happy family before."

Dimpling, Marianne beamed. "Thank you for making the arrangements," she replied. She reached up a hand to the side of his face and kissed him, unaware of how the noise suddenly died down in the parlor.

When she pulled away, she said, "If I recall, a kiss is how it all began," she murmured.

Jasper swallowed. "Courage, my sweet," he whispered, just before he dared a glance at their guests. As he feared, everyone of them was staring at him and his wife.

Far more than the three who had originally paid witness to their first kiss. At least the babies hadn't seen them. Despite the chaos, they were both sound asleep.

Marianne turned her head and blushed at the sight of so many eyes aimed in her direction. She dipped a curtsy. "Perhaps I shouldn't have worn my spectacles tonight," she said loud enough so everyone in the room could hear. "There isn't even a Cupid in sight."

Her father lifted their babe from his shoulder and held it up. "Oh, yes there is," he called out.

It was a long time before the laughter died down and the dinner chime sounded.

ABOUT THE AUTHOR

A self-described nerd and lover of science, Linda Rae spent many years as a published technical writer specializing in 3D graphics workstations, software and 3D animation (her movie credits include SHREK and SHREK 2). An interest in genealogy led to years of research on the Regency era and a desire to write fiction based in that time.

A fan of action-adventure movies, she can frequently be found at the local cinema. Although she no longer has any tropical fish, she does follow the San Jose Sharks. She makes her home in Cody, Wyoming.

For more information:
www.lindaraesande.com